Crimson Ascent

In the boundless
crimson wilderness
of Mars,
Our isolation becomes
both decree & revelation

by **KAVEE**

Disclaimer & Copyright

First Published by Kavee in 2025

Copyright © by Kaveendra Vithana

Author has asserted his right under the Copyright and Designs to be identified as the author of this work and as the creator and architect of this cosmic narrative.

This work of fiction unfolds among the stars and across the boundless expanses of the unknown. Any resemblance to actual persons, terrestrial or otherwise, living or interstellar, is entirely coincidental except where historical fact is noted.

Technological Disclaimer: All technologies, systems, and machinery depicted in this narrative are entirely hypothetical and exist solely within the realm of speculative fiction. They do not represent real-world engineering, validated scientific principles, or operational space systems.

Generative AI Contributions: This book incorporates illustrations generated using advanced artificial intelligence technology and includes editorial assistance provided by AI-based tools. These contributions have enriched the creative process and remain the property of author.

This book is sold subject to the condition that it shall not, by way of trade, lending, resale, rental, or any other circulation, be rebound or reissued in any form other than in its original published format, without the publisher's prior written consent. This condition, along with any similar restrictions, must be imposed upon any subsequent purchaser

First Edition

01-00-2459707-kdp

ISBN : 978-1-7640023-0-1

WWW.CRIMSONASCENT.COM

—For my family—

Love that grounds
Wisdom that guides
Patience that endures
Trust that never fades

This journey among the stars is written with you in my heart

Prologue

The stars have always been our silent companions, distant yet ever-present, inspiring wonder and curiosity across generations. From the first time we looked up at the night sky, humanity has been driven by an unshakable desire to explore—to understand what lies beyond the horizon and to find our place in the vast expanse of the cosmos.

Crimson Ascent is a story born from this eternal quest. Set in a future where humanity takes its first bold steps toward becoming an interplanetary species, it explores not only the physical challenges of venturing to another world but also the emotional and philosophical trials that accompany such a monumental journey.

Mars, the enigmatic red planet, becomes a stage for triumph and tragedy, unity and division, hope and despair.

This book is not just about technology or space exploration; it is about the people who dare to make the impossible possible. It delves into their fears, ambitions, and resilience, showing how the human spirit can thrive even in the harshest of environments. At its core, this story asks timeless questions: Are we truly alone in the universe? What responsibilities do we carry as explorers of new worlds? And, perhaps most importantly, how do we ensure that our future does not repeat the mistakes of our past?

As you embark on this journey, you will meet a diverse cast of characters, each bringing their own expertise, dreams, and struggles to the mission.

Their stories weave together into a narrative that celebrates the unyielding human drive to explore, to adapt, and to connect.

Whether you are a seasoned enthusiast of space exploration or simply someone drawn to tales of adventure and discovery, I invite you to step aboard the Eos Horizon and embark on a journey to ascend the Crimson world.

Together, let us venture into the unknown, guided by the belief that in the great expanse, our solitude is just an illusion.

—Kaveendra Vithana

Sydney, Australia

Table of Contents

Chapter One

DEPARTURE

D r. Elena Moreno stood at the edge of the observation platform, her gloved hands gripping the helmet in her arms. Beyond the reinforced glass, the *Eos Horizon* rose against the backdrop of a crimson and golden sunset, its sleek body a promise of humanity's future among the stars. But for Elena, the sight carried the weight of what she was leaving behind.

Behind her, the buzz of final preparations filled the air—voices over intercoms, the hum of transport carts, the measured clank of tools against metal. But Elena's focus remained fixed on two small figures pressed against the glass. Samuel, nine, and Grace, seven, waved enthusiastically, their faces lit with excitement even as tears streaked their cheeks. She raised a trembling hand in return, whispering,

"I'll come back."

It was a fragile promise—one she wasn't sure she believed herself.

A hand touched her shoulder.

"Elena," said Marcus Hayes, his voice steady.

"It's time."

Elena nodded, forcing herself to turn away from her children. As she donned her helmet and secured the seals, the isolation hit her like a physical force. Her breaths echoed within the suit, a rhythmic reminder of the distance growing between her and the life she knew.

#

The departure zone teemed with energy, a mix of exhilaration and somber resolve. Crew members in pristine white pressure suits stood in clusters, their reflective visors catching the last rays of sunlight. Technicians performed final checks on the towering spacecraft, their movements precise and purposeful. The air crackled with unspoken words, the weight of eight billion hopes resting on their shoulders.

"Attention, crew,"

 came the calm, authoritative voice of Commander Riya Kapoor. She stood at the center of the platform, her presence commanding with her matching frame. "We are moments away from history. The challenges ahead will test us in ways we cannot yet imagine. But remember why you are here—because you dared to dream of something greater."

Her gaze swept over the assembled crew, lingering on each person as if willing them to believe.

"This mission is not just for us. It's for every person back on Earth who looked to the stars and wondered what lies beyond. We carry their hopes, their dreams, and their legacy."

She raised a hand in a crisp salute.

"Crew of the *Eos Horizon*, let's make history."

The ramp to the ship's entrance extended with a low hum, and one by one, the crew began to ascend. Elena fell in step beside Marcus, her steps deliberate, weighed down by the enormity of the moment. She stole one last glance over her shoulder, her heart clenching at the sight of her children waving frantically. Then they were gone, obscured by the towering hull of the ship.

#

The *Eos Horizon* was more than a spacecraft; it was a masterpiece of human ambition and ingenuity. Its name carried deep significance, rooted in mythology and symbolizing a dawn of new beginnings. In Greek lore, *Eos* was the goddess of the dawn, opening the gates of heaven each morning to usher in the sun's light. The ship, affectionately nicknamed "Dawn" by its crew, was a testament to humanity's first step into a broader cosmos—a dawn for interplanetary exploration.

Stretching nearly half a kilometer in length, the *Eos Horizon* was a sleek monolith of reinforced alloys and ceramic composites. Its design fused elegance with functionality, an aerodynamic profile hiding the marvels within. The hybrid propulsion system, a groundbreaking blend of nuclear fusion and advanced ion thrusters, provided unprecedented speed and efficiency, halving the journey to Mars compared to earlier missions. This engineering feat not only made the ship faster but also drastically improved its energy economy, allowing for long-term sustainability in the harsh void of space.

At the heart of the vessel was *"Astraeus"* an advanced AI navigation core capable of processing astronomical data with unparalleled precision. Named after the Titan god of stars and planets, Astraeus ensured the ship remained on course, adapting dynamically to unforeseen anomalies. Its intelligence was the silent guardian of the mission, calculating and correcting with a speed and accuracy far beyond human capacity.

Inside, the *Eos Horizon* was a microcosm of Earth. Its habitats were designed for comfort and resilience, equipped with redundant life-support systems, hydroponic farms, a fully equipped medical bay and state-of-the-art research facilities. The modular construction allowed for adaptability, ensuring the ship could evolve to meet unforeseen challenges. Every corner of the vessel reflected the unity and ingenuity of a world that had come together to reach for the stars.

As it rests majestically on the launch pad ready to move away from Earth, the ship's hull caught the faint light of a distant sun, its reflective surface shimmering like a beacon of hope. The *Eos Horizon* was more than a vehicle; it was a statement of humanity's resolve, carrying the dreams of an entire planet toward an uncertain but exhilarating future.

#

The *Eos Horizon* mission had never been a straightforward endeavor. While the official narrative heralded it as humanity's next great leap, behind the scenes, it was a battleground of political conflict, financial uncertainty, and ideological warfare. The staggering cost of the mission ignited fierce global debate—was interstellar expansion a bold new frontier, or a reckless escape from Earth's mounting crises? Critics demanded that the trillions spent on Mars colonization be redirected to repair Earth's collapsing ecosystems, curb geopolitical unrest, and address the widening socioeconomic divide.

Public opinion fractured. Factions formed. Some saw the *Eos Horizon* as humanity's salvation, a way to ensure survival beyond the fragile limits of Earth. Others saw it as an elitist exodus, a lifeboat for the privileged while the rest of civilization was left to burn. Protests erupted outside UNSI headquarters, accusations of corporate profiteering flooded global media, and world leaders struggled to justify the mission amid mounting public skepticism. Every setback—every delay, budget dispute, or failed test—

became ammunition for those who opposed the endeavor. Yet, despite the turmoil, the mission moved forward. It had to.

Then, in the final months before launch, the dossier leak changed everything.

A classified report surfaced, revealing a disturbing anomaly—an unknown signal detected by NASA, ESA, CNSA, and Roscosmos. The document detailed a persistent frequency in gigahertz range, recorded not just in deep space, but in transient bursts across Earth itself. The signal's appearance in places like Antarctica's frozen wastelands and the high-altitude observatories of "Mauna Kea" defied explanation. Its pattern was too structured to be natural.

Governments and UNSI moved swiftly to suppress the findings. They dismissed the anomaly as an instrumental error, an atmospheric aberration—anything but what it truly was: a mystery. But the attempt to bury the truth only fueled the fire. The scientific community demanded answers, conspiracy theories multiplied, and speculation ran rampant. Was this evidence of extraterrestrial contact? A covert military experiment? A signal waiting to be answered?

Some began to whisper that *Eos Horizon* had never been about Mars—that its true purpose was linked to the signal, to follow it to whatever lay beyond. And if that was true, then the a string of attempted-sabotages wasn't an act of resistance—it was a warning.

Were they leaving Earth to chase the unknown, Or stepping into a fate long sown?

#

Inside the *Eos Horizon*, the atmosphere shifted. The sterile corridors gleamed under soft white lights, their silence broken only by the faint hum of the ship's systems. Crew members found their stations, strapping into seats that would cradle them through the violent ascent.

Elena's seat faced a small view-port. As she secured her harness, she caught a glimpse of Earth's horizon, the blue curve glowing faintly against the encroaching dark. Her chest tightened as memories flooded in—Samuel's questions about the stars, Grace's laughter under a canopy of trees. She gripped the armrests, grounding herself against the surge of emotion.

"T-minus ten seconds,"

The automated voice intoned, its sterile cadence slicing through the tension. The cabin became a mosaic of human emotions and coping mechanisms. Elena gripped the armrests, her knuckles white, silently repeating a mantra for calm, her breathing shallow but measured. Across from her, Marcus Hayes exuded an unsettling calm, his fingers tapping an invisible rhythm on his thigh, a habit that masked his own apprehension. Commander Riya Kapoor leaned forward in her seat, her hands clasped tightly, her dark eyes fixed ahead as if she could will the launch into success by sheer focus.

Liam, the crew's navigator, sat motionless, his expression a stoic mask of neutrality. The unflappable "poker face" he was known for, revealed nothing, but the faint movement of his fingers brushing an invisible trajectory into the air hinted at the storm of calculations in his mind. Beside him, Ada had her eyes squeezed shut, her teeth clenched tightly— an involuntary reaction to the nerves bubbling beneath her usually confident demeanor. It was her first mission into space, just as it was for many others on the crew. Her lips moved in a whispered prayer, though no one else could hear it over the rising hum of the engines.

The hum grew deeper, vibrating through the deck plates. Others exchanged fleeting glances or murmured final checks; their voices barely audible under the growing roar.

The automated voice intoned,

"T-minus five seconds."

A collective inhale swept through the crew as fear and excitement coiled together in the tight space. Even the most seasoned among them felt the weight of this moment, as the final seconds ticked away to humanity's leap into the unknown.

Elena closed her eyes, her thoughts a jumble of fear and determination. The roar of the engines were subtle but a distant rumble, growing into a deafening crescendo that rattled her entire body. The force of the launch pressed her back into her seat, her breaths shallow as the ship climbed higher, faster, piercing through the layers of Earth's atmosphere.

#

The *Eos Horizon* roared as its fusion-powered thrust-vectoring engines comes to life, their deep hum resonating through the launch pad and into the Earth's soil. A revolutionary advancement in propulsion technology, the engines harnessed the power of nuclear fusion to generate immense thrust, allowing the behemoth starship to lift vertically from the surface without reliance on conventional rocket boosters. Inside, the crew felt the faint vibrations beneath their feet as the ship began its steady ascent, the engines' precise vectoring guiding the colossal vessel skyward with an elegance that belied its size. The sheer force of the fusion drive overcame Earth's gravity effortlessly, the controlled reaction providing both power and efficiency.

As the *Eos Horizon* ascended, the relentless force of acceleration seemed to stretch time. Seconds felt like minutes, each one filled with the symphony of engines and the pounding of her own heartbeat. Then, with a suddenness that felt almost disorienting, the ship broke through the atmosphere, the crushing pressure giving way to the eerie stillness of zero gravity.

When the vibrations finally subsided, weightlessness took over. Elena opened her eyes to see Earth shrinking in the view-port, a brilliant blue sphere suspended in an endless black sea. Around her, crew-mates exchanged tentative smiles, their earlier apprehension giving way to awe.

For a moment, they allowed themselves to marvel at the view, united by the shared realization that they were no longer bound by Earth's gravity—or its limits. Yet in the back of Elena's mind, the weight of the journey ahead loomed large.

Mars awaited, with its challenges and uncertainties, and there was no turning back.

"It's beautiful," Elena whispered, her voice carrying a note of awe that resonated with those around her.

"Enjoy the view while you can,"

 Marcus remarked, his voice tinged with dry humor.

"Mars isn't nearly as pretty."

But as the faint hum of the ship's systems filled the silence, the weight of the journey ahead began to settle in. Mars was waiting, and with it, the challenges and uncertainties that would define the rest of their lives.

#

As the days stretched into weeks, the crew of the *Eos Horizon* fell into a rhythm. They navigated the constant thrum of the ship's systems, the daily regimens of maintenance and training, and the delicate balance of personalities in their confined quarters. The camaraderie that had begun to form was tempered by the underlying tension of their mission—a collective understanding that any mistake could be catastrophic.

Elena spent much of her time in the hydroponics farm, and the environmental systems module, monitoring the ship's air and water quality, which were critical to all biology inside. The routine tasks brought a sense of comfort, a tether to the scientific training she had spent years mastering. Still, her thoughts often wandered, drawn back to the faces of Samuel and Grace. She had left recordings for them—messages filled with reassurances and stories about her work—but the delay in communication meant she could not know how they were doing in her absence.

Elena Moreno was the epitome of resilience, a woman who had carved a path through the stars while raising two children on her own. As a single mother, her life had been a constant balancing act, a delicate tightrope stretched between groundbreaking scientific research and the everyday demands of raising her son, Samuel, and daughter, Grace. Her career began in the labs of Santiago, where she had quickly made a name for herself by pioneering techniques in bio-engineering crops for hostile environments. But the accolades had not come easily. Her mornings often began before dawn, helping Samuel with his homework or comforting Grace after a bad dream, before rushing to her research lab. There, she would work tirelessly, her mind focused on solving problems that could save millions of lives. At night, she would return home, exhausted but determined, ready to read bedtime stories or sit with her children under the stars, dreaming aloud about a future where her work would help humanity thrive on distant planets.

Her selection for the mission was a testament not just to her brilliance, but to her unwavering determination. The United Nations Space Initiative (UNSI) had recognized not only her scientific achievements but also her incredible capacity to persevere against all odds. Knowing the weight of her responsibilities as a mother, UNSI extended a promise of care for her children. Samuel and Grace, would be provided for in every way—education, healthcare, and emotional support—by a dedicated team committed to ensuring their well-being for life. This commitment was more than a policy; it was a lifeline. Elena sat with them before leaving, explaining the mission in simple, heartfelt terms.

"What I'm doing isn't just for me,"

she had said, holding their small hands tightly.

"It's for you, for your future, and for every child on Earth who dreams of reaching the stars."

As difficult as the separation was, Samuel and Grace had looked at her with wide, tear-filled eyes and nodded, their trust and love giving her the strength to take the next step toward the unknown.

"Earth is still there,"

David's voice interrupted her reverie one day. He floated beside her, a sealed container of coffee in one hand and a mischievous grin on his face. "I checked. It hasn't disappeared."

Elena chuckled despite herself. "That's good to know."

"You should come to the observation deck," he continued.

"Best view in the solar system."

She hesitated but eventually followed him, propelling herself through the narrow corridors to the ship's observation module. The room was small, with a curved view-port that offered an unbroken view of the stars. Beyond the window, Earth hung like a jewel in the void, its blue surface stark against the blackness of space.

"It never gets old," David said quietly, his tone shifting to something more reflective.

"We spend our lives on that tiny rock, thinking it's the center of everything. Then we come out here and realize it's just one speck among billions."

Elena nodded, her gaze fixed on the distant planet.

"It's humbling. And terrifying."

David's grin returned.

"Terrifying? Wait until you see Mars up close."

#

David Leclerc was a man who had always lived on the edge of two worlds: one of privilege and one of possibility. Born into a dynasty of Swiss industrialists, he was raised in a sprawling mansion nestled high in the Swiss Alps—a marvel of modern architecture built into the rock face itself. With floor-to-ceiling windows that overlooked miles of snow-capped peaks, the house seemed to hang between the heavens and the earth, a testament to human ingenuity and excess. Growing up, David wanted for nothing. His family's wealth spanned generations, built on cutting-edge technologies that powered industries across the globe. But despite the opulence that surrounded him, he often felt a profound disconnection from the gilded world of inherited privilege.

His love for science began as a rebellion against expectations. Unlike his peers, who indulged in the luxuries of their birthright, David spent his days immersed in books and experiments, drawn to the wonders of physics and engineering. His family, while supportive, didn't understand his fascination with the raw mechanics of the universe. "Why get your hands dirty when you can hire the best minds to do it for you?" his father had once asked. But David was restless, unsatisfied with merely benefiting from humanity's progress. He wanted to be part of it. After earning advanced degrees in astrophysics and material sciences, he shocked his family by turning down leadership of their empire. Instead, he dedicated himself to space exploration, funding groundbreaking research and pushing the limits of what was possible. "When I say I've lived on the rock," David often joked to his colleagues, "I mean it literally. But Earth is just the first step. There are other rocks out there waiting for us."

What made David unique wasn't just his intellect or his drive—it was his willingness to use his wealth as a catalyst for change. When UNSI invited him to join the *Eos Horizon* mission, it wasn't just his brilliance they sought. David brought resources and connections that could solve the mission's most daunting challenges, from securing rare materials to funding experimental technologies. But for David, the mission was never about power or prestige. It was about purpose. "Out there," he once said during a pre-launch interview, gesturing toward the stars, "money has no meaning. Only progress does." And so, the man who had lived his life suspended between privilege and passion prepared to leave behind the rock that had defined his early years, trading his alpine mansion for the red deserts of Mars, determined to help humanity take its next great leap forward.

The observation deck became a frequent retreat for Elena in the following days. There, she found a sense of peace amid the vastness of space. The stars, though cold and indifferent, seemed to whisper promises of discovery, of purpose. She began to feel a growing resolve—a determination to make this journey mean something, not just for herself but for the children she had left behind.

Ship's routine settled into a steady rhythm, the crew began to truly connect, bridging the gaps between past training sessions and the reality of living together in the confined space of the *Eos Horizon*. While many had crossed paths during UNSI training events, this was the first time all 100 members shared the same space for an extended period. Familiar faces became more than names and titles as shared meals, collaborative tasks, and late-night conversations forged bonds. Small cliques of common interests formed—engineers swapped stories about past projects, while scientists debated the mission's potential discoveries. Even the occasional awkward introduction gave way to camaraderie as the crew embraced the shared mission that united them, transforming a collection of individuals into a family of pioneers.

In the endless void of space, the concept of "night" became an ironic ritual for the crew. Without a sun to rise or set, the ship's artificial lights dimmed on schedule, signaling the start of a night that didn't truly exist. Through the view-ports, the stars blazed unblinkingly, their eternal brightness mocking the notion of darkness. It was a reminder that here, in the vacuum of space, time was a construct of humanity's need for order—an imitation of Earth's rhythm imposed on a realm where day and night held no meaning. Yet, the irony brought comfort; even a fabricated night felt like home.

But peace was fleeting aboard the *Eos Horizon*. One evening, as the crew gathered in the common area, the ship shuddered with a sudden jolt, sending unsecured items floating into the air.

"Unscheduled movement detected," Astraeus announced.

"Investigating source."

The crew exchanged uneasy glances as Riya quickly took charge.

"Everyone to your stations. Astraeus, report."

"Preliminary analysis indicates a debris collision with external shielding," the AI replied.

"No critical damage detected. Conducting further diagnostics."

Riya's tone remained calm but firm.

"Marcus, Elena, you're with me. Let's inspect the affected area."

The three of them donned their suits and made their way to the airlock. Stepping into the void of space was a surreal experience for Elena. The silence was absolute, broken only by the sound of her own breathing inside the suit. She tethered herself to the ship, her movements slow and deliberate as they approached the impact site.

The *Eos Horizon* carried a fleet of tethered drones—sleek, multi-functional devices equipped with high-resolution cameras and an array of sensors that could analyze every millimeter of the ship's exterior. Designed with precision, these probes made spacewalks redundant, offering a safer and more efficient way to monitor the ship for micrometeorite impacts, hull integrity, and radiation damages. When deployed, they danced around the *Eos Horizon* like a school of mechanical fish, their movements choreographed by the ship's AI, Astraeus.

Yet, despite their flawless coverage, there were those among the crew who longed for the old ways. Spacewalks had become less about necessity and more about immersion—an unspoken ritual for those who craved the visceral awe of floating untethered in the vastness of space. For these dreamers, stepping beyond the safety of the ship wasn't about checking the hull; it was about touching infinity. In the silence of the void, where even the hum of the *Eos Horizon* disappeared, they felt not isolation but connection—a profound sense of belonging to the endless, star-strewn expanse surrounding them.

"I was expecting worse!", Marcus said.

The damage was minor—a series of small dents along the ship's hull—but it served as a stark reminder of the dangers they faced.

"Looks like the shielding did its job," Marcus uttered, his voice crackling over the comms. "Lucky us."

"Luck has nothing to do with it," Riya replied.

"The design held up, as it should. But let's not take any chances. Document the damage, and we'll assess the need for repairs."

Elena activated her helmet camera, capturing images of the impact. As she worked, she couldn't help but feel the oppressive weight of the stars surrounding them. The vastness of space, once a source of wonder, now felt like a predator waiting for its chance to strike.

When they returned to the ship, the atmosphere was tense but controlled. Riya debriefed the crew, emphasizing the importance of vigilance.

"This was a minor incident,"

she said, her tone unwavering.

"But it won't be the last. Stay sharp, and we'll make it through."

Later that night, Elena found herself unable to sleep. She was hanging in the observation module, staring out at the endless expanse. Her reflection stared back at her, a pale, ghostly figure framed by the stars. For the first time, she allowed herself to confront the fear she had been suppressing— the fear of failure, of loss, of the unknown.

"Mars is waiting," she whispered, her voice barely audible. It was a statement, a mantra, and a plea all at once.

Behind her, the ship hummed softly, its systems a fragile lifeline connecting them to their destination. The journey was far from over, and the challenges ahead would only grow. But for now, she held onto the faint glimmer of hope that had brought her here, clinging to it as tightly as the tether that had kept her anchored in the void.

The hum of the *Eos Horizon*'s systems blended into the background of daily life, a constant reminder of the precariousness of their existence. Each passing day felt both routine and monumental, the weight of their mission punctuating even the smallest moments.

Inside the *Eos Horizon*, silence was a crafted illusion. The ship's active noise damping technology muted the mechanical roar of its various systems, leaving the living quarters bathed in a calm as serene as a distant forest. Yet, a faint hum lingered—not in the air but in the marrow, a vibration so subtle it teetered on the edge of perception. It was not a sound so much as a presence, a gentle reminder of the colossal machine cradling them through the void. Some likened it to the heartbeat of the ship, a steady pulse that soothed frayed nerves in the solitude of space. Others claimed it was the universe itself whispering through the hull, a low, eternal murmur that only the truly untethered could hear. Whatever it was, the hum became a companion, a rhythm that seeped into their bodies and dreams, grounding them even as the stars called them forward.

For Ethan Rees the hum of the *Eos Horizon*'s systems a steady anchor for his focus. Remote-viewing, once dismissed as pseudoscience, had evolved into a respected discipline, blending psychology and quantum theory, making his expertise tested on this mission. UNSI had mandated his inclusion, recognizing his abilities in the uncharted territory. Though the crew often joked about his "mind palace," they never joked about his discipline.

#

Elena spent more time immersed in her duties. The environmental systems were a constant concern—air composition, water recycling, temperature control—all meticulously monitored. It was the kind of meticulous work that demanded focus, which suited her. When she concentrated on the ship's complex systems, she could momentarily forget the uncertainties ahead.

One afternoon, Elena floated into the ship's hydroponics module, where Dr. Noah was tending to the seedlings. Tiny green shoots sprouted in nutrient-rich gel, their fragile forms stark against the sterile, metallic backdrop of the ship. The scent of greenery was faint but distinct, a reminder of Earth that felt almost out of place in the void of space.

Dr. Noah Carter was the quiet architect of life aboard the *Eos Horizon*, the agriculture specialist tasked with transforming sterile hydroponics modules into thriving ecosystems. Tall and wiry, with perpetually dirt-streaked hands and a calming presence, Noah was as much a nurturer of plants as he was of people. A farm boy turned biologist, he had spent years perfecting hydroponic techniques that could turn even the most hostile environments into green havens. His love for the work ran deep; for Noah, every seed carried a promise of resilience, every sprout a testament to hope. He spoke to his plants as he worked, coaxing life from them with a mix of science and instinct, and his colleagues often joked that the greenery responded better to him than to the nutrient solutions he meticulously prepared. But beneath his quiet demeanor lay a fierce dedication. "If we can grow life here," he often said, gesturing to the hydroponic modules lit with soft, artificial sunlight, "then Mars isn't just a frontier—it's a home waiting to claimed."

"Hey, Elena," Dr. Noah greeted her, his voice as casual as if they were back in a greenhouse on Earth.

"Come to admire my little garden?"

She smiled faintly. "Just checking on the oxygen yield. Astraeus flagged a fluctuation."

Noah snorted. "A fluctuation of, what, half a percent? These babies are doing fine. They're tougher than they look."

Elena bent closer to examine the plants. The delicate leaves quivered slightly in the artificial airflow, but their color and structure seemed healthy. "It's amazing how adaptable life can be," she mused.

"I wonder if we'll ever be as resilient as these plants."

Noah laughed. "We're getting there. You've got to admit, it's kind of poetic—bringing life to a place as barren as Mars."

Her lips curved into a smile, though her thoughts were far away. She envied the plants in a way—uncomplicated, purpose-driven, thriving in an environment that should have been hostile. For a moment, she let herself imagine a future where their colony on Mars would be just as resilient, its people rooted and thriving in a new world.

#

The day passed quietly, but as evening settled, an announcement from Astraeus broke the calm.

"Scheduled course correction approaching. All crew, prepare for inertial dampener re-calibration."

Elena joined the others in the main hub, where Riya and Marcus were already at the controls. On the large central screen, the trajectory display showed a slight deviation—barely perceptible, but enough to require adjustment.

"Manual override engaged," Riya announced.

"Liam, confirm burn calculations."

Liam Hwang was a prodigy in every sense of the word, a mathematician whose brilliance had redefined the limits of human calculation. From a young age, numbers had been his language, equations his poetry. By the time he was twelve, he had outpaced his professors, and by twenty, his orbital mechanics theories were being implemented in space programs worldwide. Now, as the *Eos Horizon*'s lead navigator, Liam's mind was a living supercomputer, capable of calculating trajectories, gravitational slingshots, and fuel efficiencies faster than the ship's AI, Astraeus, could verify them. His uncanny ability to visualize complex multidimensional pathways in his head earned him both awe and a touch of skepticism—how could one person hold so much? Quiet and introspective, Liam often seemed lost in thought, his hands sketching invisible vectors in the air. But when the ship's navigation systems required fine-tuning or when the unpredictable arose, his sharp, deliberate input was a lifeline. "Machines are good," he'd say with a faint smile, "but sometimes, it takes a human to feel the math." For Liam, navigation wasn't just a science; it was an art, a way to paint paths through the cosmos with precision and elegance.

"On it," Liam replied, his fingers flying over the console.

"Looks good. Ten-second burn, thirty percent thrust. Ready on your mark."

The crew braced themselves, securing their positions as Riya initiated the burn. The ship shuddered faintly as the thrusters fired, the sensation rippling through the cabin like a distant tremor. Elena gripped the edge of her console, her gaze fixed on the trajectory display. The thin line representing their path shifted incrementally, aligning perfectly with its intended course.

Liam's role extended far beyond the journey to Mars; his genius would be indispensable in the colony's survival and growth. Once the *Eos Horizon* landed, his mathematical expertise would be crucial for plotting safe routes for exploration rovers, optimizing launch and landing trajectories for cargo and communication satellites, and calculating energy-efficient pathways for resource extraction missions. His ability to model complex systems would also aid in predicting weather patterns in Mars' volatile atmosphere, ensuring the safety of the colony's outdoor activities. As the settlement expanded, Liam's knack for precision and foresight would help design transportation networks and guide the placement of future infrastructure. To the colony, Liam was more than a navigator—he was the architect of its connectivity with Mars and, ultimately, the stars.

"Burn complete," Riya confirmed.

"Re-calibrating dampeners. Good work, everyone."

A ripple of relief passed through the crew, though the moment was short-lived. As they began to disperse, Astraeus's voice chimed again, this time with a note of urgency.

"Unidentified anomaly detected. Scanning for details."

Riya's posture stiffened, and she turned sharply back to the console. "What kind of anomaly, Astraeus?"

"Electromagnetic fluctuation originating from external systems," the AI replied.

"Source undetermined. Further analysis required."

The air in the hub grew taut with tension. Marcus leaned over the console, his expression serious. "Could be interference from the burn. Let me run a systems check."

Elena's pulse quickened as she moved to assist. "I'll check the environmental controls, just in case."

The minutes that followed were marked by focused activity, the crew working in near silence as they searched for the source of the anomaly. When no immediate threat was identified, Riya made the call to continue monitoring while proceeding with their duties.

"Keep me updated," she said firmly, her gaze sweeping over the team.

"We don't take risks out here."

As the others returned to their stations, Elena remained in the hub, her mind racing. The anomaly was likely nothing, a minor glitch that would soon be explained away. But it had stirred something in her—a reminder of how little they truly understood about the forces at play in space.

Later that night, unable to shake her unease, Elena found herself in the observation module once more. The stars stretched endlessly before her, their cold light illuminating the darkness. Somewhere out there lay Mars, waiting, but in this moment, it felt as distant as a dream.

Her thoughts were interrupted by the sound of footsteps—floating, rather than walking. Marcus appeared in the doorway, a small tablet in hand.

"Couldn't sleep either?" he asked, his tone light but sympathetic.

Elena shook her head. "Too much on my mind. What about you?"

"Same," he admitted, holding up the tablet.

"I figured I'd run another diagnostic on the external systems. Just in case."

She gestured for him to join her, and he floated over to the view-port. They stood in companionable silence for a moment, both lost in their thoughts. Finally, Marcus spoke.

"You ever wonder if we'll find something out here we didn't expect? Something we can't explain?"

Elena glanced at him, her brow furrowing slightly. "Like what?"

He shrugged. "I don't know. We've mapped the stars, sent probes to the edges of the solar system. But being here… it feels different. Like there's more to the story than we've ever imagined."

She considered his words, the weight of them settling over her.

"I think we will,"

 she said softly.

"But whether we're ready for it is another question."

Marcus nodded, his expression thoughtful. "Fair point."

The two of them stayed there for a while longer, staring out at the endless expanse. In the vastness of space, their conversation felt small, almost insignificant. But it also felt real—a quiet acknowledgment of the unknown, and of the courage it took to face it.

The next day began with a renewed sense of purpose. Whatever unease the anomaly had caused, the crew carried on with their tasks, knowing the importance of routine in maintaining focus and sanity. For Elena, that meant returning to the environmental systems module, where the hum of machinery and Astraeus's ever-calm voice provided a strange kind of solace.

Two weeks into the voyage, Liam's meticulous oversight had kept the *Eos Horizon* on an unerringly efficient path, its engines firing with precision that felt almost choreographed. He often sat for hours in the navigation deck, tracing potential anomalies or refining adjustments proposed by Astraeus, his fingers drawing invisible arcs in the air. But just as the journey was beginning to feel routine, a faint disruption in the ship's sensor readings sent ripples of unease through the crew.

"Dr. Moreno," Astraeus said as Elena secured herself at the console, "the anomaly detected last night remains under observation. No further fluctuations have been recorded."

"Good to hear," Elena replied, though she wasn't entirely reassured.

"Run a full diagnostic on the environmental systems. I want to be sure nothing's been affected."

"Understood," Astraeus confirmed, launching into its automated process.

As the AI worked, Elena found herself drifting into thought. The anomaly, though likely benign, had unsettled her. She wondered if it had done the same for the rest of the crew. Her musings were interrupted by the arrival of David, who floated into the module with his characteristic grin.

"Morning, Elena," he greeted, holding a container of what passed for coffee aboard the *Eos Horizon*.

"How's life in the land of air and water?"

"Stable for now," she replied, offering a faint smile.

"Though I wouldn't mind an extra set of hands if you're not busy."

"Always happy to help," David said, securing himself beside her.

"What's on the agenda?"

"Just making sure everything's in order after last night. Astraeus's running a diagnostic, but a manual check never hurts."

The two of them worked in companionable silence, reviewing the system's parameters and inspecting the equipment. As they moved through their tasks, David began to hum softly, a tune Elena didn't recognize but found oddly soothing.

"Do you always sing while you work?" she asked, raising an eyebrow.

"Only when I'm trying to impress my coworkers," he replied with a wink.

Elena couldn't help but laugh. "Well, it's working. Keep it up."

Their light-hearted exchange was cut short by a sudden alert from Astraeus.

"Attention: minor irregularity detected in water filtration output. Investigating cause."

Elena's smile faded as she turned back to the console.

"Details, Astraeus?"

"The filtration system is experiencing a reduction in flow efficiency. Initial analysis suggests a partial blockage in one of the intake valves."

David frowned. "That's odd. Those valves were fine during the last check."

"Could be debris from the micro-meteoroid impact," Elena speculated. "I'll take a closer look."

She retrieved her toolkit and floated to the affected section of the module. Securing herself in place, she opened the panel to reveal the network of pipes and valves responsible for processing the ship's water supply. As she inspected the system, David hovered nearby, ready to assist.

The *Eos Horizon* offered artificial gravity in its living quarters and workspaces, a vital feature for maintaining the crew's physical health and psychological stability during the long journey. By using a rotating habitation ring combined with localized graviton projectors, the ship created a comfortable semblance of Earth-like gravity in key areas where the crew ate, slept, and worked. However, not every part of the ship enjoyed this luxury. In the sprawling cargo bays and engine compartments, artificial gravity was absent to save energy and simplify structural design. Here, crew members navigated the weightlessness by floating with tethers clipped to their suits or by using "Clingers"—a nickname for the ship's magnetic boots. The Clingers, reliable but occasionally temperamental, allowed wearers to adhere to metal surfaces with a satisfying clunk, though they required some finesse to master. For many, transitioning between the gravity zones and the free-floating areas was an unspoken rite of passage, a constant reminder of the extraordinary environment they now called home.

"Here it is," Elena said after a few minutes, locating a small cluster of particles lodged in the intake valve.

"Looks like it's just residue from the filtration media. Nothing serious."

"Good catch," David said, handing her a sterilized tool.

"Think you can clear it?"

"Shouldn't be a problem," she replied, carefully removing the blockage. Once the valve was clear, she ran a series of tests to ensure the system was functioning properly.

"Flow efficiency restored. We're back to normal."

"Nice work, Doc," David said, offering her a fist bump. She hesitated for a moment before responding, the gesture feeling strangely human in the sterile, mechanical environment of the ship.

"Don't bother checking inside the sterilizer room," David said with a knowing smirk.

"Clingers won't cling to the carbon fiber walls."

"Nice one," Elena chuckled, her voice breaking the stillness of the moment. Marcus grinned, his normally stoic face lighting up as he joined in her laughter.

As they secured the panel and returned to the console, Astraeus's voice chimed again. "Diagnostic complete. All environmental systems are operating within acceptable parameters."

"Thanks, Astraeus," Elena said, relief evident in her tone. She turned to David.

"Crisis averted—for now."

"Let's hope it stays that way," he replied.

"Though with this crew, I'm sure we can handle whatever comes our way."

#

That evening, the entire crew gathered in the common area, seeking a brief reprieve from the day's relentless demands. The space, though compact and practical, felt expansive thanks to the thin, flexible display panels seamlessly integrated into the walls. These advanced screens could mimic the textures and colors of Earth's landscapes with breathtaking clarity—lush forests swayed gently in an invisible breeze, serene oceans ebbed and flowed, and mountain peaks rose majestically under a golden sky. The illusion was near perfect, a technological marvel designed to soothe frayed nerves and evoke the comforts of home. For some, the scenes brought solace, while for others, they deepened the ache of what had been left behind.

Elena sat near the edge of the room, her thoughts distant as she toyed with a pouch of re-hydrated pasta, her appetite dulled. Beside her, Noah leaned back, quietly observing the shifting landscapes on the walls, his fingers absentmindedly tracing the edge of his chair as though trying to draw inspiration from the illusion of Earth. Across the room, Marcus and Riya were locked in an animated discussion, their voices low but charged with the energy of problem-solving. Ada and Amara sat close together, sharing whispered thoughts about the newly discovered ancient text from Göbeklitepe, while Sonja scribbled notes into her tablet, her mind seemingly elsewhere. Liam, perched near the main console, was still working on navigation adjustments, though his attention occasionally drifted to the harmonica in David's hands.

David had once again produced the small instrument, its polished surface gleaming faintly under the room's soft lights. He began to play, the haunting strains of a melody weaving through the room like a thread tying them all together. The music, raw and unembellished, carried with it a piece of Earth, a reminder of humanity's shared roots. As the final notes lingered in the air, even Astraeus's distant hum seemed to quiet, as if the ship itself was pausing to listen. For a moment, the *Eos Horizon* felt less like a vessel bound for the unknown and more like a refuge—a place where memories, hopes, and dreams converged.

"You've got quite the talent," Elena said, breaking the silence between them.

"Thanks," David replied, pausing to take a sip from his drink. "It's nothing fancy, but it keeps me sane."

"It's nice," she admitted, her voice quieter. "Reminds me of… simpler times."

He tilted his head, studying her. "Your kids, right? You talk about them sometimes."

Elena nodded, her gaze distant. "Samuel and Grace. They're still so young. I keep wondering if they'll remember me—if they'll understand why I left."

"They'll remember," David said firmly. "And when they're old enough, they'll be proud. You're doing something incredible, Elena. Don't forget that."

She looked at him, surprised by the sincerity in his voice.

"Thanks," she said after a moment. "I needed to hear that."

The two of them fell into a companionable silence, the harmonica's melody resuming as the others chatted softly around them. For a brief moment, the weight of the mission felt lighter, the vastness of space less daunting.

But as Elena lay in her bunk that night, staring at the dim glow of the overhead lights, the unease from earlier lingered at the edges of her thoughts. The anomaly. The small irregularities in the systems. They were minor, easily explained. Yet they hinted at a fragility she couldn't ignore.

Somewhere in the back of her mind, a quiet voice whispered:

This is just the beginning.

The following morning, Elena awoke to the soft *"Whisper"*, as the crew had affectionately nicknamed the gentle, rhythmic hum of the ship's systems. Alongside it came Astraeus's automated wake-up announcement, her tone calm yet commanding. "Good morning, crew. Current time: seven hundred hours. Environmental conditions remain stable. Today's schedule has been uploaded to your consoles."

Elena rubbed her eyes and gently pushed herself out of her sleeping pod, her movements fluid in the weightlessness of the *Whisper* zone. Unlike her personal room in the artificial gravity section of the ship, she had chosen to sleep in one of the gravity-free bunk pods tucked into the quieter areas of the ship's living quarters. Some crew members, like Elena, preferred the sensation of weightlessness, a deliberate choice to acclimate to the Martian low gravity they would soon face. Floating to sleep felt oddly freeing—no pressure points against her body, no need for a mattress or pillows, just the soft cocoon of a sleeping bag tethered securely to the wall.

The key to restful sleep in zero gravity was containment. Elena zipped herself into the bag each night, snug enough to prevent drifting but loose enough to mimic the comfort of a blanket. Her head was cushioned by a padded rest to prevent bobbing, and subtle elastic bands around her hips provided just enough tactile feedback to keep her anchored. For her, the weightlessness wasn't disorienting; it was soothing. Every breath felt lighter, her body untethered from Earth's constraints. As she drifted through the *Whisper* zone that morning, she marveled at how natural it had begun to feel, even as she knew others preferred the grounding pull of artificial gravity. To Elena, this was a taste of the future—floating in the quiet expanse, preparing her body and mind for the alien gravity of Mars.

#

After her morning routine—a quick meal of re-hydrated fruit and a check-in with the environmental systems—she joined the others in the main hub for their daily briefing. Riya stood at the center of the circular room, her expression as composed as ever.

"First, some good news," Riya began.

"All systems are currently operating within normal parameters. The anomaly detected two days ago has shown no further activity. Marcus and Astraeus have been running continuous diagnostics, and we've found no indication of any immediate threat."

A murmur of relief passed through the crew, though it was tempered by the lingering memory of how quickly things could change.

"However," Riya continued, her tone firm,

"we cannot afford to become complacent. Every system on this ship has been designed with redundancies, but it's our vigilance that will ensure we reach Mars in one piece. Stay sharp and report anything out of the ordinary, no matter how minor."

The crew nodded in unison, the weight of her words sinking in. As they dispersed to their stations, Leva found herself paired with Marcus for a routine inspection of the fusion core. The task required navigating to the aft section of the ship, where the massive engines powered their steady journey through the void.

Dr. Ieva Dainauskaitė was a name that resonated with the brilliance of innovation and the quiet resilience of someone who had carved her own path through life's harshest circumstances. A nuclear physicist of unparalleled expertise, Ieva had been a key member of the international team that developed the fusion engine powering the *Eos Horizon*. Born in a small town in Lithuania, her life had been marked by tragedy early on—she was orphaned at the age of five when an industrial accident claimed her parents' lives. Raised in a state-run orphanage, Ieva found solace in books, her natural aptitude for science revealing itself before she had even turned ten.

Her academic journey was meteoric. By her twenties, she was contributing to groundbreaking research in nuclear containment fields, and by thirty, she was leading projects that pushed the boundaries of fusion propulsion. Despite her accomplishments, Ieva remained deeply private, her solitary nature shaped by a life of self-reliance. She had never married and seemed to carry her independence as both a shield and a badge of honor. Her stoic demeanor belied a sharp wit and an unyielding commitment to her work. On board the *Eos Horizon*, Ieva was both revered and somewhat enigmatic, often found running meticulous diagnostics on the fusion core or quietly observing the faint glow of the reactor's containment chamber. To Ieva, the engine wasn't just technology—it was a living thing, a creation she had nurtured and perfected. "The heart of the ship," she would call it, her Lithuanian accent lending the words a certain poetic weight. For her, the *Eos Horizon* wasn't just a mission—it was the culmination of a lifetime's work and the only home she had ever truly chosen.

"Rope or Clingers?" Marcus asked with a smirk.

"Joking, right? Clingers would be useless in this jungle of cables and chaos," Ieva shot back without missing a beat.

The propulsion module was a labyrinth of cables, control panels, and glowing reactors, their faint hum filling the air. Marcus floated beside Leva, a diagnostic tablet in hand.

"Ever think about how much power it takes to move this thing?" Marcus asked as he began scanning the system.

"One miscalculation, and we'd be drifting through space forever."

"Comforting thought," Leva replied dryly, though a small smile tugged at her lips. She appreciated Marcus's blunt humor, even if it bordered on morbid.

He chuckled. "Hey, if we can laugh about it, we're still in good shape."

The inspection proceeded smoothly, with no irregularities detected. As they worked, Marcus shared stories from his past projects—everything from designing high-speed rail systems to assisting with deep-sea drilling platforms. His experiences were vast and varied, a testament to why he had been chosen for the mission.

"So what made you want to come to Mars?" Leva asked as they secured the final panel.

Marcus paused, his expression momentarily distant. "My wife," he said finally.

"She always believed humanity's future was among the stars. She passed a few years ago, but… this felt like a way to honor her dream."

Leva's chest tightened at the quiet vulnerability in his voice. "I'm sorry," she said softly.

"Sounds like she was an incredible person."

"She was," Marcus replied, a small smile crossing his lips.

"And I think she'd have loved this—being part of something bigger than herself."

Leva nodded, her own thoughts turning to the family she never had. In the quiet of the propulsion module, surrounded by the hum of machinery and the distant stars, she felt a renewed sense of purpose. They weren't just traveling to Mars—they were carrying the dreams and hopes of countless others with them.

#

That evening, as the crew gathered for their shared meal, the mood was lighter than it had been in days. David had managed to recreate a passable version of Earth-style curry using the ship's limited ingredients, and the smell alone was enough to lift everyone's spirits.

Elliot, ever the joker, leaned back theatrically and declared, 'If this is what passes for curry on Mars, the French might actually win the food debate after all,' earning groans and laughter in equal measure.

David, not missing a beat, slammed his fork onto the table in mock outrage. 'For the record, I am not French!' he announced, feigning the wounded pride of a man who'd been gravely insulted.

'French or Swiss, same difference,' Elliot quipped with a smirk.

'Blasphemy!' David shot back, dramatically clutching his chest as if he'd been struck, while the rest of the table erupted into laughter, the sound echoing through the ship like a balm for weary souls.

"You missed your calling as a chef," Riya remarked as she took a bite, her expression momentarily softening.

David grinned. "What can I say? Space farming comes with perks. Fresh cilantro, anyone?"

Laughter rippled through the group, the tension of the past days melting away. For a few precious moments, they weren't astronauts or scientists or engineers—they were simply people, sharing a meal and enjoying each other's company.

Elena found herself laughing more than she had in weeks, the sound unfamiliar but welcome. As the conversation turned to Earth, the crew shared stories of their favorite places, foods, and memories. Marcus spoke of road trips with his wife, Riya described her childhood in India, and David waxed poetic about a hidden ramen shop in Tokyo.

When it was Elena's turn, she hesitated before speaking. "There's this park near my home," she began.

"It's nothing special—just a small stretch of green with a playground. But my kids love it. We used to go there every Saturday, rain or shine. Watching them climb and run and laugh… those were the best moments."

The room grew quiet as she spoke, her voice tinged with longing. "I keep telling myself that what we're doing here will give them a better future. But some days, it's hard not to feel selfish for leaving."

"You're not selfish," Riya said firmly, her tone leaving no room for doubt.

"You're brave. And what we're doing here—it matters. Not just for us, but for them, and for everyone back on Earth."

Elena nodded, her eyes stinging with unshed tears. She wasn't sure if she believed Riya's words completely, but she wanted to. And for now, that was enough.

As the meal ended and the crew began to disperse, Elena lingered behind in the common area. Through the view-port, the stars seemed brighter tonight, their light sharp and unyielding. Somewhere out there was Mars, a speck in the distance that was growing closer with each passing day.

She pressed her hand against the glass, her reflection staring back at her. "Mars is waiting," she whispered, the words carrying a mix of hope and uncertainty. Behind her, the ship hummed softly, a fragile thread connecting them to their destination.

The journey was far from over, and the challenges ahead loomed large. But for the first time in weeks, Elena felt something she hadn't allowed herself to feel fully: a quiet, stubborn optimism.

#

The days turned into weeks, the *Eos Horizon* cruised steadily toward Mars, its crew locked in the relentless rhythm of survival and preparation. Routines provided a structure, a way to combat the isolation and monotony of the journey. But space had a way of amplifying even the smallest cracks, and the weight of their mission lingered in every interaction.

Elena spent much of her time in the lab, working with Dr.Noah on the seedling experiments. The hydroponics system was crucial to their survival—not just for providing fresh oxygen and food, but as a foundation for the sustainable agriculture they would need to establish on Mars. Watching the tiny plants grow, their vibrant green defying the sterile surroundings, gave her a sense of purpose.

"Look at this," Noah said one morning, holding up a tray of spinach seedlings.

"Fifteen percent more growth than projected. These little guys are overachievers."

Elena smiled, her fingers brushing against the leaves of another tray. "They're thriving in conditions that should be impossible. I guess they didn't get the memo."

Noah laughed, his eyes crinkling at the corners. "Exactly. They're like us—out of their element but making it work."

She glanced at him, her smile fading slightly. "Do you ever think about what happens if we don't make it? If the colony fails?"

He leaned against the workbench, his expression thoughtful. "Of course. It's hard not to. But that's why we're here, right? To give it our best shot. And even if we don't succeed, we'll have paved the way for the next attempt."

Elena nodded, though the thought did little to ease her fears. She turned her attention back to the seedlings, focusing on the task at hand. The weight of her doubts could wait; for now, there was work to be done.

#

Not everything aboard was thriving like Noah's seedlings. Just as the crew was settling into their routines, the anomaly returned two weeks later.

Elena was in the common area, reviewing environmental data on her tablet, when Astraeus's voice cut through the quiet. "Attention: electromagnetic fluctuation detected. Source: external systems."

Her stomach tightened as she looked up to see Riya already heading for the main hub. The rest of the crew followed, their movements swift but controlled. By the time Elena reached the hub, Liam, Marcus and David were at their stations, pulling up diagnostic data.

"Same pattern as before," Marcus reported, his voice clipped.

"But stronger this time."

"External interference?" Riya asked.

"Unclear," David replied. "Could be cosmic radiation, but the frequency is unusual."

David frowned, leaning over his console. "It's almost rhythmic. Like… a signal."

The room fell silent at his words. Elena felt her pulse quicken, her mind racing through the implications. A signal? From where? And from whom?

"Let's not jump to conclusions," Riya said firmly, though her tone betrayed a hint of unease.

"Marcus, isolate the source. David, run a comparison against known frequencies, Liam, make sure heading is not affected, Elena, check the environmental systems for any abnormalities."

The team moved into action, the tension in the air palpable. Elena focused on her console, scanning the environmental data for any fluctuations. Everything appeared normal, but the growing rhythm of the anomaly echoed in her thoughts.

"It's faint," David said after a few minutes, his voice breaking the silence.

"But it's definitely a pattern. Repeating every 22 seconds."

"Could it be a malfunction in our systems?" Riya asked.

Marcus shook his head. "Doubtful. The signal's coming from outside the ship."

"Then what's causing it?" Elena asked, her voice quieter than she intended.

No one answered. The rhythmic pulses continued, faint but unrelenting, a mystery that hung over them like a shadow.

"Looks like the Whisper has a cousin," someone muttered with a nervous nod.

That night, Elena found herself in the observation module once more. The stars stretched endlessly before her, their cold light offering no answers. The faint pulse of the anomaly replayed in her mind, a question she couldn't shake.

She pressed her hand against the glass, her reflection staring back at her. "What are you?" she whispered to the void.

The door behind her slid open, and Riya entered, her movements calm but deliberate. She floated beside Elena, her gaze fixed on the stars.

"You're thinking about the anomaly," Riya said, not a question but a statement.

Elena nodded. "It doesn't make sense. A signal from outside the ship? What could it be?"

Riya was silent for a moment before replying. "We don't know. But we'll figure it out. That's why we're here—to face the unknown and make sense of it."

Elena turned to look at her. "Do you ever feel like we're… unprepared? Like we've taken on something too big?"

Riya met her gaze, her expression steady. "Every day. But that's what makes it worth doing. If it were easy, someone else would have done it already."

Elena sighed, her thoughts swirling. "I just hope we're ready for whatever's out there."

"We'll face it together," Riya said firmly. "Whatever it is."

The two of them stood in silence, staring out at the stars. The rhythmic pulse of the anomaly continued in the background, a quiet reminder of the mysteries waiting for them in the vastness of space.

The rhythmic signal lingered like an unsolved equation, its faint pulses echoing in the minds of the crew. The days that followed were filled with tension as they worked tirelessly to analyze the anomaly, balancing their regular duties with the growing weight of the unknown. Despite their efforts, answers remained elusive.

Elena threw herself into her work, her days consumed by environmental monitoring and system checks. The routine provided some relief, a way to focus her thoughts on the tangible instead of the enigmatic signal that seemed to hum just outside their reach. Still, she couldn't shake the nagging feeling that the anomaly was more than a random cosmic occurrence.

#

One evening, while reviewing the latest diagnostic reports in the hydroponics module, David stepped in, his expression uncharacteristically serious.

"We might have something," he said, holding up a data tablet.

Elena's heart quickened. "What did you find?"

"It's not just electromagnetic," he began, lowering his voice as though the walls might overhear. "There's a secondary pattern buried in the noise—infrared pulses, faint but distinct."

She frowned, her mind racing. "Infrared? Could it be interference from the ship's systems?"

David shook his head. "Marcus and I ruled that out. Whatever it is, it's external. And the timing of the pulses is too regular to be natural."

Elena leaned back, the weight of his words settling over her. "You're saying it's deliberate. A signal."

"Maybe," David admitted.

"Or maybe it's something we don't understand yet. Either way, we need to figure out where it's coming from."

The next morning, the crew gathered in the main hub to review the new findings. The atmosphere was charged with anticipation and unease, each member acutely aware of the stakes.

"This is what we know," Marcus began, displaying a graph of the signal's frequency patterns on the central screen.

"The primary electromagnetic pulses are accompanied by infrared emissions. The pattern is consistent—twenty-two-second intervals, with minor fluctuations."

"Have we pinpointed the source?" Riya asked, her tone steady but intense.

"Not yet," Marcus replied. "The signal's faint, and triangulating its origin is complicated by our movement through space."

"It's possible the signal's source is static," David added. "It could be coming from a fixed location, and we're passing through its range."

Elena listened carefully, her mind racing through the implications. If the signal was deliberate, it meant someone—or something—was transmitting it. The idea sent a chill down her spine.

"What's our next step?" she asked, breaking the silence.

Riya looked around the room, her gaze settling on each crew member in turn.

"We keep investigating. This signal could be nothing, or it could be something significant. Either way, we need answers. Marcus, David, everybody else, continue your analysis. Elena, double-check the environmental systems for any indirect effects."

Her tone grew firmer as she continued, "The two systems we cannot afford to compromise are the ship's life support and navigation. They are our top priority at this stage. If you notice anything unusual, no matter how insignificant it seems, report it to me immediately."

"And if we find the source?" Marcus asked.

Riya's expression hardened. "We cross that bridge when we come to it."

#

That evening, Elena found herself in the observation module again, staring out at the endless void. The stars, so familiar and yet so distant, seemed to mock her with their silence. She pressed her hand against the glass, her reflection merging with the starscape.

"What are we walking into?" she whispered.

Behind her, the door slid open, and Marcus walked in. He carried a small cup of re-hydrated tea, its faint aroma a welcome contrast to the sterile air of the ship.

"Couldn't sleep?" he asked, offering her the cup.

She accepted it with a grateful nod. "Something like that. You?"

He shrugged, leaning against the view-port. "Thinking about the signal. Trying to make sense of it."

Elena sipped the tea, its warmth a small comfort. "Do you think it's deliberate? That someone—or something—is sending it?"

Marcus was quiet for a moment, his gaze fixed on the stars. "I don't know. But whatever it is, it's a reminder of how little we understand about this universe."

Elena nodded, her thoughts echoing his sentiment. "It's humbling. And terrifying."

"That's the job description, isn't it?" Marcus said with a faint smile.

"Facing the terrifying and trying to make sense of it."

She smiled back, though her thoughts remained heavy. "I just hope we're ready."

"We'll figure it out," he said firmly. "One way or another."

#

The days continued to pass, the signal, whisperer's cousin, a constant presence in the background of their lives. As the *Eos Horizon* drew closer to Mars, the crew's focus shifted to preparing for their arrival. Yet the mystery of the signal loomed large, an unanswered question that seemed to follow them like a shadow.

Elena found herself thinking about her children more often, their faces etched into her memory. She wondered if they were watching her progress, if they felt proud—or abandoned. The thought weighed on her, but she pushed it aside, focusing on the work that lay ahead.

One evening, as the crew gathered for another shared meal, Riya raised her glass—a small container of re-hydrated juice—to make a toast.

"To the whisperer's cousin," she said, her voice strong and resolute.

"Whatever lies ahead, we face it together."

The crew raised their glasses in unison, their voices a quiet but determined chorus. "To the whisperer's cousin."

As they drank, Elena felt a flicker of hope. The journey was far from over, and the challenges ahead were daunting. But for the first time in weeks, she felt a sense of unity, a belief that they could face whatever waited for them on Mars—and beyond.

Ada leaned back in her chair, frustration flickering across her face.

"We've got Astraeus, the most advanced AI ever built, and Liam, the human calculator. So why is this stupid signal still a mystery?"

The room erupted in laughter, the tension momentarily easing as even Riya allowed herself a small smile.

Liam, seated at the navigation console, looked up with a faint smirk, nodding as if acknowledging the challenge.

"It's not as simple as it sounds," he said, his tone calm but measured.

"A signal like this doesn't come with a neat 'from' address. It's traveling across millions—maybe billions—of kilometers, through layers of cosmic noise, gravitational distortions, and even potential interference from our own systems. Triangulation in space isn't just pointing at a source—it's like finding a single whisper in a storm the size of the galaxy. It takes time."

Ada raised an eyebrow, her lips curling into a grin. "So, the galaxy's storm wins for now?"

"For now," Liam admitted, shrugging.

"But the Whisper's cousin doesn't get to hide forever. She must show herself, or we will find, one way or the other"

\#

Despite her academic brilliance, Ada Torres was grounded and approachable, often the first to crack a joke in tense moments, her quick wit a welcome balm for the crew. Yet beneath her humor lay an unyielding determination; she viewed every puzzle, especially the enigmatic ancient scripts, as a challenge she was destined to solve. For Ada, understanding wasn't just about communication—it was about connection, bridging the gaps between time and space, and finding humanity's place among the stars.

Among the vastness of space, somewhere, faint and unyielding, the signal continued to pulse.

The steady rhythm of the signal became an unspoken presence among the crew, a subtle reminder of the mysteries they had yet to unravel. Though the anomaly posed no immediate threat, its persistence gnawed at their collective psyche. It was both fascinating and unsettling—a puzzle that demanded to be solved, yet offered no clear solution.

Elena spent her days alternating between her regular duties and assisting Liam and David with their analysis of the signal. The hydroponics module, once her sanctuary, now felt like a backdrop to the growing tension aboard the *Eos Horizon*. Even the seedlings, thriving against all odds, seemed to echo the quiet urgency that permeated the ship.

"Still no luck tracing the source," Marcus said one evening as he walked beside her in the hub. His voice carried a mix of frustration and fatigue.

"It's like chasing a ghost."

Elena glanced at the data displayed on her console. The signal's pattern remained unchanged—consistent, deliberate, and maddeningly elusive. "What if we're looking at this the wrong way?" she asked.

"Maybe it's not about the source but the message itself."

Marcus raised an eyebrow. "You think it's a message?"

"I don't know," Elena admitted. "But if it's deliberate, there has to be a reason for the pattern. What if we tried decoding it?"

David, who had been monitoring a nearby console, leaned in with growing interest.

"You're suggesting we treat it like a cipher? Not a bad idea," he said, a hint of amusement in his voice.

"We could run it through some decryption algorithms... or just hand it over to Liam," he added with a nod and a wry smile.

Liam nodded slowly. "It's worth a shot. I'll set up the parameters."

The three of them worked late into the night, as Liam was assigned a priority task critical to impending Mars landing manures. Their focus unwavering as they sifted through the data. Hours passed in a blur of calculations, algorithms, and speculation. By the time they decided to call it a night, they had made little progress, but their determination remained intact.

#

The following morning, Riya called a full crew meeting in the main hub. Her expression was unreadable as she stood before the group, her hands clasped behind her back.

"We've been monitoring the anomaly for weeks now," she began.

"While it hasn't posed a direct threat, its persistence—and the patterns we've observed—warrant further investigation. This is no longer just a curiosity. It's a priority."

She paused, letting her words sink in. "Liam, Marcus, David, and Elena have been working on analyzing the signal. I want the rest of you to assist them where possible. If there's even a chance that this signal is deliberate, we need to understand it."

"What about Mars?" one of the engineers from Marcus' team asked.

"We're less than three weeks away from arrival. Shouldn't we be focusing on the landing and setting up the colony?"

Riya's gaze hardened. "We'll continue our preparations as planned. But this anomaly could have implications we can't ignore. It's a balance, and I expect everyone to do their part."

The crew nodded, their expressions a mix of determination and apprehension. As they dispersed, Elena felt the weight of the mission settle more heavily on her shoulders. The line between discovery and danger was growing thinner with each passing day.

#

Later that evening, Elena found herself back in the observation module, the familiar starscape stretching out before her. She had come to think of this room as her refuge, a place where she could process the complexities of their journey. But tonight, the stars offered little comfort.

"What are you doing out here?" David's voice broke the silence as he walked into the room.

David glanced over her shoulder. "Just thinking. Trying to make sense of it all."

He nodded, settling beside her. "It's a lot to process, isn't it? The signal, the mission, everything we left behind."

"Sometimes I wonder if we were meant to find it," she said quietly. "Or if we're just stumbling into something we don't understand."

David tilted his head, considering her words. "Maybe it's both. Maybe this is part of what it means to explore—to face the unknown and see what's on the other side."

Elena smiled faintly. "You're always the optimist."

"Someone has to be," he replied with a grin. "Besides, I figure if the signal's been out there for who knows how long, it can wait a little longer while we figure it out."

His lighthearted remark brought a brief sense of relief, though the weight of the signal remained. As they sat in silence, the faint hum of the ship's systems seemed to blend with the pulse of the anomaly, a subtle but constant reminder of the mysteries that awaited them.

#

The days continued in much the same rhythm, the crew working tirelessly to prepare for their arrival on Mars while piecing together the puzzle of the signal. Progress was slow but steady, and though answers remained elusive, their efforts brought a sense of purpose to the journey.

Liam and Astraeus shared a connection that transcended the usual boundaries of man and machine—a bond forged not only by Liam's expertise but by his very hand in shaping the AI's foundations. With several groundbreaking patents in artificial intelligence to his name, Liam had been instrumental in crafting the algorithms that allowed Astraeus to process cosmic data and make decisions with unmatched precision. Their communication often seemed almost otherworldly to the rest of the crew, with cryptic exchanges of equations, algorithms, and variables flowing effortlessly between them as though they were speaking a language no one else could hear. Liam's natural affection for Astraeus was evident in the way he referred to it not as a tool, but almost as a colleague, a brilliant partner whose mind he understood because he had helped create it. The two were tirelessly working and reworking the intricacies of the already planned Mars descent, recalculating trajectories and contingencies with relentless focus. For Liam, each adjustment wasn't just a technical improvement but a way to refine the legacy he shared with Astraeus, ensuring their combined brilliance brought the mission safely to its next chapter.

Astraeus (pronounced *uh-STRAY-us*) was named after the Titan god of stars and planets in Greek mythology, a fitting moniker for an AI designed to navigate the vast, unpredictable expanse of space. The name evoked not only its celestial purpose but also the idea of bridging humanity's ancient fascination with the cosmos and its modern quest to explore them. Chosen after weeks of deliberation, it symbolized the unity of myth and science—a reminder of how far humanity had come and how much further it aspired to go.

At the heart of Astraeus lay a vast web of deep neural networks, meticulously trained over decades on astronomical data, spacecraft telemetry, and simulated anomalies. It was not just an AI but the culmination of humanity's most ambitious efforts in machine learning and cognitive modeling. Every decision it made was rooted in billions of data points, every calculation refined by countless iterations of supervised and unsupervised learning. This learning was guided by the input of experts like Liam Hwang, whose own research had pioneered several key advancements in artificial intelligence, ensuring Astraeus could adapt to the unpredictable challenges of interstellar travel.

Yet Astraeus' journey to the *Eos Horizon* was nearly cut short. During its final development phase at the UNSI labs, a catastrophic power surge caused a fire that threatened to wipe its core memory. The AI, housed in a reinforced data center, survived by the narrowest of margins thanks to the heroic efforts of technicians who risked their lives to stabilize the system. The damage was extensive but repairable; however, had Astraeus been lost, the *Eos Horizon* mission would have faced delays of years, possibly decades. It was a stark reminder of the fragility of progress and how close humanity had come to seeing its most advanced creation erased before it could take flight.

The accident at the UNSI labs was not only a technical crisis but a moment of profound unease for the entire mission. The catastrophic power surge, which triggered a fire in the secure data center housing Astraeus' core memory, was initially blamed on an equipment failure. However, anomalies in the incident report—an inexplicable override of safety protocols and a suspicious delay in the activation of fire suppression systems—raised the unsettling possibility of sabotage. Investigations yielded no conclusive evidence, but the specter of a deliberate attack lingered. Quiet conversations in the upper echelons of UNSI hinted at factions opposed to the mission, though no one was willing to publicly admit it.

The incident reignited an old but simmering debate about interstellar colonization. While many viewed the *Eos Horizon* as a beacon of hope and progress, a vocal minority saw it as a harbinger of potential disaster. Critics drew parallels to Earth's own history of colonization, which often brought devastation in its wake. They pointed to the diseases and exploitation that decimated indigenous populations, the loss of biodiversity as foreign species disrupted ecosystems, and the scars left on landscapes by unchecked industrial expansion. Entire cultures had been erased, their legacies reduced to artifacts in museums, and ancient forests were leveled to fuel the ambitions of the colonizers.

This historical shadow hung heavily over the mission, with detractors arguing that humanity had not learned from its past mistakes. They questioned the ethics of imposing humanity's will on Mars, a planet whose barren landscapes might harbor microbial life yet undiscovered. What right, they asked, did humanity have to exploit another world when it had so thoroughly ravaged its own? Some of these dissenters were peaceful, raising their concerns through protests and open forums. Others, however, operated in secrecy, driven by a fervent belief that they needed to stop the mission at any cost.

Eos Horizon became more than just a spacecraft—it was a lightning rod for philosophical and ethical debates about humanity's place in the universe. The suspected attack on Astraeus underscored the stakes of those debates, a reminder that the mission's greatest challenges weren't limited to the void of space but also lay in the divisions back on Earth. For the crew aboard, it was a sobering reality that not everyone shared their vision of hope and exploration. Instead, they carried with them not just the dreams of humanity's future but also the weight of its conflicted past.

Now, aboard the *Eos Horizon*, Astraeus stood as both a marvel of technology and a symbol of resilience. Its calm, calculated voice guided the crew with unerring precision, a stabilizing presence in the uncertain void. For Liam and others who had witnessed its near destruction, Astraeus was not just a tool—it was a testament to what humanity could achieve when it dared to reach for the stars, and a reminder of how much there was still to risk and gain.

As the *Eos Horizon* approached Mars, the red planet loomed larger in the view-port, its rust-colored surface stark and unyielding against the infinite black of space. The ship's cabin was quiet, save for the occasional hum of systems and the murmured voices of the crew. Standing at the observation window, Elena Moreno let out a slow breath, her fingers grazing the cool glass as if to touch the alien world before her.

"It's beautiful," she said softly, her voice tinged with awe.

"And terrifying."

Behind her, Noah Carter approached, the lines on his face etched deeper in the dim light.

"Beautiful, sure," he said, his tone half-joking, half-serious.

"But it's a barren wasteland that'll fight us every step of the way."

"That's what makes it fun."

Dr. Jonathan Myers, the chief-medical officer, leaned against a console, his sharp gaze fixed on the swirling dust storms in the distance.

"We're not just visiting—we're rewriting what it means to exist as a species."

Sonja, her arms crossed, tilted her head, her pale blue eyes scanning the view-port.

"What gets me," she said, her voice low, "is how small Earth looks now. A faint speck in the distance. Everything we've ever known, everyone we've ever loved, all crammed onto that tiny dot."

Ada Torres stepped into the room, her usual energy dampened by the magnitude of the moment.

"Maybe it's not about what we've left behind," she said, her voice steadier than she felt.

"Maybe it's about what we're carrying forward."

Noah snorted lightly, the sound breaking the tension. "Well, Ada, you better be ready to carry a lot forward. We're counting on you to find a partner and kick-start the next generation of Mars colonists. I mean, someone's gotta do it."

Ada stopped mid-step, turning to him with a raised eyebrow and a wry grin. "Oh, really? That's my job now? Fine, I'll put up a sign: 'Volunteers Wanted—Apply Within.' You interested, Noah? You could contribute to the gene pool."

Sonja laughed, the sound sharp and brief. "Yeah, Noah's kids would probably grow hydroponic crops out of their ears."

Dr. Myers joined in, his chuckle dry and understated. "And Ada's would probably decipher Martian hieroglyphs by kindergarten."

Ada smirked, leaning against the bulkhead. "As long as they don't inherit your sense of humor, I think we'll be fine."

Elena turned to face them, her expression torn between amusement and seriousness. "Focus, people. We've got a planet to land on. Let's survive our first day before we start naming colonies."

The laughter faded, replaced by a heavy silence as the crew's eyes turned back to the view-port. Mars dominated their vision now, a harsh, unforgiving expanse of rust-red sands and shadowy canyons. The faint glimmer of Earth was barely visible, a pinprick of light swallowed by the vastness of the universe. The sight was humbling, a reminder of their fragility and the monumental task ahead.

"It's not just about surviving," Noah said quietly.

"It's about creating something that lasts."

Ada nodded, her gaze unwavering as the planet loomed closer. "A future. That's what this is."

The crew fell silent, the weight of their shared mission settling over them. Mars, stark and resolute, awaited their arrival. It was a challenge unlike any humanity had faced—a blank canvas, a hostile frontier, and a fragile hope for a new beginning. And as the *Eos Horizon* drifted closer, they knew there was no turning back.

Elena stood in the observation module, her eyes fixed on the planet that would soon become their new home. Behind her, the faint pulse of the signal continued, its rhythm steady and unyielding.

"Mars is waiting," she whispered, her voice carrying a mix of anticipation and uncertainty.

And somewhere, in the depths of space, the signal waited too.

Chapter Two
ARRIVAL

Commander Riya Kapoor was not the kind of leader who sought attention. She didn't need to. Her presence was quiet yet commanding, like the steady rhythm of a heartbeat—reliable, grounding, and impossible to ignore. When her name was announced as the mission commander for the *Eos Horizon*, it didn't spark debate; it silenced it. She was the choice that felt inevitable, the leader who seemed forged for this exact moment.

Riya Kapoor's journey began in Chandigarh, India, in a modest apartment filled with books and dreams. Her mother, a schoolteacher, believed in the transformative power of knowledge. Her father, a retired Air Force pilot, carried the discipline and adventure of his career into their home. Together, they cultivated in Riya an insatiable curiosity about the world—and the universe beyond. On clear nights, the family would climb to the roof. Her father would point out constellations with a precision that seemed almost reverent.

"Look there, beta," he'd say, his finger tracing the glittering path of the Milky Way.

"That's where our stories begin." It was under that vast, star-filled canopy that Riya first said, "One day, I'm going there."

Her path to the stars was as relentless as the drive behind those words. At the Indian Institute of Technology, she graduated at the top of her class in aerospace engineering, her brilliance matched only by her work ethic. Recruited by ISRO, she quickly became a leading mind in modular habitat design for lunar missions. But for Riya, engineering blueprints wasn't enough. She wanted to step inside those habitats. She wanted to lead.

A scholarship to the United States opened new horizons. At MIT, she pursued advanced studies in aerospace engineering, where her academic brilliance and leadership potential caught the attention of the U.S. Navy. After becoming a U.S. citizen, Riya joined the Navy and climbed the ranks to become head of the Deep Space Exploration Corps. Her tenure was marked by exceptional achievements, including the development of hybrid propulsion systems and leading multiple deep-space missions. Her ability to inspire and unify diverse teams under extreme conditions earned her multiple commendations.

Her acceptance into the United Nations Space Initiative (UNSI) astronaut program was more than a milestone—it was a transformation. Riya honed her skills across disciplines: piloting, survival training, and deep-space navigation. Her first mission proved her mettle. When a thermal control system failed mid-orbit, threatening the spacecraft, Riya suited up without hesitation, venturing into the void to perform a manual bypass. She returned to the cabin, systems stabilized, with the calm demeanor of someone who'd merely adjusted a thermostat. Her crew gave her a nickname that day: "Kapoor the Unflappable."

But she wasn't unshakable. No one is. Riya's career soared, yet it came tethered to moments of profound loss. She married her UNSI colleague, Daniel Holt, an astronaut whose daring matched her own. Together, they were a team forged in the crucible of space exploration. Until the unthinkable happened. A suborbital test flight went wrong, and Daniel didn't come home.

The grief gutted her. For months, she drifted in its shadow, questioning everything. Could she continue to work in a field that had taken so much? Was space exploration worth the human cost? It was Daniel's own words that brought her back. "Pushing past the known," he had once said, "is what makes us human."

She returned to work with a renewed sense of purpose. But something had shifted. Her drive was no longer just for herself or her career—it was for humanity. Riya led a team that revolutionized habitat systems for Mars. She published groundbreaking research on psychological resilience in low-gravity environments. She wasn't just surviving her grief; she was transforming it into progress.

When UNSI began assembling the crew for the *Eos Horizon*, Riya's name rose to the top of every list. Technical expertise? Unquestionable. Leadership under pressure? Proven. But it was her humanity—her ability to inspire, to empathize, to unite—that sealed her selection. Leading humanity's first colonization mission to Mars wasn't just another challenge. For Riya Kapoor, it was the culmination of a life shaped by discipline, discovery, and the enduring belief that our greatest achievements lie beyond the known.

#

The day her selection was announced, Riya addressed the world. She stood at the podium, poised but not detached. Her voice carried the weight of the past and the promise of the future.

"This mission isn't just about science," she began, her words deliberate.

"It's about humanity. We're leaving behind our homes, our loved ones, and the world that shaped us. But we're not abandoning it. We're carrying it with us. Every lesson, every story, every hope—it all comes with us to Mars."

Her gaze swept across the room, and for a moment, it seemed as though she was speaking directly to each person watching.

"This mission will test us in ways we can't yet imagine. There will be hardships, dangers we've prepared for and others we haven't. But what defines us is how we face them—together."

She paused, her expression softening. "We are not just explorers. We are builders of the future. And that future begins now."

#

The *Eos Horizon* hovered in orbit above Mars, its shadow slicing across the planet's ochre surface. Inside the ship, the crew gathered in the main hub, the anticipation palpable. Weeks of preparation had led to this moment, and now, they were minutes away from humanity's first landing on the Red Planet.

Riya stood at the center, her voice calm but commanding as she addressed the team.

"We've trained for this. The descent will be rough, but our systems are designed to handle it. Stick to protocol, and we'll get through this."

Elena tightened the straps of her harness, her heart racing as she cast a quick glance at the others. Marcus was at his station, meticulously double-checking the ship's landing systems, his movements precise and deliberate. Beside her, David sat unusually quiet, his face lined with a seriousness that was rare for him.

Liam, however, seemed the least tense of them all. His confidence was palpable, the result of relentless preparation and a mind that had rehearsed this moment a thousand times over. He had calculated every trajectory, accounted for every variable, and with Astraeus by his side—the perfect, unerring companion—he was certain of success. To Liam, it wasn't just numbers; it was a life-saving certainty, a delicate balance of logic and trust in the systems that would guide them safely to Mars.

"Excited?" David asked, his attempt at a grin barely masking the tension in his voice.

"Terrified," Elena admitted. "But in a good way."

"Good. Means you're alive," he said, offering her a reassuring nod.

The ship jolted as the descent sequence began. Riya's voice rang out over the comms.

"Engaging thrusters. Prepare for atmospheric entry."

Most of the crew was already at their designated stations, meticulously executing their assigned tasks. Engineers monitored the ship's systems, scientists checked their equipment, and navigators worked in sync with Astraeus to ensure the descent trajectory was flawless. The rest of the crew, those without immediate responsibilities during landing, were directed to the living quarters. Their only duty now was to sit, brace, and wait—a task deceptively simple yet fraught with the weight of the moment. The lack of windows in the quarters, while initially a point of contention for some, had become a blessing. Without a direct view of the red planet rushing up to meet them, it was easier to focus inward, to calm the nerves and trust in the process.

#

The absence of children aboard the *Eos Horizon* was conspicuous, especially for those who had left their families behind. It was a decision steeped in practicality and politics. The mission designers had faced the delicate task of navigating the international treaties and laws that governed this unprecedented endeavor. Including children in a one-way mission to Mars would have sparked an avalanche of ethical debates, not to mention legal challenges from nations unwilling to condone such a risk. The consensus was clear: while the prospect of a new generation born on Mars was thrilling, the responsibility for their safety outweighed any pioneering ambitions. It was far easier, politically and morally, to leave them on Earth, safeguarded under UNSI's care, than to fight the inevitable legal battles that would arise if something went wrong.

For many aboard, the absence was bittersweet. The notion of a child's laughter echoing in the ship's corridors was an appealing yet distant dream. It was a sacrifice everyone had to make, a reminder that this mission wasn't just about the individuals on board—it was about the future of humanity. The weight of this understanding settled heavily on those now seated in the living quarters, their thoughts drifting to the lives they had left behind. In the quiet hum of the *Whisper*, each passenger braced not only for landing but for the reality of the life awaiting them on the surface of Mars.

#

"We are going in" David murmured.

The cabin shook violently as the *Eos Horizon* pierced the thin Martian atmosphere. Flames licked the edges of the view-port, a vivid display of the friction between the ship's heat shield and the planet's atmosphere. Elena gripped her harness, her knuckles white as the turbulence intensified.

"Heat shield holding," Marcus reported.

"Descent trajectory nominal." Liam's, almost machine-like tone followed.

Elena's breath came in shallow gasps as the ship continued its descent. The turbulence was relentless, every jolt and vibration a reminder of the thin line between success and disaster. She closed her eyes, focusing on the rhythm of her breathing as Riya's voice guided them through the descent.

"Approaching landing zone," Riya announced.

"Deploying retro thrusters."

The ship slowed with a sudden force, the vibrations subsiding as the thrusters fired. Elena opened her eyes to see the barren Martian surface coming into view—a vast expanse of rust-colored rock and dust, dotted with the faint outlines of the automated systems that had been sent ahead to prepare the site.

"Landing in three… two… one."

The *Eos Horizon* touched down with a heavy thud, the cabin jolting before falling still. For a moment, there was silence, broken only by the faint hum of the ship's systems. The sensation rippled through the crew, a reminder of the immense forces at play. Even though the touchdown sounded and deep inside felt hard, the magnetic suspension built into the landing gear, combined with the precision-controlled thrust vectoring engines, absorbed the shock with grace. It was as gentle as a mother resting her baby on a cushion—a feat of engineering perfection that had been tested and retested countless times in simulations but never before on Mars itself.

For those few seconds, the cabin felt suspended in a liminal space between tension and relief. The crew exchanged glances, their expressions a mix of awe and disbelief. They had made it. Against all odds, they were here—on the red planet. And then, breaking the fragile stillness, Riya's voice came over the comms, calm and steady as always.

"Ladies and gentlemen," she said, a faint note of emotion threading through her words,

"welcome to Mars."

Her words seemed to unlock the room, a ripple of cheers and laughter spreading through the cabin as the tension broke. The enormity of the moment settled over them like a warm tide. The *Eos Horizon* had carried them across millions of miles of space, defying gravity and probability, and now it rested on Martian soil.

A cheer erupted from the crew, the tension of the descent giving way to relief and exhilaration. Elena unstrapped herself, her movements shaky as she floated toward the view-port. The sight before her was surreal—a landscape that had existed only in photographs and simulations, now a reality.

"Can you believe it?" David said, his voice filled with awe as he joined her at the window.

"We're here."

Elena nodded, her throat tight with emotion.

"It's… incredible."

#

As the cheers settled into an electric hum of excitement, Ada unstrapped herself and stretched, casting a glance out the view-port at the rust-colored expanse of Mars.

"You know what," she said, her voice tinged with both joy and sarcasm, "Earth's just going to have to wait for the news."

The crew turned to her, grinning as she continued.

"What's the delay right now? About fifteen minutes each way? By the time Mission Control hears we landed safely, we'll already be unpacking and debating where to plant the first flag. Honestly, I think we've earned this little head start on history."

Astraeus's calm, measured voice filled the *Eos Horizon* as the ship settled onto the Martian surface with a faint, satisfying hum of its landing mechanisms.

"Touchdown confirmed. Location: Olympus Planitia, approximately three-hundred kilometers southeast of Olympus Mons. Current atmospheric conditions: thin carbon-dioxide rich atmosphere at approximately six-hundred pascals pressure, surface temperature minus nineteen-degrees Celsius and falling. Moderate wind activity detected, no significant hazards at present. Precautionary measures: exterior excursions are prohibited until environmental clearance is granted by Earth command. All crew are advised to remain within the vessel."

The AI continued, seamlessly transitioning to operational instructions.

"Crew may now move freely within the vessel. However, protocols mandate that all personnel remain on-board for the next forty-eight to seventy-two hours. This period will be utilized for comprehensive external scans, atmospheric sampling, and radiation assessment. Earth command will review all data before issuing clearance for exterior activities. Commander Kapoor will make an announcement in this regard later as needed"

Astraeus paused briefly, as if giving the crew a moment to absorb the information, before adding in a tone that was almost reassuring, "The *Eos Horizon*'s systems are fully operational and calibrated for extended surface habitation. All immediate needs for life support and functionality are secure. Congratulations and welcome to Mars"

#

The mandatory waiting period felt like an eternity for the crew. Excitement mingled with restlessness, each hour stretching impossibly long as they stared out at the red landscape through the ship's observation screens. Conversations ebbed and flowed, alternating between enthusiastic speculation and nervous silence. For some, the whispering hum of the ship's systems became a source of solace, a reminder of the vessel's reliability. For others, it only amplified the ache of anticipation. Every scan, every data point from Astraeus seemed to drag time further, a relentless countdown to the moment they would finally step into the history books. Even the most patient among them found themselves pacing the halls, driven by the irrepressible urge to set foot on Mars. It wasn't just a mission—it was the culmination of lifetimes of dreams and sacrifices, condensed into the longest two days they had ever known.

As the artificial gravity aboard the *Eos Horizon* was shut down, the crew experienced their first taste of Mars' reduced pull—just one third of Earth's gravity. It was a strange sensation, a peculiar lightness that made every movement feel both liberating and awkward. Elena took an experimental step, nearly overcompensating and stumbling before catching herself with a laugh.

"Okay, that's…weird," she muttered, flexing her fingers as if expecting even them to feel different. Marcus, ever the pragmatist, bounced slightly on his toes, testing the resistance.

"It's like walking in a dream," he said, though his expression betrayed how alien it felt. Ada, meanwhile, attempted an exaggerated stride, grinning as her foot rose higher than intended.

"So, this is what it feels like to be a superhero," she quipped, drawing a chuckle from the others.

Riya observed quietly from the corner, her sharp eyes assessing the crew's adjustments as the most experienced on low gravity and spacewalks.

"Take it slow," she advised, her voice steady.

"Muscle memory from Earth won't serve you here. Every step, every movement—you'll need to relearn."

Her calm voice broke through the murmurs.

"Remember, this isn't zero gravity anymore. You can't just push off and float; you need control, but not too much. Overcompensating will get you hurt."

The warning hung in the air, sobering but necessary.

"It's like learning to walk from a crawl, or learning to ride a bike," she continued, her tone measured but encouraging.

"Take it slow, focus on each movement, and your muscles will adjust. The intricacies will become second nature before you know it—but only if you respect the process.

#

On day two of the landing, Riya Kapoor stood at the front of the command center, her voice clear and steady as it echoed through the ship's comm system.

"Crew of the *Eos Horizon*, after thorough analysis by both Earth Command and our on-board systems, I am authorizing disembarkation. We are cleared to set foot on Martian soil in 30 minutes. This is a moment that will define us—not only as individuals but as representatives of humanity's aspirations."

She paused briefly, allowing the gravity of the moment to settle.

"Before we proceed, I want to emphasize a few critical instructions. MSA suits must be triple-checked for integrity, especially oxygen supply, and temperature regulation. Stick to the designated perimeter mapped out by Astraeus for initial exploration—no deviations until further notice. Communication lines must remain open at all times. Report anything unusual immediately, no matter how small it may seem."

Riya's tone softened slightly, acknowledging the mix of emotions likely coursing through the crew.

"This is more than a first step. It's a declaration. We're here to build something extraordinary, but safety is paramount. Remember, we're still learning this world, and it's unforgiving. Let's make our mark, but let's do it wisely and together."

She gave a small, confident nod, her words carrying the weight of a leader who understood both the risks and the rewards.

"Suit up, prepare your equipment, and meet at the airlock. The red horizon is waiting for us."

#

As the comm channel closed, a palpable mix of excitement and focus filled the ship. The crew began final preparations for their historic first steps onto Martian soil.

As the crew absorbed Commander Kapoor's announcement, Astraeus's calm, measured voice flowed through the comm system, adding a layer of precision to the excitement.

"Attention, crew. Before disembarkation, please ensure you report to your designated team leaders and remain with your assigned groups at all times during exterior activities. This is important for maintaining operational efficiency and safety in the Martian environment."

There was a brief pause, followed by another reminder. "For those who have not yet completed their pre-disembarkation medical and health assessments, the medical bay remains open and fully staffed. Please report immediately to ensure clearance. It is important that all personnel are in optimal physical condition before stepping into Mars' challenging atmosphere."

Dr. Jonathan Myers - Chief Medical Officer aboard *Eos Horizon* - was a name synonymous with innovation in the world of neurosurgery. Born and raised in Boston, Massachusetts, he had spent decades at the cutting edge of medicine, pioneering advancements that merged human expertise with artificial intelligence. His groundbreaking work on AI-assisted robotic surgery not only revolutionized complex neurosurgical procedures but also garnered him numerous patents and international accolades. A dedicated researcher, he had been a key consultant for UNSI's medical teams on various space missions, helping to develop protocols for medical emergencies in zero-gravity environments. Despite his immense contributions, Jonathan had never ventured into space himself—until now.

This mission marked a dramatic shift for Dr. Myers, stepping from the labs and operating rooms he had mastered into the unpredictable reality of deep space. For all his expertise, the personal experience of being in the void of space was entirely new, yet he embraced it with the same meticulous approach that had defined his career. Though initially reserved, he quickly became a respected figure among the crew, known for his calm demeanor and ability to inspire confidence. For Jonathan, this journey wasn't just about providing medical care—it was about pushing the boundaries of what human biology could achieve on a foreign planet and testing the very technologies he had helped create in the most challenging environment imaginable.

Dr. Myers led a dedicated team of five medical professionals aboard the *Eos Horizon*, each carefully selected for their expertise in fields vital to sustaining human health in the harsh conditions of space and on Mars.

The medical bay is outfitted with state-of-the-art technology, ensuring the crew's safety and well-being in even the most extreme scenarios. A full-body diagnostic scanner could perform comprehensive scans within seconds, detecting fractures, internal injuries, and illnesses with pinpoint accuracy. The bay also housed a robotic surgical unit equipped with AI-assisted precision tools, designed by Dr. Myers himself, allowing complex surgeries to be performed even in zero gravity and vibration.

The portable medical pods were a groundbreaking addition, capable of stabilizing critical patients with features such as real-time vitals monitoring, temperature regulation, and automatic administration of medication. The advanced lab station allowed the team to conduct in-depth blood, tissue, and microbiological analyses, crucial for adapting to Mars' unique biological risks.

Additionally, a regenerative tissue synthesizer was included, capable of promoting rapid healing for wounds and burns, and a pharmaceutical synthesizer provided on-demand creation of medications. The psychological evaluation suite combined immersive VR (Virtual Reality) therapy with biofeedback sensors to help manage stress, depression, and anxiety.

Together, Dr. Myers and his team represented the pinnacle of medical innovation and care, prepared to tackle the unpredictable challenges of humanity's first steps on another planet.

Dr. Myers' poster, hung on the back wall of the medical bay, was both a mantra and a reminder which read: *"To seed the colony with life anew, we must first keep the hundred true"*.

It served as a constant call to vigilance, reminding every crew member who saw it that their collective survival was the cornerstone of humanity's future on Mars.

Ada passed through the medical bay, her eyes landed on the poster. She smirked and quipped, "Dr. Myers, you should have that embroidered somewhere: 'Lowest I count is Hundred.'"

Myers, without missing a beat, looked up from his work and replied with a faint smile, "All of us should, Ada.

"Attention, crew" Astraeus broke the silence.

"Current weather update for Olympus Planitia: surface temperature is minus 18 degrees Celsius with moderate wind activity at 25 kilometers per hour. Visibility remains clear, and no significant atmospheric disturbances are forecasted for the next 12 hours. Please ensure all MSA suits are calibrated for thermal and wind resistance before disembarkation. Safety remains paramount." Astraeus's voice echoed.

The crew moved quickly to prepare for disembarkation. Each member donned their MSA (Mars Surface Activity) suits, the layers of advanced materials designed to withstand Mars' harsh conditions. The suits felt bulky compared to their shipboard uniforms, but they provided the necessary protection against the planet's thin atmosphere and extreme temperatures.

As they gathered at the airlock, Riya addressed them one final time. "This is it. Humanity's first steps on another planet. But remember, we're here to work. Stick to your assignments, follow protocol, and stay safe. Let's make history."

The airlock hissed as it depressurized, the outer door sliding open to reveal the Martian surface. Riya stepped out first, her boots sinking slightly into the dusty soil. She paused, her gaze sweeping over the horizon before turning back to the crew.

"Let's get to it," she said.

One by one, the crew followed, their movements cautious as they adjusted to Mars' lower gravity. Elena was among the last to step out, her breath catching as her boots touched the ground. The sensation was strange— both familiar and alien. She looked around, taking in the vast, barren landscape that stretched out in every direction.

"It's like a whole new world," she murmured, her voice barely audible over the comms.

"And it's ours to build," Marcus replied, his tone filled with quiet determination.

The Martian landscape stretched endlessly, a vast expanse of rust-red dust and jagged rocks under a pale, salmon-colored sky. The thin atmosphere gave the light an eerie quality, casting long shadows that made the terrain seem otherworldly. Elena stood still for a moment, letting the surreal nature of their achievement sink in.

Around her, the crew began their work. Automated rovers that had arrived months earlier stood idle, coated in fine layers of Martian dust. Their job now was to activate these machines and ensure the site was ready for the next phase of colonization. The primary habitat module, pre-assembled by the rovers, loomed in the distance like white dome against the red horizon.

#

"Dr. Moreno, how's it feel to be part of history?" David's voice crackled through her comms. He was standing nearby, a sample container in one hand and a scoop in the other, already collecting soil for analysis.

"It feels…" Elena paused, searching for the right words.

"Bigger than I thought it would. Like standing at the edge of something vast."

David chuckled.

"That's Mars for you—big, empty, and full of possibilities."

"Less talking, more working," Riya's voice interrupted, firm but not unkind.

"We have a lot to do before sunset."

The crew set to work with precision, their tasks clearly defined. Elena joined the environmental team, running diagnostics on the air filtration units within the habitat modules. These systems would be their lifeline, converting Mars' CO2-heavy atmosphere into breathable air. Inside the first dome, the airlock hissed as it sealed behind her, and she removed her helmet, her breath catching as the filtered air filled her lungs.

"Air quality stable," she reported over the comms.

"Filtration system is online."

Outside, Marcus and some of his team set up the solar arrays, carefully clearing dust from the panels and angling them to capture the faint Martian sunlight. Once aligned, the automated sun-trackers would ensure the arrays continuously adjusted to maintain optimal exposure. These solar arrays were designed to complement the nuclear fusion generators powering the habitat, providing vital redundancy to safeguard critical systems.

"Elena," Marcus called over the comms, "can you check the greenhouse systems? David and I are seeing some strange readings from the hydroponics module."

"On it," she replied, making her way to the adjacent dome. The greenhouse was a feat of engineering, its transparent walls allowing filtered sunlight to nourish the plants inside. The crops—yet to be transplanted— had been growing in *Eos Horizon* under control environment. Rows of leafy greens and budding vegetables transporting from the vessel to the greenhouse stretched before her, a stark contrast to the desolation outside.

As she checked the control systems, Elena noticed a slight drop in water pressure within the irrigation network. It wasn't critical, but it was enough to warrant attention.

"I'm seeing a minor pressure drop in the irrigation system," she reported. "Running diagnostics now."

"Keep us posted," Marcus replied.

Elena traced the issue to a partially clogged valve, likely caused by sediment in the recycled water supply. She adjusted the flow manually, then logged the anomaly for further review.

"Pressure's back to normal. I'll keep an eye on it."

"Good work," Marcus said.

"We're making progress, but let's not get complacent. This planet won't forgive mistakes."

"Sounds like something Riya would say," Elena chuckled, a faint smirk breaking through the tension.

Marcus allowed himself a brief grin. "Maybe, but she's not wrong. Mars plays for keeps."

#

As the sun dipped lower on the horizon, casting the landscape in shades of gold and crimson, the crew gathered outside the main habitat dome. The day's work was nearly done, and Riya had called for a brief meeting to review their progress.

Elena stood with the others, the Martian dust clinging to her suit like a badge of honor. Around her, the crew members looked tired but exhilarated, their faces reflecting the weight and wonder of what they had accomplished.

"We've made a strong start," Riya began, her voice carrying over the open comm channel.

"The habitats are operational, the greenhouse is stable, and the solar arrays are generating power. But this is just the beginning. Every day from here will test us in ways we can't predict. Stay sharp, stay focused, and support each other. That's how we succeed."

Her words were met with nods and murmurs of agreement. The unity among the crew was tangible, forged in the crucible of their shared mission.

As they prepared to return to the habitat, Marcus paused, his gaze fixed on the horizon. "Anyone else see that?" he asked, pointing toward a ridge in the distance.

Elena followed his gesture, her heart skipping as she spotted a faint glimmer—an unnatural flicker of light against the dusty landscape.

"Could be a reflection," she suggested, though her voice betrayed her uncertainty.

"Could be," Marcus replied, his tone cautious. "Or it could be something else."

Riya's voice cut in. "Log it for now. We'll investigate once we've secured the site. Let's head back inside."

Elena hesitated, her eyes lingering on the ridge. The flicker was gone, replaced by the stillness of the Martian dusk. She turned and followed the others, her thoughts swirling with questions.

#

On the other side, the *Eos Horizon* stood majestically in the distance, its sleek frame gleaming under the faint Martian light. Like a battle-hardened warrior who had carried its legionaries through trials and tribulations, it seemed to gaze back at them with quiet pride and unwavering majesty, a testament to the resilience of both machine and humanity.

Inside the habitat, the crew gathered for their first meal on Mars. The re-hydrated food tasted no better than it had aboard the *Eos Horizon*, but the setting made it feel different—more significant. Laughter and conversation filled the dome as the crew shared their experiences from the day.

#

The habitat dome, a space of ingenuity, stands as the first structure on Martian soil designed to sustain human life for an extended period. Constructed from modular, interlocking segments of reinforced carbon composites and polymerized glass, it creates a spacious and secure environment capable of withstanding Mars' thin atmosphere, radiation levels, and fluctuating temperatures. Its translucent roof filters out harmful solar radiation while allowing natural light to flood the interior, providing a connection to the red Martian landscape outside.

Its double-glazed glass incorporates advanced UV filtering and houses a water-filled cavity between the layers, which significantly enhances its thermal capacity. This innovative design minimizes heat transfer into the dome, maintaining stable temperatures even during the extreme fluctuations of Martian days and nights.

Suspended within the water are nano-particles that dynamically respond to environmental conditions, regulating the amount of heat that enters or escapes the dome, and to detect and block harmful radiation from penetrating. This mechanism not only ensures a consistent internal temperature but also allows the majority of sunlight to pass through, creating an ideal balance between light and heat for human habitation and plant growth.

Inside, the dome is meticulously designed to balance efficiency and comfort. The living quarters are arranged in a circular layout along the perimeter, with each crew member assigned a private room equipped with an en-suite bathroom. The dome accommodates hundred-and-twenty such quarters, each approximately 20 square meters in size. Despite their compact dimensions, the rooms are thoughtfully engineered with space-saving features like foldable furniture, integrated storage units, and customizable lighting to provide a sense of personal comfort. Positioning the quarters along the perimeter offers the added luxury of a window in each room, an intentional design choice aimed at reducing stress and promoting mental well-being by providing visual access to the Martian landscape.

The main entrance to the dorm is strategically positioned to face east, offering protection from prevailing winds in most cases. It opens directly into the level one circular corridor, which connects seamlessly to the living quarters. This layout ensures easy and unobstructed access for residents to their private rooms, eliminating the need to navigate through utility or operational areas.

The level two corridor, also circular and coaxial, connects the utility and communal areas to the core of the dome, fostering interaction and collaboration among the crew. Three radial corridors act as arterial pathways, efficiently linking the outer circular corridors to the central core. One radial corridor connects directly to the main entrance, while the other two, positioned symmetrically apart, each lead to emergency exits at their ends. This design ensures efficient evacuation routes in case of danger, enhancing the safety and functionality of the habitat.

At the core of the dome lies a large, multi-purpose communal area. This space is equipped with long tables, ergonomic seating, and thin holographic display panels lining the walls. These panels serve multiple purposes, from projecting calming Earth landscapes to hosting mission briefings and entertainment. Adjacent to this area are shared facilities, including a modular kitchen with advanced food preparation systems and a recreation zone for relaxation and light exercise.

Although the habitat dome is designed to comfortably house 100 individuals for the initial months, its layout also allows adaptability as the colony expands. After the first few months, when the crew begins constructing individual habitats, the dome will transition into a shared facility, re-purposed as a central hub for operations, dining, and leisure.

Encompassing all its facilities within a hundred-meter radius and a perimeter of over half a kilometer, the dome is far from insignificant. Yet, against the vast, desolate Martian landscape, it seems modest—an unassuming outpost of humanity amid the endless expanse of rust-red terrain.

#

The medical team, however, will remain aboard the *Eos Horizon* for the foreseeable future. This decision is rooted in the ship's state-of-the-art medical bay, which offers unparalleled diagnostic and treatment capabilities. Until the next shipment from Earth delivers the necessary supplies and equipment to establish a fully equipped medical facility on Mars, the *Eos Horizon* will serve as the primary center for medical care. This phased strategy ensures the immediate and long-term health needs of the crew are carefully addressed, providing the colony with stability and safety as it develops.

Additionally, the *Eos Horizon's* fusion engines, functioning as high-capacity generators, will be dedicated to supporting medical operations. With their immense energy reserves, they guarantee uninterrupted functionality under any circumstances, reinforcing the colony's resilience in critical moments.

The evening passed with a mix of excitement and exhaustion as the crew settled into their designated cabins. For the first time in weeks, Elena allowed herself to feel a small measure of hope. They had made it to Mars, and despite the challenges, they were off to a strong start.

But as she lay in her bunk that night, staring at the curved ceiling of the habitat dome, the image of the flicker on the ridge lingered in her mind. Was it just a trick of the light? Or was it something more?

Somewhere outside, beneath the endless Martian sky, the question remained unanswered.

#

The following day began early, the crew moving with quiet efficiency as they resumed their work. Mars' harsh environment left no room for complacency, and the tasks ahead were daunting. Solar panels needed to be fine-tuned, equipment calibrated, and the habitats reinforced against the ever-present threat of dust storms.

Elena focused on the greenhouse, her primary responsibility. The crops, though young, were vital to the colony's survival—not just for food but as a source of oxygen. She moved carefully through the rows of plants, checking their growth and adjusting the irrigation system where necessary.

#

The water supply for the initial colonization stage on Mars is a carefully planned system combining imported resources with in-situ generation and recycling. The early Mars missions and the *Eos Horizon* itself carried an initial stock of water, stored in highly insulated containers to minimize losses, ensuring an immediate supply for drinking, hygiene, and agricultural needs. Alongside this, the missions also transported a reserve of hydrogen, which would be combined with oxygen extracted from the Martian atmosphere using advanced electrolysis of Carbon Dioxide, producing additional water as required.

The habitat's closed-loop system maximizes resource efficiency by recycling gray water from sinks and showers through multi-stage filtration and reclaiming moisture from the air using humidity condensers. Even though the colony's water needs have been meticulously planned and resolved for the initial stage, with supplies calculated to sustain operations for a decade, the search for new and improved methods remains a top priority. Ideally, discovering a reliable water source on Mars—whether through subsurface ice deposits, hydrated minerals, or atmospheric extraction—would represent a breakthrough, transforming the colony's long-term prospects.

Achieving "water independence" would not only ensure the survival and growth of the settlement but also reduce reliance on costly resupply missions from Earth, marking a pivotal step toward self-sufficiency on the Red Planet.

"Morning, Doc," David's voice crackled through her comms. She turned to see him standing at the entrance, holding a sample container.

"Thought I'd swing by and see how the Martian salad's coming along."

She smiled. "Better than expected. The soil's responding well to the nutrients. It's not Earth, but it's enough."

David nodded, his gaze sweeping over the rows of green. "Amazing, isn't it? Growing life on a planet that's been dead for billions of years."

"You don't know that, but terrifying nevertheless," Elena replied.

"If anything goes wrong with these systems, we're in trouble."

"Which is why we have you," David said with a grin.

"No pressure, though."

Elena laughed softly, grateful for his easy demeanor. It was a brief reprieve from the weight of her responsibilities.

Elena leaned against the cool metal wall of the dome's bio-lab, her thoughts a tangled mix of anticipation and dread. The weight of her responsibility was immense—transforming barren Martian soil into a thriving ecosystem was no small feat, and the pressure to succeed felt as crushing as the gravity she had left behind on Earth. Every variable seemed to whisper of potential failure: the unpredictability of Martian regolith, the limits of her bio-engineered crops, and the sheer fragility of the ecosystem they were trying to create. Yet, as overwhelming as it all felt, there was comfort in knowing she wasn't alone—she had a legacy of decades of Earth's best research backing her.

As the leading expert in agricultural gene technology, Elena is the colony's most valuable asset in the fight against Mars's unforgiving environment. Her advanced engineered crops represent the cutting edge of synthetic biology, designed to withstand the challenges of Martian conditions. While the critical hurdles of low pressure and intense radiation remain unresolved, her work gives the colony hope that one day, crops might flourish directly on Martian soil exposed to the elements. For now, cultivation remains confined to the safety of a pressurized and meticulously controlled greenhouse, a lifeline that sustains the colony and symbolizes humanity's determination to thrive against the odds.

The next level of security is the stockpile of seeds, the seed vault, nestled securely within the habitat, served as a quiet beacon of reassurance for the crew. In addition to the seedlings and plants already growing in the hydroponic chambers during the journey, the vault stood as an invaluable backup. It held the promise that even if all current efforts were to fail—if crops withered or soil experiments faltered—they could start over, not just once, but several times over. Each tiny seed encapsulated humanity's determination to adapt, survive, and thrive, a safeguard against the uncertainties of life on Mars.

The *Eos Horizon's* seed vault, while not as expansive as the renowned Svalbard Global Seed Vault, is a testament to decades of meticulous research and preparation for Martian colonization. Compact yet robust, it houses a carefully curated selection of seeds, each chosen for its potential to thrive in the harsh Martian conditions. The collection includes pure, hybrid and genetically engineered varieties, spanning essential food crops like wheat, soybeans, and potatoes, alongside plants with ecological and practical roles. Genetically engineered varieties, developed specifically for Mars, feature traits like enhanced drought resistance, lower atmospheric pressure tolerance, and rapid growth cycles. These innovations are critical for establishing not just sustainable agriculture but also a thriving ecosystem.

Beyond food production, the seed vault contains species for landscaping, wind barriers, and soil improvement. Hardy shrubs and grasses are intended to stabilize loose Martian regolith, while nitrogen-fixing plants and cover crops will work in tandem with a cocktail of carefully selected microbes to enhance soil fertility. These microorganisms, brought from Earth, have been tailored to survive in the oxidized Martian soil and are expected to catalyze the transformation of the barren terrain into a medium capable of supporting life. The vault represents a vision far beyond mere survival—it is a blueprint for the gradual greening of Mars, each seed a tiny but powerful promise of the future.

"Wait," Elena said, raising her hand to halt the conversation.

A subtle pulse of the wrist display units—dubbed Orion Bands—signaled an incoming message.

Commander Riya's voice followed, firm yet steady: "All crew, please assemble in the main hub for important announcements at eleven hundred hours."

#

The Orion Bands were indispensable tools for the crew's survival, seamlessly blending communication, monitoring, and medical capabilities. These bands has built-in location and environmental awareness, tracking air quality, radiation levels, and personal health metrics with precision. In moments of distress, their needle-less drug delivery system utilized advanced micro-jet propulsion to administer medication or pain relief directly through the skin, ensuring immediate intervention. For crew members operating outside the protective domes, the bands synchronized with their visors' HUDs, projecting vital alerts and updates directly into their field of view to keep them informed and prepared.

In addition to their health and environmental monitoring functions, the bands were powerful command tools. Those in leadership roles or with special clearance could interact directly with Astraeus, the ship's AI, using the Orion Bands to issue commands or retrieve mission-critical data on the go. This capability ensured the crew could maintain control and cohesion during critical operations, whether managing resources within the habitat or navigating challenges on Mars's surface. The bands' integration into the mission's systems underscored their importance, acting as both personal lifelines and operational hubs.

Engineered from bio-mimetic materials, the Orion Bands were designed to feel as natural as a part of the skin, remaining unobtrusive even during prolonged use. Their thin, low-profile form merged effortlessly with the wearer, offering both comfort and functionality in equal measure. With an augmented holographic interface and seamless integration into mission-critical systems, the bands became an indispensable extension of the body—a constant partner in navigating and surviving the unforgiving Martian environment.

#

"That's more than a tea break," Elena murmured, her tone laced with both humor and exasperation as she glanced at the clock.

By midday, the crew gathered in the main hub to discuss their next steps. Riya stood at the central console, reviewing a map of the surrounding area. The ridge where Marcus had spotted the flicker of light was marked in red.

"We've made good progress here," Riya began, her voice steady and confident.

"The habitats are stable, and our primary systems are online. The greenhouse is operating at optimal capacity, power generation is performing as expected, and no major breakdowns have been reported. Airlocks have been thoroughly inspected and repaired, ensuring safe transitions in and out of the habitat. Logistics are progressing as planned, with equipment and storage boxes steadily being moved from the Dawn."

Riya paused briefly, with a slight smile, she added, "I hope we haven't forgotten the ship, staring at us over the hill." The crew chuckled softly, her remark breaking the tension as they all turned their thoughts to the imposing *Eos Horizon*, standing sentinel just beyond their base of operations.

Riya was glancing at her team leaders for updates. Each provided quick confirmations: tasks were assigned, systems were checked, and operations were running smoothly.

In a brief moment, Riya raised her voice, "But we can't stay in our bubble forever," her tone shifting to a determined edge.

"We need to start exploring the terrain beyond the immediate site. The ridge to the east is a natural target—it'll give us a better vantage point and help us map the area more effectively. Let's get a scouting team ready and ensure they have the resources to make a safe and productive trip. We've laid the groundwork, but there's still so much more to uncover."

#

In orbit high above the red planet, *Sentinel* and *Watcher* maintained their tireless vigil, the silent guardians of the colony. Equipped with imaging systems and atmospheric sensors, *Sentinel* constantly monitored the colony's surroundings, tracking weather patterns, dust storms, and any potential threats to the habitat. Its data fed directly into the colony's central systems, providing early warnings and ensuring the crew could respond to environmental challenges with precision.

Watcher, synchronized in orbit with its counterpart, focused on detailed terrain mapping and communications. Its high-resolution cameras captured every ridge, valley, and crater in the occupied zone, feeding critical data to ground teams planning expeditions. Acting as a communication relay, it kept the crew connected to Earth and each other, even in areas where direct signals were obstructed.

#

"I'd like to go," Marcus volunteered.

"It's close enough to be safe, and I'll take one of the rovers."

Riya nodded. "Take David with you. Two sets of eyes are better than one. Stick to the planned route, and don't take unnecessary risks."

Elena watched as the two men prepared for their excursion, a knot of unease tightening in her chest.

"Be careful out there," she said as they passed her on their way to the airlock.

"Always," Marcus replied with a reassuring smile.

The airlock hissed as it cycled, and moments later, the two men were outside, the rover's engine humming softly as they set off toward the ridge. Elena returned to her work, but her thoughts kept drifting back to the flicker of light and the possibility of what it might mean.

Time on Mars operates differently from Earth, dictated by the planet's longer rotation period and its unique orbit around the Sun. A Martian day, known as a *sol*, lasts approximately twenty four hours, thirty nine minutes, and thirty five seconds, slightly longer than an Earth day. This subtle difference accumulates over time, requiring the crew to re-calibrate their schedules regularly to stay aligned with the Martian rhythm. A Martian year, due to the planet's more elliptical orbit, spans six hundred and eighty seven Earth days, which means seasons on Mars are almost twice as long as those on Earth. The crew uses a synchronized Martian Time System (MTS), adapted to their new home, with Astraeus managing daily schedules to align work cycles with the *sol* while ensuring sufficient rest. Despite the extended days, the lack of Earth's familiar twenty-four-hour clock presents both an adjustment challenge and a mental shift, as the crew learns to embrace a new cadence of time on the red planet.

The Martian day begins with a pale, diffused light as the Sun rises, appearing smaller and dimmer than on Earth due to Mars' greater distance from the star. The sunlight, though weaker, still casts long, sharp shadows across the dusty, rust-red landscape. By midday, the sky takes on a butterscotch hue, a result of the fine Martian dust suspended in the atmosphere. As evening falls, the sunlight softens into a colder, muted glow before fading into an extended twilight, eventually giving way to the frigid, starlit darkness of the Martian night. Seasons on Mars are more extreme and drawn out due to its elliptical orbit, with spring and summer in the southern hemisphere being hotter and shorter, while autumn and winter are colder and longer. Dust storms, sometimes encompassing the entire planet, are a hallmark of Martian weather, especially during southern summer, adding a layer of unpredictability to the seasons. The crew relies on atmospheric monitoring systems to adapt their activities to the unique interplay of light and seasonal conditions, a constant reminder of the stark contrast between this alien world and their home planet.

Hours passed, and the sun hung low on the Martian horizon, casting long shadows across the barren landscape. Inside the habitat, Elena monitored the rover's telemetry on a console, the steady stream of data a small comfort.

Though an accomplished Agricultural Scientist, Elena Moreno's contributions aboard the *Eos Horizon* extend far beyond her primary role. Her prior experience on space missions has honed her understanding of advanced technologies and interdisciplinary problem-solving, making her a versatile member of the crew. Agriculture, while critical, isn't a constant, round-the-clock endeavor, and with a capable team managing the day-to-day tasks, Elena often finds herself taking on additional responsibilities. Recognizing her organizational skills and keen acumen, Riya frequently entrusts Elena with administrative duties, ranging from resource allocation to coordinating inter-team activities. It's not uncommon to see Riya, David, Marcus, and others consulting Elena on non-agricultural matters. Her ability to approach challenges from a unique perspective often provides fresh insights, sparking solutions that might otherwise be overlooked. In a crew built on collaboration, Elena has become a trusted voice beyond her expertise in agriculture, embodying adaptability and intellect in equal measure.

"Marcus, David, status update," Riya's voice came over Orion.

"Almost there," Marcus replied.

"The ridge is steeper than it looked, but the rover's handling it fine."

"Anything unusual?" Riya asked.

"Not yet," David said. "But the terrain's full of reflective surfaces. Could explain the flicker we saw."

"Stay cautious," Riya said. "We don't take chances out here."

The minutes dragged on as Elena watched their progress. The ridge came into view on the console's display—a jagged outcrop of rock that loomed over the surrounding plains. The rover stopped at the base, and Marcus and David disembarked, their suits stark against the red backdrop.

"We're climbing now," Marcus reported. "Visibility's good."

Elena leaned closer to the screen, her pulse quickening as the two men ascended the ridge. The audio feed crackled with the sound of their breathing and the crunch of their boots on the rocky surface.

"Wait," David said suddenly. "Do you see that?"

"Yeah," Marcus replied, his voice tense. "There's something up here."

Elena's heart pounded as she listened. "What is it?" she asked, her voice sharper than she intended.

"Hard to say," Marcus said.

"Looks like… some kind of metallic structure. Could be debris from an old rover."

"Or something else," David added, his tone cautious.

"Stay where you are," Riya ordered.

"Don't approach until we assess the situation."

"Copy that," Marcus said. "Standing by."

"Astraeus, analyze satellite data. Get us a view of the ground," Riya commanded, her deep, unwavering voice carrying authority that cared little whether it addressed man or machine.

"Scan complete," Astraeus replied in its calm, measured tone.

"No elevated radiation levels detected. No movements detected. No immediate threats identified to David and Marcus. Body vitals are stable, though both show an elevated pulse and blood pressure—indicative of anxiety."

Riya nodded, her eyes fixed on the console as the data streamed in. "Understood. Keep monitoring their vitals and notify me of any changes. Let's not take any chances out there."

She leaned forward slightly, her gaze sharpening as the satellite feed refreshed. "Marcus can handle pressure, but David needs reassurance. Patch me through if you see their stress rising further."

"Yes, Commander," Astraeus responded, seamlessly continuing its watch.

Elena's eyes remained fixed on the screen, her mind racing. A metallic structure on the ridge? It could be an artifact of human exploration, a piece of equipment left behind by previous missions. But the unease in her chest refused to dissipate.

"Riya, what do we do?" she asked quietly.

Riya's gaze was steady, but the tension in her jaw betrayed her concern. "We proceed carefully. Marcus, David, document what you see and take samples if possible. Do not engage with it directly."

"Understood," Marcus said. He activated his helmet camera, and the video feed appeared on the console's display. The structure came into focus—a gleaming, angular object partially embedded in the rock.

#

The advanced MSA-mounted camera system is an advance piece of equipment designed to enhance situational awareness and safety during extravehicular activities. Strategically mounted above the wearer's ears and shoulders, the cameras are positioned to create a seamless 360-degree view, ensuring comprehensive visual coverage without blind spots. These aren't just ordinary cameras; they are state-of-the-art multi-spectral systems capable of capturing images across the visible spectrum and beyond, including infrared and ultraviolet. This allows the cameras to detect heat signatures, map radiation levels, and highlight environmental hazards invisible to the human perception.

By integrating radiation mapping with visual data, the system generates real-time overlays that help the wearer navigate the harsh Martian terrain with unparalleled precision. The cameras are wirelessly linked to the crew's Orion-Belt and, critically, to the central command centre, enabling mission leaders to see exactly what the crew sees in real-time.

Additionally, the feeds from multiple crew members are combined into a coherent world model, allowing the command centre to visualize what multiple operatives on the ground experience as a unified 360-degree view. At the heart of the command centre is the *Aegis* projection deck, a holographic interface that builds the incoming data into an interactive three-dimensional model. This system enables mission leaders to use space-touch gestures and voice to manipulate, analyze, and coordinate activities with unmatched precision. Astraeus also has seamless access to this 3D world, enhancing its usability further more.

#

"It's not from Earth," David said softly.

"At least, not anything I've seen."

Elena's breath caught as the implications sank in. Whatever this was, it wasn't part of any mission she'd ever studied. The realization sent a chill through her, the weight of the unknown pressing down like gravity.

The feed from Marcus's helmet camera displayed the structure in stark detail. The metallic surface shimmered faintly under the Martian light, its angular edges too precise to be natural formations. It was partially buried in the rock, as though it had been there for years—or centuries.

"Do you see that?" Marcus said, moving closer to the object while keeping a safe distance. The surface was etched with faint patterns, symmetrical and complex.

"This doesn't look random. It's deliberate."

David crouched beside him, using his *TerraProbe*, a handheld tool designed for collecting, analyzing, and securely storing material samples, to take a small soil sample from the base of the structure.

"The soil around it is different," he said. "Looks like it's not been disturbed recently."

Riya's voice came over the comms, sharp with caution. "Document everything, but don't touch it. We need to analyze this carefully."

"Understood," Marcus replied, switching his camera to macro mode to capture close-up images of the patterns. As he worked, the faint hum of the object grew audible through the comms, a low, rhythmic vibration that made Elena's skin prickle.

"Are you hearing that?" David asked, his voice tense. "It's… pulsing."

Elena's fingers tightened on the round beveled edge of *Aegis* as they all were monitoring the feed. The rhythmic hum matched the electromagnetic pulses they'd detected earlier, a realization that sent her heart racing.

"It's the same frequency, Whisperer's Cousin"

 she said to herself, fear of drawing everyone's attention.

Having no emotions to navigate or concern for how its words might be received, Astraeus stated in its precise, monotone voice, "This frequency, along with its delays and overall pattern, closely resembles the one detected during our journey."

The room fell silent, the implications settling heavily over the crew. Riya's eyes narrowed as she processed the information, her mind already running scenarios.

"Are you certain?" she asked, her tone clipped, betraying her unease.

"Confidence level: ninety-seven-point-three-percent," Astraeus responded without hesitation, its lack of emotion amplifying the weight of its conclusion. The air in the room seemed to grow thinner, the crew exchanging uneasy glances as the significance of the pattern began to take shape.

"You're saying this thing is the source of the signal?" Marcus asked.

"Affirmative" Astraeus's tone contained solid confirmation.

Elena nodded, "It has to be. The pattern is identical."

David straightened, his posture wary. "So, what are we dealing with here? A probe? A beacon?"

"Whatever it is, we need to stay cautious," Riya said firmly.

"Marcus, David, finish documenting and return to the rover. We'll analyze the data from here."

"Copy that," Marcus replied, though his gaze lingered on the structure.

"This thing… it's incredible."

#

The protocol for informing Earth and awaiting orders is a carefully balanced system designed to ensure both autonomy and oversight. Under Riya's authority, the colony has the mandate to make immediate decisions regarding safety, health, and resource allocation, particularly when swift action is required to safeguard lives or critical systems. However, actions with broader implications—such as major resource extractions, artifact interactions, or introducing irreversible changes to Mars' environment—require Earth's approval. The communication delay, ranging between 5 to 20 minutes one-way depending on orbital positions, poses significant challenges for real-time coordination. To address this, the colony operates under a tiered protocol system: Tier One allows for autonomous action in emergencies, Tier Two involves notifying Earth and proceeding unless explicitly countermanded, and Tier Three requires a full halt until Earth responds. These measures ensure the colony can act decisively when needed while maintaining accountability for actions with long-term consequences. The protocols, while strict, are designed to adapt to the unique challenges of interplanetary colonization.

"This is uncharted territory," Riya continued, her voice steady but firm.

"The protocols are clear—any interaction with an extraterrestrial construct requires Earth's direct sanction. We document everything, every detail, and then we move out. No exceptions."

The team exchanged uneasy glances, the tension palpable. Behind them, Liam undisturbed, already running scans, his hands moving deftly over his console as the artifact's faint hum filled the silence.

#

Liam Hwang was a man of few words and even fewer expressions. His face, perpetually composed, had earned him the nickname "Poker-face" among the crew. Whether poring over complex navigational equations or maneuvering the *Eos Horizon* through a critical course correction, Liam's demeanor remained impenetrable. It wasn't arrogance or indifference—it was precision. Every thought, every calculation, seemed locked behind his calm exterior, leaving others guessing at the emotions that might flicker beneath. Some found it unsettling; others admired it. In a world of unpredictability, he must have believed emotions were best kept in check.

Yet, his silence carried weight. When Liam did speak, his words cut through the noise with the clarity of someone who had already considered every variable. It was as though his mind existed a few steps ahead of the present, processing outcomes before anyone else even saw the problem. This emotional restraint extended to moments of triumph or crisis. When the crew landed safely on Mars, cheers erupted across the ship, but Liam's expression hardly shifted. Instead, he nodded toward a display and murmured, "Just as expected." Beneath that unyielding surface, however, was a quiet confidence and an unwavering dedication to his role—a resolve that spoke volumes to those who took the time to notice.

#

Riya straightened her tone softening just enough to reassure. "Until we receive further instructions, we prioritize safety. The risks here are too great, and we can't afford to act on speculation. Let's get this documented, clean up the site, and move back to base. This isn't over, but for now, we are done."

Elena's mind raced as she watched the feed. If the structure was the source of the signal, it meant they weren't alone—someone, or something, had been here before. The implications were staggering, a revelation that could reshape humanity's understanding of the universe. But it also raised questions that filled her with unease. Who had left the structure? And why?

The return to the habitat was uneventful, but the air inside was thick with tension as the crew gathered to review the footage. The video from Marcus's camera played on the main display, every detail of the structure magnified for scrutiny.

"This changes everything," David said, his voice barely above a whisper.

"We're not the first to step foot on Mars."

"We don't know that yet," Riya countered, though her tone lacked its usual certainty.

"It could still be debris from a classified mission. We can't jump to conclusions."

Marcus shook his head in agreement.

"It looks out-of-place and didn't came from Earth. The design, the textures—it's unlike anything I've ever seen."

Elena leaned forward; her gaze fixed on the screen.

"What if it's a message? The signal could be a way of drawing attention to it."

"Or a warning," Marcus said grimly.

The room fell silent as the weight of his words settled over them. The structure, with its enigmatic patterns and unrelenting hum, felt less like a discovery and more like an enigma waiting to be unraveled.

Riya broke the silence, her voice steady but firm.

"We document, we analyze, and we proceed with caution. This mission is about survival first. Whatever this thing is, it doesn't change that."

The crew nodded, though the tension in the room remained. As the meeting dispersed, Elena lingered behind, her thoughts swirling. The structure was a mystery, one that filled her with equal parts awe and dread. It was a puzzle she couldn't ignore—but it was also a reminder of how small and vulnerable they were on this alien world.

That night, Elena lay in her bunk, staring at the curved ceiling of the habitat. Sleep eluded her as questions raced through her mind. The discovery of the structure was monumental, but it also felt like the first step into something far larger and more complex than they could comprehend.

The rhythmic hum of the signal played in her memory, a sound that seemed to echo in the stillness of the habitat. She turned over, closing her eyes and willing herself to rest. But even as exhaustion tugged at her, one thought lingered, sharp and unyielding.

What have we found?

#

The next morning, the crew's work resumed, but the atmosphere in the habitat was palpably different. The discovery on the ridge had shifted the tone of their mission. What had been a collective focus on survival and preparation was now laced with unease and speculation. The structure— alien, deliberate, and pulsing with the same signal they had detected— loomed over every conversation.

Riya, ever the steady leader, kept them on task.

"We can't let this distract us from the colony's priorities," she said during the morning briefing.

"We're here to build a foundation for humanity. Everything else is secondary. The analysis of the structure will continue, but it's not our main objective."

Elena nodded, though she found it increasingly difficult to concentrate on her assigned tasks. The greenhouse, even though completely automated, required constant human attention—checking nutrient levels, maintaining the irrigation system, and monitoring the plants' growth, during this early stages of the unknowns in Martian agriculture. Yet her thoughts kept straying to the structure. The patterns on its surface haunted her, the symmetry and precision a stark contrast to the chaos of the Martian environment.

As she calibrated the greenhouse's climate controls, David appeared in the doorway, his expression unusually serious.

"You've got to see this,"

 he said, holding a tablet.

"What is it?" Elena asked, setting down her tools.

David handed her the device, his voice lowering. "Liam ran a deep analysis of the images we took of the structure. There's more to those patterns than we thought."

Elena's eyes widened as she scanned the data. The patterns etched into the structure's surface weren't just decorative—they were organized, repeating sequences that resembled a form of language. The realization sent a shiver down her spine.

"This isn't random," she murmured. "It's a code."

"Exactly," David said.

"Marcus thinks it could be a form of communication. Ada is doing her thing to see if she can decode it."

Elena's pulse quickened. If the patterns were a language, then whoever—or whatever—had created the structure was trying to convey a message. But what was it? And why leave it here, buried on Mars?

By midday, the tension among the crew was unsettling. Marcus and Riya had convened in the main hub to review the progress on decoding the patterns. Elena joined them, her curiosity outweighing her unease.

Marcus pointed to the screen, where the patterns had been digitally reconstructed.

"We've identified repeating sequences," he explained.

"They're too consistent to be natural. It's looks like a code, but it doesn't match any known languages or mathematical sequences from Earth."

"This is Ada's territory, she is working nonstop" Marcus said.

"Could it be symbolic?" Elena asked.

"Something meant to be interpreted visually rather than phonetically?"

"It's possible," Ada said. "But without a key, we're shooting in the dark."

Riya folded her arms, her expression unreadable. "What about the signal? Could it be related to the patterns?"

"Can't say," Marcus replied. "The frequency of the signal matches the spacing of the sequences, but that doesn't prove one way or the other. It's possible the structure is broadcasting the code."

David, who had been listening from the doorway, spoke up. "A message sent out into the void, waiting for someone to find it."

"Or a beacon," Marcus added. "Calling something—or someone—back."

The room fell silent at his words, the implications hanging heavy in the air. The structure wasn't just an artifact; it was an active presence, its purpose a mystery that both intrigued and unsettled them.

#

That evening, Elena found herself back in the observation deck, staring out at the Martian horizon.

Inside the habitat dome, perched above the circular utility rooms, lies the Level 1 Observation Deck, called the *"Circle"*, offering unparalleled, three-sixty-degree views of the Martian landscape. This continuous deck, encircling the dome's perimeter, has become a favorite retreat for the crew, providing an awe-inspiring opportunity to relax or exercise while gazing out at the vast, rust-colored expanse.

The half-a-kilometer brisk walk along the circular track was popular pastime. The sweeping views, dotted with ridges and valleys, evoke a sense of wonder and solitude, often envy when described to their peers back on Earth.

Higher up, near the dome's center, sits the Level 2 Observation Deck, Elena prefers to call *"The Sky"*, is a smaller and more secluded platform. Elevated above its larger counterpart, it offers extended panoramic views, stretching further toward the Martian horizon. Looks like purposely built for Stargazing, this is an breath-taking experience, with the Martian night sky unveiling a crystal-clear tapestry of stars, connecting the observer to the boundless cosmos. The higher vantage point and its quieter atmosphere provide a more private experience, as it's often left unoccupied. The winding stairs leading to this, designed intentionally without elevators, demand extra effort to reach, which likely explains its frequent emptiness.

Both observation decks stand as architectural highlights of the dome, blending practicality with a touch of luxury. They serve not just as spaces for relaxation but as a reminder of the extraordinary achievement of standing on another world, looking out at an untouched frontier waiting to be explored.

#

The ridge where the structure had been found was barely visible in the fading light to the Level two deck, a distant silhouette against the coppery sky.

Elena placed her hand against the glass, a ritual she fondly called *"Touching Mars,"* watching as her reflection blended with the otherworldly landscape beyond.

"What are you trying to tell us?" she whispered, her breath fogging the glass.

Footsteps echoed softly on the winding stairs, growing closer until Riya appeared beside Elena. She moved to stand silently at her side, her eyes drawn to the same distant ridge. For a moment that stretched into quiet understanding, neither of them spoke.

Among the rare visitors to *"The Sky"*, Riya was one of them. She often sought solace in its seclusion, escaping the weight of leading the colony and meeting the expectations of Earth, if only for a brief moment of peace.

"Do you think we're ready for this?" Elena asked finally, her voice barely audible.

Riya's expression remained calm, but there was a flicker of uncertainty in her eyes. "I don't think anyone can be ready for something like this," she admitted.

"But we're here. And we'll face it."

Elena turned to Riya, her voice steady but laced with curiosity. "What are Earth's orders? Do they have anything to add?"

Riya sighed softly, her gaze still fixed on the horizon. "They've granted us permission to examine, but not to disturb the artifact. Still, who knows what they'll decide tomorrow. Protocols are there for a reason, let's wait and see."

Elena nodded, though the unease in her chest didn't subside. "What if it's not just a message? What if it's a warning?"

"Then we'll figure it out," Riya said firmly. "

We've come too far to turn back now."

Elena looked at her, searching for reassurance. Riya's confidence was steady, but there was a weight behind her words—a recognition of the enormity of what they had found.

As they stood in silence, the rhythmic pulse of the signal seemed to hum in the back of Elena's mind, a quiet but unyielding presence. The structure was waiting, and with it, the answers they both craved and feared.

The next morning, the crew woke to an urgent announcement from Astraeus. "Attention: electromagnetic signal strength has increased. analyzing source."

Elena sat bolt upright in her bunk, her heart racing. The signal had been faint and consistent for weeks, but an increase in strength was something new—and potentially dangerous. She quickly donned her gear and made her way to the main hub, where the others were already gathered around Aegis, the holographic projection table.

"What's happening?" Riya asked, her voice sharp.

Marcus gestured to the projection, where the signal's frequency was displayed as a series of rising peaks. "It's definitely coming from the structure. The pulse intervals are shorter, and the intensity is increasing."

"Could it be responding to something we did?" David suggested. "The scans, the proximity…, we haven't touched it, have we?"

"It's possible we might have accidentally touched it at some point," Marcus admitted, his tone uncertain.

"But honestly, there's no way to be sure. Whatever this thing is, its behavior is still beyond our understanding."

"We might have a way," Liam said, his calm voice cutting through the uncertainty.

"The MSA suits are equipped with advanced touch sensors—an array of pressure-sensitive nodes embedded in the outer layers. These sensors can detect even the slightest contact, mapping tactile responses with precision. If we correlate the touch data with the 3D models and the video logs, we should be able to determine with absolute certainty if there was any contact with the artifact."

Astraeus's voice broke the silence with its calm, precise tone.

"Analysis complete, Liam. Neither David nor Marcus made contact with the artifact. Certainty: one hundred percent."

Riya frowned, her jaw tightening as she considered their options. "How close are we to decoding the patterns?"

"Still working on it," Marcus and Ada both replied at once.

"We've made progress, but without more data, it's slow going" said Marcus.

"We don't have the luxury of time," Riya said.

"If the signal's changing, it could be a sign of escalation. We need to figure out what we're dealing with before it's too late."

David said, "It was only emitting radio waves up until now—that's why we picked it up during our journey. But with its expansion into a wider spectrum, we'll need a thorough scan to identify any additional emissions. Watcher's images from this morning confirm visible light, infrared, and ultraviolet. Before we conduct a closer inspection, we need to ensure these emissions pose no harm to us or our systems."

"All scans are complete," Astraeus reported.

"The threat level to human biology is calculated at point-two-seven percent."

"Humm, walking on Mars is more dangerous", Ada murmured.

Elena stepped forward, her voice steady despite the tension in the room.

"I'll go back to the ridge. If the signal's intensifying, it might be transmitting new information. We need a closer look."

Riya hesitated, her expression conflicted. "It's risky. If the signal's behavior is changing, we don't know what we're walking into."

"We're already in it," Elena said firmly.

"The more we know, the better chance we have of staying ahead of whatever this is."

After a moment, Riya nodded "Keep the artifact area under constant surveillance," Riya instructed firmly. "No one is to interact with or approach it without explicit permission. As of now, Earth has not granted authorization, but I trust we'll receive a directive later today."

#

Later that day Riya reviewed the latest message from Earth, her expression unreadable as the words sank in.

The directive was concise but carried significant weight:

"Proceed with caution. Use your intuition to interact with and recover the artifact if deemed necessary. Relocate the artifact if the situation demands."

It was a rare instance of Earth entrusting her and the crew with such autonomy, a recognition of their expertise and the immediacy of the situation. Riya exhaled deeply, understanding the responsibility that came with the trust placed in her.

"All right," she murmured to herself, her resolve solidifying. "Intuition with caution it is."

The rover's engine hummed softly as it carried Elena, Marcus, and David back to the ridge. The tension in the cabin was thick, none of them speaking as the barren landscape rolled by. The ridge loomed larger as they approached, its jagged outline casting sharp shadows under the Martian sun.

#

As they disembarked, the rhythmic hum of the signal became audible once more, louder and more insistent than before. Elena felt a chill run down her spine despite the heat of her suit.

She glanced nervously at the artifact, her voice edged with unease. "We should've brought security with us."

David raised an eyebrow, leaning casually against the rover.

"I wouldn't mind some company," he said, his tone light but firm.

"But security? Seriously? Look at it—it's a rock. And if it's not, and there's advanced tech in the belly, do you really think our weapons would stand a chance? They'd be rendered useless in a heartbeat."

Marcus chuckled, crossing his arms as he glanced at the "rock" in the distance.

"Yeah, David, we'd look like a bunch of monkeys holding sticks, squaring off against a fully armed US Marine. If it's advanced tech, our weapons wouldn't just be useless—they'd be downright laughable."

He shook his head, the humor in his tone barely masking the seriousness of the situation. "Still, I'd rather have sticks than nothing at all."

Marcus let out a low, weighty laugh, the kind that came from someone used to brushing off danger.

"If this thing has violent intentions, we're already sitting ducks. Armed or not, it would not make a difference."

He looked at Elena over his shoulder with a smirk, but the heaviness in his words hung in the air, settling like a quiet warning.

"Same as before," Marcus said, scanning the structure with his handheld device. "The signal's definitely stronger. It's almost like it's... reacting to us."

David crouched beside the structure, his probe in hand. "The patterns haven't changed, but the surface temperature is higher. This thing's active."

Elena moved closer, her eyes fixed on the intricate patterns etched into the metal. The symmetry was mesmerizing, the lines and curves forming a language she couldn't begin to understand. "It's like it's trying to communicate," she said softly.

"Or it's warning us off," Marcus muttered, his tone uneasy.

Marcus chuckled darkly, gesturing toward the artifact with a tilt of his head.

"Let's face it," he said, his voice carrying a mix of sarcasm and resignation, "it's either come hug me or leave me alone. If this thing's got advanced tech, it'll make its intentions pretty clear—and I doubt it's waiting on us to figure it out."

Elena crouched beside David, activating her helmet camera to document the scene.

"Let's not jump to conclusions. We don't know enough yet."

As they worked, the hum of the signal grew louder, vibrating through the ground beneath their feet. Marcus's device beeped sharply, and he frowned at the display.

"Electromagnetic levels are spiking. We need to pull back."

"Pull back, pull back!" shouted Elena, her voice cutting through the comms with urgency.

"Orion's jittery—the interference is too much!" Her eyes darted between the fluctuating readings and the artifact, the tension thick in the air as the situation teetered dangerously close to losing control.

"Wait," David said, holding up a hand. "Look at this."

Elena turned to see him pointing at a small panel on the structure, its surface glowing faintly. The glow pulsed in time with the signal, the light intensifying with each beat.

"What did you do?" Elena demanded, her tone sharp with urgency.

"Just… pushed on the surface," David remarked casually, though his wide eyes betrayed his surprise.

"It's… opening," David said, his voice tinged with awe and alarm.

The panel slid aside with a hiss, revealing a hollow compartment within the structure. Inside was a small, crystalline object, its surface shimmering with an otherworldly light.

"What is that?" Marcus asked, his voice low.

"A key," Elena said, the word slipping from her lips before she could think. She didn't know how she knew—it was a feeling, a certainty that defied explanation.

David reached toward the crystal, but Marcus grabbed his arm. "Don't touch it," he warned. "We don't know what it'll do."

"We can't just leave it here," David argued. "This could be the breakthrough we've been looking for."

Elena hesitated, torn between caution and curiosity. The crystal was beautiful, its light casting shifting patterns on the interior of the compartment. It felt… alive, as though it were aware of their presence.

"Document everything first," Elena said, her voice firm. "If we decide to take it, we need to be sure it's safe."

Riya stood at the Aegis, her gaze fixed on the intricate holographic model of the artifact and its surroundings. Beside her, the faint glow of the live feeds from Marcus, David, and Elena flickered, casting shifting shadows across her focused expression. The atmosphere in the command centre was tense but purposeful, with Astraeus's calm updates punctuating the silence.

"They're the best we've got out there," Riya said to herself.

She has given them the autonomy to make the call—Marcus, David, and Elena are the most senior officials next to Riya, and they've proven they can handle such responsibility.

The holographic model updated in real-time, mapping every movement and interaction. Riya's jaw tightened slightly as she watched the trio on the ground, fully aware that, despite their expertise, the unknown nature of the artifact left even the most seasoned leaders at the edge.

Three of them worked quickly, capturing every detail of the crystal and its surroundings. The signal continued to pulse, its intensity unwavering, as though it were waiting for their next move.

After extensive deliberation, the trio reached a cautious consensus: the crystal would be carefully extracted from its chamber. The decision wasn't taken lightly, given the chamber's mysterious mechanics, faint radiation readings, Orion's display jittery, and countless other unknowns. A robotic arm was brought into play, its precise movements controlled from a safe distance. The machine's steady grip locked onto the crystal, its multi-spectral cameras providing a detailed view as it began the slow, deliberate process of removal.

As the crystal was carefully lifted from its resting place, the chamber responded almost immediately. The metallic door slid shut with an eerie smoothness, as if it had been waiting for this exact moment. Simultaneously, the artifact's faint glow dimmed and then vanished altogether, leaving only the sound of the robotic arm retracting. It was as if the artifact had been programmed for this precise interaction—a silent acknowledgment that the crystal's removal was expected, perhaps even required. The trio exchanged uneasy glances, a mix of relief and growing curiosity settling over them as they stared at the now-dormant artifact.

"Everything's quiet. Nothing on the spectrum. Even Orion's come to its senses," Marcus said, his tone steady but showed a sign of relief laced with cautious curiosity as he glanced toward the artifact.

"Let's pack it up and go. There's nothing more for us to do here," David said firmly, glancing at the structure one last time.

"It's staying put—it's embedded into the surrounding rock plateau, almost fused with it. If there's a reason to return, we'll come back, but for now, we are done."

Back at the habitat, the crew gathered to review the footage. The discovery of the crystal had electrified the group, their earlier tension replaced by a mix of excitement and apprehension.

"This changes everything," David said, his voice filled with awe.

"Whatever this thing is, it's not just a relic. It's active. It's trying to interact with us."

"Or manipulate us," Marcus countered. "We have no idea what we're dealing with."

Elena listened quietly, her thoughts swirling. The crystal was more than a clue—it was a connection to something far larger than their mission. But the questions it raised were as daunting as the answers it promised.

"What do we do now?" she asked, turning to Riya.

The commander's expression was unreadable, her gaze fixed on the images of the crystal. "We proceed carefully," she said finally.

"No one interacts with it directly until we understand it better. And we keep it contained."

Her words carried a quiet weight, a recognition of the stakes they were now facing. The discovery of the structure had been monumental, but the crystal was something else entirely. It was a key—but to what, none of them could yet say.

#

The crystal now rested in the containment chamber away from the habitat dome, a deliberate choice to keep it safely isolated until the team could ensure it was safe to interact with. Housing something so enigmatic near 100 people felt like tempting fate, even if the crystal had shown no signs of emitting dangerous levels of radiation. Its faint, ethereal glow cast ghostly patterns across the sterile walls, adding an otherworldly unease to the room.

Encased within a transparent isolation field, it appeared almost dormant now, its rhythmic pulses reduced to barely perceptible flickers. Yet, its presence was impossible to ignore—a relic seemingly out of place and time, humming with an inscrutable purpose that both fascinated and unnerved the crew.

A few hundred meters from the main habitat dome stood the quarantine quarters, a box-shaped structure designed for high-stakes containment and research. Equipped with living quarters for four people, a fully equipped lab, and a storage area, the facility was strategically nestled in a small valley between modest ground protrusions. This carefully chosen location provided natural shielding and minimized potential risks to the primary habitat. The quarters were meticulously engineered to handle all types of biological contingencies, with interior chambers sealed against radiation, electromagnetic interference, and even unidentified environmental threats. Secure and isolated, it served as the perfect site to store and study the artifact, ensuring restricted access while safeguarding the colony from any unforeseen dangers.

#

"I'll survive," Ada said with a mock worried expression, playing up the fact that the quarantine valley— as they had come to call it—was situated on her side of the main habitat dome.

David smirked, crossing his arms.

"It's yours to decode, Ada," he said, with a playful edge.

"Having it right by your side should help, don't you think?"

Elena stood before the chamber, her gloved hands hovering above the control panel. The rest of the crew had gone to their stations, leaving her alone with the enigmatic artifact. She couldn't shake the sense of awe it inspired, but with it came an undercurrent of fear. The crystal felt alive, and she couldn't ignore the questions it raised. Who—or what—had left it here? And why?

The next day, Elena found herself standing before the crystal in the quarantine quarters, unable to tear her gaze away. There was something about it—an almost imperceptible pull, as if it were calling out to her. The faint, shifting patterns within its surface seemed alive, whispering secrets just beyond her understanding.

Her thoughts were interrupted by David's arrival. He walked slowly into the lab with a tablet in hand, his expression a mix of excitement and concern.

"I've been analyzing the footage from the ridge," he said, handing her the tablet.

"The patterns on the crystal—they're evolving."

David, with his expertise as a material scientist, spent hours conducting non-invasive scans, tests, and meticulous observations on the artifact and the crystal. Advanced spectroscopy, magnetic resonance imaging, and thermal analyses all yielded tantalizing data but no definitive answers. The material defied classification—it wasn't metallic, organic, or ceramic, nor did it align with any known terrestrial compounds. Frustration simmered beneath his calm exterior as every methodical step brought him no closer to understanding its composition.

"Terrestrial—you mean Earth," Elena nodded, her expression thoughtful as she stared at the artifact.

"We don't know what's here, let alone what's out there in the universe," she added, her voice quiet yet resolute, the weight of the unknown pressing heavily upon her words.

To delve deeper would mean taking invasive measures—breaking off a fragment, exposing the crystal to stress, or altering its structure. But such actions could trigger unpredictable, even catastrophic consequences. The crystal's dormant yet palpable energy commanded respect, a silent reminder of its mysterious origin. Caution was paramount.

"For now," David murmured to himself, his gaze fixed on the artifact within its containment field, "we study, we document—but we don't touch beyond what's necessary."

Elena frowned as she studied the screen. The etchings on the crystal's surface were indeed changing, shifting subtly with each pulse of light. The patterns seemed to grow more complex, as though responding to some unseen input.

"It's like it's adapting," she said, her voice tinged with unease.

"But to what?"

"Us, maybe," David suggested. "Or the environment. Either way, this thing isn't just sitting idle. It's doing something."

"The energy it must take to do this, even just to light up like this... I'm baffled," David said, shaking his head in disbelief.

"Even in this shielded chamber, it seems to have plenty of energy to do whatever it's doing," David said, his eyes narrowing as he studied the artifact.

"I don't think it's absorbing energy from the outside—it must have a stored energy reserve or some kind of internal power source."

"Energy as we know it," Elena added thoughtfully, her gaze fixed on the glowing artifact, her words carrying the weight of a perspective not yet fully understood.

"How little we know," David said, nodding slowly, his gaze fixed on the crystal.

Elena nodded, though the implications made her stomach twist.

Next day, the commander was in the main hub, reviewing a diagnostic report when Elena and David arrived. She glanced up as they entered, her sharp gaze immediately honing in on the tablet in Elena's hand.

"What is it?" Riya asked.

"The crystal," Elena began, holding out the tablet. "The patterns on its surface are changing. It's reacting to something."

Riya's jaw tightened as she studied the footage. "Has it affected any of our systems?"

"Not yet," David replied. "But if it's capable of adapting, we need to be ready for anything."

Riya's tone was sharp yet measured as she addressed the team. "Is this affecting health in any way? We need answers, not assumptions. Get Dr. Myers to run a full health assessment on everyone who had close interaction with the crystal. Physical symptoms, anomalies—everything. And get Dr. Tina involved. I want her to conduct mental evaluations on a randomized sample from the crew. This isn't just about physical well-being; if this thing is having any psychological impact, we need to catch it early. The last thing we need is for anyone to be affected—or worse, compromised—by this, whether it's physical or mental. Cover all the bases."

Her gaze lingered on the faint glow of the containment chamber of the video feed, her unease barely concealed. "We didn't come this far to let an unknown risk destabilize us now."

Riya continued, "It's not what we see that we need to be cautious of—it's what we don't. The unseen, the subtle shifts in behavior or thought that might escape notice until it's too late. That's why Dr. Nina's mental assessments are critical." She paused, her gaze sweeping over the room, letting the gravity of her words settle.

Riya nodded, her expression grim. "We'll increase the isolation protocols. I want full environmental monitoring around the containment chamber. If this thing makes so much as a flicker, I want to know about it."

#

Dr. Tina Verma, the colony's psychologist and behavioral specialist, was a cornerstone of UNSI's human resilience programs long before she set foot on the *Eos Horizon*. A seasoned expert in cognitive science and group dynamics, she had spent over a decade working alongside Dr. Jonathan Myers on deep-space mission readiness projects. Together, they developed protocols to ensure mental and emotional stability for crews operating under extreme isolation and stress. Their work, which ranged from designing AI-assisted therapy modules to pioneering techniques for detecting early signs of psychological strain, became the gold standard for UNSI missions. While Myers often focused on the physical, Nina's expertise delved into the complexities of the mind, making her the perfect counterpart.

Her appointment to the *Eos Horizon* mission was a natural progression, though Tina hadn't originally anticipated leaving Earth herself. It was Myers who encouraged her, pointing out the importance of her presence on such a high-stakes mission. Known for her empathetic approach and sharp analytical mind, Tina had a knack for reading between the lines of a person's words and actions. Her ability to bring calm to tense situations had earned her the crew's trust early on, making her not just a counselor but a confidante. Now, with the unknowns surrounding the artifact and its potential effects on the crew, Nina's role was more critical than ever. Her years of collaboration with Myers ensured a seamless partnership as they worked to safeguard not just the crew's bodies but their minds.

#

Later that evening, the crew gathered for their regular debriefing, though the atmosphere was far from routine. The crystal had become the unspoken center of their mission, its presence overshadowing even the practical challenges of survival on Mars.

"This discovery puts us in uncharted territory," Riya said, addressing the group.

"We've trained for the unknown, but this… this is beyond anything we could have anticipated. Our priority remains the same: the safety of this colony and its mission. But we can't ignore the potential significance of what we've found."

Marcus crossed his arms, his skepticism evident.

"It could be a Trojan horse for all we know. We're taking a massive risk even keeping it here."

David shot him a sharp look. "And what do you suggest? Leave it out there? Destroy it? This could be the most important discovery in human history."

"Or the deadliest," Marcus countered.

This was the first time a heated exchange between the two had unfolded so openly during the mission. Marcus and David had crossed paths at UNSI on couple of prior projects, where their complementing strengths in decision-making and execution had always fostered mutual respect. But here, on Mars, with stakes so high and uncertainty weighing heavy, even the smallest spark of disagreement threatened to ignite a wildfire. The crew exchanged uneasy glances, sensing that the artifact had begun to challenge not just their safety, but their unity.

"Enough," Riya said firmly, her tone silencing the room. "We'll proceed with caution. Until we know more, and especially until we know more on the health of the crew, the crystal stays in containment, and no one interacts with it directly. Understood?"

Everyone nodded, though the tension between Marcus and David lingered like static in the air. As the meeting adjourned, Elena couldn't shake the feeling that they were teetering on the edge of something monumental—or potentially catastrophic.

That night, Elena lay awake in her bunk, the faint hum of the habitat's systems doing little to soothe her nerves. The crystal's pulsing light replayed in her mind, each pattern etched into her thoughts like a fragment of an unfinished puzzle. She turned over, staring at the curved ceiling as questions swirled in her head.

Was the crystal truly a key? And if so, what would it unlock?

The rhythmic pulse of the signal seemed to echo in the back of her mind, a quiet reminder that the answers lay just beyond their reach. Somewhere outside, under the endless Martian sky, the structure waited—its purpose still shrouded in mystery.

#

The following day began with a sense of unease hanging over the crew. The crystal remained in its containment chamber, seemingly dormant, but its presence was an unspoken weight on everyone's shoulders. As the team gathered in the main hub, Riya's face betrayed none of the tension they all felt.

"We're sticking to the schedule," she announced, her tone firm.

"The priority is ensuring the habitat is fully operational and sustainable. Marcus, David, you'll focus on system checks for power and life support. Elena, continue monitoring the greenhouse. And keep an eye on the crystal's environmental impact. Let's not let this… discovery derail the mission."

The crew dispersed, though Elena could sense the distraction in each of them. The crystal's implications loomed large, casting doubt and speculation over their tasks. Still, she forced herself to focus as she joined Marcus in the power systems module, routine checks for the greenhouse energy consumption.

"You think she's downplaying it?" Marcus asked as he ran a diagnostic on power distribution arrays.

Elena sighed, her hands moving deftly over the control panel. "She's trying to keep us grounded. If we let this thing consume us, we'll lose sight of why we're here."

"Hard not to be consumed by it," Marcus said. "We came to build a colony, not play archaeologists with alien artifacts."

Elena paused, meeting his gaze. "What if the two are connected? What if understanding this thing is part of building our future here?"

Marcus shook his head, his expression hard. "Or it's the thing that destroys our future. We don't know what we're dealing with."

"That's why we have to learn," Elena countered. "We can't ignore it, Marcus. It's here for a reason."

Their conversation was interrupted by an alert on the Orion. "Power fluctuation detected," Astraeus announced.

"analyzing source."

Marcus scowled, turning his attention back to the system. "Great. As if we didn't have enough to deal with."

Elena watched as he worked, her own unease deepening. The crystal's arrival seemed to coincide with these small anomalies—first the signal, then the electromagnetic fluctuations, and now this. Coincidence, or something more?

By midday, the power systems were stabilized, and Elena returned to the greenhouse to check on the plants. The crops were thriving, their vibrant green a stark contrast to the sterile interior of the habitat. Yet even here, the presence of the crystal seemed to linger, its faint pulse echoing in her mind.

Dr. Noah was crouched by a row of spinach, inspecting the irrigation system. He glanced up as Elena entered. "How's the power situation?"

"Under control, for now," she replied.

"But it feels like everything's more fragile lately."

Noah nodded, his expression thoughtful. "It's like the crystal is amplifying everything. The signal, the environment… even our temperament."

"What do you mean?" Elena asked, crouching beside him.

He hesitated before answering. "Have you noticed how we've all been acting lately? The tension, the arguments—it's not just stress. It feels… amplified, like the crystal's affecting us."

Elena frowned, considering his words. She had noticed the growing friction among the crew, the way small disagreements seemed to escalate more quickly. "You think it's influencing us?"

Noah shrugged. "I don't know. But it's worth keeping an eye on. If this thing can change its patterns, who's to say it can't affect us, too?"

The thought sent a chill down her spine. The crystal wasn't just an object—it was active, adaptive. And if Noah was right, its influence might extend far beyond what they could measure.

Later that evening, the tension came to a head. During the crew's evening debrief, Marcus and David clashed again, their voices rising as they debated the crystal's significance.

"It's not a threat," David insisted, his tone sharp. "We need to study it, not hide from it."

"You don't know that," Marcus shot back.

"For all we know, it could be a Trojan horse waiting to take us out."

"Are you both done!" Riya's voice cut through the argument, silencing the room. She stood with her hands on the table, her expression steely.

"We're not here to fight each other. We're here to survive. The crystal stays in containment until we understand it better. That's final."

The tension lingered as the crew dispersed, the air in the habitat heavy with unspoken fears. Elena stayed behind, her gaze fixed on the central console. The live video feed of the crystal's faint light pulsed on the screen, its patterns shifting in a mesmerizing rhythm.

"What are you trying to tell us?" she murmured, her voice barely audible.

Behind her, Riya approached, her expression softening. "You did good work today," she said. "Don't let this thing consume you."

Elena turned to face her. "How can it not? Whatever this is… it changes everything."

"I know," Riya said quietly. "But we can't let it change us. Not yet."

Elena nodded, though the unease in her chest didn't dissipate. The crystal was more than a discovery—it was a challenge, a test of their resilience and unity. And as its pulse continued, steady and unyielding, she couldn't shake the feeling that they were running out of time.

"Have you seen the old movie *Gods Must Be Crazy*?" Riya asked, a faint smile on her face.

"It should be in our archives. I recommend you watch it—I think all of us should."

"Hmmm, if you insist," Elena replied, raising an eyebrow. "Is it about Mars colonization?"

Riya chuckled, shaking her head. "It's about what we're experiencing right now. A peaceful, primitive tribe in the middle of nowhere, suddenly distracted and driven to conflict over a misunderstood glass bottle."

"Ah," Elena giggled, leaning back with a smirk.

"I see the resemblance. Now I can't wait to get my hands on that movie."

#

The habitat lights dimmed to their nighttime cycle, casting soft shadows across the domes. Most of the crew had retreated to their quarters, seeking some semblance of rest after a tense day. But Elena couldn't sleep. The thought of the crystal—its pulsating light and shifting patterns—filled her mind.

She found herself drawn back to *"The Sky"* Her gaze, however, was fixed on Orion's display, the surveillance feed on the containment chamber where the isolation field shimmered faintly, a thin veil of energy separating them from the unknown. Within the chamber, the crystal rested, its glow subdued yet unwavering, as if quietly pulsing with purpose. Elena stood there in silence, her thoughts as still as her posture, watching it with an almost hypnotic intensity, as though, at any moment, it might unveil the secrets it so resolutely guarded.

Footsteps behind her climbing the stairs grew louder, and Marcus entered. He paused when he saw her, his expression unreadable. "Couldn't sleep?" he asked, stepping closer.

Elena shook her head. "It's hard to stop thinking about it."

"Yeah," Marcus said, his gaze fixed on the horizon."

She glanced at him, startled. "You feel that too?"

He nodded slowly. "I don't know how to explain it. It's not just a thing. It feels… aware."

Elena's pulse quickened. She had thought the same but hadn't dared to voice it. The crystal's presence was more than physical—it was palpable, like an unseen force that filled the room.

"We need to understand it," she said quietly. "Before it does something we can't predict."

Marcus hesitated before responding. "And if it's dangerous? What then?"

"Then we deal with it," Elena replied, her voice firm.

"But we can't act out of fear. Not yet."

Marcus sighed, running a hand over his face. "I hope you're right."

The next morning, ranking officers woke to another announcement from Astraeus.

"Attention: signal intensity remains elevated. No additional anomalies detected."

The message did little to calm the growing unease. The signal's steady presence had become a constant background hum, both literally and figuratively. As the crew gathered for the morning briefing, Riya's expression was tighter than usual.

"We've maintained containment and monitoring," she began, her tone brisk.

"But the signal's behavior hasn't changed. For now, we focus on preparing the colony. The crystal will remain under observation, and any changes must be reported immediately."

Elena noticed the glances exchanged among the crew—Marcus's wary skepticism, David's barely concealed curiosity. The lines between caution and exploration were becoming harder to define, and the strain was showing.

As the meeting adjourned, Riya pulled Elena aside. "I need you to keep an eye on everyone," she said quietly.

"The crystal's affecting more than just our systems. It's affecting us."

Elena frowned. "You think it's deliberate?"

"I don't know," Riya admitted. "But tensions are rising, and I can't risk this crew fracturing. Not now."

"Dr. Tina has assured us that her initial sample doesn't show any alarming levels of anxiety or psychological issues requiring immediate attention," she began, her gaze steady.

"Dr. Myers concurs with her assessment from a physical health standpoint—no abnormalities, no immediate signs of exposure-related effects."

She paused, her tone shifting to one of cautious deliberation. "However, Nina's deeper concern lies not in what's already present but in what's beginning to take shape. She's observing subtle behavioral shifts—not pathological, but concerning nonetheless. These aren't issues stemming directly from the crystal itself but rather from how people are reacting to it. As theories form and circulate, some are beginning to latch onto their own interpretations, subscribing to ideas that may or may not align with reality. This has the potential to fragment cohesion within the crew."

Riya paused, letting her words sink in before continuing. "Elena, the artifact's mysterious nature makes it a magnet for speculation. It's human nature to try to fill the gaps in what we don't understand, but if we're not careful, that can quickly lead to division. Nina's already pointed out how these little narratives are starting to take root—stories that can create factions if left unchecked. We can't afford to let curiosity or uncertainty pull us apart. We need to stay unified, keep communication open, and tackle the questions it raises together, as a team."

Elena nodded, though the weight of the request was heavy. The crystal wasn't just a mystery—it was a catalyst, and its influence was growing.

By midday, the signal spiked again.

Elena was in the greenhouse when Astraeus's voice interrupted her work.

"Warning: electromagnetic interference detected. Signal intensity increasing."

She dropped her tools and rushed to the main hub, where the rest of the crew was already gathered. The central display showed the signal's frequency, its peaks climbing higher with each passing moment.

"Engineering, confirm the magnetic shielding at the quarantine valley is checked!" Riya's tone was sharp, her eyes narrowing as she continued.

"Any idea why we're still picking up the signal when the artifact is inside a Faraday cage?"

Marcus nodded firmly. "It's triple-checked. The chamber containment is sound," he said, though his expression showed lingering uncertainty.

"As for the signal—we're still working on that. The leading theory right now is that the signal isn't directly emanating from the crystal itself. Instead, it seems to be all around us, embedded in the ambient. The crystal may—or may not—be influencing it."

"If the signal is all around us, what good does shielding the crystal do?" Riya questioned, her tone sharp with frustration as she paced.

Marcus hesitated, then replied carefully, "The shielding ensures containment—if the crystal is amplifying or modulating the signal in any way, we need to keep it isolated to study those effects without interference. It's not about blocking the signal entirely, but understanding its interaction with the artifact."

Riya stopped and turned, her gaze steady. "Fine, but I need more than theories. If this thing is influencing the environment, we can't afford to stay in the dark for much longer."

Riya's frown deepened, her mind racing with the implications of his words. "Keep at it," she said, her voice quieter but no less commanding.

"Do we know what's causing this, any pointers?" Riya asked gently.

Marcus shook his head. "The source is still the crystal, probably, but this level of activity—it's unprecedented."

"Is it affecting the habitat systems?" Riya asked.

"Not yet," Marcus replied. "But at this rate, it's only a matter of time."

David leaned closer to the screen, his expression a mix of awe and concern. "It's like it's… building to something."

Elena's chest tightened. The crystal's behavior was escalating, its pulses more intense, more deliberate. "We need to find out what it's trying to do," she said, her voice firm.

Riya nodded, her jaw set. "Then we go back to the location we found it. If the crystal is reacting to something, we need to understand what—and why."

"Perhaps we shouldn't have moved it from its cradle," Elena sighed, and murmured to herself.

The decision was made quickly. Riya, Marcus, and Elena would return to the ridge, while David and the others monitored the crystal from the habitat. The journey across the Martian terrain felt different this time—heavier, as though the air itself carried the weight of their discovery.

As they approached the ridge, the signal's hum grew louder, vibrating through the ground beneath their feet. The structure stood as it had before, its metallic surface gleaming faintly in the light. But something was different. The glow around the crystal's compartment was brighter, its patterns shifting more rapidly.

"It's more active than before," Marcus said, scanning the structure with his handheld device. "Energy levels are spiking."

"Keep your distance," Riya warned.

"We don't know what it's capable of."

Elena stepped closer, her eyes fixed on the crystal's compartment. The patterns were mesmerizing, their complexity almost hypnotic. She felt a pull toward it, an inexplicable urge to reach out, to understand.

"Elena," Riya said sharply, snapping her out of her trance.

"Stay back."

Elena blinked, stepping away from the structure. Her heart raced as she realized how close she had been. "I don't know what came over me," she admitted, her voice trembling.

"I'm registering dispersed energy levels," Marcus said, his brow furrowing as he studied the readings.

"The signal is all around us—there's no way to triangulate or pinpoint a specific direction. This artifact is definitely one of the sources,"

he added, raising his eyebrows, "but it's likely there are others. Probably many." His words hung in the air, the implications unsettling as the crew exchanged uneasy glances.

"I touched and pushed the door," Marcus said, his voice low and measured, "the same way as the other day when it opened to reveal the crystal. But this time, no response—just a different glow around where the door should be." He exhaled sharply, shaking his head.

"I don't think we can return the crystal, even if we wanted to. It's as if whatever mechanism allowed it to open before… is gone dead now."

Riya's expression hardened. "Then we are done here. Document everything, and we get out."

As they worked, the signal's hum grew louder, resonating through the air like a living thing. The crystal's light pulsed in time, faster and brighter, as though responding to their presence.

"Elena," Marcus said suddenly, his voice sharp.

"Look."

She turned to see the patterns on the crystal shifting again, forming shapes that were unmistakable—symbols. Words.

"It's a message," she whispered, her breath catching.

The symbols pulsed, their meaning just out of reach. And then, as suddenly as it had begun, the light dimmed, the signal fading to a low hum.

"Electromagnetic interference has reduced to background levels. No anomaly detected. Signal remains below average levels," Astraeus announced over Orion, her measured tone calming down the tense silence.

"What just happened?" Riya demanded.

"It wasn't me," they all said to themselves, almost in unison, like a well-rehearsed march, the reflexive denial silently echoing through the control room and the field.

Elena stared at the structure, her mind racing with possibilities. "It's trying to communicate," she murmured. "Or," she added after a pause, "probably we're in compliance." Her words sent a shiver through the group, the unsettling idea settling in like an unspoken truth.

ΣΘS-PG124

Chapter Three
FOUNDATIONS

The sun crept over the Martian horizon with a pale, amber glow, the weak light spreading across the barren expanse like a fleeting promise of warmth. The horizon, a blend of soft pinks, dusky oranges and deep crimsons, seemed to stretch endlessly, blending into the dusty sky in a way that only Mars could paint. It wasn't the bold brilliance of Earth's sunrise but something quieter, more ethereal—a fragile beauty born of thin air and distant light. The scattered remnants of a dust storm lingered in the atmosphere, refracting the sun's rays into muted halos, a celestial whisper of the alien world's untamed nature.

It had been nearly a month since the crew first set foot on Martian soil, yet the novelty of their alien surroundings had not diminished. The initial frenzy of establishing the habitat, securing life support systems, and setting up the greenhouse had given way to a steady rhythm of daily tasks and exploration. The crew had begun to adapt, each person finding their place in the routines and challenges of this new world. Yet, despite the growing familiarity, the harshness of Mars remained ever-present—a silent reminder of the fragility of their existence here. Each sunrise and crimson horizon was a quiet testament to their perseverance, marking time in a place where every day was a triumph against the odds.

Within the habitat, the crew stirred. Astraeus's dawn announcements had long since become a rhythm of their days, as familiar as the faint hum of the systems that surrounded them. Though subdued after the intensity of the previous day, they moved with purpose, their minds already turning to the tasks ahead.

Elena was one of the first to step out, her visor reflecting the Martian light as she made her way to the greenhouse. Inside, seedlings stretched toward the artificial glow of grow lights, tiny bursts of green in an otherwise reddish-brown world. Each plant was a testament to months of careful planning and research, and Elena inspected them with a sense of reverence, knowing that their survival meant more than just food—it meant hope.

Elsewhere, Marcus was knee-deep in technical diagnostics, calibrating the solar, communication and sensor arrays after their exposure to a fine layer of Martian dust. His sharp commands echoed across the communication channels, his no-nonsense attitude driving his team as they worked to ensure the colony's systems remained optimal. Nearby, Freja was attending to a specialized rover used for core-drilling. Her calm precision a steady counterpoint to the hum of machinery that sustained their fragile existence.

" *Surface temperatures at minus 15 degrees Celsius.*
Winds at 15 kilometers per hour, direction east-northeast.
No major dust activity detected within a 50-kilometer radius.
Visibility remains clear.
No anomalies detected. "

Occasional weather updates from Astraeus broke the silence, or the chaos, depending on the moment.

David and Riya, meanwhile, were engaged in a spirited debate, in the seclusion of Commander's cabin adjacent to the hub, discussing the latest updates from Earth and the intricacies of their evolving colony. David's curiosity met Riya's pragmatism head-on as they mapped out the coming weeks, each word underscored by the urgency of their mission.

Breaks were brief but welcome. In the common area, some crew members gathered over re-hydrated meals, sharing jokes and camaraderie to lighten the weight of their responsibilities. Others sought solitude, finding moments of peace in the habitat's quiet corners, where Earth landscapes cycled through the thin display walls, reminding them of home.

As the day progressed, the Martian dusk crept in, softening the edges of the world with hues of lavender and deep rust. The crew's movements slowed as they wound down their activities, the horizon fading into a quiet stillness. Despite the long hours and relentless work, there was a sense of accomplishment, each task a step closer to turning the barren expanse into a place they could call home. The day on Mars ended as it began—not with bold proclamations, but with quiet resilience and the unwavering resolve to forge a future on the Red Planet.

#

Few days later, Elena sat at the central console in the main hub, reviewing the images and data from the ridge. The symbols the artifact and crystal had displayed were unlike anything she'd ever seen—geometric yet fluid, with a logic that seemed to defy conventional understanding.

"You're up early," David said, walking into the room with a steaming pouch of coffee.

"I couldn't sleep," Elena admitted, her eyes fixed on the screen.

"I keep going over this. The patterns, the symbols… It's definitely a language, but it's nothing we recognize."

Elena's frustration simmered just beneath the surface, a gnawing sense of helplessness that she couldn't shake. The symbols on the artifact called to her, tantalizingly close yet incomprehensible, like a language spoken just beyond her hearing. She wanted so desperately to decipher their meaning, but lack of expertise in the field felt like a cruel limitation. It was as if she were mute, seeing something extraordinary but unable to voice it, or like being handcuffed and chained, her potential shackled by the confines of her own knowledge. The weight of the unknown pressed heavily on her, amplifying the urgency to understand what lay before her.

"What's Ada's take on this?" David asked, leaning back slightly.

"Ada's not like us," Elena said, a faint smile tugging at her lips as she glanced toward the quiet scientist.

"She takes the symbols, the patterns, all of it, much more academically. She won't say a word until she's absolutely certain."

Elena sighed, leaning back against the edge of the console.

"But me? I can't wait that long. That's just who I am. I need to act, to try something—anything—while the answers are still forming. Sitting on my hands, hoping for clarity, just isn't in my nature."

She laughed softly, her voice carrying a mix of admiration and frustration. "Guess that's why Ada and I make a decent team—her patience, my impulsiveness. Balance, or something like it."

David leaned over her shoulder, his curiosity outweighing his fatigue.

"Maybe it's not meant for us to understand yet. Maybe it's just the first step."

Elena glanced at him, her brow furrowed. "First step to what?"

He shrugged, his expression thoughtful. "To whatever comes next."

By midday, the crew convened for their daily briefing. Riya stood at the head of the table, her expression as steady as ever, though her eyes betrayed a hint of fatigue.

"Yesterday's events don't change today's priorities," Riya began, her voice resolute, cutting through the tension in the room.

"The colony must be fully operational. We've made progress, but there's still work to do. Marcus, Elena—keep fortifying the habitats and double-check that all systems are stable. Dr. Noah, your focus remains on the greenhouse. We can't afford setbacks there. And everyone—stay vigilant. If you notice anything unusual or experience any abnormalities in your tasks, report them immediately.

Even though Riya don't usually explicitly list every crew member and their assigned tasks, everyone knew exactly what their priorities were and how to execute them with minimal supervision. It was a testament to the rigorous training and the trust she placed in her team. Months of preparation had drilled into them not just the technical skills required for their roles, but also the self-reliance and adaptability essential for survival on Mars. Each crew member moved with purpose, seamlessly tackling their responsibilities, whether it was maintaining the habitat, analyzing data, or tending to the critical systems. Riya's leadership wasn't about micromanagement—it was about fostering competence and confidence, ensuring every individual could step up when it mattered most.

The crew nodded, though the tension in the room was profound. The crystal was a constant presence now, its influence extending beyond the containment chamber. Each of them felt its pull, its enigmatic hum lingering in the back of their minds.

#

Akira and Marcus worked side by side in the communication systems module, their movements efficient despite the unspoken tension between them. The communication arrays required re-calibration after the previous day's signal spikes, and the process was delicate.

Akira Nakamura, the second engineer on the *Eos Horizon*, carried a unique blend of heritage and expertise that made him indispensable to the mission. At forty two years old, Akira's tall frame and Japanese features, inherited from his maternal lineage, were complemented by the ruggedness of his American grandfather. His grandfather, a mechanic in the post-war era, had instilled in him an early love for machines. This passion drove Akira to become an electro-mechanical engineer with a specialty in maintaining and optimizing complex systems. His previous experience on a moon mission had earned him a reputation for ingenuity under pressure, a quality Riya greatly valued. Known for his constant smile and an easy-going demeanor, Akira was a calming presence, even in the most tense situations.

#

Dr. Sophia Martinez, the colony's biochemist, brought her own brilliance to the team. At thirty seven, she was a powerhouse of intellect and compassion, having spearheaded projects on Earth to develop sustainable biochemical systems for extreme environments. Her sharp mind and warm personality had drawn Akira's attention long before the *Eos Horizon* mission. Their relationship, which began in the laboratories of UNSI, had evolved into a deep bond over shared ambitions and late-night conversations about life on Mars. During recruitment, their relationship was flagged as a potential concern but was ultimately encouraged by UNSI, which recognized the importance of building emotional connections within the first 100 colonists. The organization understood that such partnerships would naturally form as the colony matured, contributing to its long-term stability and growth.

Together, Akira and Sophia became the embodiment of what UNSI envisioned for the colony's future: collaboration, resilience, and the forging of new bonds. Despite their busy schedules, they always found moments to support and encourage one another. Whether it was Akira fine-tuning the habitat's life-support systems or Sophia troubleshooting nutrient cycles for the agricultural domes, they worked seamlessly, their relationship a quiet yet powerful cornerstone of their lives on Mars. For the crew, their partnership served as a reminder that even in the vast loneliness of space, human connection could thrive and inspire hope for the future.

"Do you think we're even close to understanding it?" Marcus asked as he adjusted the angle of a panel.

"The crystal?" Akira replied, tightening a bolt.

"No. But I think it's trying to tell us something."

Marcus glanced at him, surprised to see this is not Elena talking. However, his skepticism evident, "Or it's manipulating us. We can't assume its intentions are good."

Akira paused, meeting his gaze. "We can't assume they're bad either. If it wanted to harm us, don't you think it would've done something by now?"

"Maybe," Marcus admitted, though his expression remained guarded. "But that doesn't mean we lower the guard."

#

In the greenhouse, Dr.Noah found solace in his work. The crops were thriving, their growth steady despite the challenges of the Martian environment. He knelt beside a row of lettuce, checking it's root system and noting the progress in his log.

Yet even here, the crystal's presence lingered. Noah couldn't shake the feeling that it was watching them, observing their every move. He glanced toward the lab, where the isolation chamber pulsed faintly in the distance.

"Are you trying to harm us?" he muttered under his breath.

By evening, the habitats were secure, the all systems stabilized, and the crew gathered for their first collective meal in days. The tension had eased slightly, replaced by a cautious optimism that they could handle whatever came next.

"Shall we take a count?" Sonja's commanding voice cut through the chaos, where hundred people sat at tables, talking about a thousand different things all at once.

A ripple of giggles followed her suggestion. "Sonja is one, and I'm hundred," David quipped, grinning.

"Where's everyone else?"

The room relaxed briefly, the humor a welcome reprieve, but Riya quickly brought them back to reality. "We're all so consumed with our day-to-day work," she said, her tone different, stark contrast to the usual,

"it's easy to start taking things—and each other—for granted. That's a dangerous mindset out here. If we don't keep an eye on one another, it's only a matter of time before someone goes missing—or worse."

"I'm just saying because I felt it aligned," Riya said, her tone light and her expression playful.

"This isn't the briefing table, nor is it my command. I'd hate to disturb your meal," she added with a huge smile, her attempt to ease the tension drawing a few chuckles from the crew.

Riya raised her glass—a pouch of re-hydrated juice—and addressed the team. "We've made progress," she said.

"The habitats are stable, the greenhouse is thriving, and the power systems are holding. We've faced challenges, but we've met them. And we'll continue to."

The crew raised their glasses in unison, their voices a quiet chorus. "To the colony."

Elena felt a flicker of hope as she sipped her drink. They were building something here, despite the uncertainties. Yet as she glanced toward the lab, where the crystal's faint light pulsed steadily, she couldn't shake the feeling that their greatest challenge had yet to reveal itself.

#

The following days passed in a blur of Labor and cautious optimism. The crew threw themselves into their work, each task a step toward solidifying the colony's foundations. Yet, like a shadow cast by the Martian sun, the crystal's presence lingered, its enigmatic hum a constant reminder of the unknown.

The crystal's hum was subtle, barely audible, yet its presence was unmistakable, like a quiet whisper that resonated just beneath the surface of perception. It wasn't merely a sound—it was a sensation, an almost tactile awareness that lingered in the air. The experience was akin to being submerged in water, where the surrounding warmth or chill blurs the boundary between what is felt internally and externally. It seeped into their consciousness, unbidden, leaving its mark in ways that were hard to articulate.

David, Liam, Ada and the rest of the team had poured over data and observations, confirming that the hum's origin wasn't the crystal itself. Instead, it seemed to be a phenomenon that interacted with the crystal, as though the two were intrinsically linked—a system rather than a singularity. Despite their calculations, the nature of this interaction remained elusive, adding another layer to the growing enigma.

Some of the crew had begun to acclimate to what they jokingly referred to as "*Whisperer's cousin*," the hum blending into their daily lives like background noise.

The *Whisperer*, that subtle subliminal sensation once omnipresent aboard the *Eos Horizon*, now felt like a distant memory. Its near-imperceptible hum had been a constant companion during their journey, a faint presence that many had come to associate with the ship itself. But now, on Mars, the Whisperer was no more.

In its place, they said, "the cousin" had claimed the throne.

#

Yet for others, it remained a source of unease, a constant, intangible presence they couldn't reconcile. It was a reminder that, even in the quiet, Mars had its own voice—one they couldn't shake off.

Elena's days were consumed by the greenhouse and plethora of scientific research on seeds, seedlings, plants and everything to do with plant-life. The crops—spinach, lettuce, and potatoes—were responding well to the enriched Martian soil and the precisely calibrated irrigation system. She monitored every variable, her focus unyielding as she sought to ensure the colony's survival. Yet even here, amid the vibrant green rows, the crystal's influence felt close, as if its light reached into every corner of the habitat.

The agriculture team, essential to the colony's survival, had affectionately become known as *The Greens*, a name that reflected both their life-sustaining work and the vibrant greens flourished in the greenhouse, standing in stark contrast to the crimson expanse of the Martian skies and beyond

Dr. Noah joined her often, offering his own insights as they worked side by side. "Did you notice the irrigation pressure spike yesterday?" he asked one afternoon, crouching beside a tray of seedlings.

"I did," Elena replied, her hands deftly adjusting a valve. "I traced it back to a clog in the filter system. Nothing major."

Noah nodded, though his expression remained pensive. "Still, it's odd. We didn't have these issues before the crystal."

"Filter clogging, nothing out of the ordinary," Elena countered, her focus unwavering as she continued with her task.

Elena paused, reconsidering his words. "You think it's related?"

"Maybe," he said, standing and dusting his hands off. "Or maybe I'm just seeing connections where there aren't any."

"You saw the jellified nutrients within the filters, right? Have you ever seen our nutrient mix do that? I mean, ever?" Noah's voice carried a sharp edge.

She smiled faintly. "Paranoia or insight—it's a fine line out here."

#

The second harvest of lettuce and tomatoes marked a significant milestone for the crew, a triumph born of careful planning and tireless dedication. The lettuce had completed its 30-day growth cycle in the bio-dome's nutrient-rich hydroponic system, while the tomatoes, on their 75-day cycle, ripened in perfect synchronization. The first harvest had been reserved for rigorous testing, ensuring the crops were safe for consumption and free from contaminants or unexpected changes due to Martian conditions. Now, with the second yield ready, the crew could finally enjoy the fruits of their labor—literally and figuratively.

This also reminds the colony that its closing to three months since landing.

As Elena inspected the freshly picked produce, her pride was evident. The lettuce leaves were crisp and vibrant, their green hues a stark contrast to the dusty red world outside. The tomatoes, plump and juicy, felt like a small miracle.

"It's incredible," Elena said, holding a cluster of tomatoes up to the light.

"We're eating food grown on Mars. This is history, and we're living it." The excitement spread quickly, and soon discussions erupted in the common area about what to do with the bounty. Marcus, never the practical joker, suggested eating the lettuce like chips, but David had a better idea.

"We have flour. We have tomatoes. Why not make a pizza?" he said, a mischievous glint in his eye.

The idea caught on like wildfire. As the dough was kneaded and shaped, laughter and anticipation filled the habitat. A makeshift kitchen came alive with activity as the tomatoes were sliced and turned into a simple sauce, and the lettuce was set aside for a fresh side salad. Even those who rarely cooked found themselves pitching in with the orders of Elliot, the excitement of a freshly cooked meal igniting a collective joy.

To the crew's delight, Riya stood in the makeshift kitchen wearing an apron, her usual commanding presence replaced by a playful demeanor as she took instructions from Elliot. A rare smile lit up her face, and a hint of flour dusted her cheek, making her seem more grounded, more human. She moved with a mix of amusement and determination, fully immersed in the moment and savoring the chance to step away from the weight of leadership, if only briefly.

When the pizza emerged from the compact oven and resting on Eliot's hand, its aroma wafting through the air, the crew gathered eagerly, their faces lighting up in childlike wonder. "This is what we needed," Sonja said, taking her first bite and savoring the flavor. For a moment, the crew forgot the vastness of space and the challenges ahead. They were simply humans, sharing a meal and relishing a slice of normalcy in the extraordinary.

#

Elliot Graham, brought an unexpected blend of culinary artistry and technical brilliance to the mission. Born in Hertfordshire, England, Elliot's journey was anything but conventional. Joined as a robotic engineer for UNSI, he had spent years designing precision systems for automated space operations, his work instrumental in enhancing robotic efficiency for lunar and Martian missions. Yet, despite his technical accomplishments, Elliot found his true passion in an entirely different field. After leaving UNSI, he purchased a small tavern in his hometown, transforming it into a culinary hot-spot. His inventive dishes quickly gained recognition, leading to the creation of a global franchise that made him quite wealthy.

Despite his financial success and global fame, Elliot never strayed far from the kitchen. To him, cooking was more than a profession; it was a way to connect with people and bring joy through simple, well-crafted meals. Whether serving a pint and pie to locals or preparing haute cuisine for international food critics, Elliot's talent was undeniable. His unique path made him an unconventional choice for the *Eos Horizon* mission, but UNSI recognized his dual capabilities as a rare asset. A skilled robotic engineer and a world-class chef, he embodied versatility and adaptability—qualities critical for the challenges of Mars colonization.

While the *Eos Horizon* journey did not initially require a dedicated chef, as the crew relied on Thermal-Rehydration Meal Packs" or heat-and-eat meals, Elliot's presence was a calculated investment in the future. UNSI anticipated that as the colony began cultivating its own food, the need for a chef to inspire creativity in meals and bring a sense of normalcy to Martian life would grow. Elliot embraced the mission with characteristic enthusiasm, dreaming not only of feeding the first Martian colonists but also of establishing a tavern on the red planet—*Elliot Alehouse*—as he jokingly called, a gathering place where stories could be shared, and the colony's spirit nourished. For now, he lent his ingenuity to both the kitchen and the engineering bay, eager to contribute wherever he was needed.

#

"Let's see what's on for today", he pointed to the tablet on the far side of the table, as Marcus and his team focused on expanding the habitat's infrastructure. The solar arrays, critical to supplementing the nuclear fusion power supply, required constant maintenance to keep them free of Martian dust. The construction of additional storage modules and emergency shelters was also underway, each structure painstakingly assembled by hand and machine.

The crew's "*KinetiFrame Exosuits*" were pivotal in tackling the physically demanding tasks of structure assembly on the Martian surface. These advanced exoskeleton units augmented human strength and endurance, allowing the wearers to lift and maneuver heavy components with precision while minimizing strain. Powered by compact solid-state-graphene cells and integrated motion-assist technology, the *KinetiFrame* exosuits adapted to the wearer's movements, providing support in real time. Each suit featured a reinforced frame, built-in stabilization gyros, and a modular tool-set that could be configured for specific tasks like drilling, welding, or even excavating.

Building the colony's first large storage structure was a monumental challenge. The uneven terrain, riddled with rocky outcrops and layers of loose regolith, demanded meticulous groundwork before any construction could begin. The exosuits were instrumental in preparing the site, as crew members carried heavy structural panels, installed anchoring systems, and secured modular storage units. Despite the suits' enhancements, the work was grueling. The thin atmosphere and Martian dust added layers of complexity, requiring frequent maintenance of both equipment and personal resolve. Yet, the colony's cutting-edge innovations, like vibration-dampening tools and geo-fencing probes, ensured the foundation was stable.

As the storage structure's skeleton rose against the crimson horizon, there was a shared sense of triumph. The *KinetiFrame* exosuits had turned an otherwise insurmountable task into a testament to human ingenuity and teamwork, standing as a symbol of their ability to adapt and thrive in the harshest conditions.

"Hold that steady," Marcus called to one of the engineers as they secured a beam in place. The habitat expansion was grueling work, the thin atmosphere and low gravity presenting challenges that no amount of Earth-based training could fully prepare them for.

As they worked, Marcus couldn't shake the sense that they were racing against an invisible clock. The crystal, though contained, felt like a dormant volcano—quiet for now, but capable of erupting without warning.

#

The evenings were a rare respite. The crew gathered for meals, their laughter and stories a temporary escape from the weight of their mission. Yet even in these moments of camaraderie, the crystal was a topic they couldn't avoid.

"I've been running simulations on the patterns," Liam said one evening, his voice breaking the relaxed atmosphere.

"There's definitely a logic to them, but it's nothing I've seen before. It's like it's deliberately avoiding anything we'd recognize."

"It's alien," David said, leaning forward. "We can't expect it to make sense to us."

"Maybe," Marcus replied. "Or maybe it's testing us—seeing how far we can go before we understand."

Elena frowned, her thoughts turning over his words. "And if we don't understand? What happens then?"

The room fell silent, the question hanging heavy in the air.

Days later, the crystal's dormancy shifted again!

#

Elena was in the greenhouse when Astraeus's voice interrupted her work.

"Warning: environmental fluctuations detected. Source: unknown."

Her heart jumped as she rushed to the central console. The data on the screen showed a subtle but undeniable shift in the habitat's atmospheric pressure and temperature. It wasn't critical, but it was enough to set off alarms.

"What's causing this?" she asked, her voice sharp.

"analyzing," Astraeus replied.

"Preliminary data indicates a pattern aligned to electromagnetic activity from the crystal."

Elena's stomach tightened. The crystal was no longer just passive—it was interacting with its environment in ways they couldn't control.

The crew convened in the main hub, their faces tense as they reviewed the data. Riya stood at the head of the table, her composure strained but intact.

"This is the first time the crystal's behavior has directly impacted the habitat," she said.

"We need to understand what's happening and why. Marcus, Liam, I want a full diagnostic of every system. Elena, monitor the greenhouse for any abnormalities. And no one approaches the crystal without my authorization."

The crew nodded, though the tension was palpable. The crystal's activity was escalating, and the implications were impossible to ignore.

Liam and Marcus worked late into the night accompanied by Elena, combing through the habitat's systems for any signs of instability. The data was exhaustive, each variable a potential clue to the crystal's influence. Yet the deeper they delved, the more questions they uncovered.

"It's like it's probing," Marcus said, his voice low as they reviewed another set of readings.

"Testing how much it can affect without breaking anything."

Elena nodded, her brow furrowed. "But why? What's it trying to achieve?"

Marcus didn't answer. The silence stretched between them, heavy with unspoken fears.

That night, as the crew settled into their bunks, the crystal pulsed faintly in its containment chamber. Its light was steady, almost hypnotic, as though it were waiting—for what, none of them could say.

Elena lay awake, her thoughts racing. The crystal was more than an object; it was an active force, shaping their environment and their mission in ways they couldn't predict. And as its pulse echoed in her mind, one thought rose above the rest.

What are you trying to tell us?

#

The days following the crystal's environmental fluctuations were marked by an uneasy rhythm. The crew worked tirelessly, their focus split between sustaining the colony and deciphering the crystal's behavior. The line between routine and anomaly blurred, every small irregularity in the habitat's systems scrutinized for connections to the artifact.

Elena found herself caught in the middle, her responsibilities to the greenhouse competing with the growing demands of the crystal's mysteries. She spent hours in the lab, poring over data with David, trying to make sense of the symbols and patterns that the crystal continued to produce.

"It's evolving," David said one evening, pointing to a new set of symbols displayed on the lab console.

"These patterns weren't there two days ago."

"They're more intricate," Elena observed, leaning closer. "It's like it's building on the previous sequences."

"Or it's learning," David added, his tone grim. "And we're the test subjects."

"Any progress on the symbols, Ada?" Elena asked, turning to her—not with expectation, but as if looking for a straw to grasp in raging waters.

Ada's expression said it all—a quiet mix of defeat and silent apology, the weight of uncertainty settling between them.

Elena glanced at Liam, her unease deepening. "You really think it's sentient?"

Liam hesitated before replying.

"I think it's operating on a level we don't understand. Whether that's intelligence, programmed or pure instinct… I'm not sure."

The thought sent a chill through Elena. The crystal wasn't just reacting—it was changing, adapting. And the implications were far more complex than any of them were prepared for.

"We have no damn idea what it displays or even sounds like!" Liam exploded, his voice echoing through the room as he shoved his chair aside and rose abruptly. Striding to the wall, he pressed his palms flat against it, pushing as if sheer force could make the answers materialize. His tone was sharp, frustration bubbling over the calm veneer he typically maintained.

"We don't even know how anything like this is possible—no visible power source, nothing! It's completely impenetrable to all of our diagnostic tools. No radiation, no emissions—nothing passes through! And we still can't figure out what the hell this thing is—living or machine!"

He exhaled sharply, his chest rising and falling as he ran a hand through his hair. The outburst hung in the air, catching the others off guard. Liam wasn't one to let his emotions show, but it was clear that the artifact—the maddening, incomprehensible artifact—was testing his limits in ways nothing ever had.

Elena stepped forward, her hand hovering just above Liam's shoulder, but she hesitated. She'd never seen this side of him before, and uncertainty gripped her—how do you console someone who rarely lets their emotions show?

"We all feel the same, Liam," she said softly, her voice steady but laced with empathy.

"If anyone can figure this out, it's you. But for now… take a rest. I mean all of us should. That's enough for now."

Her words hung in the air, a quiet attempt to diffuse the tension, offering a moment of reprieve from the enigma that had consumed them.

"I was asking for a challenge," Liam muttered, exhaling deeply as he straightened up.

"I got one." His voice steadied, the frustration melting into quiet determination as he composed himself in no time, ready to face the enigma with renewed focus. But for now, he retired to his quarters.

#

In the greenhouse, Elena found a brief reprieve from the constant questions surrounding the crystal. The crops were thriving, their vibrant growth a testament to the colony's careful planning. Yet even here, the artifact's presence loomed, its influence felt in subtle ways.

She knelt beside a row of potatoes, carefully examining the leaves for nutrition deficiency or other abnormalities as David entered. He carried a tablet, his expression thoughtful.

"Any changes?" he asked, crouching beside her.

"None here," Elena replied, wiping her hands on her suit.

"But I've been noticing something strange with the nutrient levels. They're fluctuating more than they should."

David frowned, pulling up the greenhouse's data on his tablet.

"Could be related to the environmental shifts. The crystal's electromagnetic field might be affecting the soil chemistry."

"Great," Elena muttered, her frustration breaking through. "As if we didn't have enough to deal with."

David gave her a sympathetic smile. "At least the plants are still growing. That's something."

"We don't know yet—it could just be the pumps or the sensors," David said, his voice calm and measured as he tried to console Elena.

"A routine inspection and cleanup might be all it takes to fix it." He offered a reassuring smile, though the uncertainty lingered in his eyes, mirroring the doubt she was trying to push aside.

Elena nodded, though the weight of the unknown pressed heavily on her. The greenhouse was their lifeline, a fragile ecosystem that couldn't afford disruptions. If the crystal's influence extended here, it would put everything they had built at risk.

#

The colony's diet was thoughtfully designed to ensure balanced nutrition, with proteins being a critical component of their meals. Alongside the fresh produce from the greenhouse, the crew relied on their carefully curated stock of protein sources. Vacuum-sealed cuts of meat, sustainably produced and pre-packed on Earth, provided an occasional indulgence, bringing a touch of home to their Martian tables. Additionally, a robust supply of plant-based proteins—soy, lentils, and various types of peas— ensured a versatile foundation for daily meals.

Artificially engineered eggs, sausage and bacon, a marvel of modern food engineering, played a significant role in the colony's diet. Packed with essential amino acids and designed for long shelf life, they were incredibly versatile, finding their way into omelets, baked goods, and even Elliot's famous Martian pancakes. These protein options were not just about sustenance; they were about maintaining the health and energy levels of the crew as they took on the physical and mental demands of building a colony from scratch.

Elliot skilfully blended these protein sources with the fresh vegetables, creating meals that were both nutritious and satisfying. His latest dish—a stir-fry combining soy chunks, kale, and freshly harvested radishes—had quickly become a favorite, offering a hearty meal after long days of work. The careful balance of these proteins, coupled with the burgeoning harvests, ensured that the crew remained strong and resilient, ready to tackle the challenges of their new home on the red planet.

#

After the day's break or finishing up a meal, most of the crew gravitated to *The Circle*, seeking its serenity and the chance to relax and stretch. The open, panoramic views of the Martian landscape offered a rare sense of calm, while the gentle hum of the habitat faded into the background, making it the perfect space to unwind and recharge.

Some stretched out on beach chairs, soaking in the tranquil atmosphere, while others briskly walked the circular track, their steps echoing softly in the stillness. A few leaned casually on the rail, chatting with colleagues as they gazed out at the endless crimson horizon. Marcus, often referred to *The Circle* as the "Malibu Beach of Mars," claiming that the relaxed crowd and the sweeping expanse reminded him of home. Some started to call this simply *Beach*, and the crew couldn't help but smile at the comparison, finding a touch of Earth in their Martian sanctuary.

It wasn't this serene all the time.

#

As the days stretched on, the crew's tension grew, creeping into their routines like an unwelcome shadow. The weight of the unknown, and the sheer isolation of Mars began to wear on even the most resilient among them. Being away from loved ones, probably forever, was a lot to take in, and the weight of that realization pressed heavily on everyone. Nobody had truly been prepared for the ultimatum of leaving Earth behind—its familiar skies, its bustling life, and the people they cared for. The finality of their journey, once masked by the excitement of exploration, now loomed over them, a quiet but persistent reminder of all they had sacrificed for the promise of a new frontier.

Day in day out, conversations grew sharper, silences heavier, and the once-tranquil camaraderie of the colony began to fray. Small disagreements quickly escalated into arguments, as the strain of their mission, fueled by doubt and fear, became impossible to separate from any potential influence by the crystal.

Even Riya, usually a bastion of calm, seemed on edge, her orders more clipped and her patience thinner than usual.

"We need to address this," Elena said one evening during a private conversation with Riya in the main hub.

"The crystal isn't just affecting our systems—it's affecting us. People are talking about this everywhere"

Riya leaned back in her chair, her expression weary.

"I've noticed. But what do you suggest? Destroy it? Abandon it? We don't even know if that's possible."

"I'm not saying we get rid of it," Elena said carefully.

"But we need to understand it better. The longer we wait, the more it destabilizes everything—our environment, our relationships, our mission."

Riya nodded slowly, her gaze distant.

"You're right. We can't let this continue. But if we're going to escalate our investigation, we need to do it carefully. No risks we can't afford."

Elena agreed, though a part of her wondered if they were already past the point of no return.

A breakthrough came late one night.

Elena was in the lab with Liam, their eyes bleary from hours of reviewing data. The crystal's patterns had grown increasingly complex, the sequences resembling a mathematical language that defied traditional decoding methods.

"What if we're looking at this wrong?" Liam said suddenly, his voice cutting through the silence.

Elena blinked, startled. "What do you mean?"

"We've been trying to decode this as a static message," Liam explained, pulling up a new set of simulations.

"But what if it's dynamic? A conversation, not a statement?"

Elena's heart quickened as she considered his words. "If it's a conversation… then it's waiting for a response."

"Exactly," Liam said, his fingers flying over the console.

"If we input a basic pattern—something universal, like the Fibonacci sequence—it might respond."

"That's risky," Elena said, her tone cautious. "What if we trigger something we can't control?"

Liam met her gaze, his expression resolute. "If we don't take risks, we'll never understand it."

After a moment's hesitation, Elena nodded. "This is unlike of you Liam, but I like it, Let's do it. But carefully."

"How are we supposed to input anything to the crystal?" Elena asked abruptly, her tone a mix of curiosity and frustration.

Then, with a wry smile, she added, "What do we do—wave a piece of paper at it and hope it notices?" Her remark drew a few chuckles, though the underlying question hung in the air, unanswered.

"We already have an interface to 'poke' the crystal," Liam said with a nod.

"It translates digital commands into electromagnetic pulses projected toward it."

"Like playing music?" Elena asked, raising an eyebrow.

"You may say so," Liam replied, raising a hand as if to pre-empt further questions.

"In fact, we've already tried playing music through it, but… no luck so far."

"Was it Mozart?" Elena teased with a wink.

"A bunch of composers, actually," Liam said, in an emotionless tone. "Still nothing."

The sequence was inputted into the containment field's interface. For a moment, nothing happened. Then, the crystal's light pulsed brighter, its patterns shifting in real-time.

"It's doing something," Liam said, his voice steady and mechanical.

The new patterns were more intricate, their logic clearer as they built on the Fibonacci sequence. It was as if the crystal was acknowledging their input, its symbols aligning with the mathematical foundation they had provided.

Elena felt a chill run through her. The crystal wasn't just adapting—it was communicating.

"What now?" she asked, her voice barely above a whisper.

Liam stared at the screen, his expression unreadable.

"Now we know how to get its attention."

#

The following morning, the crew gathered to review the breakthrough. The hub was filled with a mix of excitement and apprehension, the discovery reigniting their sense of purpose but deepening the mystery of the crystal.

"It's not just a message," Liam said, addressing the group. "It's a dialogue. And it's waiting for us to continue."

David leaned forward, his expression intense. "What if it's guiding us? Leading us to something bigger?"

"Or manipulating us," Marcus suggested. "We can't assume its intentions are benign."

Elena listened quietly, her thoughts racing. The crystal's behavior was a revelation, but it also felt like a turning point—one that could either propel their mission forward or unravel everything they had built.

"We proceed carefully," Riya said, her tone firm.

"No assumptions, no risks we can't control. This is uncharted territory, and we need to treat it as such."

The crew nodded, though the tension in the room was palpable. The crystal's influence had shifted again, its presence no longer just a mystery but a force that was shaping their mission—and their future.

The crystal's response changed everything. What had been a silent enigma now felt like an active participant in their mission, its patterns growing more intricate and deliberate with each new interaction. The breakthrough energized the crew, but it also deepened the divide between those who saw the crystal as an opportunity and those who saw it as a threat.

Riya called a meeting in the main hub the next evening, her expression a mask of calm authority. The crew gathered around the central console; their faces lit by the faint glow of the crystal's latest patterns displayed on the screen.

"We need to establish clear protocols for how we proceed," Riya began.

"This is uncharted territory, and every step we take must be deliberate. David, Marcus, Elena and Liam will lead the analysis. The rest of us will focus on maintaining the colony and monitoring for any changes in the crystal's behavior."

"And what happens if it escalates again?" Marcus asked, his arms crossed.

Riya met his gaze, her voice steady. "We contain it. No direct interaction unless absolutely necessary. We're here to survive, not to gamble."

The room fell silent as her words sank in. The crystal's potential was undeniable, but so were the risks.

#

The greenhouse bustled with its usual quiet energy as Elena's team tended to the growing crops. The artificial sunlamps cast a golden glow over the rows of lettuce, tomatoes, and kale, creating a tranquil environment that belied the exacting work required to sustain their harvest cadence. Sienna Matsuda, one of Elena's most dedicated team members, was perched on a maintenance platform, adjusting a misaligned grow light. Her focus was intense, her hands deftly maneuvering the fixture into place. But a single misstep sent her plummeting.

The Orion band strapped to her wrist immediately detected the fall, its sensors registering the rapid descent, the impact, and her vitals spiking with distress. The band's AI system acted instantly, injecting a calibrated dose of painkillers into her body within seconds, dulling the pain before it could overwhelm her.

Orion alerted, and monotone voice of the Astraeus followed:

"Medical emergency detected. Crew member Sienna Matsuda requires immediate assistance. Pain management activated. Please attend immediately."

Elena froze, her heart sinking as she saw Sienna lying still on the greenhouse floor.

Within moments, a medical team arrived with a stretcher. Sienna, conscious but in visible discomfort, was stabilized and transported back to *Eos Horizon*—the first time many had set foot on the starship since landing. As the hatch sealed behind them, the familiar hum of the ship's systems, "Whisper," was noticeably absent, as the ship is now on auxiliary fusion core, supporting the medical bay and other vital systems on-board, which is a much smaller, noise and vibration free device.

Dr. Amir Qureshi, the Trauma Surgeon, met them in the medical bay, his calm professionalism cutting through the tension. Sienna was placed into the total-body scanner, an advanced piece of equipment capable of rendering detailed, real-time images of the body's internal structures. As the scanner moved over her, the room grew silent. The results were clear:

multiple fractures, including several ribs, a broken wrist, and damage to her lower spine. Though serious, Dr. Qureshi reassured the team.

"She's fortunate," he said, his voice steady. "Everything we're seeing is recoverable with the technology we have here. The pain management from Orion helped stabilize her early. But she'll need time—and an intense rehabilitation plan."

Sienna, pale but determined, managed a weak smile. "Guess I'll have to sit out the next harvest," she joked, though her voice trembled. Dr. Qureshi nodded, his expression softening.

"Maybe for a while. But you'll be back in no time, stronger than ever."

The incident was a sobering reminder of the risks inherent in their work and the necessity of their advanced medical capabilities. As the medical team began preparations for Sienna's recovery, the rest of the crew reflected on how *Eos Horizon* remained not just their lifeline to Mars, but their sanctuary in times of crisis. The sight of the starship, its corridors, spaces and lighting with purpose, rekindled a sense of unity and resilience among them.

#

Dr. Amir Qureshi was no stranger to chaos. A seasoned trauma surgeon from Pakistan, he had spent years in war zones, where life and death were separated by mere seconds and steady hands. His expertise in emergency medicine made him invaluable to the *Eos Horizon* mission, but it was his composure under pressure that truly set him apart.

Before Mars, before the colony, he had already made history—being among the first Pakistanis to travel to space as part of a Pakistan-American joint mission. That experience had given him a perspective few others shared, a deep understanding of both the frailty and resilience of the human body in the void. Now, on the Red Planet, far from the battlefield hospitals and the weightlessness of Earth's orbit, he faced a new kind of challenge—keeping humanity alive in a place never meant for it.

In the days that followed, the team's work intensified. Marcus and David joined Liam and Ada, designed a series of input patterns to test the crystal's responsiveness, while Elena focused on monitoring its environmental impact. The artifact's behavior was as mesmerizing as it was unsettling—its patterns growing more complex with each interaction, as though it were learning from them.

One evening, as Elena reviewed the latest data in the lab, David entered with a tablet in hand.

"You're not going to believe this," he said, his voice tinged with excitement.

She looked up, her curiosity piqued. "What is it?"

David set the tablet on the counter, displaying a set of newly decoded patterns.

"These symbols—they're coordinates!"

Elena's breath caught. "Coordinates? To what?"

"That's the question," David replied. "They're local, though. Somewhere within a ten-kilometer radius."

She stared at the screen, her mind racing. The crystal wasn't just communicating—it was directing them. But to what end?

"We need to show this to Riya," she said, her voice firm.

The revelation of the coordinates reignited tensions among the crew. While some saw it as an opportunity to uncover more about the crystal's purpose, others—like Marcus—viewed it as a potential trap.

"This is exactly how we get ourselves killed," Marcus said during the next briefing, his tone sharp.

"Following breadcrumbs left by something we don't understand? It's reckless."

He paused, scanning the room, then continued with a firm voice.

"We were trained in the military exactly for this scenario—to recognize these traps and avoid getting ambushed. Half of us here have military training already, so this should be clear as day. We don't walk blindly into what's obviously a setup. We assess, adapt, and outmaneuver. Anything less, and we're just serving ourselves up on a platter."

"Concerns noted, but we can't ignore it," David argued. "Whether the crystal is guiding us or not, if anything out there we have to find."

Riya turned to Liam, her expression steady but tinged with curiosity.

"Liam, what do you think of the coordinates?"

Liam glanced at the console; his expression as inscrutable as ever.

"As you know, we don't have GPS-like coordinates on Mars. Navigation here relies on satellite-based triangulation and dead reckoning—for now."

He continued, "What we received and analyzed were four vectors. When we use the artifact that housed the crystal as the origin point, two vectors intersect. When we use the quarantine valley as the origin point, the other two intersect."

He leaned back slightly. "Both intersections overlap exactly".

"If that's a coincidence, it's one hell of a coincidence."

Liam's tone remained calm but deliberate as he added, "For simplicity, we can call them coordinates—local, within ten kilometers from here. That's the data."

He paused, then added with a faint shrug, "What to do with it, though—that's outside my wheelhouse. I'm afraid I can't help you there."

Riya nodded thoughtfully, her gaze lingering on Liam for a moment longer. She appreciated his precision, even if his nonchalance sometimes left others uneasy.

"Fair enough," she replied, her mind already racing ahead to consider the possibilities.

"We'll investigate these 'coordinates,'" she said, pausing to weigh the word carefully before continuing,

"but we do it on our terms. No unnecessary risks, no direct contact until we're certain it's safe. Marcus, you'll lead the team."

Her tone was firm, leaving no room for debate.

"Yes Ma'am. And we go prepared for anything", Marcus frowned but nodded, his reluctance clear.

#

Marcus Hayes began his journey as a dedicated member of the United States Marine Corps, serving with distinction as part of the Marine Wing Support Squadrons (MWSS). In this capacity, he participated in missions that challenged both his resilience and tactical ingenuity, instilling in him a profound sense of discipline, camaraderie, and unwavering determination to solve problems under pressure. Following an honorable discharge—his record decorated with commendations for leadership and resourcefulness—Marcus pursued a degree in mechanical engineering, driven by a passion for innovation. He later joined UNSI, where his military-honed grit seamlessly complements the precision and creativity demanded by groundbreaking aerospace projects.

Beneath Marcus's tough exterior looks and outspoken attitude, was a deeply compassionate and selfless man shaped by his upbringing. The youngest of four siblings, he grew up in a modest, middle-class household with three sisters, the eldest of whom had down syndrome. Resources were always scarce, as their parents worked tirelessly to support the family and care for their eldest daughter's special needs. Marcus was on casual work while schooling to support the family in every which way he could. While his two other sisters eventually got married and moved out, Marcus stayed behind, taking on the role of caregiver for his eldest sister. He supported her not just financially, but also physically and emotionally, shouldering the weight of her care even as he sacrificed building a life for himself.

His parents, whose love for each other was their anchor, passed away shortly after Marcus enlisted in the military. Farther was first, then mother within a very short period of his demise. This loss only deepened his resolve to remain by his sister's side, becoming her primary support system through the years. When the sister passed away eventually, Marcus redirected the love and dedication he'd poured into her care into a new purpose: service to the UNSI and, ultimately, the mission to Mars. It was his way of honoring the values his family had instilled in him—selflessness, resilience, and an unwavering commitment to those in need.

#

The expedition to the coordinates took place the next morning. Marcus, Elena, and two other crew members loaded a rover with equipment and set off across the Martian terrain. The journey was tense, the landscape barren and unchanging as they followed the mapped route.

Marcus has two junior engineers in his team, each bringing a unique blend of military discipline and technical aptitude to the colony. Stafford "Staff" Carter, twenty-nine, was a former Air Force technician who specialized in maintaining and troubleshooting advanced experimental aircraft systems. His sharp analytical mind and hands-on experience with complex machinery made him a natural fit for the demanding work of constructing and maintaining the colony's infrastructure. Despite his junior status, Staff quickly gained a reputation for his keen attention to detail and unwavering commitment to the mission.

Alongside Staff, was Riley Cho, twenty-seven, an avionics engineer for US Navy, with a background in electronics and communications. Having served on several naval expeditions, Riley was adept at adapting to high-pressure environments and handling intricate systems under duress. Her calm demeanor and quick thinking were assets to the team, complementing Staff's technical precision. Both shared a sense of camaraderie with Marcus, their military backgrounds creating an unspoken bond of mutual respect and understanding. Together, they formed a cohesive unit, working tirelessly to ensure the colony's engineering challenges were met with skill and determination.

#

Six security members, usually assigned to surveillance and escort duties throughout the colony, were partially re-tasked for other critical responsibilities. Moreover, two had reported mild digestive discomfort after consuming a recent meal of Martian-grown produce. While it was the first instance of greenhouse food causing such a reaction, the medical team was quick to investigate. All systems and protocols in the greenhouse had been cleared of contamination, so the issue was believed to stem from individual sensitivities to the fresh produce rather than a systemic problem.

With security personnel reduced, Marcus asked Staff, and Riley to fill in as additional support for the excursion. Their military backgrounds made them natural candidates for this role, even if the call to duty was unexpected.

"We'll be fine," Marcus assured the team as they geared up, his voice calm yet commanding.

Staff's hands moved deftly as he checked the integrity of their exosuits, while Riley double-checked the calibration of the multi-spectrum cameras mounted on their MSA suites. Despite the change in their assignment, they approached the task with the same dedication and precision that had earned them their place in the colony. It was an unexpected blend of engineering expertise and operational readiness, but it was a reminder of how versatile the team needed to be on this untamed world.

#

The coordinates led them to a shallow depression at the base of a ridge. At the center of the depression was another structure—slightly larger than the first but similar in design, its metallic surface partially buried in red dust.

"This is it," Marcus said, his voice low as he stepped out of the rover, the red dust of Mars swirling lightly around his boots. His eyes scanned the horizon, settling on the ominous silhouette ahead. After a moment, he exhaled, his tone laced with dry humor.

"We've got enough problems with one. Now we have two to deal with—double trouble."

Riley, stepping out behind him, gave a wry chuckle, her visor reflecting the faint glow of the Martian sunrise.

"Well, at least it keeps each-other company," she replied, her voice tinged with equal parts humor and nervous anticipation.

Staff adjusted his gear, glancing at Marcus.

"Let's just hope it's not trouble squared," he muttered, his usual sharp wit dulled by the growing tension.

For a brief moment, Elena giggled too—a light, fleeting sound that seemed almost out of place amidst the tension. If it was sincere, she wouldn't even know. It felt more like her body's involuntary attempt to diffuse the weight pressing down on them, a reflex rather than a conscious choice. The sound lingered in the air for a heartbeat before fading, leaving an odd silence in its wake, as if the room itself was unsure how to respond.

Their enthusiasm was noticeably muted, a blunt contrast to the excitement surrounding the discovery of the first artifact. It was as if they already knew what to expect and weren't particularly fond of the finding.

Marcus smirked faintly, his hand instinctively resting on the rover's panel.

"Let's get to work. Whatever this is, it's not solving itself."

Elena followed, her heart pounding nevertheless as she approached the structure. It lacked the intricate patterns of the first artifact, but its shape and material were unmistakably similar.

"Let's document everything," Marcus said.

"No touching until we know what we're dealing with."

Elena knelt beside the structure, scanning it with her hand-held device. The readings were similar to the first artifact—elevated electromagnetic activity, faint heat signatures, and a subtle hum that seemed to resonate through the air.

"It's inactive," she said, though her voice betrayed her uncertainty. "What do we know" she murmured.

As they worked, the tension among the team grew. The artifact's stillness was unnerving, its presence a silent question that none of them could answer. Yet even as they documented every detail, Elena couldn't shake the feeling that they were being watched—not by the crew, but by something unseen.

The return to the habitat was subdued. The new artifact was too large to bring back, though Marcus and Staff were confident it wasn't fused or lodged beyond the point of eventual mobilization. but they had collected extensive data and samples for further analysis. The discovery deepened the mystery of the crystal, raising more questions than answers.

In the main hub, Riya reviewed their findings with a frown. "Another structure. Same signal. But no clear purpose."

"It's connected to the crystal," Elena said.

"The patterns, the materials—it's all part of the same system. Whatever left this behind, it wasn't random."

Riya nodded, though her expression remained guarded.

"We'll continue the analysis. But we don't let this distract us from the mission. The colony comes first."

The crew dispersed; their conversations subdued. The discovery of the second artifact was monumental, but it also felt like the beginning of something far larger—and far more sinister.

That night, as Elena lay in her bunk, she couldn't stop thinking about the artifact. Its presence, its silence, its connection to the crystal—it all felt like pieces of a puzzle just out of reach. She stared at the curved ceiling, her thoughts a whirlwind of speculation and unease.

The crystal pulsed faintly in the lab, its light steady and unyielding. Somewhere in the depths of her mind, Elena felt its presence—not malevolent, but insistent.

It was waiting.

For what?

#

The following week brought a flurry of activity as the crew focused on reinforcing the colony's foundations. The initial euphoria of their discoveries was tempered by the sobering reality of survival on Mars. With the crystal and the second artifact occupying much of their minds, Riya pushed the team to maintain their focus on the essentials.

Elena and Dr. Noah spent long hours in the greenhouse, expanding the system to accommodate additional crops. The original plan had called for a second greenhouse module to be activated after six months, but with the crops thriving and the colony's food reserves shrinking faster than anticipated, they decided to accelerate the timeline.

Marcus stepped into the greenhouse, his presence unmistakable. His expression carrying the weight of unspoken thoughts. It was clear—he wasn't just here for a routine check-in. He needed to talk. He needed company.

"It's Elliot's fault—he made us want to eat more," Elena joked with a mock complaint, a playful grin spreading across her face.

"Totally!" Noah chimed in from a far. Marcus chuckled.

"This module's going to push our power systems harder," Marcus said, leaning casually against the doorway as Elena focused on fine-tuning the irrigation system.

"We're monitoring it," she replied, her tone brisk, not looking up.

"The colony's fusion generators can handle the load, but I'll make the necessary adjustments to keep the strain minimal."

Marcus crossed his arms, his expression thoughtful. "It's not the fusion generators I'm worried about," he said, his voice steady but edged with concern.

"It's the infrastructure—the grid and the backups. If the fusion generators go dark, the solar arrays and batteries will have to carry the weight. And pushing those too hard... well, that's not a scenario we want to test."

Noah crouched beside a row of newly transplanted seedlings, his gloved hands carefully packing the soil around their roots.

"These crops will be worth it. We've got enough stored nutrients to double our yield if the second greenhouse holds steady."

Elena nodded, though her thoughts remained divided. The greenhouse represented hope and stability, a symbol of humanity's ability to adapt. But the looming presence of the crystal cast a shadow over their work, a constant reminder of how precarious their situation was.

#

Meanwhile, Marcus led a team to construct additional storage modules and reinforce the habitat's exterior. The Martian dust storms—an ever-present threat—had already left fine layers of grit on the habitat's surface, and the team worked tirelessly to ensure the colony could withstand stronger weather events.

"Structural integrity is holding," Marcus reported to Riya during a midday check-in.

"But the seals on the secondary airlocks need reinforcing. A strong storm could compromise them."

"Make it a priority," Riya said. "We can't afford any weak points."

Using materials stored in the colony's supply caches, Marcus and his team devised new bracing systems for the airlocks. The work was tedious, the weightlessness of their suits making precision work challenging, but the team pressed on. By the end of the day, the secondary airlocks were secured, and Marcus allowed himself a rare moment of satisfaction.

"It's not elegant," he said to one of his engineers, "but it'll hold."

#

Power generation remained one of the colony's most critical challenges. The solar arrays required daily maintenance to keep them clear of Martian dust, and the fusion reactors—while stable—needed constant monitoring to ensure it operated within safe parameters.

Marcus worked closely with the engineers to refine the colony's energy grid. They reconfigured the solar array's tracking systems to maximize efficiency and introduced a redundancy circuit to ensure that critical systems could switch to backup in case of a failure.

The colony's sewer system is an achievement in sustainability, meticulously designed to support life on Mars while minimizing waste. Utilizing advanced filtering techniques, the system separates water and nutrients from the waste stream, re-purposing both for agricultural use in the greenhouse. The reclaimed water undergoes additional purification, including microbial removal, ensuring it is safe for irrigation and, if necessary, drinkable. However, with the colony stockpiled with a multi-year water supply, using reclaimed water for consumption remains a contingency rather than an immediate need. The remaining solids are processed into a material virtually indistinguishable from soil, free of harmful contaminants and safe for dispersal into the Martian ground. The system is fully automatic, having own power banks to withstand up to a month without connecting to the grid. This semi-closed-loop system significantly reduces dependency on Earth-based resources, supporting the colony's mission to establish a sustainable, self-sufficient ecosystem on the red planet.

"It's a balancing act," Marcus explained to Elena as they reviewed the latest energy reports.

"The more we rely on solar, the less strain on the reactor. But if the weather turns, we'll need to shift everything back."

"We're in better shape than I thought we'd be," Elena said, her tone hopeful. "The redundancy gives us breathing room."

"For now," Marcus replied.

"But this planet has a way of surprising us."

With a growing sense that the crystal's presence might not be an isolated anomaly, Riya ordered part of the team to enhance the colony's communications array. The expansion wasn't just about maintaining a reliable link with Earth; it was a strategic move to extend the colony's ability to monitor the electromagnetic fluctuations. By increasing sensitivity and range, the array would provide a clearer picture of any surrounding signals or disturbances, offering critical insights into the enigmatic phenomena that seemed to be unfolding around them.

"Adding these sensor and antennas will give us better resolution on the crystal's signal," David explained as he and another engineer installed additional antennae on the habitat's exterior. "If there are more artifacts out there, we'll pick them up."

"And if the signal changes again?" Riya asked, watching from the airlock.

"Then we'll be ready," David said, though his tone was less certain.

#

As part of their efforts to ensure the colony's survival, Riya initiated a series of crisis simulations to test the crew's readiness for emergencies. These scenarios ranged from sudden dust storms cutting off solar power to equipment malfunctions in the greenhouse.

One afternoon, the alarm blared through the habitat, signaling the start of a simulated reactor failure. Marcus and his team rushed to the reactor module, getting into protective gear and running through the emergency protocols.

"Coolant levels stabilizing," one of the engineers reported as Marcus adjusted the flow controls. "Backup systems are online."

Riya observed from the central console, nodding as the team resolved the issue within the allotted time.

"Good work," she said over the comms. "We'll run another scenario tomorrow. Let's be ready."

Elena and Noah's team faced their own test when a simulated rupture in the greenhouse's irrigation system forced them to reroute water supplies. The challenge highlighted weak points in the system, which they worked late into the night to address.

"These drills aren't just for show," Riya said during the evening debrief.

"This planet won't wait for us to get comfortable. Stay sharp."

Amid the relentless pace of work, Riya recognized the need to bolster the crew's morale. One evening, she surprised the team by setting up a shared movie night in the common area, screening an old Earth film onto the habitat wall.

The laughter and conversation that followed were a rare reprieve, a reminder of their shared humanity amid the alien landscape. Even Marcus allowed himself a brief smile as the crew exchanged jokes and stories long after the credits rolled.

"It's easy to forget why we're here," Riya said quietly to Elena as they cleaned up. "Moments like this remind us."

"Thanks for doing that. We needed it," Elena said, her tone genuine. She glanced at Riya and added with a chuckle,

"I remember you told me about this movie some time ago, but I have to admit—I never got around to watching it. Now I see the resemblance."

Riya gave a faint smile, acknowledging Elena's words with a silent nod, her expression thoughtful as the moment hung lightly between them.

Elena nodded, her thoughts briefly turning to Earth. The colony was their home now, but the ties to their past remained strong. It was those ties—family, friends, and the promise of a future—that drove them forward.

#

The foundations of the colony were stronger than ever, but the challenges ahead loomed large. The crystal's influence continued to grow, its patterns evolving with each interaction. And though the crew had built a stable base on Mars, the unknowns they faced—both external and internal—were impossible to ignore.

As the sun set over the Martian horizon, casting long shadows across the habitat, Elena stood in the observation module, staring out at the endless expanse of red dust and rock. Somewhere out there, the crystal and its secrets waited, their meaning still just out of reach.

The days stretched into weeks, the monotony of Labor punctuated by the unspoken tension surrounding the crystal. The colony was taking shape, a fragile but functional foothold on an alien world. The habitats were secure, the greenhouse expanded, and the energy systems reinforced to withstand the planet's unpredictable conditions. Yet, for all their progress, there was a sense that they were building atop something vast and unknowable, the crystal and its symbols a constant reminder of the mysteries they hadn't yet unraveled.

Elena's nights were restless. The crystal's patterns haunted her dreams, the shapes twisting into something almost comprehensible before slipping away. Each morning, she awoke with the same nagging thought: they were missing something. The crystal was waiting for them to understand, but it felt as though they were speaking two different languages.

Marcus had grown quieter over the past days. He worked with grim efficiency, his focus unwavering, but Elena noticed how often his gaze lingered on the lab's containment chamber as he passed by. Despite his outward pragmatism, the crystal's presence was clearly affecting him too.

David, on the other hand, seemed energized by the discovery. He spent hours in the lab, running simulations and testing inputs, his excitement tempered only by Riya's insistence on caution. He often spoke to Elena about the potential implications of their work—how the crystal might represent a turning point for humanity.

"Imagine what this could mean," he said one evening as they worked in the greenhouse.

"If it's a guide, a blueprint… it could show us how to thrive here. Maybe even beyond."

"And if it's a trap?" Elena countered, her voice low. "If it's manipulating us into doing something we don't understand?"

David hesitated, then shrugged.

"That's the risk, isn't it? Every leap forward starts with a question we can't fully answer."

She didn't respond, her hands busy moving through the rows of plants, gently rubbing the leaves as if they were the delicate skin of a newborn infant. Her mind, just as engaged, seemed to lovingly observe every detail, almost expecting the plants to respond in kind—a quiet, wordless exchange. The plants, at least, provided a semblance of stability—a quiet reassurance that some things still grew steadily amidst the chaos. Their thriving presence was a small but meaningful victory against the odds. Yet even here, the crystal's influence felt inescapable. Subtle but persistent anomalies in the soil's nutrient levels continued to defy explanation, an unsettling reminder that nothing in the colony was entirely untouched by its existence.

Riya remained a steady presence, her leadership keeping the crew grounded even as tensions rose. She divided her time between overseeing the colony's expansion and mediating the growing friction among the team. It was clear that the pressure was wearing on her, though she rarely let it show.

#

One evening, as Elena reviewed the latest data in the main hub, Riya approached her, a mug of steaming tea in hand. She set it down beside Elena's console and leaned against the edge of the table.

"You've been working nonstop," Riya said. "Take a break."

Elena looked up, startled. "I'm fine. There's just so much to do."

"There will always be more to do," Riya replied. "But if we burn ourselves out, none of it will matter."

Elena nodded reluctantly, her gaze drifting to the crystal's faint glow on the screen.

"Do you ever feel like we're being pulled in two directions? Building the colony, but also… whatever this is?"

Riya followed her gaze, her expression calm but unreadable.

"Every day," she said softly.

"But we can't lose sight of why we're here. The crystal is important, yes. But if we let it tear us apart—if we perish because we lose ourselves—none of it will matter in the end."

"And if the two are connected?" Elena asked softly.

Riya didn't answer immediately. When she finally spoke, her voice was quieter. "Then we'll face it. Together."

The words stayed with Elena as she returned to her bunk that night. The crystal's pulse echoed faintly in her thoughts, a rhythm she couldn't ignore. It wasn't just a presence—it was a force, shaping their mission in ways they were only beginning to understand.

#

As the habitat settled into its nightly stillness, Elena stared at the curved ceiling above her, the weight of their discoveries pressing heavily on her. Somewhere in the Martian wilderness, the second artifact lay dormant, its purpose as inscrutable as the crystal's. The two were connected, she was certain of that. But what tied them together remained a mystery.

She closed her eyes, exhaustion finally overtaking her. Yet even in sleep, the questions persisted, weaving through her dreams like threads in an unfinished tapestry.

So far, they had discovered two structures: the first revealed a crystal inside, while the second remained dormant. Was it empty, or had they simply not figured out how to unlock it? If a second crystal lay hidden within, was it the same as the first, or something entirely different? How would it differ in form, function, or purpose? The possibilities seemed endless, and the dunes surrounding the colony seemed to whisper of more secrets waiting to be unearthed.

A hundred questions lingered in everyone's minds, gnawing at their focus. Without clarity, speculation became the only constant—a fragile thread tethering their curiosity to reality, yet one that threatened to unravel into chaos.

What had they uncovered? And what would it cost them to find out?

#

The colony settled into a rhythm that mirrored the Martian days—busy, focused, and ever underpinned by the quiet hum of the crystal. The routines they'd built, though necessary, felt fragile, as if any disruption might unravel the tenuous sense of stability they had achieved.

Elena continued to pour herself into her work. The second greenhouse module was now fully operational, and the crops were thriving under the care of meticulously calibrated systems. Each leaf, each sprouting potato, was a small triumph against the unforgiving landscape. Yet even these victories were tempered by the looming question of the crystal's role in their survival—or their undoing.

The crew's interactions grew more strained as days passed. Arguments, once rare, now flared with increasing frequency. Small disputes over resources or schedules escalated into heated debates, the tension thick enough to permeate the air. Riya worked tirelessly to mediate, but even she couldn't silence the gnawing unease that gripped them all.

One evening, as the crew gathered for a shared meal in the common area, Marcus's voice cut through the low hum of conversation.

"We're losing focus," he said, his tone sharp.

"This mission was supposed to be about survival—about building something sustainable. But instead, we're playing *Indiana Jones*, chasing mysteries we don't understand."

David, seated across the table, bristled. "The crystal isn't just a mystery. It's part of this planet, part of why we're here. Ignoring it would be irresponsible."

"Irresponsible is putting the colony at risk because you can't let go of your pet project," Marcus shot back.

"Enough," Riya interjected, her voice firm. "This isn't the time or place for this discussion."

But the tension lingered, the air heavy with unspoken words. Elena sat in silence; her appetite forgotten as she stared at her plate. The rift between Marcus and David was growing, and she feared it was only a matter of time before it erupted into something they couldn't contain.

After the meal, Riya pulled Marcus aside.

"I need you to keep your focus on the mission," she said, her tone measured but firm.

"The crystal is part of what we're dealing with, whether we like it or not. You don't have to agree with David, but I need you to work with him."

Marcus nodded reluctantly. "I'll do my job. But if this thing jeopardizes the colony…"

"It won't," Riya said, cutting him off. "Because we won't let it."

\#

Later that night, Elena found herself drawn back to the *"The Sky"*. The Martian landscape stretched out before her, its desolation both beautiful and unnerving. The ridge where the second artifact had been discovered loomed in the distance, a dark silhouette against the faint light of the rising sun.

The faint hum of the crystal echoed in her mind, as it always did now. She pressed her hand against the cold glass, her reflection merging with the red horizon.

"What do you want from us?" she whispered.

The deck was hers alone until David stepped in. He didn't speak at first, simply standing beside her and staring out at the same view.

"You feel it too, don't you?" he said finally.

Elena hesitated before nodding. "It's like it's always there. Watching, waiting."

David glanced at her, his expression thoughtful. "Do you think we're the first to find it?"

"The first humans, maybe," she replied. "But something—or someone—put it here."

"And we're supposed to figure out why," David said, his voice quiet.

"It's like we're part of a test."

Elena turned to face him. "What if we fail?"

David didn't answer. The silence between them was heavy with the weight of their shared fears.

"I enjoy the crimson," Elena whispered, her voice soft and reflective, just loud enough to carry the message. "Until I can't."

#

The following day, Riya announced a new initiative to map the surrounding terrain more extensively. With the discovery of the second artifact, it had become clear that the colony was situated within a network of unknown artifacts. The team divided into pairs, each assigned a sector to survey using drones and rovers.

Elena and Marcus were paired together, their task to explore a stretch of rocky plains extending beyond the ridge. The rover's engine hummed softly as they navigated the uneven terrain, the silence between them broken only by the occasional beep of the on-board instruments.

"This area's been untouched," Marcus said, scanning the horizon.

"No signs of erosion patterns that would suggest anything recent."

"Yet the artifacts are here," Elena replied.

"That means someone—or something—was here long before us."

Marcus frowned, his grip tightening on the controls.

"I still think we're playing with fire. These things weren't left here by accident."

"I've seen monkeys touch electrical cables and get fried all the time," Marcus said, his tone balancing somewhere between genuine caution and biting sarcasm.

Elena chuckled, trying to stifle an all-out laugh. The statement might have been biased, but she couldn't deny how comparable it was.

Elena didn't argue, she couldn't. She felt the same unease but didn't see the point in voicing it. Instead, she focused on the survey equipment, logging soil samples and geological readings.

As the rover crested a small hill, they both froze. Below them, nestled in a shallow basin, was another metallic structure. Unlike the others, this one was larger, its angular edges partially buried in the Martian soil. It shimmered faintly under the weak sunlight, its surface marred by centuries of dust and wind.

"Another one," Marcus said, his voice low, laced more with disappointment than excitement. "And it's bigger than the last."

Elena activated the rover's camera, capturing the scene. "We need to tell Riya."

Marcus nodded but didn't take his eyes off the structure. "And we need to be ready for whatever this thing brings."

The scouting teams eventually discovered several more structures within the designated search grid. Some were similar in size to the first, while others varied, some larger, some smaller. Despite these differences, all the structures appeared to be made from the same enigmatic material, adorned with similar markings. Each radiated the same faint glow and emitted the same subtle hum, their shared characteristics deepening the mystery and raising more questions than answers.

The discovery of more artifacts sent ripples through the colony. It was clear now that the crystal and the artifacts were part of a larger system, a network whose purpose remained maddeningly out of reach. The crew's work continued, but the strain of balancing survival with the pursuit of answers grew heavier with each passing day.

As the Martian sun set once more, casting long shadows across the habitat, Elena sat alone in the greenhouse. The plants swayed gently under the artificial breeze of the ventilation system, their vibrant green a stark contrast to the red wasteland outside.

She closed her eyes, the hum of the crystal echoing faintly in her mind. It wasn't just a sound—it was a call, a question, a force that demanded to be understood.

And for the first time, she wondered if understanding it would cost them everything.

"Why you make this hard"

Chapter Four

FRACTURES

Ada Torres carried a quiet resilience that belied the weight of the personal sacrifices she had made for the mission. A linguist and code specialist, her expertise lay in deciphering ancient texts and lost languages, a skill honed through years of studying forgotten civilizations. With an academic background in archaeology, she had spent much of her career piecing together fragmented histories, decoding symbols that once held the knowledge of entire cultures.

Newly married to her husband, Carlos, a fellow archaeologist, their bond had been forged through years of shared expeditions, challenging digs, and late-night conversations under starlit skies. Both orphans raised in similar circumstances in nearby cities of Mexico, they had an innate understanding of each other, a shared sense of purpose and independence that drew them together. Their connection was seamless, almost unspoken—a rhythm born of mutual respect and a deep appreciation for each other's strengths.

While their friends dreamed of crossing the border at any cost, Ada and Carlos focused on their education alone, determined to carve out a different way out. Their dedication paid off when both earned scholarships to universities on the other side of the border, a testament to their perseverance and shared values. It was during field studies in the vast plains of Utah that their paths finally crossed.

When the opportunity to join the Mars mission arose, the decision was both agonizing and inevitable. They had sat together for hours, weighing the enormity of the choice. Carlos had understood immediately; he always did.

"This is bigger than us," he'd said softly, his words echoing what they both already knew. That understanding, the same one that had made them such a strong pair, also made their parting achingly clear. It was difficult to leave someone who truly knew you, but it was that very understanding made the separation possible. Carlos had stayed behind, continuing their work on Earth, while Ada carried their shared passion to the stars, knowing that every step she took was for something greater than herself.

Carlos worked in archaeological sites across the globe, where star-studded skies were a familiar companion. Yet now, stargazing felt different—what was once a shared passion had become a solitary ritual. Whenever he found a quiet moment, he would tilt his gaze upward, his thoughts reaching far beyond the shimmering expanse. Among those distant lights, he imagined Ada, his beloved, carrying their shared dreams to the red planet.

The weight of their separation lingered, but within it, he found a quiet solace. A deep certainty settled in his heart—she was safe. The bond that had connected them so deeply on Earth seemed to stretch across the vastness of space, unbroken. He knew this was a one-way journey, and Ada shouldn't have to live alone. In the end, Carlos made the choice for both of them—to legally separate, giving Ada the freedom to step fully into her future. It wasn't an easy decision, but it was necessary.

Carlos's love for Ada had never been about possession. Love, he knew, was not about holding on, but about letting go so it could flourish. He wasn't sentimental, but he loved her in the quietest, purest way—like watching the stars, knowing she was out there, shining in her own place in the universe. Despite the ache of absence, he knew she was exactly where she was meant to be, and somehow, that knowledge made the stars shine a little brighter.

#

"Ada," David called, catching her attention. "We need more of you."

"You could have had Carlos too, but you didn't," she whispered with a sigh, her words barely audible but heavy with emotion.

"I heard it," David responded softly, his tone measured yet laced with regret. "I know you both were upset with me about that. I understand."

He hesitated for a moment, then added, "But you also know I'm the reason you're here. I could only do so much."

His explanation was kinder than she expected, his voice steady but carrying a trace of sorrow buried deep, an acknowledgment of the choices made, and the opportunities lost.

"I'm already more," Ada quipped with a grin, also an agreement with what David said.

"Jokes aside," David pressed, "do you think having more of these artifacts makes it easier or harder?"

Ada paused thoughtfully before responding.

"We had to wait for the *Rosetta-Stone* to be discovered before hieroglyphics were anything more than pretty pictures. I don't see a *Rosetta-Stone* here, at least not yet. But having more symbols, more occurrences—it increases the chances of finding patterns, of making sense of this, if that's even a possibility."

She hesitated, then chuckled softly. "But honestly, some things might just be meant to remain undecipherable. I'm just being realistic."

#

The discovery of multiple artifacts marked a somber turning point for the colony. The once-steady rhythm of daily life gave way to a simmering tension, the unspoken divide among the crew widening with each new revelation. The artifacts were no longer anomalies—they were part of a system, a cluster that seemed to stretch across the red planet. But with every new discovery, the questions grew sharper, and the answers more elusive.

Sentinel and *Watcher* could only faintly detect the structures of the artifacts on its own, and even then, only after they were first identified and marked through ground observation. These artifacts—enigmatic and elusive—are now widely believed to be scattered across the Red Planet, hidden beyond the reach of even the colony's most advanced imaging and sensory technology, in orbit and on ground. Their obscurity lends credence to the pervasive nature of the signal, or the ambient sensation that had enveloped the colony since they landed here.

Destroying the crystal, if it were even possible, now seems unlikely to have any meaningful impact on the larger alien system that appeared to blanket the planet. With no definitive way to dismantle or alter its influence, the colony faced two stark and uncertain choices: to study the artifacts and attempt to uncover their secrets, or to ignore them altogether and prioritize survival. For now, both options remain subjects of heated debate, shrouded in uncertainty and risk on either choice.

It started subtly at first: curt exchanges during work, averted gazes during meals. The crew, bound together by a shared purpose, now seemed to fracture along invisible lines. Marcus and David clashed openly, their debates about the artifacts escalating into full-blown arguments.

"This isn't just a science project!" Marcus shouted one afternoon in the main hub, his voice echoing through the cramped space.

"Every minute we spend chasing these things, we're neglecting the colony. Our survival comes first!"

"And these artifacts might be the key to that survival!" David fired back, his face flushed with frustration.

"They're part of this planet—part of our survival. You can't just ignore them."

Riya stepped between them, her voice firm. "Enough. We're not here to argue. We're here to work. Both of you need to focus on your tasks and leave the speculation for later."

The room fell silent, but the tension lingered. Riya's command was enough to quell the immediate conflict, but the underlying divisions remained, festering just below the surface.

Elena tried to avoid taking sides, but it was becoming increasingly difficult. She understood Marcus's caution—every discovery seemed to destabilize the colony further. But she also couldn't ignore the pull of the artifacts, the sense that they were on the cusp of something monumental.

Her days in the greenhouse provided little solace. The crops continued to thrive, but anomalies in the nutrient and filtration systems persisted, subtle fluctuations that defied explanation. It was as though the artifacts were reaching into every corner of the colony, their influence growing with each passing day.

#

One evening, as she worked alone in the greenhouse, Marcus appeared in the doorway. He leaned against the frame, his expression unreadable.

"We need to talk," he said.

Elena set down her tools, wiping her hands on her jumpsuit. "About what?"

"About this," he replied, gesturing vaguely toward the habitat around them. "The artifacts, the crystal… all of it. It's tearing us apart."

She sighed, crossing her arms. "You think I don't see that? But what do you want me to do? Pretend they don't exist?"

"No," Marcus said, his tone softening. "But we need to be realistic. These things are a distraction. Every time we engage with them, something else goes wrong—systems fail, people argue. It's a pattern, Elena. And it's only going to get worse."

"And if ignoring them puts us at greater risk?" she countered. "What if understanding them is the only way to survive here?"

Marcus hesitated, his jaw tightening. "I don't have the answers. But I know this—if we keep chasing shadows, we'll lose sight of what matters."

Elena didn't respond. She couldn't argue with his logic, but she also couldn't shake the feeling that the artifacts were more than distractions—they were the key to something larger, something they couldn't afford to ignore.

#

The fractures within the crew deepened after a near-fatal accident in the rover bay. What was supposed to be a routine maintenance task turned into a crisis in an instant. Riley had been inspecting the pressure regulators on one of the rovers, ensuring the seals were intact before the next scheduled surface excursion. The work was tedious but necessary—one unnoticed crack in a valve could mean a slow leak, an invisible threat until it was too late. She was adjusting a connection when, without warning, a pressurized valve failed catastrophically. The high-pressure gas, meant to stabilize the rover's environmental systems, burst free with the force of an explosion, sending a deafening hiss through the bay. The shock-wave lifted Riley off her feet, hurling her backward like a rag doll. She slammed into the bulkhead with a sickening crunch, her suit scraping against the metal before she crumpled to the floor. The warning alarms blared to life, the flashing red lights casting eerie shadows on the walls.

Marcus and Riya reacted instantly. Marcus lunged forward, sealing the compromised valve with a quick clamp before the situation could spiral further. Riya, moving with practiced urgency, was already at Riley's side, flipping her over to check for injuries. The first thing she saw was the tear in Riley's suit—a jagged gash along her side, hissing as precious oxygen escaped into the thin Martian air. The HUD on Riley's helmet flickered erratically, her vitals unstable.

"Suit breach—oxygen dropping," Riya called out, her voice tense but controlled. Marcus was beside her in seconds, retrieving a patch kit from his belt. His hands were steady as he pressed the seal over the rupture, securing it in place. Riley gasped, struggling to regain her breath, her eyes wide with shock. The emergency oxygen reserve in her suit kicked in, but she was still dangerously close to passing out.

"Stay with me, Riley," Marcus urged, gripping her shoulder.

By the time they got her to the medical bay, the immediate crisis had passed, but the damage was done. Riley would recover—her injuries were painful but not life-threatening. But the incident left more than just bruises. The tension that had been simmering beneath the surface of the colony erupted in full force. The blame game began almost immediately. Some accused the engineers of negligence, questioning whether proper checks had been overlooked. Others pointed fingers at the colony's leadership, arguing that rushed schedules and limited resources had created a dangerous work environment. Marcus, already under strain from previous conflicts within the crew, found himself caught in the middle. "The valve should never have failed like that," he said in the debriefing, frustration evident in his voice.

"Either it was a material defect, or someone missed a stress fracture during inspection." No one wanted to admit fault, but the whispers spread through the colony like wildfire.

The accident became a catalyst for deeper divisions, exposing fractures that had long been ignored. Trust, once tenuous, now hung by a thread. Some crew members demanded stricter oversight, while others resented the implication that they were careless. Riley, recovering in the infirmary, could feel the weight of the rift growing even from her bed. The colony was supposed to be a unified front, the first step toward humanity's future on Mars. But in the wake of the accident, it became clear that survival was about more than just engineering and science—it was about people, and people were messy.

#

Elena gazed at the Martian soil at the greenhouse, a fragile lifeline sculpted with care—enriched, balanced, made to nurture life where none should thrive. Yet, no amount of precision or science could mend the fractures splintering between them. Like hairline cracks in glass, invisible at first, they deepened with every unspoken word, every lingering resentment. The colony was built to survive the harshest world, but it was the weight of human hearts, not the barren land, that threatened to break it apart.

"It's these distractions," Marcus said during the emergency debriefing.

"We're stretched too thin, trying to do too much. This was bound to happen."

"And how do you know the artifacts had anything to do with this?" David snapped.

"Equipment fails—it happens."

"Not like this," Marcus shot back, his voice sharp with frustration.

"We've been cutting corners, pushing limits—all because of these damn artifacts. We're diverting our focus, our resources, everything we have, and for what? It's putting the entire colony at risk."

Riya silenced them with a sharp look. "This isn't the time for arguments. We investigate what happened, fix the problem, and make sure it doesn't happen again. That's the priority."

The meeting ended, but the damage was done. The crew retreated to their tasks, their interactions strained and guarded.

#

Elena found herself caught in the middle more often than she wanted to admit. Marcus's hard-edged pragmatism clashed with David's relentless curiosity, and though Riya tried to keep the peace, there was only so much mediation could do when the very ground they stood on seemed to divide them. The artifacts had become more than objects—they were lines in the sand, separating the crew into factions, straining relationships that once felt unbreakable. The weight of it pressed on Elena, settling into her bones like the cold that seeped through the colony's metal walls at night.

That night, sleep eluded her, the tension in her mind refusing to settle. Restless, she wandered into the *"The Sky"*, drawn to the only thing vast enough to make human conflict feel small. The Martian landscape stretched before her, endless and silent, its emptiness a total contrast to the storm of emotions raging within the colony. She pressed her forehead against the glass, her breath fogging the surface in soft, fleeting patterns. Outside, the vastness of the planet swallowed all sound, all movement, leaving only the quiet hum of life-support systems and the steady rhythm of her own breathing.

The colony's solar-powered luminaries cast gentle pools of golden light across the barren land, fragile halos in an ocean of black. Designed to withstand the relentless dust storms and bitter cold, the lights spread in soft circles, illuminating the rust-colored soil and jagged rocks in muted contrast. From a distance, they resembled tiny beacons, trembling yet resolute, their glow refusing to be consumed by the abyss. But even their light could only reach so far. Beyond them, the darkness stretched infinitely, a void indifferent to human struggle, indifferent to everything.

She watched as the Martian wind stirred the dust, sending faint, restless shadows flickering across the illuminated ground. The motion was hypnotic, a slow, ghostly dance that seemed almost sentient, as if Mars itself was whispering, acknowledging its visitors with a silent, knowing presence. Elena let out a breath she hadn't realized she was holding. Here, beneath the cold and unfeeling sky, the weight of their conflicts seemed smaller, like echoes lost in a universe too vast to care. Yet the fractures within the crew, no matter how insignificant they seemed against the endless night, still had the power to break them.

"We can't keep going like this," she murmured.

She heard footsteps and Riya stepped inside. She stood silently beside Elena, her gaze fixed on the horizon, engulfed in the darkness.

"I've been thinking the same thing," Riya said at last, her tone grave.

"The fractures are growing. If we don't find a way to come together, this colony won't survive."

Elena kept staring into the night, her thoughts unraveling like threads caught in an unseen current. The darkness stretched endlessly before her, silent and vast, but it was not the emptiness outside that unsettled her most. For a fleeting moment, she wondered—which abyss was deeper? The one beyond the dome, cold and indifferent, or the one growing within the colony, fed by fear, doubt, and quiet betrayals? Out there, the night was simply the absence of light. In here, it was something far more insidious—a shadow creeping between them, born not of the cosmos, but of human nature.

After few seconds, she nodded, her chest tight. "But how do we fix it? The artifacts… they've changed everything."

"They have," Riya agreed. "But we can't let them define us. We have to find a way to balance exploration with survival. Otherwise, we'll lose both."

The two women stood in silence, the weight of their shared fears hanging between them. Outside, the Martian night stretched on, vast and unyielding. The answers felt as distant as the stars, and the fractures within the colony seemed to deepen with every passing day.

#

The fractures within the crew became more visible, like hairline cracks spreading through an overburdened structure. It wasn't just Marcus and David anymore—others were choosing sides, their perspectives on the artifacts and the mission hardening into quiet resentments. Even Riya, the unflinching leader, was beginning to show signs of strain.

Elena noticed it in the way Riya hesitated before giving orders, the moments of silence where there had once been decisiveness. It wasn't indecision—it was exhaustion, a weariness that settled over the entire colony like the omnipresent Martian dust. The rift between survival and discovery, between pragmatism and curiosity, was pulling them apart.

A week after Riley's accident, the tension reached a boiling point during a meeting in the main hub. The crew gathered around the central console to discuss their findings from one of the artifacts. Riya stood at the head of the table, her expression unreadable as the latest data scrolled across the screen.

"The artifact's electromagnetic emissions are consistent with the crystal's," Marcus said, his tone clipped. "But it's inactive. No response to any of our input patterns."

"It's dormant now," David said, leaning forward. "But that doesn't mean it's dead. We just haven't found the right way to engage with it."

"Or it's not meant to be engaged with at all," Marcus shot back. "Maybe leaving it alone is the best thing we can do."

"We don't know that," David argued. "These artifacts are part of something larger. If we ignore them, we're ignoring the key to understanding this planet."

"And while we're on a goose chase in the name of '*understanding*,' the colony is falling apart," Marcus snapped.

"You saw what happened with Riley. How many more accidents before we realize these things are a distraction?"

"That's enough," Riya said, her voice cutting through the argument like a blade.

"Both of you."

The room fell silent, the tension intense. Riya's gaze swept across the table, her tone measured but firm. "We're here to survive. That means maintaining the colony and exploring what's around us. But if we let these artifacts divide us, we'll fail at both."

Her words hung in the air, but the undercurrent of discord remained. The meeting continued, but the damage was done—fractures widened, alliances hardened, and the fragile sense of unity within the crew eroded further.

The colony was increasingly divided, with two distinct schools of thought emerging—each a fault line that deepened with every passing day. Even those who wished to remain neutral found themselves walking on unstable ground, where any misstep risked pulling them into the chasm between the two factions. On one side, the survivalists argued that nothing mattered more than the colony's stability. They saw Mars as an untamed frontier where infrastructure, safety, and resource management had to take precedence. Every breath was borrowed from a life-support system, every meal a calculated allocation of nutrients, and every decision a step toward long-term survival. To them, the artifacts were an unnecessary distraction, an indulgence they couldn't afford when even a single oversight could mean death.

On the other side, the scientists and explorers viewed the artifacts as the very reason they had come to Mars in the first place. To ignore them—to turn away from the possibility of a civilization that had once existed here—was to reject the greatest scientific opportunity in human history. Yes, it required resources, and yes, it was dangerous, but what was the point of surviving if they didn't uncover the truth? The discoveries they were making could redefine humanity's understanding of the universe, and for them, the pursuit of knowledge was worth the risk. The divide between these two ideologies was no longer a quiet undercurrent—it had become a schism, a fracture in the very foundation of the colony.

And Riya stood in the center of it all, bearing the weight of both sides while trying to hold everything together. The pressure from Earth was relentless—mission control, sponsors, and research institutions sent daily transmissions, each more insistent than the last. They demanded updates, results, and progress, treating the study of the artifacts as the colony's primary objective. They had invested billions into this mission, and they expected breakthroughs. But they weren't the ones rationing water. They weren't the ones repairing airlocks after dust storms or dealing with the psychological toll of isolation. Earth saw Mars as a laboratory, but for Riya and the crew, it was home—a fragile, unyielding home where survival required constant vigilance.

Every decision she made felt like a compromise, a battle between what was necessary and what was expected. She was tired—exhausted in a way that went beyond sleepless nights. She had taken on the role of mediator, leader, and liaison, but the fractures were widening faster than she could mend them. The weight of their future pressed against her ribs like an unseen force, suffocating in its intensity. How much longer could she keep them from breaking apart? And if they did, would there be anything left to salvage? The answer loomed over her like the Martian night—vast, unrelenting, and utterly indifferent.

#

Elena tried to focus on her work in the greenhouse, but even here, the tension found her. The crops were thriving, their growth steady despite the subtle anomalies in the nutrient systems. She knelt beside a row of potatoes, her hands moving mechanically as she checked for signs of stress. The routine, once comforting, now felt hollow.

The greenhouse was the heart of the colony, a carefully controlled oasis amidst the barren Martian landscape. It was divided into sections, each tailored for different agricultural methods. The hydroponic systems, suspended in neat rows, provided a constant supply of leafy greens, herbs, and vine crops, their roots immersed in nutrient-rich water. Alongside them, soil-based cultivation thrived in designated areas, where crops like potatoes and wheat pushed through carefully treated Martian soil. This soil, once inhospitable, had been painstakingly balanced with nutrients and inoculated with Earth's microbes to create a viable growing medium. A sophisticated monitoring system constantly analyzed moisture levels, nutrient composition, and plant health, ensuring that every plant received exactly what it needed to flourish.

Beyond simply sustaining the colony, the greenhouse served as a hub for agricultural innovation. A state-of-the-art research lab nestled within its structure allowed scientists to experiment with hybrid crops, genetic engineering, and adaptive farming techniques suited for the Martian environment. Researchers worked to develop plant strains that could thrive under lower gravity and higher radiation levels, pushing the boundaries of human knowledge in space agriculture. The controlled climate, regulated to mimic the ideal conditions for each crop, allowed for year-round cultivation, making the colony more self-sufficient with each harvest.

The plants grew indifferent to the fractures within the colony. They didn't care about human disputes, ambitions, or regrets. They simply stretched toward the artificial sunlight, took in the nutrients provided, and thrived at their own pace—oblivious to the weight of human thoughts, emotions, and struggles.

#

David entered, his footsteps soft on the metallic floor. "I thought I'd find you here," he said, crouching beside her.

"I needed to clear my head," Elena replied without looking up.

He nodded, his expression thoughtful. "It's getting worse, isn't it?"

She sighed, setting down her tools.

"I don't know how much longer we can keep this up. The colony, the artifacts… it's too much."

"It was easy planning back on Earth," David said, his voice tinged with frustration and reflection.

"We thought, 'We Go, Grow, and Glow.'

But out here barely four months? A colony is so much more—more complicated, more fragile, more demanding than any of us imagined.”

David leaned against the wall, his gaze distant.

“You ever think about why we were chosen for this mission?”

Elena frowned. “What do you mean?”

He gestured vaguely around them.

“We’re the best of the best, right? Handpicked for our skills, our ability to handle pressure. But maybe that’s not enough. Maybe this mission was doomed from the start.”

“You don’t really believe that,” Elena said softly.

“I don’t know what I believe anymore,” David admitted.

“But I do know this—if we give up on the artifacts, we’re giving up on what makes this mission more than just survival.”

Elena didn’t respond. She wanted to believe in the artifacts, to see them as something greater than the burden they had become. But the fractures within the crew made it hard to hope.

#

Another breaking point came two days later.

A sudden systems failure in the power grid plunged the habitat into darkness, the air filled with the shrill wail of emergency alarms. Elena scrambled to the central console, her heart pounding as she scanned the readouts.

“Backup systems are online,” Astraeus announced, her voice calm despite the chaos. “Primary power grid compromised. Cause: unknown.”

The crew gathered in the main hub, their voices a cacophony of confusion and accusations.

"This is what I was talking about!" Marcus shouted, his face flushed red with anger, almost blending into the Martian backdrop.

"We've been neglecting the systems for too long, and now look at where we are. This is on all of us." His words echoed through the room, heavy with frustration and the weight of unspoken blame.

"We don't know if this is the artifact's doing," David countered, his voice rising to meet Marcus's frustration.

"It could just be the systems failing. But artifacts affecting the grid? We've seen it happen before—just not on this scale." His tone wavered between reason and concern, the uncertainty gnawing at him as he tried to make sense of the unfolding chaos.

"And you still want to keep engaging with them?" Marcus shot back.

"How many more failures before you see what's happening?"

"Isn't it your responsibility to keep the systems in check?" David pounded the table, his voice cutting through the tense air like a knife.

"If something's to be blamed, it's the engineering team. Tell me I'm wrong. You keep pointing fingers at the artifacts, but you're neglecting your job. And when something goes wrong, the artifacts are always your scapegoat!"

His words landed hard, the tension in the room palpable as the weight of the accusation hung in the air.

Marcus took a step forward, his fists clenched tightly at his sides.

"A distraction is a distraction, engineering or not," he growled, his voice low but brimming with barely restrained fury.

"Before you start pointing fingers at my team, maybe take a good look at the resources we're pouring into this treasure hunt! My people are stretched thin, trying to keep a grid running that's being ignored because everyone's too busy deciphering symbols and poking glowing rocks."

His voice was a mix of fury and frustration, the words laced with an unmistakable edge.

"This needs to end—one way or the other."

The room was thick with tension, the echo of Marcus' final words hanging in the air. Around them, the hum of the systems seemed louder, a constant reminder of the stakes at hand.

The argument spiraled further, voices clashing like a storm. Marcus jabbed a finger toward David, while David's retorts cut back like a blade. Others chimed in, their words blending into a cacophony of overlapping protests, theories, and accusations. The tension in the room was palpable, the air thick with frustration and simmering anger.

Riya stepped forward, her eyes blazing with authority, her presence commanding instant attention. Her expression was thunderous, her jaw set like steel.

"Enough!" she bellowed, her voice echoing through the room like a crack of lightning. The chaotic blur of voices ceased immediately; the silence that followed almost deafening.

She let the quiet hang for a moment, her sharp gaze cutting across the room, meeting each set of eyes in turn.

"This isn't who we are," she said, her voice quieter now but no less firm. "We solve problems. We don't let them consume us."

Her words carried the weight of her authority and the undeniable truth of their shared mission. Her words carried weight, but the fractures remained. The crew dispersed to their tasks, their interactions terse and strained. The power grid was restored, but the damage to their unity lingered.

#

That evening, Elena climbed the winding stairs to *"The Sky"*, her steps slow and deliberate. Reaching the glass, she stood motionless for a moment before leaning in, her eyes fixed on the Martian dusk. The stars were faint, their dim light struggling against the reddish haze that clung to the horizon. She pressed her forehead against the cool surface of the glass, the rhythmic motion of gently bumping it betraying her restless thoughts.

She exhaled, her breath fogging against the glass, soft, fleeting clouds that blurred the view just as much as her own thoughts. She had known this journey would demand sacrifices, but knowing it hadn't made it easier. Earth was an entire world away—her children were an entire lifetime away. She had left them behind, promising that she would return, that her mission would mean something. And now, that promise felt like a cruel lie. The colony was unraveling, its people fracturing under pressure, their survival no longer guaranteed. There was no return trip, no contingency plan—only the brutal truth that Mars had never promised them a future, only a chance to carve one out of its unforgiving dust.

Her fingers tightened into fists against the railing as she wrestled with the guilt that never truly left her. Had she been selfish? Had she justified it too easily—telling herself that pushing humanity forward was worth the cost? Every transmission from Earth had been a reminder of what she'd left behind. The birthdays she missed, the bedtime stories that would never be hers to tell again. Her children were growing up beneath an Earth sky, while she stood here, trapped beneath an alien one, unable to even tell them if she would make it back.

For the first time, doubt settled in Elena's stomach like a slab of cold iron, heavy and lifeless. It pressed against her ribs, coiling tight like a dead weight dragging her down, suffocating in its quiet persistence. She had carried uncertainty before, but never like this—never so visceral, so unshakable. It sat within her, dark and unrelenting, like a shadow stretching endlessly across the Martian dust, impossible to outrun.

Had she been wrong to come here? To chase the stars while leaving her children beneath an Earth she might never see again? The weight of her choices pressed against her chest, heavier than the gravity that bound her to this barren world. Was this the price of ambition—a sacrifice that could never be undone? A mother torn between the future and the past, between duty and love, between the infinite and the irrevocable. Perhaps humanity was always meant to struggle against the impossible, to reach for the unknown, only to find itself lost in the void.

She let out a shaky breath, watching the vapor dissolve into nothing. Outside, the luminaries cast their steady, golden glow over the barren ground, small circles of light clinging to the darkness. A fragile illusion of control in a world that cared nothing for them. It struck her then—how much like those lights they were. Flickering. Vulnerable. Holding on in defiance of the void. And yet, despite everything, she could not bring herself to regret it entirely. Because if she was to be stranded here, if she was to lose everything for the sake of this mission, then at the very least, it had to mean something.

"You wouldn't break it," came a faint voice from the corner.

Startled, Elena spun around, her heart skipping a beat. She had assumed she was alone in the quiet space of *"The Sky"*. The voice was soft but unmistakable, and as she turned, her surprise deepened.

"You may try a hammer, not your forehead, my dear."

The voice was calm—but devoid of humor. It carried no warmth, only the quiet weight of observation, as if stating an inevitable truth. The words hung in the air like dust unsettled by a distant tremor, lingering just long enough to remind Elena that even in solitude, she wasn't alone.

There, on the floor, at the far end, sat Riya, her legs pulled tightly to her chest as if trying to make herself disappear into the smallest possible space. It was a total contrast to the commanding presence Riya had always known, a woman who had held the colony together through sheer will and strength—sometimes with a single word. Seeing her commander like this—vulnerable, retreating from the world—shattered something inside Elena. Tears welled in her eyes and began falling, uncontrollable and silent, streaking her cheeks as she stood frozen in place.

"Come here, have a seat," Riya said softly, her voice still calm, her tone gentle and compassionate despite the weight she so clearly carried. She patted the floor beside her, offering a place not just to sit but to share in the moment.

Both sat quietly, sharing the space and time, their gazes fixed on the endless expanse beyond the glass. The silence between them felt profound, almost sacred, as if they were transcending to a different dimension—one untouched by the weight of their responsibilities. No words could offer the comfort they both needed, and none were attempted. The stillness became their solace, a fragile yet unspoken comfort forming in the quiet hum of *"The Sky"*.

#

The fractures within the crew felt as vast as the expanse before them. Survival and discovery, caution and curiosity—these weren't just differences in opinion. They were fault lines, dividing them in ways that felt impossible to repair.

The division within the colony deepened, splitting the crew into two starkly opposing factions. Those who supported investigating the artifacts argued that ignoring such discoveries was tantamount to defying Earth's directive. They believed the artifacts held the key to understanding Mars' secrets and possibly even advancing humanity. For them, resistance to this mission was seen as a challenge not only to Riya's authority but to Earth's orders, subtly accusing their detractors of insubordination.

On the other side, frustration and fear brewed. Many crew members openly expressed their concerns that the artifact investigations jeopardized the colony's safety and future.

"This isn't what we signed up for," became a common refrain, spoken in mess halls and murmured in hallways. Their focus was survival and colony-building, not engaging with enigmatic objects of unknown origin. As paranoia and mistrust grew, even mundane tasks became battlegrounds for tension.

Arguments escalated into outright confrontations, culminating in a series of fistfights that left several crew members injured and needing medical attention. The six-person security team, typically tasked with perimeter defense and observation, was forced to redirect their efforts to maintain order within the habitat. What once was a self-policing comradeship, built on trust and mutual respect, had devolved into a well-policed gang driven by fear and violence. This shift left the colony vulnerable, as their external vigilance waned.

Once-cohesive teams began to fracture more and more. Cadence in daily operations faltered, communication became stilted, and the empathy that had once bound the crew was all but lost. The habitat, a sanctuary of unity and purpose, now felt like a powder keg, one wrong spark away from explosion. Riya watched the disintegration with mounting concern, knowing that restoring trust and focus would be her most critical challenge yet.

Somewhere in the distance, the crystal pulsed faintly, its rhythm steady and unyielding. Its presence was both a comfort and a threat, a reminder of the unknown forces shaping their mission.

Elena closed her eyes, the hum of the crystal echoing in her mind. It wasn't just the crew that was fractured—it was the mission itself, split between survival and the endless questions posed by the artifacts.

And as the habitat settled into uneasy stillness, one thought lingered in her mind: How long before the cracks become irreparable, or is it already happened?

The days after the power grid failure, the colony steeped in a heavy silence. Even routine tasks felt strained as the crew moved through the habitat, their faces drawn with exhaustion and frustration. The fractures in their unity, once subtle, were now glaringly apparent. Every interaction seemed weighted with unspoken resentments, and even the most mundane conversations felt charged.

#

Elena focused on the greenhouse, pouring herself into the physical labor as a way to quiet her racing thoughts. With methodical precision, she measured nutrient levels, adjusted irrigation valves, and meticulously documented the latest growth rates. She even took measurements of the leaves, stems, and the tiniest buds beginning to emerge—details that weren't strictly necessary but offered her a sense of control. There was comfort in devoting her attention to the innocence of the plants, a way to momentarily escape the complexities and tensions unfolding elsewhere. In the midst of uncertainty, the crops stood as a small, tangible success, and she clung to their steady growth like a lifeline.

As she worked, Marcus entered, his expression as grim as ever. He carried a toolbox, but Elena knew he wasn't just here to fix the pumps—anyone on his team could have done that. No, Marcus had come for something else, something heavier than faulty machinery. The weight in his shoulders wasn't just from the day's work but from the unspoken tensions fracturing the colony.

"Water flow's been inconsistent," he said, setting the toolbox on the counter with a dull thud, the sound punctuating the silence between them. "I'll check the pumps."

Elena nodded, her gaze still fixed on the rows of leafy greens, hands moving with practiced precision as she inspected the hydroponic roots. "Thanks."

She knew what was coming. The conversation they'd been avoiding for too long—the one about sides, about survival, about the growing divide within the colony. He wasn't here just to turn wrenches. He was here to remind her that soon, she would have to choose.

The silence between them was thick, the recent arguments hanging unspoken in the air. Marcus knelt beside the main irrigation unit, unscrewing a panel and inspecting the machinery inside. The hum of the system filled the greenhouse, a constant backdrop to their uneasy truce.

After a few minutes, Marcus broke the silence. "I know you don't agree with me about the artifacts."

Elena looked up, startled. "It's not about agreeing or disagreeing. It's about balance. We can't ignore them, but we can't let them consume us either."

Marcus snorted softly, his head still inside the irrigation panel. "Balance doesn't seem to be our strong suit lately."

She didn't argue. He wasn't wrong. The colony felt like it was teetering on a knife's edge, every decision threatening to push them over.

As Marcus replaced the parts and stood, he glanced at her, his expression softer. "I know we're all trying. But if we don't figure this out soon…"

Elena finished his sentence in her mind: "We might not last". She nodded, the weight of his words settling heavily on her shoulders.

Later that day, Riya called another meeting in the main hub. The crew assembled around the central console, their faces etched with exhaustion and wariness. The power grid failure had been a wake-up call, and Riya's determination to address the growing fractures was clear.

"We need to re-calibrate," she began, her tone firm but measured.

"The last few weeks have been chaotic, and we've lost sight of what matters most: each other. The artifacts are important, but they're not our only priority. We have to find a way to work together."

David leaned forward, his expression tight. "How do we do that when half the crew thinks the artifacts are a threat and the other half sees them as our best hope?"

Marcus scowled but said nothing, his silence louder than any argument.

Riya held up a hand.

"We don't have to agree on everything, but we do have to respect each other's perspectives. The artifacts are part of our mission, whether we like it or not. Ignoring them isn't an option, but neither is letting them distract us from the colony's needs."

"And what happens if the artifacts destabilize us further?" Marcus asked, his voice low but firm.

"We can't afford another systems failure."

Riya stood at the center of the room, her voice cutting through the tension like a blade. Her gaze swept across the faces of the crew—some still flushed with anger, others avoiding her eyes entirely. She took a deep breath, letting the weight of her words sink in before she spoke.

"The trades you've mastered—the ones you were chosen for—don't matter anymore," she began, her tone firm yet resolute.

"Out here, on this planet, titles and specialties mean little if we can't function as a collective. Yes, we have skilled people for critical tasks, and those skills are invaluable. But if we want to survive—if we want to grow—we have to embrace more than our expertise."

She paused, letting her words hang in the air, before continuing.

"We all have to be engineers, medics, farmers. We all have to clean up our own messes. This isn't a company, and none of us are employees. This is a colony. Our colony. And the only way this works is if we share responsibilities, learn from one another, and step up where we're needed."

Riya's voice softened, but her conviction remained. "Those of you with knowledge—teach it. Those who need help—ask for it. Expertise will always matter, but out here, willingness to adapt matters more. Let's stop acting like a group of strangers trying to fulfill a job description and start being what we need to be—a responsible community."

She folded her arms, letting the room sit in silence, her words leaving no room for debate. In her eyes, this was not just a directive—it was a necessity for their survival.

"When we have a problem", Riya paused.

"Then we address it as a team," she continued. "Together. No more finger-pointing, no more blame. We're in this for the long haul, and we won't survive if we don't find a way to work past this."

The room was silent, her words hanging in the air. Slowly, the crew nodded, though the tension remained. It wasn't a resolution, but it was a step—fragile, tentative, but a step, nonetheless.

#

In the days that followed, the crew worked to repair the damage to the power grid and reinforce their systems against future failures. The work was grueling but necessary, a reminder of the fragility of their existence on Mars. Each task required precision and focus, and for a brief time, the shared effort brought a semblance of unity.

Elena worked closely with Marcus on the greenhouse systems, their earlier conversation forming the basis for an uneasy truce. They focused on the tangible—checking water flow, calibrating nutrient dispensers, and repairing minor leaks in the irrigation lines. The crops continued to thrive, their steady growth a quiet reassurance against the backdrop of the colony's larger struggles.

Meanwhile, David and a few engineers from Marcus team worked on enhancing the habitat's electromagnetic shielding. The artifacts' influence on the colony's systems was still poorly understood, but the shielding was a precautionary measure designed to mitigate any potential disruptions. The work was painstaking, requiring hours of meticulous adjustments and tests.

"We're seeing less interference already," David reported during an evening briefing.

"The shielding isn't perfect, but it's stabilizing the grid."

Marcus nodded grudgingly. "It's a start."

Riya, nodded. "Good work. Let's keep building on this progress."

Despite these efforts, the fractures within the crew continued to linger. Small disagreements flared into heated arguments, and the once-steady rhythm of life in the colony felt increasingly precarious. The artifacts were at the heart of every conflict, their enigmatic presence a source of both wonder and fear.

One evening, Elena found herself in the lab, staring at the display, showing crystal in its containment chamber. Its faint light pulsed steadily, the patterns on its surface shifting in ways that seemed almost deliberate. She couldn't shake the feeling that it was watching them, its silence more telling than words.

"What are you trying to tell us?" she whispered.

The door slid open, and Riya stepped inside. She joined Elena at the console, her gaze fixed on the crystal.

"It's beautiful, isn't it?" Riya said softly.

Elena nodded. "And terrifying."

Riya sighed, crossing her arms. "It's like it's waiting for something. But for what?"

"I don't know," Elena admitted. "But whatever it is, it's tearing us apart."

"We're already dealing with the mess its mere presence is causing," she said, her voice low.

"I can't even imagine how bad it'll get if these artifacts actually start interfering."

Riya's expression hardened. "Then we can't let it. Whatever this thing is, we're stronger together. We have to be."

Elena wanted to believe her, but the fractures in the crew felt deeper than ever. The crystal's light reflected faintly in the glass, a silent reminder of the mysteries that continued to elude them.

#

The fractures within the colony have shown no slowing down. What had once been a united team working toward a common goal was now a group divided by mistrust, clashing priorities, and the weight of their isolation.

Elena tried to stay neutral, pouring herself into her work in the greenhouse. The crops continued to thrive, but even here, the undercurrent of discord seeped in. Conversations that had once been light-hearted and collaborative now felt guarded, every word carefully chosen to avoid sparking an argument.

One morning, as Elena strolling through the corridor, she overheard a heated exchange in the main hub. Marcus and David's voices carried through the thin walls, their argument escalating quickly.

"We can't keep dedicating resources to your science project!" Marcus shouted.

"Every hour spent on them is an hour taken away from what really matters—keeping this colony alive."

"And ignoring them puts us at risk in other ways!" David fired back. "They're part of this planet, Marcus. We can't just pretend they don't exist."

"We're not pretending—they're a distraction, plain and simple," Marcus snapped.

"You're so obsessed with your theories that you're blind to the bigger picture."

Elena sighed, turning back to her work. The arguments were becoming more frequent, the same points repeated over and over without resolution.

It was exhausting, and she wanted to avoid confrontations at all costs.

Later that day, the crew gathered for the scheduled briefing.

The Hub used to be a place filled with excitement, amusement, laughter, and comfort. Daily briefings and meetings were something everyone looked forward to, a chance to connect and share. Now, a call for a briefing feels more like a dose of bitter medicine—something no one wants but can't avoid.

Riya stood at the head of the table, her posture rigid and her expression unreadable. The tension in the room was thick, the air heavy with unspoken grievances.

"We're stretched thin," Riya began, her voice calm but firm.

"I know that. The power grid is stable for now, the greenhouse is producing, and our oxygen levels are steady… for now!"

"Fractures within this team are putting all of that at risk. We need to address this, now."

Marcus leaned back in his chair, his arms crossed. "Then let's start by prioritizing what actually matters. The artifacts can wait."

David shook his head, his frustration evident. "We've been over this. The artifacts are part of what matters."

"And chasing them is reckless!" Marcus snapped.

"Every time we divert resources, we compromise the systems that keep us alive."

The argument flared again, their voices overlapping in a cacophony of frustration. Riya let it go for a moment, then raised her hand, silencing the room.

"This isn't about choosing one or the other," she said sharply. "It's about balance. Marcus, your concerns are valid, but we can't ignore the artifacts. David, your work is important, but it can't come at the expense of the colony's stability. Both of you need to focus on your tasks—and stop tearing each other apart."

Her words carried weight, but the room remained tense. The fractures within the crew were deeper than ever, and it was clear that words alone wouldn't be enough to mend them.

That night, Elena sat alone at *"The Sky"*, her gaze fixed on the barren Martian expanse. The ridge where the artifacts rested loomed in the distance, cloaked in the deep shadows of the Martian night. Even its vague silhouette, barely discernible in the darkness, was a stark reminder of the mysteries that lingered unanswered—a weight that seemed to press against her as heavily as the silence surrounding her.

Over her shoulder, Elena could see the quarantine valley, its faintly illuminated outline against the darkness. She stared for a moment, her voice barely above a whisper as she murmured…

"What are you all talking about?"

Then, with a sharper edge, she added…

"You all arc planning to take over!"

Her words hung in the air, a mix of disbelief and suspicion as though addressing a thought too wild to fully articulate.

#

The next morning, Riya called another meeting in the main hub. The crew assembled reluctantly, their faces drawn with exhaustion and irritation. Riya stood at the head of the table, her expression hard as she addressed them.

"We're running out of time," she began, her voice calm but firm.

"The fractures in this crew are jeopardizing everything we've built. We survived Riley's accident, but we won't survive another failure like that unless we start working together."

"We should all remember," Riya said firmly, her gaze sweeping across the room,

"Earth could send us supplies under the best of circumstances, but they're not taking any of us back. This is it. We have only each other to rely on— no babysitting, no return to parents. We all have to understand the gravity of that. No one alone will survive this world." She paused, letting her words sink in before continuing.

"Learn to forgive and forget. We don't have the luxury of choosing our neighbors or escaping to another neighborhood. This colony stands—or falls—together."

"We've all left our loved ones behind," Riya continued, her voice steady at first but softening as the weight of her words settled over the room.

"We've brought with us their hope—humanity's hope." She paused, her gaze falling as if searching for strength.

"If an argument... or a fistfight can jeopardize that..." Her voice faltered, uncharacteristically stumbling, a rare crack in the unyielding resolve that defined her. The room fell silent, her vulnerability striking deeper than any command could.

Her words hung in the air, the uncommanding tone weighed down with unspoken truths. Marcus folded his arms tightly across his chest, his gaze fixed on the table as though avoiding her eyes might ease the tension. Across from him, David sat rigidly, his jaw clenched, the muscles in his face betraying the emotions he was trying to hold back. The silence that followed was thick, each person grappling with their own thoughts, the enormity of her words pressing down on them all.

"Marcus," Riya said, her tone snapping back to its commanding edge as swiftly as it had faltered. She turned to him, her gaze unwavering.

"You've made valid points about the need to prioritize the colony's systems. I won't argue with that—our survival depends on them. But shutting down the artifacts entirely isn't the answer. We don't know enough about their influence to dismiss them outright. From your military background, you know better than anyone that awareness of the environment is key to survival. Like it or not, the network of artifacts is a part of this environment, and ignoring them could cost us more than we're prepared to lose." Her voice carried not a suggestion, but a deliberate command.

"And David," Riya said, shifting her focus to him, her tone unwavering.

"Your work with the artifacts is important, but it cannot come at the expense of the colony's stability. If we have to shift resources one way or the other, we do so as the situation demands. That might mean all 100 of us working on the mystery—or none at all. If the artifacts are affecting our systems, we need to understand how, and we need to do it quickly. First, we live   everything else comes after. And living might mean fixing a drain or decoding a signal. Whatever it takes, we prioritize survival first." Her words carried the weight of leadership, leaving no doubt about what was expected.

David opened his mouth to respond, but Riya held up a hand, cutting him off.

"This isn't a debate. It's a directive. We're addressing both priorities, and I expect full cooperation from everyone."

The room fell silent, the tension thick and palpable. It was a sobering reflection of what was at stake—insulting enough for everyone to take personally, a stinging indictment of their immaturity. It was the kind of moment that demanded a captain's speech, one capable of melting even the bravest soldier to their knees. Slowly but surely, the weight of Riya's words sank in, like a red-hot lead ball dropping into their collective conscience. The crew nodded, whether in genuine agreement or reluctant compliance was unclear.

With a sharp, dismissive gesture, Riya sent them back to their tasks. They dispersed without a word, the strain still evident in their interactions, but the gravity of the situation left little room for anything else.

That night, Elena sat alone in the greenhouse, the hum of the irrigation system the only sound. The crops swayed gently under the artificial lights, their vibrant green a stark contrast to the red wasteland outside.

She closed her eyes, the tension of the day settled heavily on her. The crew was unraveling, their differences still lingering. And the artifacts—their faint hum, their enigmatic patterns—felt like the catalyst for everything.

Somewhere in the distance, the crystal pulsed faintly in its containment chamber, its light steady and unyielding. Elena couldn't shake the feeling that it was watching, waiting for something she couldn't yet understand.

#

The next day began in silence, the crew's routines mechanical and subdued. Even the hum of the habitat's systems seemed quieter, as though the environment itself were responding to their strained relationships. Elena carried out her work in the greenhouse, focusing on the simple rhythms of planting, watering, and monitoring. The plants, at least, remained unaffected by the fractures dividing the team.

Her solitude was broken when Marcus entered, his footsteps heavier than usual. He carried a tablet, his jaw set in a tight line. Without a word, he handed it to her. The screen displayed a detailed report on the habitat's pressurized systems.

"We found another weak point in the greenhouse airlocks," he said. "It's stable for now, but we'll need to reinforce it."

Elena scanned the report, nodding. "How soon can it be fixed?"

"Within the week," Marcus replied. "Assuming we get your team's assistance."

She caught the edge in his voice but chose not to engage. Instead, she handed the tablet back with a calm, neutral tone.

"Thanks for letting me know. Keep us updated on your schedule—we'll all be hands on deck to your orders."

He hesitated, his expression softening. "I know you're stuck in the middle of all this. And I know I can come across as… difficult. But I'm trying to keep us alive."

"I know," Elena said quietly. "And so is David. You're just looking at the same problem from different angles."

Marcus nodded reluctantly. "Let's hope one of us is right."

"I am sure both of you are right!, Now, you just have to convince each other to feel it"

#

In the lab, David was engrossed in his latest analysis of the crystal. The patterns on its surface had shifted again, their complexity deepening in ways that defied any predictable logic. Elena joined him after finishing her work in the greenhouse, her curiosity outweighing her exhaustion.

"Any progress?" she asked, leaning over the console.

David shook his head, his brow furrowed. "Not in the way I hoped. The patterns are evolving, but they're not random. There's an order to them—it's just not one we understand."

Elena studied the screen, the symbols twisting and re-forming in mesmerizing sequences. "Do you think it's trying to communicate with us?"

"I think it's reacting to us," David replied.

"Every input we've tried, every observation we've made—it all seems to feed back into the system."

"And what happens when it finishes reacting?" she asked.

David didn't answer immediately. When he finally spoke, his voice was quiet. "I don't know. But whatever it is, it's bigger than us."

The crystal sat in the quarantine quarters; an enigma wrapped in impossible physics. Smooth yet faceted in ways that defied natural formation, it pulsed with a faint inner light—one that subtly shifted across the electromagnetic spectrum. David had seen materials fluoresce before, had worked with compounds that responded to energy inputs, but this was different. The crystal wasn't merely reflecting or refracting light; it was generating it, emitting full-spectrum signals that spanned from radio waves to ultraviolet. That alone was astonishing, but what truly unsettled him was the lack of any visible power source. There were no conduits, no apparent energy reserves, nothing to suggest how it sustained such a complex output. For something to generate signals at this range and intensity, the energy demands would be enormous—far beyond anything their colony's fusion reactor could provide. And yet, it persisted, as if defying the very need for energy input at all.

Elena stood beside him, arms crossed, studying the shifting hues within the crystal's core.

"Could it be drawing power from the vacuum?" she murmured, her voice quiet but edged with something close to awe.

"Or something we haven't even identified yet?" The thought sent a shiver through David—not from fear, but from the sheer vastness of what it implied.

Humanity had spent centuries refining its understanding of physics, building pillars of knowledge that defined the boundaries of existence. Energy could not be created from nothing. Every reaction required an equal and opposite force. Entropy was an inevitable tide. These laws were the foundation upon which civilizations had risen, equations that had carried humanity from fire-lit caves to the stars. And yet, here—buried beneath the Martian soil—stood something that defied all of it. The crystal did not consume fuel, did not harness solar radiation, did not tether itself to any known force of nature. It simply *was*, radiating its impossible signals, whispering in spectra far beyond human perception. The realization clawed at the edges of David's mind, unraveling the certainty he had carried since the day he first looked through a telescope and believed the universe could be understood.

If the crystal was drawing energy from the vacuum—if it was tapping into some hidden reservoir of power woven into the very fabric of space—then everything humanity thought it knew was incomplete, perhaps even primitive. Maybe they had only been scratching at the surface of reality, tracing shadows cast by something far greater. Or worse—what if they had been looking at the universe *all wrong*? What if their science, their precious laws, were nothing more than the stories of children, grasping at a truth too vast to fit within the fragile pages of their understanding? The thought sent a chill through him, colder than the Martian night outside. He looked at the crystal, its glow unwavering, and in that moment, he felt small—not in the way a scientist marvels at the cosmos, but in the way an explorer stares into the abyss, realizing the map ends here, and beyond it lies only the unknown.!

The days stretched into an uneasy rhythm. The crew threw themselves into their work, but the tension was never far beneath the surface. Every interaction felt like a test, each decision a potential spark to ignite the simmering discord. The fractures were no longer just personal—they were structural, woven into the fabric of the colony itself.

Meanwhile, Marcus and his team focused on reinforcing the habitat's pressurized systems. The repairs were slow and painstaking, each adjustment requiring meticulous precision. The main airlock was the priority, its structural integrity compromised by micro-fractures that had gone unnoticed until the recent inspection.

"We're running out of time," Marcus muttered as he welded a new brace into place. "This should've been addressed weeks ago."

One of the engineers glanced at him, her voice hesitant. "You think the artifacts are distracting us too much?"

"I think we've lost sight of what matters," Marcus replied. "Every minute we spend chasing those things is a minute we're not spending on keeping this colony alive."

The engineer nodded, though her expression was uneasy.

#

That night, Elena found herself at *"The Sky"* once again. The Martian landscape stretched out before her, its desolation stark and unchanging.

The ridge where the third artifact lay loomed in the distance, its dark silhouette a reminder of the questions they couldn't answer.

The faint hum of the crystal echoed in her mind, its rhythm steady and unyielding. It wasn't just a discovery—it was a force, shaping their mission and their relationships in ways none of them fully understood. And as much as she wanted to believe in Riya's vision of unity, the fractures within the crew felt irreparable.

Crystal pulsed faintly in the distance, its glow shifting like the breath of something ancient and patient. Its patterns were not random; they evolved, deliberate yet unknowable, as if tracing the rhythm of an unseen design. It was waiting for them—or perhaps, testing them.

God tests his disciples for faith, asking them to walk blindly into the unknown, to trust in the unseen. A teacher tests students, not to punish, but to reveal what they have learned, what they are ready to understand. A survivalist tests his followers, forcing them to endure, to adapt, to prove their resilience against the unyielding forces of nature. And now, the crystal—silent, enigmatic—tested them, too. But for what? Faith? Knowledge? Strength? Or something beyond the reach of human comprehension?

Or perhaps it was not a test at all. Perhaps it was calculating, watching, measuring them not as students but as something far more insignificant. Like a pest controller fumigates a nest, indifferent to the creatures within. Like a builder levels the land, unbothered by what once stood there. Or like a child, aimless and curious, pounding on a line of ants simply because they are there. The thought settled into Elena's bones like ice. The crystal pulsed again—steady, patient, waiting. And for the first time, she wondered if humanity was not being invited into some higher knowledge, but instead standing unknowingly on the precipice of erasure.

Are we crashing somebody's party, uninvited and unwelcome? The thought slithered through Elena's mind like a whisper from the void, chilling in its simplicity. Humanity had come to Mars with the arrogance of pioneers, planting their flags, building their shelters, claiming the barren soil as if it had been waiting for them all along. But what if it hadn't? What if they weren't the first? What if they weren't even meant to be here?

The crystal pulsed again in its confinement—a slow, rhythmic flicker, neither welcoming nor hostile, but indifferent, as though humanity's presence was nothing more than static noise in a grander design. A signal ignored. A whisper unanswered. Or worse, an intrusion noted, cataloged, and left to be dealt with in due time.

She pressed her hand against the glass, her breath fogging the surface. The answers felt as distant as the stars; she whispered...

"We have no home to return, you know that!"

Chapter Five

DISCOVERY

D r. Sonja, the colony's geologist, was surveying a sector of rocky terrain near the habitat, using ground-penetrating radar to map subsurface formations. Her objective was simple: identify potential mineral deposits or underground features that might support the colony's resource needs. She hadn't expected to find anything significant.

Among the colony's high-priority tasks, exploration holds significant value for both the short and long term. For UNSI, exploration is tied to its vested interest in Martian mineral extraction—a key element in securing funding for the mission. The potential for valuable resources beneath the Martian surface has long been a driving force behind such initiatives, making exploration a critical component of their broader objectives.

From the colony's standpoint, however, exploration serves a more immediate purpose. Covering more ground not only expands their understanding of the environment but also provides a sense of security about their habitat. Knowing what lies beyond the ridges isn't just practical—it's deeply ingrained in human psychology, an intrinsic need to uncover the unknown.

Foremost among exploration's goals, however, is the search for water—a discovery that would mark a turning point for long-term survival on Mars. While years of satellite observations and robotic probes have provided indirect evidence of sub-surface water, no accessible or sizable deposits have been found. These indications remain speculative, a tantalizing possibility rather than a proven resource. For the colony, the quest for water isn't just about survival—it's about turning Mars from a hostile frontier into a sustainable home.

#

Dr. Sonja Eriksson, age fifty-eight, hails from Uppsala, Sweden, where she grew up surrounded by academia and natural beauty. A celebrated geologist, she carved her reputation through groundbreaking work in resource mapping, eventually securing a spot on the UNSI mission to Mars.

However, her inclusion wasn't without controversy. Married to an American engineer from Texas, Mr. Tomas Eriksson, the two, affectionately known as the *Eriksson Duo* within the industry circles, are billionaires who own a global oil empire and hold minor shares in UNSI. Their financial ties to the mission drew sharp criticism from the media, accusing them of positioning themselves for future domination of Mars's resources.

Despite the headlines, a lesser-known truth about the *Eriksson Duo* paints a much different picture. Both Sonja and her husband have dedicated most of their wealth to philanthropy and humanitarian efforts. Over the years, they've built infrastructure and cities in underprivileged regions and funded the education of countless children, offering them opportunities for a better life. Their commitment to philanthropy and social progress has left an indelible mark on some of the world's least fortunate areas, though their altruism often goes overlooked in the shadow of their corporate empire.

Mr. Eriksson, now seventy-eight, is a retired professor who taught at multiple universities, despite having the luxury to retire into the most expensive place on earth but instead sharing his expertise and mentoring a new generation of engineers. When Sonja left for Mars, he gave her a heartfelt farewell, understanding the importance of her role in humanity's greatest exploration. "At my age," he had said, "I can do more good staying here on Earth than going to Mars." His unwavering support for her mission, coupled with his continued work in education and philanthropy, highlights the true legacy of the Eriksson Duo—a partnership that values progress for humanity above all else.

Despite their celebrity status in billionaire circles, Sonja and Thomas Eriksson maintained an intensely private family life, shielding their children from the public eye. The roots of their partnership trace back to a serendipitous meeting when Sonja was just beginning her career.

She joined one of Thomas's offshore oil exploration companies as an intern, initially a small cog in the massive machinery of his empire. Their paths crossed on a deep-sea oil platform near Antarctica, where Sonja's brilliance and unshakable confidence shone through. Ignoring the dismissive attitudes of her superiors—many with decades of experience in oil exploration—Sonja trusted her instincts and used her unconventional methods to pinpoint one of the richest oil deposits ever discovered on Earth. Her discovery reshaped the industry and caught the eye of Thomas Eriksson, who was not only impressed by her results but by her defiance of convention.

In a rare gesture for an industry mogul, Thomas offered Sonja stake in the newly discovered deposit, making her a partner in the venture. Overnight, she became a millionaire, and with her newfound resources, she refined her groundbreaking exploration techniques, leveraging cutting-edge technology she helped design with her team. Her unconventional approach quickly cemented her as a trailblazer in the industry, and it wasn't long before she stepped onto the billionaire stage, her reputation rivaling Thomas's.

Their professional partnership blossomed into something more, and Sonja eventually became Mrs. Eriksson, combining their fortunes and their passions. Together, they built an empire that wasn't just about wealth but about pushing boundaries—in exploration, technology, and humanitarian efforts. Despite their staggering success, they remained dedicated to creating a legacy defined not by their financial power but by the lasting impact of their work on the world and beyond.

Both being billionaires and deeply embedded in the most influential circles on Earth, Sonja Eriksson and David Leclerc were undoubtedly the two most powerful figures on the team. Their combined financial resources and political leverage were instrumental in making *Eos Horizon's* lift-off a reality. Erickson's wealth and reputation as a pioneer in resource exploration, paired with David's connections and persuasive vision for humanity's interplanetary future, formed a foundation that no mission sponsor could ignore. Together, they navigated the complex web of politics, funding, and public perception, ensuring that the mission moved from an ambitious concept to a historic reality.

Despite their deep-rooted involvement in the mission, only a handful of the colony knew the extent of Sonja and David's contributions. They preferred it that way, choosing to focus on their roles within the team rather than their influence behind the scenes.

#

"Dr. Sonja!" Freja shouted, her voice raised.

Freja Vikström, Sonja's handpicked assistant, had worked closely with her for years, developing a deep understanding of Sonja's methods and expectations.

"This can't be normal!", Freja added.

She reviewed the radar data together, a particular anomaly caught her attention. A dense, reflective layer beneath the surface—consistent with the signature of frozen water.

Her pulse quickened as she reviewed the data, her fingers hovering over the console to verify the readings once more. The deposit sprawled beneath the Martian surface, a vast expanse stretching kilometers below the rust-colored soil. Water—pristine and likely untouched for millions of years.

To reach this conclusion, she employed a sophisticated array of tools. Quantum Sensing Technology provided unparalleled precision, while Electromagnetic Induction Imaging mapped the subtle conductivity variations indicative of liquid water. Traditional Ground Penetrating Radar (GPR) added depth and clarity, revealing the geological layers. When anomalous reflections appeared, she turned to Neutron Spectroscopy to detect hydrogen signatures and Infrared Spectroscopy to confirm water's unique absorption wavelengths. One by one, the results aligned, pointing unmistakably to a monumental discovery.

Her hand trembled as she touched Orion.

"Riya," she said, her voice barely containing the thrill coursing through her.

"You need to see this. It's a subsurface ice deposit—one of the largest I've ever seen!"

#

The discovery electrified the colony. Water independence had always been a critical goal, and the prospect of accessing a local source instead of relying solely on reserves brought a rare moment of optimism. Within hours, an excavation team was assembled, their equipment loaded onto rovers as they prepared to extract and analyze samples.

Marcus led the operation, his focus sharp despite the ongoing tensions within the crew. Elena joined the team, her curiosity outweighing her usual hesitations. David stayed behind, engrossed in his work with the crystal, though he kept a watchful eye on the team's progress through the habitat's monitoring systems.

This was an excitement Riya, Elena, David, Marcus, and the others hadn't felt in what seemed like an eternity. In fact, none of them could easily recall the last time they had been this thrilled, this energized by the prospect of discovery. It was a rare moment that cut through the strain and uncertainty, reminding them why they had embarked on this mission in the first place.

#

Marcus approached Sonja with a wide grin, his voice booming with playful enthusiasm.

"Hey, Sonja, our hero!" he exclaimed, his tone light enough to brighten even the dullest Martian day.

It almost looked like he was about to sweep her into a hug or lift her off the ground in celebration. Instead, with their bulky MSA suits limiting any grand gestures, they settled for a wrist or shoulder bump—the closest thing to friendship Mars would allow.

"Tell me, tell me—how far do we have to drill?" Marcus asked, practically bouncing with excitement, his eyes gleaming with a renewed energy that had been absent for far too long.

He was like a child on Christmas morning, hands itching to tear into a long-awaited gift, or a gamer hovering over a freshly unwrapped console, unable to resist the thrill of pressing the power button for the first time. The weight of the colony's struggles, the endless debates, the fractures between them—none of it seemed to exist in this moment. Right now, there was only the raw exhilaration of discovery, the rush of *doing* rather than debating. It was as if he had found his purpose again, and nothing— not caution, not logic, not even the unknown—was going to slow him down.

"Hold on to your hat, cowboy. We've got a lot to do," Sonja said with a smirk, handing him the tablet.

"First, I need you to get a core drilling done. The location is marked, and I've already sent the coordinates to your drill rig. Start with the grid pattern I've designed—sixteen holes to begin with."

"Sixteen!" Marcus exclaimed; his playful tone was underscored by a mock look of disbelief. Despite already knowing the details of the grid and the core-drilling plan, he couldn't help but feign surprise, his excitement bubbling over. It was refreshing to see him so animated, leaving behind the weight of the colony's responsibilities, if only for a moment. His enthusiasm was contagious, and even Sonja couldn't help but smile as she watched him dive headfirst into the task.

#

Riya and the others arrived at the site moments later, their eyes scanning the equipment already in motion.

"Hey, Sonja, you did great," Riya said, her tone warm with genuine praise.

Sonja nodded, her focus already on the next steps.

"We still need an extraction plan," she replied.

"Marcus is already on the core-drilling—it'll give us a better idea of the extent and depth of the deposit. Once we have that data, we can pinpoint the best spot for the main extraction point." Her calm, methodical explanation reflected her years of expertise, grounding the team with a sense of direction amidst the excitement.

"How can I help?" David asked, stepping closer to Sonja.

"Get Liam to work on a piping route," Sonja replied quickly, her mind already running through the logistics.

"Actually, even before that, have him map a path between the utility dome and this site. If there are any boulders or obstacles, get the robotic excavator to clear them out. And place some lighting along the way—this is going to be a day-and-night operation, especially with the unpredictable weather."

"We need to mobilize while the conditions hold."

She paused briefly, as though remembering something crucial.

"Oh, and make sure a shelter is set up nearby so the crew has a place to relax and recharge. Marcus is with the drilling team, and I need him focused, leading his team without distractions."

Her tone was direct, but there was a faint undercurrent of urgency, a reflection of the stakes at hand.

The excavation site was a stark, windswept plain marked by the distinctive red hues of Martian soil. The radar-guided drills bored into the ground with mechanical precision, their vibrations resonating through the rover's equipment. As the team worked, the atmosphere was one of cautious hope—this discovery could change everything.

Marcus was at the helm, leading the team overseeing the core-drilling operation with his usual precision and focus. Nearby, Sonja, Freja, and a handful of others inspected the core samples as they were brought to the surface, analyzing them with keen attention to detail. The operation had been running nonstop for two days, meticulously organized with a shift plan that ensured the crew had ample rest.

#

Freja Vikström had always been drawn to the unseen—the silent stories etched in mineral grains, the traces of ancient worlds preserved in the chemistry of rocks. Growing up in Stockholm, she preferred the wild coastlines and dense forests to the confines of home, fascinated by landscapes shaped long before humans existed. With a marine biologist mother and an aerospace engineer father, curiosity was woven into her nature. She pursued *Planetary Geochemistry and Exobiology* at Uppsala University, later earning a doctorate at Cal-tech, where she specialized in extremophiles—life forms thriving in Earth's most hostile environments, analogues for what might once have survived on Mars. Her research took her to sulfuric hot springs, Arctic tundras, and deep-sea hydrothermal vents, always chasing the question: *Could life have ever endured beyond Earth?*

Despite her professional success, Freja's personal life had been as unstable as the chemical reactions she studied. She had loved a man who burned too brightly—an artist, a dreamer, but an addict. For years, she tried to pull him back from the edge, only to realize that addiction had a gravity even love couldn't escape. Walking away felt like abandoning him, but it was also the first breath of freedom she had taken in years. Needing distance, she sought refuge in isolation, joining a deep-sea oil exploration platform owned by the *Eriksson Duo*. There, amid the endless churn of waves and the relentless bite of the wind, she immersed herself in resource analysis, high-pressure chemistry, and remote sensing—skills that would later prove invaluable on Mars.

It was on that platform that she met Sonja, one of its owners and the colony's future lead geologist. Sonja saw something in Freja—more than just expertise, but an instinct for survival in the most unforgiving places. They became an unshakable team, their minds aligned in the pursuit of knowledge against nature's indifference. When Sonja was selected for the Mars mission, she didn't just recommend Freja—she insisted on her inclusion, a decision that no one dared challenge given Freja's proven expertise. The ocean had stripped her down, demanded everything, but Mars—Mars would take more. And this time, she wasn't just running. She was ready.

#

"Freja, get the core samples analyzed—I'm heading to the lab," Sonja shouted over her shoulder, her voice sharp and urgent as she strode toward the exit.

"Let me know if you need anything."

She didn't wait for a response, already locking her focus on Riya, who stood waiting by the rover. The colony had no room for hesitation, and neither did she.

Despite the grueling schedule, the excitement was intense. Every colonist, no matter their role, seemed eager to pitch in, swept up in the shared anticipation of discovery. The tension and divisions that had once plagued the colony felt like a distant memory, replaced by a renewed sense of unity and purpose. For the first time in what felt like months, the colony was moving as one.

Riya called David and Elena to the command center on the morning of the second day of drilling. Her tone was sharp and decisive, leaving no room for debate.

"David, you'll take over the day-to-day maintenance. Elena, you'll work with Liam and provide support to Sonja," she instructed, her gaze steady.

"I was working on the logistics for Sonja—" David began, but Riya cut him off mid-sentence.

"I know. That's almost going smooth, which is exactly why it's easier for Elena to take over," she said firmly.

She leaned slightly forward, her tone softening just enough to emphasize the importance of her next words.

"The maintenance is critical, and we can't afford any oversights. Marcus cannot be pulled away from the drilling, and you're the best person to handle this, right?"

David exhaled, his jaw tightening slightly before nodding. "Yes, ma'am," he said, his voice resolute. There was no arguing with her logic, and the weight of responsibility settled squarely on his shoulders.

With no concerning news from the drill site, the excitement continued to ripple through the colony, fueling conversations and speculation. As the day turned to dusk, the Martian sky shifted into its signature hues of crimson and gold, casting a surreal glow over the habitat.

#

For the first time in a very long while, Elena climbed the stairs to *"The Sky"* with a sense of joy and purpose. Her steps were lighter, her spirit buoyed by the renewed excitement coursing through the colony. As she reached the deck, the directional-presence aware sound system, synced with Orion, began playing her chosen anthem—*"It's My Life"*—the familiar tune filling the space around her.

The music grew ever more audible over the deck, carrying its vibrant rhythm into the air. Elena closed her eyes, letting the beat take over. She flipped her head to the rhythm, her hip swaying with an energy that had been absent for too long. For a moment, the tension, the mysteries, and the weight of Mars all dissolved, leaving only her, the music, and the open expanse of the crimson horizon.

Elena's senses tingled, a subtle awareness creeping in that she wasn't alone. Time seemed to stretch endlessly as the song continued to play, each beat filling her with what felt like an eternity of joy. Reluctantly, she cracked her eyes open, only to catch a faint silhouette through her lids. The moment shifted, as if hitting a concrete wall.

Opening her eyes fully, she saw Riya leaning casually against the perimeter balustrade, a calm smile softening her face. Before Elena could process the change in mood, she noticed Riya tapping her fingers rhythmically on the bevel, her head moving ever so slightly in sync with the music.

For Elena, the trance was broken—but in a good way. Letting the tune finish its course, she acknowledged the moment's end, knowing the song would fade soon enough. She walked toward Riya, her steps light.

"Why stop?" Riya asked, her tone teasing. "I could've joined you."

With a smile, Elena replied, "I had my moment."

Riya chuckled, the nostalgia flickering behind her eyes.

"It was an anthem back in the day—came out in around turn of the century, way before I was even a teenager. But it stuck. It was one of those songs that made you feel like you had control over your destiny, like you were the one calling the shots. *It's now or never, I ain't gonna live forever*'—it was rebellious, defiant. It was about carving your own path, no matter what people said."

She exhaled, a wistful smile tugging at the corner of her lips.

"It's funny… back then, it felt like a rally cry for reckless youth. Now? Feels more like a survival mantra."

The two stood for a moment, looking at each other with a shared understanding, a quiet compassion that spoke volumes. In the midst of the challenges and chaos, this simple exchange reminded them both of something vital—they still had hope.

"I know what you did," Elena said, breaking the silence.

"If you're talking about David," Riya replied with a small shrug, "good on me, then."

Elena smiled knowingly. "You handle things so cleverly. I wouldn't have even thought of it."

"We all have our roles to play," Riya said, her voice steady yet kind. "Seems like we're both doing okay."

The two women turned their gazes outward to the Martian horizon, the music fading, leaving only the quiet hum of *"The Sky"* and the unspoken bond between them.

#

Third day on the drill site, the mood shifted.

Marcus noticed it first. The drills were encountering an unusual resistance, their progress slowing despite the uniform consistency of the ice. The readings from the subsurface scanner began to fluctuate, erratic spikes appearing amidst the otherwise stable data.

"What's causing that?" Sonja asked, frowning at the monitor.

Marcus shook his head, his brow furrowed with uncertainty. "I don't know. This is the final hole, and it's the shallowest of them all. Could be a denser layer beneath the ice. Let's proceed carefully."

"It can't be," Sonja interrupted, her voice calm but firm. She nodded toward the data in her hand. "I see water much deeper than that. The ground-penetrating radar shows a density change, yes, but it's consistent with water all the way down." Her confidence brought a momentary stillness to the team, the weight of a discovery hanging in the air.

Minutes later, the drill hit something solid. The vibrations stopped abruptly, the machine emitting a low hum as it struggled against the obstruction.

"Withdraw the drill and secure the borehole," Marcus commanded, his voice steady but firm. "We need eyes in this."

The team deployed a remotely-operated vehicle (ROV), a compact yet highly advanced machine bristling with sensors designed to probe the unseen depths. Equipped with multi-spectrum imaging, chemical analyses, and sonar mapping, it could detect temperature shifts, mineral compositions, and subtle variations in rock density—each data point a clue in unraveling the geological mysteries hidden below. As the ROV descended, its instruments continuously fed back real-time telemetry, painting a clearer picture of the terrain beneath them. Every reading, every scan, helped piece together the ancient story of Mars, one fragment of data at a time.

The ROV descended cautiously through the frozen layers of ice, its progress marked by the occasional crunch as it grazed the borehole walls. The team watched intently as the live feed transmitted grainy yet revealing images from the depths.

It didn't take long to uncover the source of the resistance—a smooth, unmistakable blackish-metallic like object embedded within the ice. The object's surface shimmered faintly under the ROV's lights, its presence alien and undeniable, sending a wave of unease rippling through the team.

#

"Last thing I expected to see," Marcus muttered, his tone heavy with disappointment as he stared at the live feed. His jaw tightened, the excitement from moments earlier now replaced with a grim sense of inevitability.

Watching closely at the monitor, "Looks like the diamond-impregnated ceramic cutting teeth haven't even scratched it," Marcus continued, his tone laced with equal parts amusement and frustration. He leaned back, running his fingers over the mangled drill head, the once-pristine cutting teeth now rendered useless.

"So much for breaking it apart—or sending a sample for lab analysis," he added, the weight of the artifact's impenetrability sinking in, a silent declaration of defeat.

Elena leaned in closely, peeking over his shoulder. She staired at the object for a moment longer, then nodded, her expression firm. "That much is certain," she confirmed, her voice steady but tinged with curiosity.

Sonja broke the tension with a bright tone. "We've successfully completed the grid—congratulations, team!"

She paused, scanning the data on her tablet. "All 16 boreholes are penetrating the ice layer—some deep, some not so much. Now we can pinpoint the best site to drill and line the water extraction hole."

"Yes, I agree," Marcus added, nodding at the display.

"This is a vast deposit by the looks of it. Avoiding the artifact and drilling through the ice shouldn't be a problem." His voice carried a mixture of relief and determination as the plan began to solidify.

"Let's pack up and withdraw," Sonja said, her voice calm but purposeful. "I need to work on this data, and before long, we'll be back."

Her tone carried an assurance that pinned hope to her words, a quiet conviction that steadied the uncertainty lingering in the air. Even in the face of the unknown, Sonja never wavered—a trait that made her not just a leader, but an anchor in the shifting tides of discovery.

#

It seems that the discovery of the artifact embedded in the ice hasn't caused the ripple effect across the colony that one might have anticipated. Its location deep below ground, combined with the vast expanse of the ice deposit offering plenty of opportunities to drill elsewhere, has diminished its immediate significance. With practical solutions readily available to bypass the artifact, its presence has been more of a curiosity than a true game-changer—for now.

Riya had instructed the drill team and those who had worked tirelessly for three days on the water extraction project to take a day off, assigning tasks to others to keep the workflow steady. At first, this sparked envy among the rest of the colony, but it wasn't long before they were seeing getting into routine work.

Elena spotted Marcus climbing into a rover and called out, waving to catch his attention.

"On a picnic?" she teased, raising an eyebrow.

Marcus glanced over, a faint smile tugging at the corner of his lips.

"See, that's the irony on Mars," he said, his tone laced with dry humor.

"Everywhere looks the same. Whatever place you pick, it's no different from another."

His expression grew more serious as he turned back to adjust his gear.

"We don't exactly know how to spend a holiday here. It's easier to just… do something useful. So, I'm heading down to the drill site to stockpile the temporary shelter, getting things ready for the next phase," he explained, his voice steady with purpose.

Elena nodded, watching as the rover hummed to life.

"Don't overdo it," she called after him, but Marcus was already on his way, the faint tracks of the rover trailing behind in the red dust.

All of this is about to change next morning.

#

Riya called the team together, her usual air of composure giving way to something more urgent. Once the routine updates were out of the way—supply levels, maintenance reports, mission schedules—she wasted no time getting to the heart of the matter.

Her tone sharpened as she turned to Sonja, who had spent the last few days buried in data, piecing together the findings from the drill program.

"Alright, Sonja," Riya said, leaning forward, her eyes scanning the geologist's expression for any telltale signs of hesitation. "What did you find?"

The room fell into silence, anticipation thick in the air. Whatever Sonja had uncovered, it wasn't just numbers on a report—it was something that could change everything.

"I'll let Sonja explain," Riya said, stepping back and gesturing for her to take the floor.

Sonja stood, holding a tablet in her hands.

"Well," she began, "the good news is we can drill pretty much anywhere in the grid and extract water. The deposit is vast."

She paused, glancing at the room before continuing.

"What's less entertaining is this: the best location for extraction is at the last hole we drilled—hole sixteen—where the artifact is. It has the shallowest depth to penetrate and shows the clearest ice deposit compared to the other locations. From the other samples, we've found varying degrees of debris and heavy metals, but no detectable microbes. However, the ice core samples from hole sixteen look promising. This may or may not mean anything, but it's worth noting."

She sat back down, the room heavy with silence. Riya picked up where she left off.

"David and his team, who are analyzing the artifact, believe hole sixteen should be expanded and the artifact retrieved."

A collective hiss rippled through the room. Some reacted with excitement at the prospect of uncovering a Martian artifact, while others muttered in despair, clearly uneasy. Riya raised her hand, silenced the group.

"It's a single effort," she said, her voice calm but commanding.

"We get the water and the artifact. The artifact is the smallest we've encountered so far, and it can be extracted through the same hole we need for water retrieval. It's efficient, and it aligns with our objectives."

The room quieted again, though the unease remained palpable. Marcus sat still; his expression unreadable but his thoughts clearly elsewhere. As an engineer, he understood that this was the best course of action given the circumstances. Logically, it made sense to drill at hole sixteen and retrieve both resources in one effort.

But his unease wasn't about logistics. It was about the artifact itself. A lingering doubt tugged at his mind, a question he couldn't shake: what if retrieving it is a mistake? What if surfacing this long-buried artifact bring more trouble than they could foresee?

Riya broke the silence again, her gaze settling on Marcus.

"Marcus, do you agree with this plan?" she asked, her tone steady but probing.

Marcus hesitated, his fingers tapping lightly on the table as if weighing the unspoken concerns in his mind. Finally, he nodded, though his expression remained reserved.

"I understand," he said simply, his voice calm but lacking enthusiasm.

The room stayed silent for a beat longer, as though everyone felt the weight of his restrained agreement. Marcus leaned back in his chair, his thoughts already spinning. He understood the logic, the efficiency, the necessity—but none of it quelled the unease gnawing at him. Whatever lay buried alongside the ice, he wasn't sure they were ready to face it.

Elena wasn't sure either. The potential risks—it all felt like a step into the unknown. But amidst her uncertainty, there was one thing she found herself oddly relieved about: Marcus and David had finally agreed on something. It had been a long time since the two had seen eye to eye on anything, their clashing perspectives often a source of tension. For once, they were aligned, even if it was over something as precarious as this plan. That, at least, gave her a sliver of hope that the team could move forward together.

#

They day passed as those who were assigned to the water extraction project prepared themselves. Marcus called for series of meetings with various skilled people on the extraction plans. Plans for such an extraction was anticipated, and in fact prepared for, at UNSI. They have number of scenarios modeled, and few dozens of plans meticulously detailed to suite the circumstances. Marcus' main responsibility is to pick the right plan and execute. However, he wanted everybody involved to go through, including Riya, so no small detail overlooked.

Marcus broke the silence, his voice steady but filled with respect.

"Dr. Sonja, you have more experience with this kind of stuff than everyone else here combined," he said, meeting her gaze.

"And as the project manager on this operation, I think you should take over this meeting. I believe it's the right call." His words carried the weight of his confidence in her

With a warm smile, Sonja stepped forward, her presence commanding but approachable.

"Right, if you insist," she said, her tone light with humor.

"But just so we're clear, I've never dug a hole on another planet before—first for me." Her joke broke through the tension, drawing a few chuckles from the team.

"Okay, first things first," Sonja began, her tone steady and authoritative.

"We'll have a safety briefing tomorrow morning before we commence. Safety protocols are already in place, and let me remind you—you've all been trained on this countless times back at UNSI."

She glanced around the room, ensuring everyone was attentive before continuing. "We've simulated water extraction with numerous models and scenarios, built on years of research back on Earth. Hundreds of PhDs and countless hours of study have gone into this process."

She paused briefly, then added, "From all that work, we've selected two models we think are best suited for our current conditions. What we'll be utilizing tomorrow is the *PyroTherma* head, which uses ion-wave conduction from an in-situ plasmoid core..."

She trailed off, catching the confused looks in the room and chuckled.

"Okay, okay—without boring you to death, just think of it as a red-hot iron that melts the ice as it's pushed in. The result? Melted water filling the intrusion. That's the part that matters."

"This tech, ladies and gentlemen, is Sonja's baby," Marcus said, his voice carrying a mix of admiration and humor.

"She designed this and used it in plenty of similar scenarios in her enterprise back on Earth. Of course," he added with a chuckle, "She's got countless babies like this."

The crew laughed lightly, the tension in the room easing as the moment highlighted Sonja's expertise and the team's shared confidence in her leadership.

Sonja stepped in with a smile, adding to the playful tone.

"Well, what's the second solution? Thanks for asking," she said, adding a touch of drama to lighten the room.

"If we encounter any issues with the *PyroTherma* technology—like destabilization of the ice layer, for instance—then we won't be able to proceed. That said, the head is equipped with advanced sensors and AI to provide us with prior warnings, so nothing catastrophic should happen."

She paused, letting the seriousness of her words settle before continuing.

"If it does come to that, we'll have to resort to the age-old method: an open-cut mine, just like the old days. That option would be time and resource-intensive—not to mention far less efficient—but it's our fallback, nevertheless."

The room was quiet, the gravity of the backup plan clear. Despite her calm delivery, it was evident to everyone that avoiding the fallback was critical to their success.

A few of the crew couldn't help but recall the pile of containers and massive machinery stacked in a sheltered depression nearby, left behind by earlier unmanned supply missions. Most had passed by countless times without a second thought, assuming it was just another collection of supplies. But only a select few knew the truth—those hulking pieces of equipment were mining machines, quietly waiting for the day they might be called into action.

#

The day the operation began as a less of a dramatic spectacle and more of a well-rehearsed dance. Every detail had been meticulously planned, and the team moved with precision, each member knowing exactly what to do next. The atmosphere buzzed with quiet confidence, the result of countless simulations and thorough preparations.

Riya, overseeing it all from the command station, was comfortable allocating a third of the colony to the operation, trusting the remaining crew to manage the daily tasks back at the habitat. It was a delicate balance, but seamless coordination spoke to the discipline and unity the mission demanded. The tension of the unknown still lingered, but for now, the colony operated like a finely tuned machine.

After two days of tireless work in shifts, the team finally managed to enlarge hole sixteen and sink a massive casing, two meters in diameter, lined with engineered plastic material which can withstand the harsh Martian environment, into the ground. The operation was executed with precision, and the casing now stood firm at the target depth of hundred and twenty meters, its bottom securely anchored in place.

Lurking just a few meters below the casing's end, however, was the enigmatic artifact—a presence that weighed heavily on everyone's minds but was pointedly left unspoken. Whether out of unease or silent agreement, nobody acknowledged its existence aloud, choosing instead to focus on the task at hand as if ignoring it might lessen its significance.

#

As Sonja called for a cease to the drilling, the associated machinery was meticulously dismantled and transported back to the colony's storage facilities. The team wasted no time transitioning to the next phase. Over the course of three more days, they completed the above-ground installations, including the setup of massive suction pumps capable of drawing water from the newly secured borehole.

For now, the decision was made to use a bowser system to transport the extracted water to the habitat. It was a temporary solution, offering flexibility while the debate over a permanent pipeline—whether to route it above or below ground—continued. The arrangement provided the team some much-needed breathing room, allowing them to focus on operational stability without rushing into a longer-term infrastructure project prematurely.

None could escape the inevitable dawn of the day that everyone had silently dreaded—the day of the unspoken. Riya called a meeting, the atmosphere heavy with unacknowledged tension. After carefully assessing the progress of the project and expressing heartfelt gratitude to those who had worked tirelessly to bring it to completion, she shifted the focus.

"Either we can continue to keep our eyes closed to what's beneath," she said, her tone calm but firm, "or we can do something about it." Her words were measured, an effort to ease the unease in the room.

Turning to Marcus, she added decisively, "We agreed to bring the artifact to the surface. It's time."

Marcus hesitated for a moment, the weight of the decision visible in his expression.

Finally, he gave a reluctant nod. "Yes," he said, his voice low but steady.

"We have to do what we have to do."

He added, "Let's secure the perimeter and mend the road. The bowsers are automated, sure, but even they wouldn't mind a smooth ride."

His attempt at humor felt a bit dry, the joke landing awkwardly in the heavy atmosphere. Still, it was not hard to see the effort, understanding he was trying in his own way to ease the tension. He paused briefly before continuing, his tone turning more serious.

"We'll begin the extraction first thing tomorrow morning."

#

As the Martian dusk began to cast its deep crimson hues over the harsh landscape, the colony slowly came alive with movement. Crew members returned to the habitat, washing off the day's grit, gathering for meals, and engaging in light-hearted conversations. The atmosphere, once heavy with tension and division, had begun to soften. Laughter mingled with the sound of clinking dishes, and the quiet hum of camaraderie filled the air.

The water extraction project had not only provided the promise of a sustainable future but had also rekindled a sense of unity among the colonists.

With newfound purpose and the reassurance of water security, the colony seemed to breathe again, stirring with a renewed sense of life. Laughter lingered a little longer over meals, casual conversations stretched into the late afternoon, and for the first time in a long while, the crew allowed themselves to relax. One by one, they withdrew into their quarters, settling in for what promised to be a rare, uninterrupted night of rest.

All except one.

#

Elena lay awake, trapped in a restless battle with sleep that refused to come. She tossed and turned, shifting positions as if searching for some elusive comfort that remained just out of reach. Pillows were gathered, then discarded. Blankets were kicked away, then pulled back in frustration. No matter what she tried, her mind refused to quiet, her thoughts circling like a storm that had no intention of passing.

Then, finally, she drifted off.

For a moment, that is.

Sleep came like a fragile whisper, barely settling at last, she thought...

Elena was jolted awake—a sudden, visceral pull, as if some unseen force had yanked her from sleep. She shot upright, breath sharp, pulse pounding in her ears. For a disorienting moment, she couldn't tell if she was still trapped in a dream or if her feet were truly pressing against the cold, solid floor.

"Why me?" she whispered into the stillness, her own voice unsettling in the emptiness of the room.

She lay back down, trying to roll into every possible position on the bed again, searching for some comfort in vain. Frustrated, she finally got up and began wandering out of her room, her feet instinctively leading her toward *"The Sky"*, her sanctuary of solace.

As she climbed the steps, fingers brushed every surface she passed—walls, railings, even the cool metal of a doorway—desperately grounding herself, as if to confirm she wasn't sleepwalking. The stillness of the colony pressed against her, but her steps were deliberate, her mind racing with questions that refused to let her rest.

Elena froze, her half-closed eyes widening in shock as she reached *"The Sky"* and saw a small group already gathered there, standing silently as though they'd been waiting for her.

Her pulse quickened, and in a moment's shake, nervousness and embarrassment flooded her. She glanced down at herself—her night suit suddenly feeling like a glaring reminder of her unpreparedness. Standing before her were Riya, David, Marcus, Ada, and Liam, all dressed more appropriately, certainly more aptly than her, their presence composed and deliberate. Elena's cheeks flushed as she struggled to reconcile the casual state she'd arrived in with the seriousness of the moment unfolding before her.

David immediately stepped forward, offering his jacket with a poker face. Before Elena could respond, Riya moved closer, placing a comforting arm around her shoulders, pulling Elena towards her.

"It's alright," she said, her tone calm and reassuring.

"We weren't sure whether to wake you up in the middle of the night, but it looks like that's sorted now."

Her warmth and understanding helped ease some of Elena's nerves, grounding her in the moment despite her lingering embarrassment.

David, sensing Elena's confusion, decided to bring her out of suspension.

"Elena," he began, his voice steady but laced with urgency, "The crystal is connected to you—for how much and to what extent, we don't know yet."

Before she could respond, David continued, his tone measured but serious.

"Liam and I have been holding this for a couple of days, waiting until we were absolutely certain"

"Among all the things the *crystal math* spits out, your name stands out." He turned to Liam, pulling him into the spotlight.

Liam hesitated, clearly not prepared for the attention, but quickly picked his words.

"Most of what we've been decoding are vectors—patterns building up to a kind of map. It's universal, not just Martian ground but extending beyond, into the cosmos. But then, we found a recurring sequence of numbers, something that didn't fit with the vector theory, or anything else for that matter."

He paused, searching for the right way to explain.

"So, we asked Ada to take a look, thinking it might have some connection to her research so far."

Ada shook her head, her tone calm yet electrified with significance.

"Since Liam had tried everything else" she said, her voice deliberate.

"I thought, why not give it a shot with logo-graphs and ancient texts? It seemed like a long shot."

She continued, "With some effort, I managed to map the sequence against cuneiform texts from ancient Mesopotamia. And… it worked!"

"I verified it multiple ways," Liam couldn't help himself, his tone firm and assured.

"Ada's basis for the cuneiform mapping is solid."

He gestured toward the tablet, his enthusiasm bubbling over as he continued.

"Ada discovered that the wedge-shaped forms in the sequence create recursive patterns—patterns that mirror fractals when plotted on a graph. And when we analyzed it further, it led us to a base-eight framework!"

Liam's exhaustive explanation carried an unmistakable certainty, his agreement with Ada's work shining through in every word. His excitement was palpable, a rare glimpse of passion that underscored just how groundbreaking the discovery could be.

"Liam has been running the figure sequences against everything we have," David said, frustration lingering in his tone.

"Nothing matched."

He exhaled before continuing. "Then, yesterday, Dr. Amir took one look at it and—half-joking—said it looked like a PCR pattern."

A silence hung in the room as the weight of his next words settled over them.

"That gave Liam the idea to analyze the sequences as if they were genetic markers", he nodded.

"With nothing to lose, Liam ran a comparison against our DNA database," David continued, his voice steady but laced with urgency.

"And it matched with one record—one hundred percent."

His gaze locked onto Elena. "With your DNA, Elena. That's not a coincidence."

Elena dropped on her knees!

Riya was quick to kneel beside Elena, her movements deliberate yet tender. Without hesitation, she wrapped her arms around Elena, pulling her close and letting her rest against her chest. Hugging her tightly, Riya held her as though comforting her own child, her touch radiating warmth and reassurance. She whispered softly, her words inaudible to the others.

The room fell into a tense silence as the words settled. All eyes were on Elena, the weight of this revelation pressing heavily into the space.

It took a while for Elena to pull herself out of the torrent of emotions that had overtaken her. Her breathing steadied, the sobs subsiding into silence as she clung to Riya's embrace, as though anchoring herself to the present. Slowly, she lifted her gaze, her tear-streaked face turning toward the others, an unspoken determination in her eyes—a need to reconnect with the moment and face the reality unfolding around her.

"I had a calling in the dream," Elena said, her voice trembling and breaking the thick silence, the weight of her words pulling every eye toward her.

"The crystal needs to go to the waterhole," she added firmly, her gaze unwavering.

"That's what we'll do, first thing in the morning."

Marcus agreed, his tone confident and assured. For a brief moment, he seemed to forget Riya's authority and decision-making role, his words carrying an uncharacteristic finality.

More strikingly, his sudden shift in stance starkly contrasted with his long-standing objections to the artifact and his strong opinions against any dealings with it. Marcus had been one of the staunchest critics, and if anyone had seemed unlikely to propose this course of action, it would be him.

The room shifted awkwardly as everyone exchanged surprised glances, unsure how to react to Marcus's abrupt declaration.

Riya, noticing the tension, quickly stepped in.

"Marcus made the right call," she said, her voice steady and decisive.

"We'll do exactly that."

Her words brought the room back into focus, her approval dissolving the unease and reaffirming her command.

#

The morning briefing buzzed with anticipation, the team eager to hear updates and plans for the continuation of the water extraction project. The atmosphere was charged with optimism.

Riya entered the room, her face betraying exhaustion, the telltale signs of a sleepless night etched in her expression. Yet, despite the fatigue, her presence was commanding. There was determination in her eyes, an energy that seemed to come from some deeper reserve.

"The team will take a break today," Riya announced, her tone calm but deliberate, catching the crew off guard. A murmur of amusement rippled through the group; their curiosity immediately piqued.

"We have a slight change of plans," she continued, her voice steady but carrying an undercurrent of significance.

"Marcus will lead a small team on a special mission, and until we receive an update from his team, the rest of us will focus on our day-to-day tasks."

She glanced over the gathering, her sharp gaze scanning the room as though searching for a reaction—an unspoken question hanging in the air.

"For those who want to know," Riya began, her tone measured but firm, "the crystal will be taken to the artifact at the water extraction site. All our research on the artifact so far builds up to a map—a network of coordinates. We need further tests to validate what we've found, and today's mission is part of that effort. Marcus and his team will be conducting one of these tests."

Riya shared only what was necessary, carefully treading the line between transparency and control. She provided just enough information to keep speculation at bay, ensuring the crew remained focused without feeding the kind of uncertainty that could spiral into panic. Yet, she held back the full scope of the mission—not out of deception, but out of necessity. Some truths, if revealed too soon, would only ignite fear rather than prepare them.

Elena stood beside the wall, her shoulder pressed against its cold, unyielding surface. She leaned into it, as if grounding herself against the weight of her thoughts, her mind drifting in endless loops. The hum of the colony around her faded into the background—just distant voices and mechanical murmurs, none of it reaching her.

She was visibly shaken from the previous night. The exhaustion from lack of sleep weighed heavily on her, amplifying the anxiety that had been gnawing at her since the revelation. The overwhelming sense of being thrust into the spotlight, of becoming the singular focus out of hundred colonists, left her feeling vulnerable and exposed. Depression lingered at the edges of her thoughts, making it difficult to separate the weight of her emotions from the magnitude of the situation. She kept her head low, trying to disappear into the crowd, even as she wrestled with the unsettling reality that she could no longer avoid.

The meeting adjourned, and the room emptied as people scattered, their murmurs fading into the distance. Elena remained still, lost in the undertow of her thoughts, drifting somewhere far beyond the confines of the colony.

She barely registered Riya's presence until a firm but gentle hand rested on her shoulder. The touch pulled her back, grounding her in the moment. She exhaled sharply, suddenly aware of how far away she had been—not in distance, but in thought.

"You must rest," Riya said, her tone soft but insistent, choosing not to acknowledge Elena's distraction outright. It was less an order, more a quiet attempt at persuasion.

Elena let out a hollow sigh, shaking her head slightly. "I think we all do…" she murmured, her voice edged with exhaustion.

She glanced toward the empty room before adding, almost as an afterthought, "…once this is finished."

#

Elena found herself unsure of what she truly wanted, a complete contrast to the enthusiasm and curiosity she once felt. The thought of being at the water extraction site to witness the outcome—something she would have eagerly anticipated—now left her conflicted. The weight of uncertainty pressed down on her, not just about the mission or the crystal, but about her own place in all of it. She wasn't even sure what to do in the next minute, the next hour, or even the days ahead.

She tried immersing herself in the greenhouse, seeking solace in the plants she'd always found comfort in, but their quiet growth failed to calm her racing thoughts. She went for a walk outside, hoping the Martian expanse might offer clarity, but the emptiness only seemed to mirror her own. She climbed to *"The Sky"*, looking for peace in its panoramic views, but the vastness of the horizon only amplified her restlessness. Finally, she retreated to her quarters, packing herself away from the world, but even there, the unease followed her, refusing to let her be.

#

Back at the water extraction site—now affectionately dubbed *"the waterhole"*—Sonja and David stood waiting for Marcus and his team to arrive with the crystal. The atmosphere was charged with anticipation, though a subtle tension lingered beneath the surface. Marcus insisted on following a slew of protocols before mobilizing the artifact. He was strict about not cutting any corners, knowing the stakes were far too high.

Minutes stretched into what felt like days for David, the anticipation gnawing at his usually calm character. Finally, the team arrived, carrying a sleek, space-grade Pelican case that housed the crystal. The case itself was meticulously engineered, designed for utmost security and stability. Inside, the crystal was carefully suspended within a magnetically levitated cylindrical chamber, preventing any physical contact or unnecessary vibrations.

The built-in display on the front of the case registered a spike, revealing activity on the spectrum analyzer.

"Activity was increasing as it reaches here," Marcus remarked, his tone neutral but edged with unease.

Then, almost to himself, he added, "What'll happen next? I just hope we live long enough to learn."

His grim joke hung in the air, met with silence from the others. No one even cracked a smile; the tension was too thick, and the implications of the artifact's behavior were far too heavy to entertain levity. All eyes remained fixed on the case, each person silently bracing for what was to come.

As they carefully began lowering the crystal out of its magnetic confinement and into the borehole, the hum grew louder, a low, resonant vibration that seemed to echo in their chests. The glow intensified, casting flickering, alien light against the walls of the borehole, and the crystal itself appeared to pulse with energy, growing more and more dynamic with each passing moment.

The ice above the artifact, already cleared, exposed its raw form—still mostly embedded within the thick layers below.

The crystal was bustling with activity, but the artifact bellow was all mute and dormant.

Like the Martian landscape itself, the stillness was about to change.

While in the habitat, sounds were echoing in Elena's head.

"It's a key"

She pressed her palms firmly against her ears, as if trying to physically squeeze out the sounds that echoed relentlessly inside her head.

A knock on her cabin door pulled her from the spiral of her mind. She wasn't expecting anyone, nor was she in the mood for company. Yet, when the display on the wall lit up, showing Riya standing at her door, Elena hesitated. Ignoring the commander of the colony wasn't exactly an option, even under her current state of mind. But with Riya, it wasn't just about rank—she was much more than a leader to Elena.

Somehow, Riya had become a source of comfort, a steady presence amidst the chaos. Elena already felt like a child looking up to her mother when Riya was around. Sighing softly, she stood up, brushing her hair back and trying to compose herself before opening the door.

"I'm tired. Can I join?" Riya's voice was soft, almost pleading, a tone so unexpected it caught Elena completely by surprise.

Contrary to what she had expected—a command, a status check, or even a word of encouragement—the vulnerability in Riya's tone disarmed her. For a moment, Elena just stood there, uncertain how to respond, the weight of her own turmoil momentarily replaced by a flicker of connection. She stepped aside, nodding silently, allowing Riya to enter.

Both sat on the bed, each on opposite sides, their backs against the bed-head, facing the display on the front. The screen flickered with information about various systems—status updates, metrics, and graphs—but neither paid it any real attention. For both, the data blurred into meaningless shapes, their thoughts elsewhere, heavy and unspoken.

"Aren't you supposed to be elsewhere?" Elena asked, her voice almost stumbling over the words.

"I'm exactly where I needed to be," Riya responded firmly, her tone steady but kind.

"The team knows what to do," she added after a pause, her gaze softening.

"Do you?"

That question broke something inside Elena. The emotions she had been trying to suppress erupted in an uncontrollable wave, and she burst into tears, her body shaking as the weight she carried finally spilled over.

Without hesitation, Riya pulled her close, dragging Elena onto her shoulder. She gently tapped her head, slow and rhythmic, like a mother soothing a child in distress. Her presence was calming, her silent reassurance more powerful than any words could have been. The two sat there in the dim light, one pouring out everything she'd been holding back, and the other offering the quiet strength needed to hold her together.

#

A meeting was called just before daybreak, the crisp morning air still heavy with the weight of anticipation. Riya and the team from the waterhole stood waiting at the front of the room, their enthusiasm intense as the rest of the colony slowly assembled. From the corner of her eye, Riya caught a glimpse of Elena leaning quietly against a doorway at the far end, her posture subdued but present—a quiet reassurance that she was there.

Unusual for a status meeting, a box of dehydrated juice sat conspicuously on the table, drawing a few curious glances. Riya stepped forward, picking up a glass of water and emptying the contents of a satchel into it. As the liquid swirled and turned vibrant, she raised the glass high, her voice steady and proud.

"Let's drink to the achievement," she said, her gaze sweeping the room, inviting them all to share in the moment.

The waterhole team was visibly cheerful, their energy infectious as they exchanged knowing smiles and hushed whispers. In stern contrast, the rest of the crew looked almost dumbfounded, their expressions a mix of confusion and curiosity as they tried to process the unexpected celebration.

"Let's save everyone from the suspense," Riya said with a faint smile, her voice steady as she gestured toward the front of the room.

"Sonja, Marcus—go ahead and explain."

"I've seen nothing like it before," Sonja began, her voice carrying just the right amount of drama to pull everyone in.

"And that's something, considering I've seen thousands of drill holes in my career."

The room leaned forward slightly; curiosity piqued.

"Let's cut to it," Marcus interjected, his tone expressive, laced with intrigue.

"The crystal… it was a key."

His words hung in the air for a moment, the weight of them sinking in as the room exchanged puzzled and expectant glances, waiting for the revelation to unfold.

The words landed like an arrow shot through the room, straight to Elena. Her eyes widened, her mouth falling slightly open, as if the weight of the revelation had physically struck her. It wasn't exactly a surprise—deep down, she had already knew within her. But hearing it spoken aloud brought a sense of closure, a realization that she could not escape the role the crystal—and perhaps herself—was destined to play.

With a nudge of encouragement from Sonja, Marcus found his voice and began, his tone animated and unrestrained.

Marcus leaned forward, eyes gleaming with an almost reckless excitement.

"The moment that crystal hit the artifact—BOOM—it came to life, like flipping a switch on something that had been waiting, just waiting, biding its time for who knows how long." His voice picked up speed, hands flying as he spoke, like even words couldn't keep up with what he was trying to describe.

"Nah, scratch that—this wasn't no simple switch flip. This was a whole damn beast waking up! Like a generator kicking in full throttle, or hell, a starship revving up for liftoff. That hum? That wasn't just sound. You felt it—deep—shaking the walls, rattling through your chest, like the whole damn planet just took a breath and decided to move."

He let the silence stretch for a moment, his gaze darting around the room, feeding off the tension.

Trying to keep his excitement in check, he took a breath. "And for a split second? We thought we were done. Like we'd just triggered some ancient, buried system that was about to wipe us off the map. It felt like standing next to a bomb, heart pounding, waiting—not sure if the countdown had already hit zero or if we were just too late to hear it.”

He exhaled sharply, the adrenaline still thrumming beneath his skin.

“But it didn't explode. It… woke up.”

The way he shot out the words, less burdened and almost playful, drew some nervous chuckles from the group. But his vivid description left no doubt about the intensity of the moment, and the room buzzed with unease and intrigue.

“All of that,” Marcus continued, “was just for a moment. Everything calmed down after, and then we saw it—the artifact lit up with the same kind of symbols, shimmer, and light. It was alive, in a way we'd never seen before.” He paused, his expression growing more serious.

“So we thought, hey, let's pull the crystal out, stop whatever was happening. And we did.” Marcus hesitated, raising an eyebrow as the room held its collective breath.

“Only, it wasn't meant to stop. The pull didn't stop the activity. But then, something else happened—the water surrounding it started melting.”

Sonja stepped in, her voice calm but laced with unease.

“At first, I thought the water would keep melting and the entire site would collapse into a sinkhole. That's what my education and experience wanted me to believe.”

Marcus picked up again, his tone a mix of dry humor and gravity.

“It didn't. Thank the stars. But honestly? Even if it had—man, we wouldn't have been able to do a damn thing but stand there and go down with it—just a bunch of fools staring at our own doom saying, 'damn, guess this is it.'”

His words landed with a weight that pressed into the room, silencing any lingering chuckles as the gravity of their discovery began to fully sink in.

"The artifact was melting just enough water, probably about a meter around its vicinity," Sonja explained, her voice measured as she recounted the phenomenon.

"And it was suspending on that water, like an ice cube floating perfectly in equilibrium."

She paused, her gaze sweeping the room before continuing.

"After leaving it for a few hours to do its thing, we didn't notice much change. The water temperature stabilized at around eighteen degrees Celsius, while the surrounding ice remained well below freezing."

Sonja's tone shifted, a mix of awe and curiosity creeping in.

"It's almost like my *PyroTherma* head—except it's from a thousand years in the future. Doing the same thing, but with no visible power source and so much more control. Almost with… a kind of grace."

Her words lingered, the comparison driving home just how far beyond their understanding the artifact truly was.

She added, "Now it's just a matter of pumping the water out. It's like an ordinary well—except this one comes with technology that melts just enough water as we consume it."

While the rest of the team erupted in cheers, finally allowing themselves a moment of joy and relief from the relentless uncertainties and tension, Elena remained in the same posture, leaning silently against the wall. Her thoughts were far away, lost in a tangle of questions and emotions that the celebration couldn't reach.

She barely noticed the sounds of laughter and clinking glasses around her until the sharp snap of two fingers slipping in front of her face jolted her from the trance.

"Is our Elena here?" Marcus asked in a playful tone, his other arm slung casually over David's shoulder—a sight so unexpected it momentarily distracted everyone nearby.

Elena, still trying to settle from her trance, forced a smile, though it felt more like an effort than an expression.

"I'm… not so sure," she replied, her voice soft and distant, the words slipping out almost involuntarily.

"I have to go," Elena said abruptly, her voice wavering as she turned away from Marcus and David.

Without waiting for a response, she disappeared into the corridor, her steps quick and purposeful. The cheerful atmosphere for the two seemed to dim slightly in her absence, exchanging uneasy glances, unsure whether to follow or let her be.

Behind them, Riya's calm voice broke the silence. "She needs time, you know it," it was more of a pledge than an order.

Chapter Six
CRISIS

The Martian dawn unfolded in its quiet, unhurried way, casting the horizon in muted shades of dusty gold and rust-red. There was no grand spectacle, no brilliance—just the steady, indifferent turning of a world that had long existed without them. Inside the habitat, the colonists moved with calm efficiency, their motions purposeful yet lighter than they had been in days. After the rift between opposing ideologies had frayed trust, this return to routine felt like a fragile but necessary truce.

The discovery of the waterhole had changed everything. It was more than just a resource; it was proof—proof that survival here was not just a dream, proof that Mars had something to offer beyond dust and struggle. The steady hum of the habitat's systems filled the air, a rhythmic reassurance, a heartbeat in this foreign land. For the first time in what felt like forever, life on Mars felt almost… ordinary.

Elena found a quiet serenity in the greenhouse, though some whispered it was a self-imposed imprisonment. Surrounded by the gentle presence of the plants she so carefully nurtured, she spent her days from dawn to dusk tending to the crops in solitude. Noah had become a regular companion, his presence a fixture in the quiet space.

Though Dr. Noah held seniority in both age and academic tenure, Elena's contributions to research far outpaced his. While she had earned her doctorate long after him, her relentless pursuit of discovery had led to a wealth of published papers, groundbreaking studies, and a few dozen patents tied to her research. Dr. Noah, on the other hand, was a man of the field—quite literally. His roots traced back to his farm-boy upbringing, a past that shaped his preference for hands-on work over theoretical study. Splitting his time between agricultural research and lecturing at Cornell University, he thrived in the practical application of science, where soil, crops, and climate data spoke louder than lab results.

Despite their different approaches, mutual respect anchored their relationship. They understood each other's strengths, recognizing where one's expertise began and the other's took over. Elena knew when to defer to Noah's field instincts, while he trusted her data-driven precision in pushing the boundaries of their research. They didn't always agree, but they never had to—because in the end, they could depend on each other when it mattered most.

During recent times, Noah's attempts at conversation with Elena were mostly one-sided, a steady stream of words that filled the stillness, even as it was clear that Elena preferred the silence. Yet, Noah didn't seem to mind—or perhaps he simply chose not to notice. He carried on with his musings, observations, and occasional jokes, as if the act of speaking itself was enough. It had become a ritual for him, one he never failed to uphold, and in its own way, it created a balance between them, unspoken yet understood.

The warm, controlled air of the greenhouse hums with life, the scent of damp soil and chlorophyll filling the space. Rows of experimental crops stretch beneath the artificial lights, their green a striking contrast against the red world outside. Dr. Noah kneels beside a row of wheat, carefully inspecting the golden stalks while Elena stands nearby, arms crossed, her gaze distant.

Noah running a hand through the wheat stalks, "You see this? This right here is what I was talking about last week. The hybrid took better than I expected—look at that stem structure. Stronger, denser, and it's holding moisture better than batch three. That's a damn miracle considering what we started with." He plucks a kernel, rolls it between his fingers, inspecting its texture.

Elena nodded, "Mm."

Oblivious to her lack of engagement, grinning as he gestures to the wheat, Noah continued.

"Now, the key here wasn't just the modified root system, but the microbial inoculant we introduced. You remember how batch two kept yellowing too soon? Turns out, the nitrogen fixation wasn't efficient enough—had to tweak the bacterial strain to mimic a terrestrial rhizosphere better. And guess what? It worked."

He chuckles to himself, standing up, wiping his hands on his pants.

"That's good.", Elena was blinking, barely following

Noah continued, energized, gestured animatedly.

"Good?… Elena, this is phenomenal! We're talking about wheat that can grow in a closed Martian ecosystem with minimal input, better resilience to CO_2 fluctuations, and—get this—I ran some projections, and if we scale this up, we could increase yield by twenty percent with less water. You know what that means?"

Elena with a half-hearted shrug, "More wheat?"

With a laugh and shaking his head, Noah said, "More food, Elena. More security. This could be the breakthrough we need for long-term sustainability here. We're not just surviving anymore—we're building something." He steps back, admiring the crops as if they were a work of art.

Elena quietly gazed, still distant, "Yeah."

Finally noticing her silence, tilts his head, "You okay?"

Blinking, then finally meeting his gaze, Elena whispered, "Just tired."

Noah paused, then nodded, giving her an understanding smile, "Yeah, I get that. But hey, if we keep this up, we'll be eating real Martian bread soon. Just you wait."

Elena gives a faint, tired smile—more out of politeness than enthusiasm. Noah, still beaming with excitement, turns back to the wheat, already launching into another enthusiastic explanation. She lets him talk, his voice filling the space where her own thoughts have begun to drown her in silence.

#

Meanwhile, David and the team studying the crystal and artifacts clearly noticed her silence, and her continued absence from the lab.

"Elena should have been a part of the water project," Ada whispered to Liam as they worked.

Without breaking his focus or glancing up, Liam replied curtly, "She was."

"No, she wasn't," Ada countered, leaning in slightly. "She wasn't there the day the crystal was used at the site."

"She must have been busy," Liam responded casually, still focused on his task, his tone making it clear he had no interest in the conversation.

Ada, lowering her pitch to maintain the gossip, added, "It's not just us talking."

It didn't take long for a few others to overhear and join the conversation, their whispers elevated until the chatter snowballed into a full-blown nuisance. Liam, his patience worn thin, finally snapped.

"Can you take it elsewhere?" he said sharply, dissolving the unwelcome gathering with a single sentence.

The group dispersed awkwardly, leaving Liam to his work, though the unspoken questions about Elena lingered in the air.

David had tried to reach Elena at the greenhouse several times, his concern mounting with each unwelcome attempt. But her message was abundantly clear—she preferred solitude. Realizing the boundaries she had set, whether intentionally or not, David eventually gave up, opting to respect her need for space. Even so, he couldn't shake the lingering worry. How long would she remain withdrawn? And would she ever return to being the vibrant, capable person they had all grown to admire?

"I haven't seen Elena in the greenhouse today," Marcus asked Staff, catching him as he returned from a recent filter change in the greenhouse.

"She was there," Staff replied, adjusting his equipment.

"I saw her near the far end of the potato section. I think they're testing a new nutrient formula or something. The filters seem to clog a little too often lately," he added, shrugging.

Marcus nodded thoughtfully but said nothing, the brief exchange leaving him with uncertainty about Elena's reclusive routine.

Eos Horizon stood silently in its resting place, like Sphinx in the desert, overlooking the colony like a watchful parent observing children at play.

"What brings you here?" Dr. Myers greeted warmly as Riya stepped through the airlock of *Eos Horizon*.

His wide smile radiated genuine warmth and affection, the kind that came with the relief of knowing Riya wasn't visiting the sickbay for treatment. Visits to the ship were rare, usually only happening when medical attention required—absence of people, Myers often remarked was a good sign. After all, no visitors typically meant everything was running smoothly, a quiet success in the harsh Martian environment.

For Riya, the sight of Myers's friendly attitude brought a small but needed sense of relief. In his presence, she felt a rare touch of comfort, knowing she had found someone she could talk to—an uncommon luxury for a leader constantly carrying the weight of the colony on her shoulders.

Both of them sat on the sofa across from each other, the small coffee table between them lending a sense of casual intimacy to the conversation. They were in Dr. Myers's private quarters, a space of quiet and personal comfort aboard the *Eos Horizon*.

Dr. Myers had prepared coffee for Riya and tea for himself, the beverages a perfect reflection of their individual tastes. Thanks to the ship's system, everyone's personal drinking preferences were logged, making it as simple as pressing a button on the dispenser to craft the exact drink each person preferred. Riya cradled the warm cup in her hands, appreciating the small but meaningful gesture as they settled into the moment.

Riya's visits to Dr. Myers were rare, and when they happen, Myers knew immediately they weren't casual. Her presence in his quarters carried an unspoken weight, a signal that something significant was on her mind.

"It's Elena, isn't it?" Myers asked, his tone gentle yet probing as he leaned forward slightly, his eyebrows raised in curiosity.

"Yes," Riya replied with a sigh. "I'm worried."

"Do you think she's… impaired?" Myers asked, his brow furrowing, his question carrying a weight that only added to Riya's concern.

"I don't know," Riya admitted, her voice steady but tinged with unease.

"She's sound in her day-to-day work, no slip-ups there. But she's too absorbed in the greenhouse—almost consumed by it. And that's why I'm worried." She paused, her fingers tracing the edge of her coffee cup.

"It's not just her focus; it's the way she's shut herself off from everything else. I can't tell if it's coping or something more."

Myers paused for a moment, his expression thoughtful. "Our systems continuously monitor the vitals of all individuals," he said, his tone measured.

"Through Orion, we're keeping track of their parameters—heart rate, stress levels, sleep cycles. Medically, there's nothing concerning about Elena. She's perfectly healthy."

He leaned back slightly, his gaze shifting as he considered his next words.

"However," he added, his voice softening, "psychology is a very different matter. Withdrawal, especially prolonged, is not a good sign. It can be a coping mechanism, yes, but it can also be a precursor to something deeper. Something we need to watch closely."

Myers's calm appearance didn't mask the seriousness of his concern, his words lingering heavily in the room.

Riya paused, her body sinking deeper into the cushion as though testing its ability to bear the weight of what she was about to say. She adjusted her posture subtly, her fingers tracing the edge of her coffee cup, buying a moment of quiet before speaking. The silence between them grew heavier, the air charged with the significance of the words she was preparing to release.

"There's something you need to know," Riya said, her eyes serious and unwavering.

Dr. Myers listened intently, his eyes fixed on Riya as she recounted the events at *"The Sky"* with a mix of care and enthusiasm. Her words painted a vivid picture of Elena's emotional meltdown that night—the way she had crumbled under the weight of it all—and the slow, steady withdrawal from the society that followed.

Myers nodded occasionally, his expression a careful balance of professionalism and genuine concern, processing every detail with the precision of a man who understood that no part of this story could be overlooked.

With his forehead slightly raised, Dr. Myers leaned back thoughtfully and added, "So, this is the backstory to our water independence."

His words carried a mix of gravity and irony, acknowledging the monumental progress they had made while hinting at the personal toll it had taken on Elena.

"I don't know what to say," Myers admitted, nodding slowly as he exhaled a heavy breath.

"We'd typically call something like this a delusion—a known psychological condition, one that can be treated. And we're well equipped for that," he added, his tone measured but thoughtful.

He paused, rubbing his temple, a flicker of doubt crossing his face. "But I'm not so sure anymore."

His gaze drifted to the cup in his hands. "How can we call it a delusion when I'm sitting here, sipping tea made from the very water that so-called delusion resolved?"

His voice carried the weight of confusion, a man of science grappling with the inexplicable, caught between logic and the uncharted depths of the unknown.

"We give her time," Myers said, his voice steady but compassionate as he leaned forward slightly.

"And let's keep a close eye on her." His words carried a quiet resolve.

"Label a sane as lost to reason, simply for what we fail to understand, is a grave and reckless mistake," Myers added, his voice weighted with meaning as Riya rose to leave. His words lingered in the air, heavy with an unspoken plea for compassion and caution. It was more than a reminder—it was a profound acknowledgment of the fragile path where human nature intersected with the mysteries and unknowns that now stood at their doorstep.

Riya nodded slightly, a gesture of both acknowledgment and gratitude. The conversation had offered her a sense of clarity, and though the burden of leadership remained, sharing it, even briefly, left her feeling a little lighter. As she stepped out of Myers's quarters, she allowed herself a quiet exhale, appreciating the rare moment of companionship and support.

#

Elena was an unmistakable figure in the greenhouse, her presence as constant as the plants she nurtured. Some believed she had rediscovered her purpose in her roots as an agricultural scientist, pouring herself into the work that sustained the colony. Yet, her lack of interaction with others and her deliberate avoidance of the crystal, the lab and the rest of it, gave rise to rumors, gossip, and endless stories—fodder for a colony eager to fill the void with speculation and intrigue.

For Elena, the plants were her solace—a quiet refuge from the noise of the colony. Attending to a row of carrots that had finally shown signs of recovery, she might have thought they needed her more than anything else. The faint but unmistakable scent of soil filled the air, grounding her in a way the sterile metal walls of the habitat never could. She adjusted the irrigation settings, now fed by the precious Martian well, her movements precise and deliberate. Even though the water seemed abundant, she was careful not to waste a single drop, mindful of the fragile balance they were striving to maintain.

From the corner of her eye, she noticed Sabine entering, her face brightened by an uncharacteristic smile.

"Guess what?" Sabine said, holding up a tablet.

"The bio-dome data has been reviewed, and while the experiment failed, we've identified three gene expressions that might make the next batch of crops more resilient."

Elena allowed herself a faint smile, her gaze lifting from the tablet. "Good," she said simply, her tone measured but calm and abrupt.

"It's more than good," Sabine said in a low tone, her voice carrying a faint note of exasperation as she withdrew the table.

"It's a road-map. We might actually be onto something here." Her words hung in the air, charged with a mix of excitement and cautious optimism.

#

Dr. Sabine Falk, age forty-one, was born beneath the watchful towers of Heidelberg, her childhood steeped in the sterile scent of laboratories and the hum of research discussions at the dinner table. Her parents, both renowned biochemists, spent their lives decoding the intricate chemistry of pharmaceuticals, hoping to heal the body. But Sabine? She was drawn to something older, something more primal—the quiet resilience of life itself. While others saw soil as dirt, she saw it as history, memory, and the very essence of survival. She didn't want to alter human cells in test tubes; she wanted to bend nature to her will, to craft plants that could defy extinction.

She pursued Plant Biotechnology & Genetics at Göttingen, later earning a PhD in Agricultural Science from Wageningen University, a temple of agricultural innovation. There, her research became an obsession—genetic resilience, life forged under scarcity, the dream of crops that could survive where life had no right to exist. Her work took her to the sun-scorched deserts of Africa and the Middle East, where she coaxed wheat from dust, summoned green from sand, and whispered instructions into the very DNA of plants. She stood among the ruins of failed farms and made the soil breathe again. This was her power, her creation, her dominion.

It was this mastery that led her to Mars. Her name became known in the highest scientific circles, her breakthroughs landing her a lead role in the Mars Agriculture and Sustainability Program, which brought her to UNSI's attention. If humanity was to survive beyond Earth, they would need to rewrite the language of life itself, and Sabine was more than willing to wield the pen.

But for all the life she nurtured, her own had slipped through her fingers. A string of failed relationships, a marriage that wilted like an over-watered seedling. She had loved once—fiercely—but never more than her work. Her hands, meant for lovers, were always buried in soil and petri dishes instead.

She had a daughter—a piece of herself—but lost her, not to death, but to a court ruling that deemed her too devoted to her lab to be a mother. It stung, but deep down, she understood. She could cultivate life, but she was never meant to hold onto it.

The power to manipulate genes, to make crops withstand the impossible, made her feel godlike—not in arrogance, but in creation itself. She had no need for men; her love affair was with evolution, her desire written in the twisting strands of DNA. While others sought comfort in human touch, she found divinity in the quiet germination of a seed, in the resilience of life that bent—but never broke.

#

Across the habitat, Riya Kapoor was reviewing the colony's weekly status report in the command center. Supplies were holding steady, thanks to careful rationing, but the margins were thin. The colony's reliance on the artifact and crystal for purified water had stabilized some processes, but the unknowns surrounding them still made her uneasy.

Scientists are still grappling with the technology surrounding the artifacts, making little progress in unraveling their mysteries. Even Sabine, with her extensive expertise in resource exploration and extraction, finds herself at odds with the mechanism behind the water production at the waterhole. The process defies her understanding, leaving her uncertain about its long-term sustainability.

The colony's water supply remains entirely dependent on the artifact for melting and purification, a precarious reliance that leaves her uneasy. While Sabine has the skills and contingency plans to implement an alternative method, she knows it would be far less efficient and significantly less elegant than the current process. For now, they are at the mercy of the artifact, a fragile reality that underscores the colony's vulnerability.

Despite the uncertainties and their tenuous grasp of the situation, there were no significant changes in the colony, except for the shifting weather and the ever-present crimson hues of the Martian landscape. The air grew heavier with each passing day, thick with unspoken tension, and something else—a calm before the storm.

A storm, or so they thought—figuratively!

"Noah," Marcus's voice cut through the quiet of the greenhouse, sliding across the space like a sudden gust.

"Is everything around here secured?" he asked, his tone sharp as his eyes scanned the area, methodically checking for anything out of place.

"Storm, you mean?" Noah replied, glancing up from his work. His tone was steady.

"All good, nothing to report," he added, giving a slight nod toward the greenhouse systems.

"We'll be ready to switch to emergency mode at a moment's notice" he paused, "and evacuate."

His words were calm, but the undertone of preparedness was clear, matching the quiet vigilance that hung over the colony.

Marcus's eyes flickered to the far corner of the greenhouse, catching a subtle movement. There she was—Elena—her head slowly lifting, her gaze meeting his.

"El... er—"

The words stalled in his throat, tangled between hesitation and something deeper, something he wasn't ready to name. His breath hitched. A battle waged inside him—one he wasn't sure he wanted to win.

For a moment, he stood frozen, as if forcing the words out would unravel something he wasn't prepared to face. Then, with a heavy sigh, he turned abruptly, his steps quick, unsteady. He didn't look back.

Within seconds, he was gone—fading into the distance, leaving nothing but silence in his wake.

Elena had once been like a sister to Marcus, someone he could always rely on, someone who understood him without the need for words. Now, she felt so distant, as though she belonged to another world entirely. The feeling of detachment reminded him of when his two sisters had eventually moved out of his life—similar in its ache, yet different in its weight. This wasn't a natural parting; it was a growing void, one he didn't know how to bridge.

The change weighed heavily on Marcus as he made his way toward the quarantine valley, his steps steady but his mind restless. He couldn't shake the thought of how much Elena had withdrawn, leaving behind a silence that felt almost impenetrable. He wanted to reach her, to understand, but the space between them seemed wider than ever, and he didn't know if that ever could be fixed.

As much as Elena pushed others away, she got exactly what she asked for. David, Marcus, and even Riya had begun to carry on as if she wasn't part of the team. Greenhouse briefings, once her domain, were now mostly handled by Noah and Sabine, while Elena sat quietly at the far end of the briefing room, only attending because it was unavoidable. Her presence was more shadow than substance, a stark reminder of how much she had withdrawn.

Riya, watching from a distance, carried the quiet patience of a loving mother. She had expected Elena to eventually reach out, to come to her when ready. But as the days stretched on, Riya found herself waiting, her hope tempered by the growing distance that seemed harder and harder to stitch.

#

Outside, the Martian sky began to shift, a subtle but profound change rippling through the atmosphere—something different, something the colony had never experienced before. The familiar hues of crimson and gold gave way to an unsettling haze, as if the planet itself was awakening, ready to reveal a new set of mysteries. The stillness, once a comforting constant, now carried an undercurrent of unease, a quiet but undeniable warning that something was brewing on the horizon.

At first, it was nothing—just a deepening of the ever-present Martian haze, a whisper on the horizon that blended too easily into the rust-colored sky. They had seen storms before, had weathered the planet's brutal tempests more than once since landing. But this one was different.

The warning came not from instinct, but from the cold, unwavering certainty of data. The sensors caught it first—air pressure plummeting, wind speeds climbing, dust density rising beyond normal parameters. Streams of numbers flooded into the command centre, silent but urgent, a whisper turning into a scream.

Marcus entered, his face carved in stone, a tablet gripped tightly in his hands. He didn't waste time.

"Commander."

Riya looked up instantly. Marcus rarely called her that. Not in casual conversation, not even in tense mission debriefs. The title was reserved for moments when the situation demanded absolute authority—when there was no room for argument or hesitation.

A slow dread settled in her chest. "What is it?"

Marcus exhaled, jaw tightening as he passed her the tablet.

"The storm we were expecting… it's not what we thought. It's the biggest one ever recorded."

Riya's eyes traced the screen, and her breath stalled.

The storm wasn't just big. It was colossal.

A churning behemoth, stretching thousands of kilometers across the planet, a dust leviathan whose winds roared at speeds that could shred their external structures apart like brittle glass. It was moving fast—too fast. The colony, their fragile sanctuary against an unforgiving world, was directly in its path.

The room felt smaller, heavier. For a single, terrible moment, the weight of it hung in the air—an invisible force pressing against them like the coming wind.

"How long do we have?" she asked.

"About six hours," Marcus replied.

"Maybe less if it accelerates."

Riya's mind raced. She activated the habitat's alert system, her voice calm but firm as she addressed the colony.

"Attention, everyone. A major dust storm is approaching. All outdoor activities are suspended immediately. Return to the habitat and secure all systems. This is not a drill. Repeat This is not a drill"

The storm arrived faster than anyone had anticipated. The Martian sky turned from rust-red to an ominous shade of gray, then black. Winds howled around the habitat, carrying with them the fine, abrasive dust that coated every surface it touched. The solar arrays were the first to succumb, their panels quickly buried under layers of sediment.

Inside, the colonists worked with focused urgency to secure the habitat. Marcus led the effort to protect the power systems, Cutting off the solar and redirecting all energy flow to the nuclear backup reactor. Elena, Noah and the team reinforced the greenhouse seals, their movements precise despite the rising tension.

"This storm isn't just big—it's relentless," Sabine said, her voice strained as she tightened a bolt.

"If it lasts too long, we'll lose more than the solar panels."

Elena didn't reply. She knew what Sabine meant. The crops, already stressed from the failed bio-dome experiment, wouldn't survive prolonged disruption.

All hundred colonists were swiftly withdrawn into the habitat as soon as their emergency outdoor activities were completed.

#

The colony has a meticulously designed emergency plan, prepared to address everything from dangerous threats to catastrophic, life-wiping scenarios. Yet, no amount of planning or rehearsing could truly compare to the reality of living through such an event.

At *Threat Level 1*, protocol dictated that everyone be contained inside the habitat dome.

For a *Threat Level 2* situation, access to deck areas would be strictly prohibited, and movement would be limited to the ground floor.

At *Threat Level 3*, the highest alert, colonists would be confined to their individual cabins, restrained if necessary.

These cabins, designed with survival in mind, were constructed from carbon-fiber-infused metal alloy, coated with a special ceramic layer on the exterior for added durability and temperature resistance. In the event of a catastrophic failure of the habitat dome, the cabins, which are individually sealed, offer a fighting chance for survival against extensive external forces. Each cabin equipped with enough water, oxygen, and food to sustain a grown adult for up to 10 days.

Beyond that window, a reality too grim to dwell on. In such a situation, where the last bastion of safety failed, no living being would endure. The cabins are the final lifeline.

At best of times, Earth could launch a salvage mission—which would take months to reach them. The engineered cabins, designed for resilience but not indefinite survival, could hold out for ten days at most. Simple math. Brutal reality. The numbers left no room for hope—only the harsh countdown to a fate they couldn't outrun.

This is still a level one threat, at least for now!

#

The storm raged on, sustaining itself at a steady level. Astraeus reported only minor external damage—nothing critical for now. Major sites, including the waterhole, greenhouse, fusion block, quarantine valley, and of course *Eos Horizon* had been sealed shut well in advance, their defenses holding against the relentless onslaught.

Inside the habitat, however, the colonists couldn't escape the ceaseless reminders of the danger outside. The scoring, grinding, and ripping noises of the storm clawed at the dome, a stark and unyielding symphony of Mars's hostility. Each sound was a jarring reminder of how fragile life was beyond the walls, a thin barrier separating survival from oblivion.

Riya ordered Astraeus to activate the dome's active noise cancellation system, hoping the silence would ease the nerves of those less hardened to the chaos outside. But she didn't want them completely detached from reality either. She encouraged them to visit the Circle—the Level One deck—where they could deactivate the noise filters, engage their in-ear auditory assistance, and experience the storm's full fury firsthand. Six months on this planet had bred a false sense of security, a dangerous complacency that worried her more than the storm itself.

The signs had been building—small medical incidents creeping up in frequency. Crew members stumbling over rocks, forgetting to check MSA seals properly, minor lapses that led to air leaks and breathing difficulties. Others had been less fortunate—rover rollovers, fractures from careless missteps on uneven ground. No single event was catastrophic, but together, they formed a troubling pattern, an erosion of caution that could one day cost them more than a broken bone. They needed to remember where they were. Riya hadn't wanted the storm to be their teacher, but if Mars had chosen this moment to remind them of its merciless nature, she wouldn't waste the lesson.

#

By the second day of the storm, the colony was running entirely on nuclear power. The backup reactor held steady, but the strain was evident in the flickering lights and occasional system hiccups. Crops in the greenhouse began to wilt as the ventilation system struggled to maintain proper humidity and temperature.

Riya called a meeting in the command center, her expression grim as she addressed the team.

"We need a plan to minimize losses. Prioritize the greenhouse, water and the food reserves. Marcus, what's the reactor's status?"

"It's stable for now," Marcus replied, "but it wasn't designed for this level of sustained use. If the storm doesn't ease soon…"

He didn't need to finish. Everyone in the room understood the implications. He eased the tension mentioning, they would use the other two reactors, on backup, which could sustain the dome and important infrastructure for quite some time.

"*Ship?*" she asked, her tone sharp with concern.

"Stable," Marcus assured her.

"The landing gear was dropped into the emergency position—it's got a low center of gravity to keep it balanced."

"We've activated the dome's medical bay," Dr. Myers added with a faint smile, his attempt at lightening the mood obvious.

"Just don't go breaking any bones, and we'll be fine." His words were casual, meant to calm the nerves, but the underlying tension in the room was unmistakable.

Riya acknowledged, with a comforting gesture.

"David," turning to him Riya asked. "Any changes with the artifact?"

David hesitated. "The signals have intensified," he admitted. "They're erratic—almost chaotic. The crystal's patterns are shifting too."

"What does that mean?" Marcus asked, his frustration evident.

"Is it causing the storm?"

"I don't know," David said, his tone defensive.

"But I'm monitoring it. We'll figure it out."

"Figure it out faster," Marcus snapped.

"We don't have time for this."

"Enough," Riya said sharply, silencing them both.

"We'll address the artifact after we stabilize the habitat. For now, focus on keeping us alive."

#

As the storm raged on, tensions within the colony spiked. Every task became a source of friction, every decision second-guessed. The artifact's signals continued to intensify, their frequency fluctuating in ways that disrupted the habitat's systems. Lights flickered, consoles froze, and the air recyclers emitted occasional bursts of static.

Without access to the lab in the quarantine valley, David's only option was remote monitoring. He stared at the artifact through the live feed, its glow pulsing with a strange, erratic rhythm. The crystal, now more active than ever, seemed to intensify its behavior, as if engaging in some silent conversation with its counterparts across the mysterious network. The synchronized hum had grown louder, reverberating like a low, ominous chant that seemed to resonate deep within the walls—and within David himself.

"David," Liam was requesting attention, his voice tight with urgency.

"It's not just reacting to the storm. Looks like it's syncing, perhaps amplifying it."

David turned sharply; his brows furrowed. "How do you know?"

Liam pointed at the data streams scrolling rapidly across his screen.

"The electromagnetic patterns," he explained.

"They're mirroring the storm's trajectory. The artifact isn't just responding—it's in sync with it!"

David's eyes narrowed as he processed Liam's words, the weight of the revelation settling like a heavy stone in the pit of his stomach. This was no coincidence—it was a connection.

The revelation sent a ripple of fear through the room. If the artifact was influencing the storm, their situation was far more precarious than they had realized. And as the storm showed no signs of abating, the question loomed over them like a shadow: what else might the artifact be capable of?

The news spread quickly throughout the dome—it was impossible to contain. Using the habitat dome's lab as a makeshift artifact monitoring station meant that nothing stayed under wraps for long. With a pack of increasingly restless individuals confined in close quarters, maintaining secrecy was futile.

#

Later into the night, Riya was summoned to the lab. A request for her presence was never casual—it always meant serious business. Inside, David, Marcus, and the rest were already waiting in tense suspension, anticipating her arrival. As the first officer, David had the authority and trust to make most decisions independently, backed by the crew's support. But when Riya was called in, it signaled that the situation had escalated far beyond routine matters. This wasn't something to be taken lightly.

"Are we at *Level 3* already?" Riya demanded as she rushed into the room, her voice cutting through the tense atmosphere.

"Not yet," David replied sharply, his tone steady but laced with an unsettling certainty.

"But we don't know for sure."

It was the kind of confidence that came from too much knowledge and too little control—precisely the kind no one wanted to hear in that moment. The unease in the room deepened, the weight of the unknown pressing down on everyone present.

He continued, "With enough certainty, we can say the crystal is linked— and it appears to be escalating the storm!"

"And we think that's the cause of the storm itself!"

A sharp silence fell over the room, so still that a needle dropping could have been heard.

Riya finally broke it, her tone firm. "Explain. What makes you say that?"

"Liam," David signed, stepping aside giving way for Liam to take the lead. All eyes shifted to him, the weight of the moment pressing heavily as Liam prepared to speak.

Most of the colony had retired to their cabins, with only a few still awake—and even fewer present in the room. In a way, the quiet of the night had provided a sense of privacy, an opportunity for a discussion of this gravity to unfold without the distractions of a full, restless colony. The subdued atmosphere seemed almost fitting for the weight of the conversation that was about to take place.

"The electromagnetic waves generated by the crystal seem to match the storm," Liam started, his tone steady but heavy with concern.

"They're slightly off right now, but they're moving toward perfect synchronization" he continued.

"It's as if the waves are wrapping around and intertwining with the storm, merging to the point where the signal becomes indistinguishable from the storm itself," David seems to translate what Liam was telling, and then glancing toward Liam for confirmation.

"It's not just electromagnetic waves," Liam interrupted, pointing to the display beside him.

"Thermals, and a significant portion of the spectrum, are also in sync."

The screen showed a swirling, intricate visualization of particles and waves, tangled together like an impossibly complex ball of yarn. It was mesmerizing, yet deeply unsettling—a chaotic dance that seemed to defy comprehension.

"It's just a matter of time," Liam said, his voice unsteady, betraying his usual calm.

"The energy levels will hit resonance, and when they do, the storm will peak."

Though his tone lacked polish, the gravity of his words was undeniable. It was clear that beneath his exterior, Liam was shaken, the implications of what he was describing weighing heavily on him—and everyone else in the room.

"Astraeus, what's the certainty?" Riya asked, her voice steady but edged with unease, as if she were seeking solace from the cold logic of a machine.

"With the calculated rate, the peak will occur in exactly 47 minutes. Certainty: 98.7 percent" Astraeus responded, its voice indeed cold and detached, offering no comfort in its precision.

Knowing this already, everyone else in the room seemed to have come to terms with the inevitability of it, their expressions resigned to the facts. Except for Riya. Her face remained taut, her eyes scanning the room as if searching for an alternative, unwilling to accept what felt like an unavoidable outcome.

"We can't be sitting ducks!" Riya's voice pierced through the tense silence, sharp and defiant, yet unwilling to accept.

"What do we have on the table, David, Marcus?" Riya shouted, her tone urgent, commanding action even as the weight of the situation bore down on her.

Unlike his usual tough exterior and unflinching expression, Marcus looked visibly shaken, his expression betraying an acceptance of the inevitable.

"We have a backup fusion core at the quarantine valley," he began, his voice steady but hollow.

"It can be… hacked to detonate. That would definitely disrupt the crystal's activity, though I have my doubts it would destroy it entirely."

David picked up where Marcus left off, his tone pragmatic yet grim.

"The shock-wave would disrupt the storm, at least in theory. It gives us a chance of survival."

"At what cost?" Riya demanded, her voice sharp.

David exhaled heavily before answering.

"Almost all our infrastructure would be destroyed, sparing the living cubes. We'd have to refuge there for ten days—the radiation levels should subside by then. We've got a cache of supplies buried underground specifically for emergencies like this. The waterhole should remain intact due to its distance, but everything else…" He trailed off, the implications hanging heavy in the air.

The room was silent for a moment, the weight of a decision pressing down on Riya.

"If that's the best cause of survival, lets…" she couldn't finish her sentence, Elena raised her voice from the darkness of the far end of the corridor.

#

"Let it be," Elena's voice rang out from the shadows at the far end of the corridor. It was clear, commanding, and authoritative—unlike the withdrawn woman they had in recent weeks, and even more striking at Riya's presence!

All eyes turned toward the sound of her voice, and within moments, Elena emerged, rushing into the room and stepping out of the eerie darkness of the corridor.

"The crystal," Elena began, her voice resonating with a newfound confidence that silenced the room.

"It's containing the storm."

She stepped further into the light, her eyes sharp and unwavering. "If it wasn't here, we'd already be wiped out!"

"And you know how!" David exclaimed.

"In your dreams?" Marcus blurted out, his voice rising involuntarily, the words spilling out before he could consider how offensive and inappropriate they sounded.

"Yes and no," Elena replied, her face devoid of expression as she pointed toward the display behind Liam.

"You already know that the electromagnetic forces are intertwined with the storm," she began, her tone calm but firm.

"When you interpolate the data from the very beginning of the storm, you'll notice something significant—the forces have been growing alongside the storm, subtly influencing its trajectory, almost as if guiding it."

She paused for a moment, letting the weight of her words settle before continuing.

"And if you look closely, you'll notice something unusual—the storm's energy levels remain remarkably stable, holding at a steady state. Yet, the crystal's influence wavers, fluctuating unpredictably, as if it's straining to contain something—to keep the chaos wrapped within a controlled envelope, but barely managing to hold on."

Her explanation was deliberate, each word carefully chosen, as if she were assembling a puzzle piece by piece for the room to understand.

"It's easy to jump to the conclusion that the electromagnetic forces are causing the storm, driving it to resonate at dangerous levels," she continued.

Elena nodded slightly in Liam's direction. "And Liam is absolutely correct in his analysis. Without understanding the crystal's role, it's easy to view it as a threat."

Unbeknown to the others, Liam had been quietly working at the console, his hands moving swiftly, almost like a magician performing a trick. Suddenly, he interrupted the discussion, his voice breaking through with urgency.

"Elena is right," he said, not looking up from the console. "The storm hasn't grown beyond a certain level. It's been sustaining itself for hours now, but the electromagnetic energy surrounding it has increased—and it's reaching overwhelming levels!"

The room sighed as Liam's revelation added a new confidence to the already tense discussion.

"Let the crystal do what it's designed for," Elena said confidently.

"We'll be fine."

"Shall we release the containment on the crystal?" Marcus asked, his tone unusually compliant, almost hesitant, like a child caught in mischief trying to make amends. It was a contrast to the confident, survival-driven soldier everyone expected him to be.

"No need," Elena responded, shaking her head gently.

"We won't be restraining it in any way." Then, to everyone's surprise, she smiled—a calm, reassuring gesture.

Trying to regain the hold of the situation, Riya turned to the room.

"David, Liam, everyone here—anything to add?" she asked, her tone firm but open.

"What Elena says is sound," David replied, his voice steady and measured.

He glanced briefly at the others before continuing, "Even if we are to blow it up, our survival chances would be grim, confined to the cubes."

He paused, letting his words settle in the room.

"We should let it unfold. I trust that's our best course of action."

His voice carried a quiet assurance, a steady presence amidst the tension, leaving no doubt about his stance.

"Then we wait," Riya declared firmly.

Turning to Elena, she paused deliberately before speaking.

"And you, young lady," she said, her tone sharp but not unkind, "We have to talk."

Elena met her gaze with a slight nod of acknowledgment.

"Yes, Ma'am," she replied softly, having a faint smile on her lips.

Riya scanned the room, taking in the exhaustion etched into every face before exhaling sharply.

"We're all running on fumes—get some rest. There's nothing more we can do for now." Her voice carried a quiet finality, a reluctant acknowledgment of their helplessness.

Without another word, Elena turned and disappeared into the corridor, her steps quiet but resolute.

Only a few could have anticipated what seemed to be unfolding the next day. The storm, once raging, had subsided to strong gusts—still too unsafe for venturing outside but a clear sign of improvement. The rest of the colony woke to the pleasant surprise of a weather forecast that promised calmer conditions soon, hinting at the prospect of stepping outside once again. Optimism began to creep into the atmosphere, replacing the tension of the days before.

If only they knew—it had all hinged on a single moment's decision, and the calm they were beginning to embrace had teetered on the edge of catastrophe.

It wasn't difficult for Riya to spot Elena at the corner of her eye, sitting quietly at a table, sipping her morning tea.

Without hesitation, Riya brewed her coffee, walked over, and sat down directly across from her, not bothering to ask for permission.

"You're welcome," Elena said, a faint hint of sarcasm in her voice as she nodded toward Riya.

"Where have you been?" Riya asked, her tone steady but weighted, the simple question distilling the past few months into a single moment.

"Right here" Elena replied, her voice calm but distant. She paused, her gaze lingering on her cup before looking up.

"I know," she added softly, her lips curving into a faint smile.

"Thanks for not giving up on me." Her tone carried a quiet sincerity, the weight of the past subtly woven into her words.

"What did you expect, throw you out without a helmet?" Riya said with a playful smirk, her tone light and teasing. She was trying to ease the tension, offering a warm welcome to the girl she had feared might have lost forever to the Martian dust.

Riya didn't fail to catch, out of the corner of her eye, Dr. Myers watching them from a distance. His expression was calm, and as he turned to walk away, a smile crept across his face, a silent acknowledgment of the moment he was dearly anticipating.

#

The day passed as the storm continued to recede, with everyone in the colony busy planning or preparing for the massive cleanup ahead.

Elena, however, had found herself at *"The Sky"*, a space that had almost become alien to her. Time seemed to slip away unnoticed as she stood there, quietly simmering in the serene presence of the moment. The Martian expanse stretched endlessly before her, and for the first time in a long while, she allowed herself to simply exist and let time fly.

She soon realized she wasn't alone. Riya, David, and Marcus had also gathered there on their own accord, each gravitating to their own corner of *"The Sky"*. Without words, they shared the stillness, the four of them basking in the unspoken tranquility of the moment. It was a rare, fragile reprieve—just shimmering in the now.

"I know an explanation is in demand," Elena said, breaking the silence. Her voice was steady but carried a hint of vulnerability. She turned her back to the setting sun, the fiery hues casting a warm glow on her body, as she tried to catch a glimpse of the others.

Almost in perfect sync, the three of them—Riya, David, and Marcus—turned toward her, their movements eerily choreographed, like a silent dance.

"Welcome back," David said softly, a compassionate look in his eyes.

"Worth the wait," Marcus added with a warm smile.

"I like a good story," Riya said, stepping closer, her tone light but her words carrying a deeper invitation. She stopped just short of Elena, her presence reassuring, as if to say she was ready to listen—no matter what the story might hold.

"Not sure where to start," Elena nodded, her voice quiet.

"That's as good place as any to start a story," Marcus chuckled, his tone light but curious. "I'm intrigued already."

"We've made a lot of progress with the markings on the crystal," David chimed in, his voice steady, slipping into the role of uninvited storyteller.

"Ever since the day we found your DNA marker on it, Ada's been cracking the code. Her hunch about the cuneiform choreography! Pure genius. The decoding has been pointing to an elaborate star map—which, sure, we already knew—but now..." He paused for emphasis, his eyes glinting with excitement.

"With a means to, well, sort of communicate with the crystal, what we're uncovering is nothing short of astonishing," David continued, his voice carrying the weight of their collective discovery.

"It's not just a map—it's something far more intricate than we ever imagined." His enthusiasm was infectious, pulling the room's attention entirely into the unfolding mystery.

"Now the problem is we have too much information, most of it without any clear correlation," David added, his tone laced with both frustration and awe.

"It's like handing Orion to an ancient tribe—we don't know what fits where or how to even begin using any of it."

"I think I can help," Elena said with a faint but familiar smile.

"The crystal operates on principles that delve into the quantum realm," Elena began, her tone calm but deliberate.

"It's no surprise that we don't understand most of it. Our classical way of thinking—the frameworks we're accustomed to—just can't grasp phenomena at this level."

She paused, searching for the right way to express the abstract nature of what she meant.

"It's not that we lack the intelligence; it's that we've been using our brains to solve problems in a way that doesn't align with this kind of reality."

"The crystal," she continued, her voice steady but weighted with significance, "isn't just a singular entity. It's connected to many others—a network, one that seems to operate on a scale far beyond what we can currently comprehend."

"As I said," Elena continued, her voice carrying a quiet intensity, "it's beyond the reality we understand—it moves within the quantum domain, though I lack the words or explanations to fully grasp it."

"There the rules are fundamentally different from anything we're used to." She paused, her lips curling into a faint smile.

"Which is why our electromagnetic confinement for the crystal is laughable," she said, the humor in her voice tempered by the gravity of her point. It wasn't mockery, but a candid acknowledgment of how little they truly understood the artifact's nature, or the forces at play.

"Some are similar, some slightly different. Each artifact has a task it was made for."

She noticed the raised eyebrows around her and quickly added, "Yes, they were made to sustain life. I'm not sure who made those, yet," she admitted, her tone calm but deliberate.

"And yes," she continued, almost like sensing what others about to ask!, "not just life on Mars, but on other places as well." She let her words hang for a moment, watching as the weight of the revelation sank into the room.

"You already know how the artifact at the waterhole is being used," Elena said, glancing at each person in turn, her gaze steady.

"That particular artifact was created to melt ice, filter it, and make it ready for consumption. It's not coincidence; it's purpose."

"When we touched the artifacts, and the crystal," Elena began, her tone measured but firm, "it took our DNA. It connected with those of us who came into contact with it on a deeper level—on what, for lack of a better term, I'd call a quantum world. Through this connection, it has learned how our biology works, adapting itself to sustain us."

"That information was then sent to the artifact at the waterhole," Elena continued, her voice calm but deliberate. "That's how it knew the exact temperatures and filtration levels our bodies require. It wasn't random—it was tailored for us."

She paused, letting the weight of her words settle before adding, "However, for it to activate, the crystal needed to touch it, as a key. Almost like a confirmation of our need—a signal that we were here, and that it was time to respond."

Her explanation carried a sense of eerie precision, the pieces of the puzzle coming together in a way that felt both awe-inspiring and deeply unsettling.

It was hard to gauge what the others were thinking; all three sat frozen, their eyes wider than usual and their mouths slightly ajar. The weight of Elena's words seemed to hang in the air, leaving them stunned, struggling to process the enormity of what she had just revealed.

Elena wasn't bothered by their stunned reactions. She seemed like the kid returning from first day of grade school, eager to share the experience, completely unaware of the weight her words carried for those around her.

"When the storm began to brew," Elena explained, her tone steady, "the crystal attuned itself to it, trying to calm it down. As you already know, this wasn't just an ordinary storm—it was a grave one, far beyond anything we'd faced before. The artifacts, working together, struggled to keep it under control."

She paused, her gaze unwavering as she continued, "The crystal wasn't designed to eliminate—it was designed to sustain life. Each artifact in the network has its own purpose, individually designed and tuned to protect life from the harshness of its environment. That's what they are meant to do, even in the face of chaos like this."

"If the crystal is the key," Marcus pondered, his voice thoughtful but laced with skepticism, "what are the odds that we'd find it on the very first artifact we encountered?"

Elena smiled faintly; her expression calm but knowing. "What makes you think that's the only crystal?" she asked, her tone almost teasing.

She leaned forward slightly, her gaze meeting Marcus's.

"If we had touched another artifact first, it would have revealed the crystal to us then. But once we've been given the crystal, any further interactions with other artifacts won't yield another. One crystal is enough—it's designed that way."

Her explanation carried a quiet certainty, a clarity that made the improbable seem deliberate, as though every part of the process had been meticulously planned by forces beyond their understanding—a higher intelligence.

"You know all of this... how?" David finally asked, his voice cutting through the room like a scalpel. It was the question everyone had been avoiding, the elephant in the room that could no longer be ignored.

"I know I should have come clean earlier," Elena admitted, her voice steady but tinged with regret. She looked toward Marcus, her gaze softening.

"Marcus, if you don't remember, it was you who touched the artifact first—and the crystal—before I did. But the crystal found it was easier to connect with me than struggling with you," she said, pausing for a moment as her words hung in the air.

"It could have been someone else, but I just happened to be the one."

As Elena spoke, Marcus felt a quick flashback surge through his mind—a memory he had buried and dismissed. Around the time of the first artifact's discovery, he had struggled to sleep, plagued by restless nights and an odd sense of unease. He remembered fleeting, vivid dreams he couldn't quite piece together, and a nagging sensation that something was trying to reach him.

Elena hesitated briefly, gathering her thoughts. "The crystal took time," she continued, her voice quieter now.

"To... tune to me. While it was trying, it came to me in fragments— glances, nightmares, and... delusions. At least, that's what I thought they were at the time."

Her words were measured but heavy, the room silent as the others processed the weight of her confession.

"The night I stood here with all of you," Elena began, her finger pointed to the floor as if the memory were etched beneath it, "something cracked through me—like it shattered a barrier I didn't know existed."

Her voice wavered, not from uncertainty, but from the weight of what she was about to say.

"It reached me. It showed me glimpses of its story—fragments, whispers—and then it asked me… no, it insisted me to bring the crystal to the artifact at the waterhole." She hesitated, the silence stretching between them. She paused, her voice faltering slightly.

"I was resisting the urge, but it was so strong. It felt like it could physically pull me out of bed—almost, or at least that's how it felt. And then… I was persuaded to come to *"The Sky"* almost involuntarily"

She made a heavy sigh, her shoulders slumping slightly. "You saw what happened here.."

Riya, overwhelmed with a flood of guilt, struggled to contain her emotions. The realization that she hadn't been able to break through to Elena during her time of need weighed heavily on her. Unable to find the words, she stepped closer and gently patted Elena's shoulder. The gesture, though meant to comfort Elena, felt as much like an attempt to console herself for not being there for her when it mattered most.

Elena looked at Riya with a faint smile of gratitude.

"You tried," she said softly, as of she was trying to ease some of the weight Riya had.

Recalling something important, she added, "As soon as the crystal could connect with me, it accessed my memories. Through me, it recognized

Ada's strength in cuneiform, and it used that to try and reveal itself in a way she could understand."

Elena held her hand up, stopping any further assumptions.

"That's all Ada," she said firmly, her voice steady.

"Her genius to understand, to interpret—it's what made the connection possible.

"It could have gone wasted, if not Ada.." she added.

Her expression grew more thoughtful as she continued.

"The crystal doesn't know our language—it only has access to some universal context. It wasn't programmed to learn or adapt. It's not intelligent, not in the way we think. It's just a tool, doing exactly what it was designed to do."

A revelation and simplicity that made them to think how they missed something obvious all along. The clarity in Elena's explanation seemed to pull back a veil, exposing a truth that had been right in front of them yet remained unnoticed until now.

"For me, it was a different story," Elena began, her voice tinged with both weariness and vulnerability. She paused, letting out a heavy sigh as she searched for the words to describe what had clearly been a deeply personal struggle.

"I was overwhelmed—completely buried under the weight of the information it was pouring into me," she continued, her tone faltering slightly.

"It wasn't just that. I felt exposed... naked, as if it had torn through the most private corners of my memories, maybe even my consciousness itself. It wasn't just accessing me—it was invading me… I thought."

She took a shaky breath, her hands trembling slightly as she clasped them together.

"It was like ripping away something precious, something I thought belonged only to me. My thoughts, my feelings, my essence—it wasn't mine anymore. And then, as if that wasn't enough, it was like being thrown on a stage in front of an audience, expected to sing a song I had never learned and never wanted to. It was humiliating, disorienting... and terrifying."

Elena's voice dropped, the rawness of her words hanging in the air, cutting through the room. The weight of her confession left the others silent, their own discomfort evident as they tried to process the depth of her experience.

Elena continued, her voice carrying the weight of her struggle.

"I was trying to be normal, or at least not show myself as some lunatic or crackpot. But the harder I tried, the more my vulnerability showed. My only resolution was to withdraw. I thought I just needed time—time to piece myself together—but it wasn't easy. And honestly, I was convinced it would never be the same again."

She paused for a moment, her gaze distant, then added with a forced smile, "Until you all decided to destroy the crystal."

Her smile faded as her tone grew sharp.

"We wouldn't have succeeded in destroying the crystal, but we would have eliminated our only chance of surviving the storm."

Elena straightened slightly, her words cutting through the silence.

"The detonation would have created a crater, burying the artifact under tons of debris. The electromagnetic interference would have momentarily disrupted the crystal's ability to talk to it's network, tame the storm. And in those few minutes of absence..." She paused for emphasis, her eyes sweeping across the room. "That's all the storm would have needed to overwhelm the habitat."

Her conclusion hit like a thunder, sending all three of them upright in their chairs, their faces a mix of shock and unease. The realization of how close they had come to catastrophe left the room heavy with tension, the silence almost deafening.

Riya was struggling to find the words, a total contrast to her usual composed demeanor. Her lips parted slightly, but the weight of the moment seemed to steal her voice.

Finally, she managed to ask, "What it want from us?"

Elena met her gaze, her expression calm yet knowing.

"Survive"

"It wants us not to get killed" she said with a faint smile, nodding slightly as if the answer were both simple and profound.

Crimson Ascent

Chapter Seven
REVELATION

In the lab, David and Elena sat side by side, their faces illuminated by the flickering monitors. The artifact and crystal were still, but their silence was deceptive. Both emitted faint signals that defied analysis, their patterns just out of reach.

"It's not random," David said, his voice laced with frustration, his fingers raking through his hair as he leaned heavily over the console. The chaotic dance of data streams on the screen seemed almost mocking, an enigmatic puzzle that refused to yield its secrets.

"The signals—they're too structured. There's a system here, but we're missing something. Something obvious, maybe."

His words hung in the air, taut with tension. He glanced sideways at Elena, her figure illuminated by the soft glow of the monitor. She stood with her arms crossed, her gaze locked onto the data with an unyielding intensity. Her silence wasn't indifference; it was the kind of quiet that spoke of gears turning, thoughts aligning, ideas forming just beyond the edge of articulation.

David felt his frustration deepen, though not because of her quiet disposition. His glance lingered a moment longer, and in that brief hesitation, he saw himself as a child again, staring at a confusing schoolbook question and glancing hopefully at the teacher for an answer. He wasn't asking Elena outright, but everything about his posture, his tone, the flicker of desperation in his eyes, was a silent plea for her to break the code he couldn't.

Elena walked towards a corner and waved David over, her expression tight with exasperation.

"Don't look at me like I'm your interpreter—or some noble teacher with all the answers… David," she said, her tone edged with frustration, and a struggle to keep the conversation quiet.

"I'm not the crystal whisperer!" There was a faint bite to her words, but beneath the sharpness, an undercurrent of worry flickered—a concern she couldn't entirely mask.

"I only know so much," Elena said, her voice firm but edged with weariness.

"And when I do, everyone else will too. I promise."

David looked at her with an apologetic expression, raising his palms in a gesture of surrender. As he backed away, he added a mock facial expression.

Elena shook her head slowly, her lips pressed together in exasperation, the kind of look that said she was both annoyed and mildly amused.

Elena walked towards Ada, leaning gently over her shoulder to glance at her work. She offered a few quiet pointers, her tone calm and encouraging. With a reassuring pat on Ada's shoulder, she added, "You're doing great," her voice carrying genuine warmth and support.

#

Elsewhere, tension within the colony was mounting. The storm had left the greenhouse in disarray—a leaking airlock, fractured irrigation lines, and struggling crops threatened their fragile food supply. The reactor, already operating at its limits, groaned under the strain, forcing the colony to implement strict rationing measures. Tempers flared, patience wore thin, and the once-steady rhythm of life on Mars faltered under the weight of growing frustration.

During a routine trip to the waterhole for an environmental assessment, Elena's attention was caught by the distant flag of a rover, a barely visible speck near the direction of one of the artifacts.

Curious, she searched Orion to identify its operator and saw it was Marcus. What struck her was that Marcus had no scheduled work in the area. While no distress signal had been registered, something about the situation unsettled her, prompting her to investigate.

As she approached, her unease grew. Marcus was outside the rover, standing motionless, his gaze locked on the artifact. His posture was unnerving, as though he were in a trance. Disturbing thoughts flooded Elena's mind, and without hesitation, she quickened her pace. Reaching him from back, she struck hard on his shoulder, her voice sharp and anxious.

"Marcus!" she shouted, bracing for the worst, her heart racing as she tried to pull him back to the present.

"You wanna fight? Let's fight," Marcus said, breaking the tension with a wide grin as he dropped into a playful martial arts stance.

His mock-serious expression was betrayed by the giggles bubbling under his breath, a clear attempt to diffuse the situation and lighten the mood.

"You monkey, you gave me a heart attack," Elena said, her tone shifting to one of relief, though a trace of annoyance lingered. She exhaled deeply, trying to steady herself before continuing.

"What are you doing here?" she asked, her voice firm but curious as she eyed him suspiciously.

This was unlike Marcus—mocking a situation in such a playful manner wasn't his style. His usual composure, even in tense moments, was absent, replaced by an oddly carefree manner. Elena's suspicion grew, her mind racing with possibilities. *What is he trying to hide?* she wondered, her gaze narrowing as she studied him more closely, searching for clues in his behavior.

"Look," Marcus said, his tone unusually casual as he gestured toward the artifact.

"I was... giving myself to it. Letting it access my brain."

He paused, his expression a mix of amusement and something harder to read.

"I'm kinda jealous of you being the one it selected," he added, his voice hovering somewhere between sincerity and mockery, leaving Elena struggling to decipher whether he was being genuine or just making light of the situation.

Elena faintly smiled, her eyes meeting his with a hint of weariness.

"You don't want to be the one," she said softly.

"Trust me." Her voice was steady, carrying the quiet weight of experience—a warning wrapped in simplicity.

Elena let the moment hang for a beat before softening. "Anyway… how's it going for you?" A faint smile tugged at her lips, an attempt to shift the focus.

Marcus exhaled, shaking his head. "Dead as dead meat."

For a second, silence. Then, laughter—sharp, unrestrained, breaking through the tension like sunlight through a storm. Whatever weight had lingered between them dissolved, their steps naturally falling in sync as they made their way back to the rovers, the dust rising softly beneath their boots.

#

Elena couldn't escape the overwhelming attention that had transformed her life in the colony. It was as if she had become a celebrity, or even a superhero, in the eyes of her peers. Everywhere she went, she felt the weight of expectations pressing down on her, the apathy of her earlier days now replaced by constant demands.

The lab seemed to hinge entirely on her presence. The moment she walked in, she was bombarded with a thousand and one questions, each more urgent than the last. Every piece of work appeared to require her signature or approval before anyone could proceed. Even Liam, whose meticulousness was unmatched, seemed to wait for Elena to review his calculations and sign off on his findings before moving forward.

Nobody seemed to empathize with the weight she carried. The constant stream of questions, some complex and others so niche they felt like riddles, left her rattled, grappling to piece together answers on the spot. The worst moments weren't when she didn't know the answers—it was when she didn't even understand the questions. That hollow feeling of inadequacy bitten at her, compounded by the unspoken expectation that Elena always had the solutions.

Her shoulders bore the invisible burden of being the colony's go-to problem solver, but few paused to consider how much of herself she poured into their needs. Every approval she gave, every problem she dissected, took a piece of her. She could feel it, a quiet erosion of energy and confidence that left her doubting if she was truly up to the task.

Yet, she didn't voice these fears. She couldn't. The colony needed her steady hand, her calm expression, even if inside, she felt anything but.

Liam and David were captivated by the vast reservoir of data the Crystal seemed to have transmitted on Elena. At first, she agreed it was the logical course of action to let them investigate—after all, understanding the phenomenon could benefit the entire colony. She complied willingly, allowing them to apply their techniques and methods, believing in the greater good of their research.

But as time wore on, the lines blurred. She began to feel less like a person and more like a test subject—a lab rat under constant scrutiny. Every glance, every question, every probe into her thoughts left her feeling increasingly alienated, as though the Crystal had reduced her to an enigmatic puzzle to be solved rather than a valued member of the team. Slowly but surely, the weight of it consumed her, filling her days with unease and a growing resentment she couldn't entirely shake.

The greenhouse, once her sanctuary, had also become another stage for her role as the colony's reluctant figurehead. Noah hovered nearby, constantly seeking her input on schedules and projects. Even mundane tasks like checking nutrient levels, approving growth projections, and reviewing hybrid seed experiments seemed to halt until she gave her nod of approval.

Sabine, who was always in absolute control of her work, now stood adrift, uncertainty clouding her usual judgment. For once, she wasn't leading— she was waiting. Waiting for Elena to show the way.

Her mealtime, which should have been a reprieve, offered little respite. Whenever she entered the dining area, people gravitated toward her. Even if no words were exchanged, the colony seemed to find comfort just sitting near her, as though her silent presence alone was enough to inspire or reassure them.

"The Sky", her once-constant refuge, was no longer the quiet escape she had relied on. Every time she climbed the steps, all four-hundred of them; she found it filled with people. What used to be a space for solitude had transformed into a bustling hub, with people eager to be near her, consciously or not. Elena could hardly remember the last time she found herself alone up there, left only to her thoughts and the vast Martian horizon.

While the attention was born out of admiration and reliance, it left her feeling suffocated, the quiet parts of her life stolen by the pedestal she had been placed on.

#

Riya and Dr. Myers seemed to be the only ones who hadn't changed in their attitude toward Elena. They treated her no differently than they had before the crystal and the artifacts turned her into the colony's reluctant celebrity. One day, Elena decided it's time to do something about it. Passing by Riya's room, she saw the door half-open, and Dr. Myers seated inside. Without hesitation, she knocked softly, then stepped in, closing the door behind her.

It was clear from her expression that she needed them both, so Myers stayed where he was, sensing his presence was important.

"I need help," Elena said lightly, her voice calm but carrying the weight of unspoken struggles.

"From a Commander or from a Doctor?" Riya asked, matching Elena's tone with equal lightness, though her sharp eyes didn't miss the strain beneath Elena's exterior.

Dr. Myers adopted a mock-serious tone, tilting his head slightly as he asked, "Would you mind having a look at my patients' records? Might save me a lot of trouble."

All three burst into laughter, the sound cutting through the tension like a breath of fresh air.

Elena couldn't help but laugh, shaking her head in disbelief. She had never seen Dr. Myers make a joke before, let alone laugh out loud like this. The unexpected humor felt like a breeze lifting off a veil, releasing a weight.

"We were talking about you, Elena," Dr. Myers resumed, his tone softening as the laughter faded.

"We were worried it took you this long to talk about it."

His words lingered for a moment, their sincerity cutting through the lightheartedness. It suddenly became clear to Elena that Myers's earlier joke wasn't just humor—it was an invitation, a gentle nudge for her to open up freely, without fear of judgment. The warmth in his voice and the understanding in Riya's expression made her feel, perhaps for the first time in a long while, that she doesn't have to carry this burden alone.

"It's hard to be the chosen one when I don't have any control over what I can or cannot do," Elena began, her voice heavy with frustration, her expression dark. She let out a bitter laugh, more of a grim acknowledgment than any sign of humor.

"The crystal poured a horde of information into me, so much so that I don't know how to process it, let alone communicate it. And it's all one-way. I have no way to ask anything from the crystal—nothing. It only 'talks' when it wants to, and when it does, it's overwhelming."

She paused, her hands trembling slightly as she clenched them into fists on her lap.

"I'm just a pawn in the game—nothing more, nothing less. Yet the colony… they look at me like I'm their Savior. They expect me to be the oracle, the one with all the answers."

Her voice cracked, and she quickly looked down at the floor, as though ashamed to admit the next part.

"I want to shout at them sometimes," she continued, her words spilling out faster now.

"I want to scream that I'm not their fairy queen, and I'm not some wizard with a magic wand either. I can't just wave my hand and make everything better. I can't, can I? I fear one day I might actually explode and voice it all, and then what?"

Her eyes glistened as she glanced between Riya and Dr. Myers. Her voice softened, but the weight of her struggle didn't.

"I don't know how much more of this I can take," she admitted, her vulnerability laid bare. "I just… I needed to say this to someone who wouldn't judge me."

Elena's words poured out like a flood, every sentence a reflection of the pressure and stress that had been building within her. Both Riya and Dr. Myers listened intently, their expressions filled with empathy, letting her unload the burden she had carried for far too long.

Elena exhaled slowly, the tension visibly leaving her shoulders. For the first time in what felt like forever, she felt a small measure of relief, as if the weight pressing down on her chest had finally eased.

For a moment, the room was silent. Then, breaking the stillness, Dr. Myers spoke, his voice calm but thoughtful. "I think the colony should know," he said, a wrinkle forming on his temple as he leaned forward slightly.

"Know what?" Elena asked, her brow furrowing.

"Know that you're not a fairy queen or a wizard," Myers replied, his lips curving into a teasing smile.

"And that you don't have a magic wand."

The tension in the room softened as Elena chuckled, shaking her head. The humor was exactly what she needed, a lightness in contrast to the burden she had just shared.

Myers raised his hand, gesturing toward Riya. "I think you should be the one to tell them," he said, his tone serious but suggestive.

"Let the colony know that this is just Elena. Nothing more, nothing less."

Riya met his gaze, then looked at Elena with a quiet nod of acknowledgment.

"Leave it with me," she said, her voice steady. The resolve in her words was clear—she would make sure the colony understood, that Elena wasn't a mystical figure with all the answers; she was simply one of them, doing her best in impossible circumstances.

#

It didn't take long for Riya's request to spread throughout the colony: everyone was to gather aboard the *Eos Horizon* four past mid day!

The announcement came as a surprise to most, as no prior meetings were held inside the ship since they landed. In fact, many of the colonists hadn't set foot on the ship since disembarking.

For them, the prospect stirred mixed emotions—curiosity, anticipation, and a hint of unease—as they tried to guess the significance of this unexpected event.

As a man of numbers and logic, Liam had already guessed the purpose of the meeting, his quiet confidence setting him apart from the rest.

While Ada and her companions chit-chatted, tossing around wild guesses in the dark, Liam sat back, watching them with faint amusement. It was as if he was enjoying the sight of them trying to solve a puzzle whose answer he already knew.

In truth, though he hadn't deliberately withheld anything—he simply didn't feel the need to engage. If anyone had thought to ask, he would have told them without hesitation. But as they speculated, Liam remained content in his silent detachment, letting the chatter wash over him.

As the time arrived, it seemed everyone had taken the ramp to the elevators and climbed into the belly of the ship. The space felt a little cramped—an unease shared by many who had grown used to the openness of the dome and the boundless expanse of the Martian landscape outside.

But as they stood there waiting something to unfold, a sense of nostalgia crept in. Not long ago, this very space had been their refuge, their sanctuary from the perils of the cosmos. For months, they had lived within these walls, traveling through the stars, shielded from the vast emptiness of space.

What had once been their sanctuary—a fortress that carried them safely through the void to this alien world—now felt confined, its walls closing in as the vastness of Mars began to feel more like home.

"Welcome, everyone!" Dr. Myers greeted aloud, his voice echoing in the room. It was fitting for him to take the lead, given that he and his team were the ones who constantly occupied this space while the rest of the colony busied themselves in the habitat below. Behind him, Riya was noticed weaving through the crowd, her presence commanding attention as she made her way to the center.

"This is our seventh month on Mars," she began bluntly, breaking the suspense with a straightforward statement.

The room shifted slightly, murmurs rising as everyone exchanged glances. Faces were filled with curiosity, confusion, and even faint amusement, as if trying to make sense of why seven months mattered. Why not six months? Why not wait until a year? The unspoken questions hung in the air, expressed in their puzzled faces and faint, murmured speculations. The atmosphere was a mix of anticipation and unease, the significance of her words yet to be revealed.

"Seems like you all forgot," Riya said with a sly smile, her tone light but teasing.

"Mars has 24-month years, so this marks the end of Spring."

She continued, "For those who are curious, six months for summer, five-and-a-half for Fall and Five months for Winter!"

She paused, her gaze sweeping the room, catching the flickers of realization on a few faces.

"We still have time to get used to it, though," she added with a grin, her attempt to ease the tension drawing a few chuckles from the crowd. The reminder, simple as it was, shifted the mood, adding a touch of familiarity to the alien calendar they now lived by.

The room erupted into clapping and cheering as the shroud of mystery was finally lifted, a collective wave of relief and excitement spreading through the crowd. Riya, smiling, raised her arm and gestured toward the crates stacked neatly in the corner, packed full of dehydrated drinks of different flavors.

"And over there," she added with a playful grin, pointing to a table laden with freshly prepared *Elias' Pizzas*, as he was lifting the cover, their unmistakable aroma filling the air.

The revelation was met with more cheers and laughter, and murmurs of "Where on Mars did they cook that?" rippled through the crowd. The surprise feast, prepared in secret, was a welcome and joyous break from the tension of their daily routines. It was a rare moment of shared celebration, a reminder of their humanity amidst the challenges of their Martian existence.

"Let's drink to the colony down there," Riya said, picking up a cup and raising it high as she pointed out the window toward the Martian surface and the habitat dome at the distance. Her gesture carried both pride and gratitude, and the room fell momentarily quiet before erupting into applause and cheers. Cups clinked, and a wave of camaraderie swept through the group, a collective acknowledgment of their shared journey and the resilience of those working tirelessly over the months.

Riya let the joy settle for a moment, the hum of laughter and chatter gradually fading. Then, stepping forward, she raised her voice, drawing everyone's attention.

"We've been through a lot. We all know that," she began, her tone steady, commanding the room. She paused briefly, waiting for the crowd to quiet completely before continuing.

"Elena is signing autographs, if anyone's interested!" she caught everyone off-guard, her face completely devoid of emotion, delivering the line with such deadpan seriousness that it took a moment for everyone to process.

The room fell into an awkward silence, eyes darting between Riya and Elena. A few people tried to suppress nervous laughter, while others exchanged embarrassing glances, unsure how to react.

Elena, uncharacteristically, sat silently having a faintest trace of a smile playing on her lips, her reaction far calmer than anyone had expected. Riya had successfully put the room—and Elena—on the spot, her dry humor defusing the tension in a way only she could manage.

Riya stepped forward, her presence commanding as she raised a hand to quiet the murmurs in the room. The weight of her gaze swept across the gathered crew, silencing even the faintest whispers. When she spoke, her voice was low and deliberate, carrying a gravity that demanded attention.

"I want Elena to tell me what to do tomorrow," she began, her tone deep and unwavering. A pause followed, heavy and intentional.

"But that's not happening—not because I can't ask her, but because she cannot comply."

The room tensed; the air thick with anticipation as Riya's words landed.

"She has gone through a lot—yes, far more—than any of us have since the day we landed here, seven months ago," Riya continued, her voice resonating with both respect and frustration.

"I know we're all tired. We're all desperate. And yes, we're all hoping for a miracle, given everything this desolate world has thrown at us."

Her eyes narrowed slightly, her tone sharpening as she added, "If Elena happened to be that miracle, I'd gladly hand over command and let her lead you. I'd step down without hesitation."

She paused again, her words hanging heavy in the silence.

"But unfortunately, and I hate to disappoint some of you—she's not. She's just one of us."

Her voice softened, but the strength behind it remained.

"And that means, for better or worse, you're stuck with me as your commander—for now." Her words sliced through the tension, wiping across the room like a cleansing wind.

Riya's gaze lingered on the crowd, ensuring her message sank in.

"Stop treating her as *the one*," she said firmly, her voice calm but resolute.

"Because she's not. She doesn't have all the answers, and it's unfair to place that burden on her shoulders."

The room was silent, her words striking deep. Riya had spoken as a leader, not only defending Elena but also grounding the colony in the harsh realities they all shared. It wasn't a dismissal of hope, but a call for unity, a reminder that their survival depended on collective effort—not mythical saviors.

Riya straightened her posture, letting her commanding presence fill the room as she continued, her tone deliberate and heavy with purpose.

"We are ever grateful for..." She paused for a moment, her eyes scanning the room, adding weight to her words. "The artifacts. And for whoever placed them here."

The room seemed to hold its breath, some expecting Elena's name to follow. But Riya pressed on.

"Without that system in place, we would already been wiped out. The artifacts have given us a lifeline—there's no denying that." She paused again, letting the gravity of the statement sink in.

"And more than that, they've given us something we didn't plan for—an assurance, however abstract, that we're not here to struggle completely alone. We have help. How it comes, in what form, and when... nobody knows."

Her voice shifted, becoming sharper, more resolute. "But let me be clear—if the network of artifacts helps us, that's a bonus, not a guarantee. We are essentially on our own, just as we trained to be on this mission, back on Earth. All those years of training, all the simulations, all the science and math—that is what we must rely on. That is our savior."

Riya's gaze swept across the room, her voice growing firmer. "Artifacts, if anything, happen to be allies—ones who may or may not choose to notice us in danger. They are not a solution, not a crutch, and certainly not a replacement for our own capabilities."

She paused for effect, allowing the weight of her words to settle over the crowd.

"What we do know for certain is this: the artifacts are not our enemy. They've shown that much already."

She glanced around, letting the tension ease slightly before adding, "But just as radiation can be harnessed for medical tools and can help in extraordinary ways, it can kill you if not being careful, we still take precautions when handling it. We respect it. We treat it with care. And that is how I want this colony to handle the artifacts."

Her voice sharpened again, commanding the room's full attention.

"The precautions we've put in place will not be lifted. This isn't up for debate. You won't be hanging the crystal like a mirror-ball in the middle of the habitat dome... The artifacts are to be treated with respect, caution, and awareness of the unknowns we still face."

She stepped back slightly, giving the room a moment to absorb her words, her steady gaze ensuring that her message was fully understood. This wasn't just an address—it was a command, a call for discipline and collective accountability.

She leaned forward slightly, picking up her cup and taking a measured sip. Holding it in one hand, she began again, her voice calm but deliberate.

"You think Elena can talk to the crystal, get answers, and call for help whenever she wants?" She paused, her gaze scanning the room.

"That's not the case I am afraid. And yes, that's disappointing, isn't it?"

Her voice grew firmer, slicing through the quiet.

"But make no mistake—that's the reality we're dealing with. The crystal chose her not because she's special or destined, but because she happened to be among the first to come across it. It could have been Marcus, Ada, Liam—anyone."

She placed the cup back on the table, her tone shifting, laced with empathy. "The toll of becoming that contact hasn't been easy for her. It wouldn't be easy for anyone if it happened to them."

Riya's voice deepened, carrying a quiet intensity. "Imagine living day after day with nightmares that pull you off bed. Imagine fighting to keep going without sleep, and all the while, trying to convince yourself—and everyone else—that you're not insane."

Her gaze hardened slightly, sweeping across the room as she continued.

"Think of an eight-year-old being forced to read, learn and lecture university-level studies. Wouldn't be easy, would it?"

She let the question hang, giving the crowd a moment to consider it.

"That's what it's been like for Elena. She's been poured a ton of data—maybe even knowledge—that she can't fully comprehend. She can't even figure out how to communicate it properly. And yet, we expect her to have all the answers, to be our savior, to carry the burden of our survival."

Riya's words landed like a heavy weight, leaving the room silent as her steady gaze ensured no one missed the gravity of what she was saying.

"You know what she knows," Riya continued, her voice steady and deliberate. "If there's anything she can understand or even pass on, she will tell us. At this moment, though, Ada"—she paused, gesturing toward Ada—"this one here probably understands the crystal better than Elena does."

She waited for the murmurs to settle before continuing.

"Ada has learned to read the symbols. She's devised a scientific method, one that's systematic and thorough. If you're looking for a superhero, we have two of them right here. Ada, to decode the symbols, and Liam, to make sense of them in a mathematical framework."

Riya glanced at Liam, giving him a subtle nod.

"They're slowly building an understanding—perhaps even a method to communicate with the network. Maybe, one day, we'll have a knowledge base to work from."

Her tone shifted slightly, growing lighter but still firm.

"Now, if you want specific questions about agriculture, the latest in genetic engineering for seeds, or inspiration on what the future of Martian farming could look like, then talk to Elena. That's her domain."

She let her words settle, her gaze sweeping across the room.

"All I'm asking is for you to be realistic. Trust what each of you are skilled at and depend on those skills first. The expertise you bring is our strength—not fantasies about someone saving us single-handedly."

Riya's voice deepened with conviction.

"I believe this much should be clear now: Elena didn't save the colony. The colony was saved by all of us—by collaboration, by the collective effort of everyone here."

She paused; her eyes sharp as they scanned the room.

"Yes, we got help at the waterhole. And yes, we were protected through the storm. But those are just two instances. Imagine how many lives have been saved by the medical team in this very room." She scanned for the medical team, nodding appreciatively in their direction.

"So, remember Elena as someone who disembarked from this ship with you—as one of you. Not a celebrity, not a wizard who can summon a genie and save us all. She is part of this team, nothing more, nothing less."

Riya paused for a moment, letting her words sink in, before adding with a smile, "And if you haven't noticed, there's a rare treat of ice cream melting in the corner."

She pointed toward the table, her tone lightening. "Let's not waste it."

Her final words brought a ripple of laughter and a sense of ease to the room, shifting the atmosphere back to camaraderie and reminding them of their shared humanity amidst the challenges.

It took some time, but Elena eventually found her peace in the colony—not as a superhero, but as the calm and dedicated agriculturist she had always been. She returned to her role of supporting the colony, not through mythical feats, but by helping with administration, decision-making, and the steady work she had mastered.

Her time in the lab became more balanced, as the teams in both the lab and the greenhouse gradually returned to trusting their own instincts first. They consulted her only when necessary, respecting her expertise without overwhelming her with every detail. The shift allowed Elena to regain a sense of normalcy, rediscovering the quiet satisfaction of her work and the rhythm of being part of a collective effort. It was no longer about carrying the weight of the colony on her shoulders but about contributing alongside everyone else—exactly as it should be.

#

On a routine perimeter scouting mission, Elena found herself standing on the edge of a massive, jagged cliff, the Martian landscape sprawling endlessly before her. Below, the ground seemed to ripple like water, darkened by shadows that moved in unnatural patterns. The artifact was there, glowing faintly in the distance, its hum resonating like a heartbeat she could feel in her chest. As she leaned closer, the ground beneath her feet gave way without warning. She felt herself plummeting, the air rushing past her in an icy torrent, her arms flailing helplessly as the abyss opened wide to swallow her whole.

The sensation of the fall was visceral, her stomach lurching as she plunged deeper into the void. The artifact's hum grew louder, almost deafening, and its light flared, casting strange, fragmented images into her mind— faces, places, and symbols she couldn't comprehend. Just as the abyss seemed ready to claim her, she awoke with a start, her breath ragged and uneven.

Her eyes darted around frantically, taking in the familiar walls of her quarters. Linen was tangled around her legs, the bed a chaotic mess, as though she had physically fought against the dream. Her hands were gripping the edges of the bed tightly, her knuckles white, her body trembling. Still clutching the bed, she gasped for air, her mind struggling to separate the dream's intensity from reality. The sense of falling lingered, an aftershock that left her clutching her chest, trying to calm the erratic beat of her heart.

Elena slowly released her grip, staring at her hands as if they might explain the terror she'd just endured. It was just a dream, she reminded herself, but the lingering unease told her it wasn't that simple. The crystal's hold on her thoughts seemed inescapable, its presence haunting her even in the sanctuary of sleep.

Elena sat on the edge of her bed, foot resting on the floor as of trying to anchor on to reality, her breath still uneven, chest movements amplified, beads of sweat clinging to her temples. She felt fully awake, her senses sharp, yet her mind was swimming in the aftermath of the dream. It wasn't just a dream, she thought—it was more than that. The crystal was trying to communicate something, its presence lingering in her mind like an uninvited guest. A warning? A command? The messages were fragmented, tangled with feelings she couldn't grasp, like trying to grasp water with her hands.

Her thoughts turned to Sonja and the recent excavations on the southern plateau. The scans had revealed something extraordinary—regular patterns etched not very deep below the surface, almost geometric in their precision. These weren't natural formations; they couldn't be. Sonja had described them as anomalies, but to Elena, they felt like echoes of something ancient and deliberate.

The science forum had been abuzz with the findings, the colony's best minds pouring over the data, debating its implications. Riya had been particularly insistent on pursuing the expedition, her determination fueled by Earth's growing interest in the site. That curiosity had turned into something more—a near-obsessive fascination that raised as many questions as it did unease.

Elena had reviewed the scans herself, spending long hours analyzing the data late into the nights. The patterns stirred something deep within her—a faint sense of familiarity paired with a creeping discomfort she couldn't shake. It was as though the patterns themselves resisted her understanding, teasing her with glimpses of meaning only to retreat into obscurity.

Elena's thoughts spiraled as the uneasiness from her vivid dream refused to dissipate. It felt less like a dream and more like a meticulously crafted projection, one that burrowed into the recesses of her mind with calculated precision. And then, as though the crystal itself had tugged on a thread of her memory, a forgotten moment from years ago surfaced—a chilling reminder of a past she had buried.

It was the incident with Grace, her little girl, who had nearly been kidnapped after kindergarten. Elena had almost erased the ordeal from her mind, perhaps as a way to shield herself from the terror of those days. The authorities had told her later it was a well-coordinated attempt, orchestrated by individuals hired by a corporation desperate to gain access to her research on low-pressure tissue growth. They had approached her with lucrative offers first, then threats, and finally, a chilling act of desperation—a botched abduction attempt. Though investigators found circumstantial connections to the company, no charges were ever brought forward. The shadowy force behind the incident vanished, just as the company itself went bankrupt shortly after.

The details still haunted Elena: Grace had climbed a tree outside the school gate that day, a spontaneous act of childhood whimsy. Moments later, a black suburban pulled up, and four men in black suits emerged with military precision. They surrounded the tree, coaxing, cajoling, and eventually shaking it to dislodge her. But Grace, oblivious to the chaos below, had been in a world of her own. When Elena spoke to her afterward, Grace described a fairy perched on a branch who promised her a beautiful doll. She hadn't even noticed the men or the frantic scene unfolding beneath her.

What happened next was equally bizarre. The crowd gathering to protect Grace had forced the kidnappers to flee, their plans undone. As the black suburban sped off, Grace slip from the tree—nearly three meters—landing gracefully on the pavement without a single scratch. When Elena questioned her later, Grace spoke of floating down gently, like the fairy had guided her. Psychiatrists dismissed it as a coping mechanism, a child's way of reframing a traumatic event. But to Elena, it was more than coincidence. The timing, the escape, the untouched landing—it was uncanny, inexplicable, and unsettlingly perfect.

Now, as Elena wrestled with the memory, she couldn't ignore the parallels with her present situation. The crystal, with its inscrutable signals and elusive warnings, seemed to tap into something deeper—an awareness of patterns she couldn't yet grasp. Was it a coincidence that this memory had surfaced now? Or was it another piece of a puzzle she didn't yet understand? The thought lingered, heavy and unrelenting, as she tried to shake the eerie sensation creeping into her bones.

For what's it worth, the crystal wasn't happy, she thought, with Sonja's work or the colony's growing focus on the southern plateau. There was a sense of intrusion, of pushing boundaries not meant to be crossed. Elena pressed her palms against her temples, trying to suppress the surge of unease rising within her. The crystal wasn't just silent; it was watching, and perhaps waiting for the right moment to act.

#

"Elena!" someone called, the urgency in the voice slicing through her groggy haze. It took a moment for her to place the voice—it was David, standing behind her.

She blinked rapidly, attempting to steady herself. The realization hit her like a jolt—she had dozed off, slumped over her workstation, still seated in the chair that now felt uncomfortably warm. She straightened quickly, trying to act naturally, her heart pounding at the thought of anyone noticing. Her eyes darted around the room, scanning for witnesses, but it seemed no one had caught her lapse in focus.

Feigning concentration, she mumbled, "Give me a second… just finishing this up." She tapped aimlessly at the console, hoping to sell the illusion of diligence. When she finally turned toward David, her expression was composed, or so she hoped.

"Yes, what is it?" she asked, her tone brisk.

To her relief, David didn't seem to notice her slip. At least, not outwardly. He looked his usual self, a mix of earnestness and barely concealed curiosity. Still, there was something about the way his brow twitched that made her wonder if he knew more than he let on.

"Sonja needs you at the plateau," David said, leaning casually against the edge of her desk. "They've taken some core samples, and it looks like they've found a fossil of some sort. She wants you to have a look."

"A fossil?" Elena's interest piqued, momentarily overriding her embarrassment.

"Yeah," David replied, gesturing toward the door.

"I'm heading there now. You can join me if you want." It wasn't so much a request as an invitation, one that Elena couldn't bring herself to decline, despite her exhaustion.

She nodded, pushing herself up from the chair, her body stiff from the awkward nap she had stolen. As they left together, she silently thanked the stars—or the crystal, or whatever force was in play—that David hasn't noticed! The thought lingered briefly as her focus shifted to the mystery waiting at the plateau.

#

While they were riding the rover, the rhythmic crunch of Martian soil under the wheels, and motors' roar was the only sound between them until David broke the silence.

"The Crystal is bothering you again," he said, his tone unreadable.

Elena blinked, caught off guard. Was that a question? A statement? An invitation to share? She couldn't tell. Her thoughts spiraled as she tried to parse his intent. If it was a question, did he expect an answer? If it wasn't, was he merely voicing his observation, leaving her to carry the weight of the silence?

Her mind wandered back to the restless nights, the cryptic dreams, the inexplicable pull the artifact seemed to exert on her psyche. She felt exposed, as though David could see through her veneer of control. Her lips parted as if to speak, but the words tangled in her throat. Instead, she let the silence linger, hoping it would shield her from further probing.

David didn't press. He seemed content to leave the statement hanging in the air, giving her space or perhaps testing her resolve. Either way, the unspoken tension stretched between them, thick and deep.

#

The plateau loomed into view, the towering drill rig casting a long shadow across the barren landscape. It stood like a giant sentry, poking into the ground with an air of defiance, as if daring the planet to give up its secrets. The scene broke the spell of their silence, both of them pausing to take it in.

Elena jumped off the rover, her boots crunching against the dusty Martian soil. The temporary shelter at the work-site offered minimal relief from the harsh environment, but it was enough to house Sonja and her team as they huddled over their latest discovery.

"This is it," Sonja said, holding out a small, delicate fragment encased in a protective encasement.

"Very fragile, like it's ready to crumble into dust at the slightest touch. Not even sure it's worth taking back to the lab. It's practically dissolving in our fingers."

Elena leaned closer, her trained eyes scanning the tiny piece. The fragment, though faintly textured and pale, bore an undeniable resemblance to a fossil. Its edges were irregular but seemed deliberate, shaped by something other than random geology.

"We've got photos in situ," Sonja added, her tone cautiously optimistic. She tapped on a portable console, bringing up an image captured by the drill-head camera—a striking shot of the fragment nestled in the substrate, illuminated by the rig's lights.

Elena nodded, taking it all in. "How far are we from the underground patterns?" she asked, her voice steady, though her mind buzzed with possibilities.

Sonja checked a digital readout on her wrist-mounted Orion band.

"We'll hit the first cluster in a few minutes," she replied, gesturing toward the towering drill rig. Its steady hum punctuated the tense silence, a mechanical sentinel digging deeper into the unknown.

The three of them—Elena, Sonja, and David—stood just outside the shelter, their eyes fixed on the drill as it worked tirelessly. The workers in the distance moved with precision, each action a cog in the complex machine of discovery. The anticipation was palpable, an electric charge in the thin Martian air as they waited, breaths bated, for what might surface next.

A deep, resonating crunch echoed from the drill, a sound that cut through the steady hum of the work-site. It wasn't the usual noise of substrate giving way—it was something far more stubborn, like the drill had struck an unyielding barrier. The rig trembled briefly, its systems straining to adapt to the unexpected resistance.

Sonja approached, her expression a mix of curiosity and unease.

"We've tried everything," she reported, her voice edged with frustration.

"Diamond tips, high-energy lasers, plasmas, even sonic-detonations. Whatever's down there... it doesn't budge." She glanced at Elena, her worry palpable.

David, standing nearby, folded his arms thoughtfully. "It could be another artifact," he suggested, his tone speculative but with previous experience.

"Maybe," Sonja admitted, rubbing her temple as if trying to work through the implications. "The hardness certainly gives it that vibe. But the underground scans aren't consistent. The density readings are... sporadic, almost patchy. It doesn't align with what we've seen before."

Elena crouched near the drill's readout console, studying the data. Her brow furrowed.

"So, if it's not an artifact, what are we dealing with? A naturally occurring anomaly?"

"I doubt it's natural," Sonja said, her gaze locked on the drill.

"It's too deliberate, too… resistant. But if it's not another artifact, then it's something else entirely."

#

The tension was thick, each of them running scenarios in their minds. The drill's mechanisms strained again, the vibrations subtly traveling through the ground beneath their boots. Whatever lay below was not going to give up its secrets easily.

"Cut it! Shut it down!" Sonja's voice rang out, sharp and commanding, as she stepped forward, her palm slicing the air at an angle in a universal gesture to stop. The urgency in her tone left no room for hesitation.

The drill operator, startled but responsive, hit the controls, and the towering rig groaned to a halt. The vibrations that had been coursing through the ground subsided, leaving an unsettling silence in their wake. Sonja's eyes darted to the drill head monitor, where the live feed showed the unyielding surface that had thwarted their efforts. She bit her lip, her mind racing.

"Something's not right," she muttered, more to herself than anyone else, but her words carried to Elena and David, who had moved closer.

"What made you stop?" Elena asked, her gaze flitting between Sonja and the monitor.

Sonja gestured at the screen. "Look at the patterns. They've shifted. That... that wasn't there a moment ago."

David leaned in, squinting at the feed. A subtle but undeniable change had occurred—an intricate pattern of lines and faintly glowing nodes had emerged, barely perceptible but impossible to ignore.

"It's reacting," David said, his voice low and steady, though his widening eyes betrayed his unease.

"Whatever it is, it doesn't seem to appreciate what we are doing."

"This doesn't seem to look like the artifact," Sonja said, her finger hovering over the drill-head video feed. Her tone was a mix of curiosity and unease as she leaned closer to the monitor. The image displayed a surface that seemed too organized to be natural but markedly different from the material they had encountered with the artifact. It shimmered faintly, its texture an intricate lattice of ridges and valleys.

"It's a surface of some sort," she continued, glancing at Elena and David. "But definitely not the same composition or structure as the artifact. Look at the symmetry—it's almost... engineered."

Elena frowned, her gaze fixed on the screen.

"Engineered or not, it's deep enough to suggest it's been buried for eons. Could it be part of a larger network, something connected to the artifact indirectly?"

David shook his head, a skeptical expression on his face.

"If it is, it's hiding its hand well. The artifact responded immediately when we approached it. This thing, whatever it is, seems... dormant. At least for now."

Sonja crossed her arms, her brow furrowed in thought. "Dormant or cautious? The deeper we go, the stranger it gets. And this material—this isn't something our tools are going to cut through anytime soon."

Elena glanced at the drill operator and then back at the feed.

"Then we'll need to change our approach. If this isn't the artifact, we need to figure out what it is before we risk going further. The colony's safety comes first."

Sonja nodded, but her eyes lingered on the monitor, a spark of determination flickering beneath her apprehension. "Agreed. But whatever this is, it's not just another rock. We're onto something for sure."

#

"I do not feel good. Can you take me back, David?" Elena's voice was faint, almost pleading.

"Of course, let's move out," David complied without hesitation, his tone soft but steady as he energized the rover for departure.

"You haven't had sleep for a while, have you?" David asked gently as they drove back toward the colony.

Elena hesitated, unsure of how to respond. The truth hung in the air, obvious yet unspoken. Her silence was answer enough. David didn't press her further, though it was clear he'd already pieced together her struggle. He had seen her slumped at the desk earlier, her exhaustion betraying her despite her efforts to appear composed. But he chose not to bring it up, sparing her any further embarrassment.

"The crystal is trying to tell me something," Elena admitted after a long silence, her voice barely above a whisper.

"And I'm not sure what it is."

David glanced at her, his brows knitting in thought.

"You get the dreams because it might be the best state of your mind for the crystal to reach you. But… it doesn't have to be."

Elena turned to him, confused. "What do you mean?"

"Calm your mind, like what monks do," David replied, his voice carrying a measured calmness.

Elena blinked at him, the simplicity of his suggestion clashing with the enormity of her frustration.

"Meditation you mean, can you teach me?" she asked, a faint trace of hope in her voice.

David chuckled softly, though there was a tinge of disappointment in it.

"You don't have to ask, if I knew. But I don't."

They lapsed into silence again before David spoke, his tone contemplative.

"I guess… if you can let your mind sync to the crystal—don't ask me how—it should find it easier to reach you."

Elena's lips pressed into a thin line, her thoughts racing as she stared out at the Martian horizon. Could it really be that simple? Could calming her overworked, frayed mind be the key to understanding the enigmatic artifact? The thought was both comforting and maddening in its uncertainty.

"I think we have a solution," David announced, his voice laced with newfound enthusiasm. There was an energy in his tone that immediately caught Elena's attention.

"Ethan."

"Ethan? How?" Elena raised an eyebrow, her curiosity quickly morphing into skepticism.

"Was he a monk or something?"

David tried to suppress a laugh but failed, a chuckle slipping out.

"Not sure about his past, but he's trained in remote viewing," he explained, his grin fading into something more serious.

"In fact, he's already tried to reach the crystal."

Elena's eyes widened, her surprise evident. "Really? And when exactly did this happen?"

David's tone deepened, adding weight to his words.

"While you were away," he admitted, letting the moment hang in the air.

Her thoughts raced. How much had happened during her withdrawal? What had she missed while she was caught up in her own struggles? The realization unsettled her.

David continued, "It didn't work out, though. But I'm sure Ethan might know a thing or two about meditation—calming the mind and all that."

He tilted his head, a playful glint in his eye. "I wouldn't mind joining his class, you know. A little zen could do us all some good."

Elena couldn't help but smirk, though her mind was already wandering. Ethan, with his enigmatic skills, might just be the unlikely key to unraveling the connection to the crystal. It was a thought she hadn't entertained before, but in the chaos of Mars, stranger things had already proven possible.

#

Every member of the colony had a documented and meticulously selected skill set, each one critical to the operation of the *Eos Horizon* and the colony on Mars. These trades and disciplines were not secrets; they were widely known and discussed among the crew, fostering a mutual respect for one-another's expertise. It was a team of specialists, each individual bringing one or more mastery.

Ethan Rees, however, was the glaring exception. His official role was listed simply as "Remote Viewer," a title that drew more questions than answers. Most didn't even know what it meant, and those who did considered it an oddity, a relic of some classified Cold War experiment rather than a practical skill for an interplanetary mission. Whispers filled the colony—speculations that Ethan wasn't truly part of the mission, but a covert operative planted by the CIA, NASA, or some other shadowy government organization. Why would remote viewing—whatever that entailed—be necessary for a Martian colony? The mystery clung to him like Martian dust to boots, and the questions only deepened the more people speculated.

Despite the swirling rumors and veiled skepticism, Ethan's appearance was neutralizing. He was unerringly friendly, always quick with a smile or a light-hearted comment that seemed to diffuse tension wherever he went. Ethan made a point of pitching wherever he could, be it hauling equipment, assisting with logistics, or simply lending a patient ear to a crew-mate venting their frustrations. If the rumors bothered him, he never let it show, and his easy-going nature gradually won over many of the skeptics. But even as Ethan built friendships and trust, the enigma of his true purpose lingered, a silent question in every interaction.

#

Elena ascended the spiral stairs to *"The Sky"*, her steps measured, her thoughts a tangled web of anticipation. As she reached the top, she paused, drawing in a deep breath. Uncertainty prickled at her—an alien event, she mused, fitting for an alien world. Yet, as her eyes took in the space, *"The Sky"'s* serene atmosphere welcomed her like an old friend. The panoramic backdrop stretched endlessly, the Martian landscape ablaze with crimson hues, its distant ridges softened under the dome's light-filtering panels, blending the stark reality of the terrain with an almost dreamlike tranquility.

She stepped inside, her eyes scanning the open space, and immediately noticed a small group gathered near the central observation window. Ethan, David, and, to her surprise, Ada were standing in a loose circle, their postures relaxed yet purposeful. Their faint murmurs of chit-chat carried the tone of people waiting for someone.

Ethan was leaning casually against the railing, usual ease about him as he gestured animatedly. David stood nearby, his arms crossed, nodding occasionally with a slight grin that hinted at some ongoing inside joke. Ada, however, caught Elena's attention the most. She rarely ventured into spaces like these, preferring the focused solitude of her work, yet here she was, leaning in slightly to the conversation with an unusually relaxed manner.

It was clear they were expecting her. As their heads turned in unison at her arrival, Elena felt a mix of curiosity and apprehension settle over her. Whatever this impromptu gathering was about, it was bound to be something that would linger long after the conversation ended.

"Ethan the Mystical… at your service, Ma'am,"

Ethan declared, stepping in front of Elena with a flourish. He bent slightly at the waist, extending one arm in an exaggerated gesture like a performer in a royal court. His mock formality was punctuated by a playful grin, the kind that dared you not to laugh.

Ethan's theatrics had the intended effect, pulling Elena out of her whirlwind of tension and worry. A smile broke through her otherwise composed mood, and before she knew it, she found herself playing along. Adopting a mock regal stance, she straightened her back, lifted her chin, and pretended to hold the edges of an imaginary royal gown.

"Peasant,"

She intoned with dramatic flair, her voice laced with amusement,

"unless you impress me today, you shan't live to see the sunlight."

Her eyes sparkled as she met Ethan's gaze, her tone both playful and commanding.

The others in the room chuckled, the light-hearted exchange breaking through the seriousness that had loomed over their gathering. For a brief moment, *"The Sky"* wasn't just a place for plans and deliberation—it was a haven where laughter could echo across the dome.

David and Ada burst into uncontrollable laughter, their attempts to stifle it only resulting in fits of snorting and wheezing. The scene was so absurd, so perfectly ridiculous, that every effort to regain composure failed miserably. David clutched his stomach, wincing in mock agony from the ache of laughing too hard, while Ada leaned against the railing, tears streaming down her face.

Ethan, seized the moment. With a dramatic flourish, he bowed low, extending an arm toward Elena as though presenting her to an unseen audience. In a voice dripping with theatrical gravitas, he proclaimed,

"Her Majesty, the Queen of the Crystal, Ruler of Cosmos and Protector of All That Grows, commands it! And I, her humble servant, the Mystical Ethan, shall carry out her decree!"

He turned to David and Ada, pointing an accusatory finger at their crumpled forms.

"You, jesters of the dome! For your failure to uphold the decorum of this court, you are hereby condemned to the depths of the…", looked like he was looking for words, "… waterhole!". His voice echoed through *"The Sky"* with a melodramatic finality.

David managed to gasp out between peals of laughter,

"I'll take… the sentence… if it means… no more royal drama!"

Ada waved a weak hand in surrender, her face red as she howled with laughter. The playful chaos brought an unexpected levity to the room, turning it into a rarc, shared moment of joy.

It took a while for the laughter to subside and for the group to remember why they had gathered in *"The Sky"*. The light-heartedness lingered in the air like an echo, but David knew it was time to bring everyone back to the gravity of their purpose. Seizing the moment, he straightened his posture and cleared his throat, his voice carrying a steady authority.

"Alright, folks," David began, glancing around the room.

"Let's focus. We're here for a reason. Ethan has joined us to guide us in calming our minds—otherwise known as meditation."

He cast a quick, approving glance at Ethan before continuing. "Ada has shown a keen interest in the subject and apparently has some experience from back home."

Ethan offered a small, almost humble nod as David gestured toward him.

"And let me add," David said, his tone gaining weight, "Ethan's no stranger to this. He's been to India, Thailand, Sri Lanka, and a few other places where meditation isn't just a concept but a discipline. He's here to share what he's learned."

David paused, letting his words settle. "I'll be honest—I don't know what will come out of this. But I do know we need to try. If we follow Ethan's guidance, maybe we'll come away with something valuable…"

Ethan raised a hand, interrupting David mid-sentence. His usual playful appearance was gone, replaced by a voice that was calm yet carried an unexpected weight.

"Do not expect anything," Ethan said, his tone almost reverent.

"That's the key. Let go of expectations. Only then can your mind truly be free to explore."

The room grew quiet, the playful energy replaced by a collective sense of curiosity and intrigue. Even Elena, who had entered feeling wary and tense, found herself leaning in, drawn by the depth in Ethan's words. It was a moment charged with quiet potential, a small step toward something none of them could yet fully understand.

Ethan gestured to the center of *"The Sky"*, his voice calm but commanding enough to guide the group's focus.

"We should sit in a circle, keeping enough space between the four of us," he instructed, his hand sweeping the floor in an inviting motion.

Ada, wasting no time, gracefully folded herself into a meditative posture, her legs crossed and her hands resting lightly on her knees. Her ease gave away her prior experience, and a faint, knowing smile played on her lips.

"Perfect," Ethan said, nodding toward Ada.

"Follow her lead."

Without hesitation, Ethan settled into his place, his movements fluid and deliberate. David and Elena exchanged a brief glance before following suit, each finding their spot in the circle. David mirrored Ethan's posture without much difficulty, his natural dexterity serving him well.

Elena, however, fidgeted as she tried to mimic Ada, struggling to fold her legs into the meditative position. The effort made her appear more like someone preparing for a rigorous exercise routine than a calming session of introspection. Seeing her frustration, Ethan leaned slightly toward her, his tone soft but reassuring.

"Just be comfortable," he said gently.

"This isn't about doing it perfectly. It's about finding your balance."

Elena exhaled a small, relieved laugh and shifted her position, finally settled into something that felt manageable. She glanced at Ada, who offered an encouraging smile, and then at Ethan, whose calm appearance seemed to fill the space.

"Alright," he began, "close your eyes for the next two minutes. Visualize the crystal in your mind. Considering how closely you've worked with it every day, I doubt it will be difficult to picture."

After two minutes, Ethan gently prompted them to open their eyes. His gaze settled on David first. "So, what did you experience?" he asked.

David rubbed the back of his neck, a sheepish grin crossing his face.

"Well, I caught a glimpse of the crystal for just a second, but that's about it. The rest... it was just nonsense. Random flashes, like my brain throwing a reel of chaotic images at me."

Ethan nodded, his expression unreadable, then turned to Elena. Her surprise was evident as she began to speak, her tone laced with disbelief.

"I couldn't see it at all," she admitted, her brows furrowed.

"And that's shocking, honestly. I mean, it's haunting my thoughts, even invading my dreams, but the moment I try to focus on it... nothing."

Her voice trailed off, confusion written all over her face.

Ethan simply smiled, a knowing glint in his eyes.

"Interesting," he murmured, his tone inviting curiosity rather than judgment.

Ada knew was her turn and had a winning simile, "I could see it quite a few times, but as soon as I focus, it blurs away though"

"What you've just experienced is an exercise—a realization," Ethan said, his voice calm but carrying a weight of understanding.

"Our minds are like untamed rivers, constantly flowing, often in directions we don't expect or want."

He leaned forward slightly, his hands resting loosely on his knees, and continued, "We cannot control our minds. Not easily, anyway. It resists direction. The more you try to force it, the more it rebels. It's like grasping at smoke—the harder you clutch, the further it drifts."

Ethan's gaze moved from David to Elena and finally to Ada, his expression thoughtful.

"This isn't a failure. It's simply the nature of the mind. The first step is realizing that you're not here to wrestle with it. You're here to let it be—to let it settle, like muddy water becoming clear when left undisturbed."

The group sat quietly, digesting his words, the weight of his insight pressing gently but firmly on their thoughts. Ethan's voice broke the silence again, softer this time.

"And when it does settle, maybe—just maybe—you'll find what you're looking for."

"Now, the practice," Ethan continued, his tone calm yet commanding enough to draw their full attention.

"I want you all to close your eyes again, just for two minutes. But this time, there's no trying. No effort to visualize anything. Let your mind flow the way it wants, without interference."

He glanced around the circle, his gaze softening as he continued, "Think of yourself as an observer—a person sitting quietly on the bank of a river, simply watching it flow. You're not trying to control the current or change its course. If a fish swims by, you don't reach for it or try to understand it. You simply note, 'That's a fish,' and watch it swim and disappear downstream."

Ethan's voice lowered slightly, creating an almost hypnotic rhythm.

"Let the thoughts come, if they must. Let them pass, if they will. Don't grab onto them, and don't push them away. Just notice, and let them drift as they may. Remember—you're on the riverbank, not in the water."

The group closed their eyes, the room falling into an expectant silence. The faint hum of the colony and the filtered Martian light became the only background, grounding them in the moment as they began the exercise.

"It's time"

Elena heard a voice, the unmistakable calm tone of Ethan. Her eyes fluttered open, and she noticed the others doing the same. Ethan looked around the circle, his gaze landing on Ada first.

"Can you guess how long it was?" he asked, his lips curling into a knowing smile.

Ada tilted her head, considering. "A little more than two minutes?" she ventured, her tone uncertain.

Elena blinked in surprise. Two minutes give or take, she had expected exactly that—just a brief pause in time. But the subtle tension in Ethan's expression told her otherwise.

"It was twenty-five minutes," Ethan revealed, his words cutting through the air like a gentle revelation. The weight of the realization sank in, and Elena's brows shot up. A faint murmur passed between David and Ada as they exchanged glances, both equally astonished.

Ethan chuckled softly.

"Einstein said time is relative," he added, leaning back slightly with an amused twinkle in his eye.

"I think you might agree with him now, right?" His question lingered in the quiet, and each of them sat with their own thoughts, the exercise having bent their perception of time in a way none of them had expected.

"I'd like you to practice this as often as you can," Ethan added, his tone steady but encouraging.

"The more you practice, the more victories you'll achieve."

He paused for a moment, letting the thought settle before continuing, "But don't overdo it. Overdoing doesn't help anything. An athlete can exhaust themselves, risk injury, or even break mentally if they over-train for something like a hundred-meter sprint. The same goes for meditation—it's about consistency, not intensity."

Ethan's eyes scanned the group, his faint smile softening the weight of his words.

"There's no single activity called 'Meditation,'" he explained.

"There is, however, a shared goal—to allow your mind to do its thing while you simply observe. That's it. No judgment, no interference. Just be the passive observer. There are countless ways, rooted in ancient traditions, to reach that state. What I showed you today is just one of them."

He let the silence linger for a heartbeat, the room feeling heavier with thought. Then, almost as if to lighten the mood, he added with a glimmer of amusement, "Don't rush it. Meditation doesn't work overnight— unless you're born with it."

His faint smile grew slightly mischievous as he concluded, "And if you are, you'd never know unless you start doing."

Ethan sighed softly and stood up, brushing off his knees as if marking the end of a session. Everyone followed his lead, though there was an almost palpable reluctance in the room, an unspoken yearning for more. The collective sense of peace they had discovered lingered, fragile and fleeting, like a dream interrupted too soon.

Elena felt as though she'd been plucked from a tranquil river, thrust back onto the rocky banks. The stillness she'd found in her mind was a reprieve she hadn't realized she needed, and now it was gone, leaving her with an ache for the calm she had just touched. Ethan should have let it last longer, she thought, feeling a hint of frustration mingled with her newfound appreciation for the practice.

Ada's mind raced with eager anticipation. This was different from any meditative experience she'd had before—raw, unforced, and deeply satisfying. It wasn't about discipline or focus; it was pure, unadulterated peace, and it felt like a gift she hadn't expected to find. She was anxious to try again, to sink into that pleasure once more.

David, a man of science and discipline, was caught in a different loop. For him, it wasn't just about the sensation; it was about the potential. He wanted to continue—not because he sought the peace it offered, but because he was curious. What would happen if they pushed further? Could this practice yield insights, open doors in the mind, or reveal something about their connection to the crystal? His desire to experiment, to understand, was almost as strong as his need to experience it again.

#

Sonja sat hunched over her workstation in the lab, the soft glow of the monitors illuminating her focused expression. The data streams from the plateau's recent drilling operation were layered and dense, a tapestry of numbers and visuals that demanded her meticulous attention. Each data-set held potential clues, what's under the Martian soil.

Back at the dome, the engineering team finally caught a breather, refocusing their energy on routine maintenance. The hum of tools and chatter echoed through the habitat as they tightened bolts, re-calibrated systems, and inspected the intricate network that kept their fragile world alive. For the first time in weeks, there was a semblance of normalcy—an illusion of control.

Yet, deep within the borehole, the alien structure rested. Its presence, unyielding and enigmatic, loomed like a shadow in the collective unconscious of the colony. Though it was left undisturbed for now, the subtle unease it evoked lingered in the background of everyone's thoughts. No one could say for sure if it had already been disrupted, if the mere act of reaching it had set something in motion. The colony, preoccupied with the immediate demands of survival, seemed to push the thought aside, dismissing it as a worry for another day.

But Sonja, alone in the lab, couldn't shake the sense that they had poked at something far beyond their understanding—and that it might not be at rest for much longer. A live feed from the borehole occupied the corner of her screen, a persistent reminder of the alien structure's presence. Sonja's eyes flicked to it, drawn by a nearly imperceptible movement. The structure wasn't entirely still—there were subtle shifts, so minute that only the micrometer scale on her display registered the changes. It was almost as if the material itself was breathing, alive in ways she couldn't yet comprehend.

#

Ada, David, and Elena met with each other close to a ritualistic manner, their voices low but steady as they exchanged their experiences from the day in day out. There were no groundbreaking revelations, no sudden epiphanies to share. But for Elena, something had shifted.

She leaned back in her chair, a faint smile touching her lips.

"It's strange," she began, her tone introspective.

"I wouldn't call it life-changing—at least not yet. But this... this calmness in my mind. It feels like a dam broke somewhere, and now everything just flows. No resistance, no chaos as it's as it supposed to be. It's... addictive," she admitted, glancing at them with a mix of wonder and trepidation.

"Like a narcotic, perhaps."

Ada tilted her head, intrigued. "Addictive in what way?" she asked, her curiosity piqued.

"It's not something I can fully explain," Elena replied. "It's like finding a hidden room in your mind you didn't know existed, a place where all the noise fades. And once you've been there, you want to go back. Over and over."

David nodded thoughtfully, his analytical side kicking in.

"Maybe it's not just calmness," he said.

"Maybe it's clarity. The kind that makes everything else feel... distant."

Elena's faint smile grew. "Whatever it is, it's exactly what I needed."

She continued, her voice steady but reflective.

"The technique... I've started practicing it at night, too," Elena said, glancing between Ada and David.

"When a nightmare wakes me up—and they still do, believe me—it used to feel impossible to calm myself down, let alone get back to sleep. It was an ordeal, every single time."

Her gaze drifted toward the window, where the faint glow of Mars' horizon cast long shadows in the room.

"But now," she went on, "it's different. I still get the nightmares, but they don't hold the same grip on me. I can sit up, breathe, and use the technique to ease my mind. And then... I just drift back to sleep."

She looked at them, a faint smile crossing her lips. "No stress. Just... peace."

Ada leaned forward, intrigued. "That's incredible," she said.

"It's like you've found a way to take control of something that used to control you."

David nodded, his expression thoughtful.

"And maybe that's the real power of it," he said.

"Not eliminating the fear, but learning how to live with it without letting it dominate you."

Elena nodded in agreement, her smile growing.

"Exactly. It's not about silencing the noise; it's about turning down the volume."

"Noise," Marcus asked as he stopped and turned to them, he was passing by on some work, his face a mix of urgency and mild annoyance.

"We're working on some emergency repairs. I hope you wouldn't mind a little noise," he added, his tone carrying a hint of displeasure.

All three—Elena, Ada, and David—burst into laughter, their amusement catching Marcus off guard. His brow furrowed slightly as he glanced between them, unsure whether the joke was on him or something he'd been working on. The uncertainty gnawed at him, leaving an unsettling feeling that something was happening under his nose, just out of reach.

Elena, noticing his discomfort, quickly spoke, her voice light. "That's fine, Marcus. We were just talking about our meditation practice." Her smile was warm but teasing.

"Remember? You didn't want to be a part of it?"

Marcus let out a breath, visibly relieved to know they weren't laughing at him or his work.

"Ah," he said, his tone shifting to one of mock dismissal.

"The woo-woo thing." He turned to David, pointing an accusatory finger.

"You too? You're into this?" He made an exaggerated gesture of spinning his finger near his temple, miming madness.

David, undisturbed, leaned back with a small smirk. "Science is all about crazy things, Marcus," he replied.

"Until we understand them, everything seems crazy."

Marcus opened his mouth as if to counter but then stopped, the logic was catching him slowly but surely. He narrowed his eyes in mock suspicion, muttering, "Alright. Just don't expect me to start sitting cross-legged any time soon."

The laughter that followed was genuine this time, diffusing the moment entirely.

#

Elena appeared radiant, exuding an energy that was impossible to ignore. Her movements were purposeful, her focus sharper than ever, and her appearance carried a newfound serenity. She was calm, quiet, and collected—no longer flustered by the usual chaos or minor irritations. Her colleagues in the lab noticed it first, marveling at her ability to remain unbothered even in the face of setbacks. But it wasn't just the lab; her transformation was evident in the greenhouse and everywhere else she went. It was as though Elena had discovered a better version of herself, a version that inspired those around her. Her peaceful confidence left others curious and even a little envious of the change.

"Elena," came the unmistakable voice of Riya from behind, steady yet warm.

Elena turned, recognizing her instantly. "Hope I'm not interrupting anything urgent," Riya added with a faint smile, her tone light but purposeful.

Elena returned the smile, her nod signaling compliance. "Not at all."

"Good. Let's take a walk," Riya suggested.

Elena didn't hesitate, falling into step beside her. Their conversation began with casual chit-chat—updates on the greenhouse, shared observations about the colony's recent activities. The banter flowed easily, a mix of the professional and the personal.

Before long, they found themselves at *The Circle*. The usually bustling area was unexpectedly quiet, offering an air of calm that felt almost intentional. Without much effort, they selected a secluded corner, two opposing settees framing a modest coffee table.

On the way, they grabbed two steaming cups of coffee, the warmth a small comfort against the sterile chill of the habitat. Settling into the soft cushions, the two women sat facing each other, their gazes steady yet curious, the unspoken weight of a deeper conversation lingering in the air.

Riya began with a warm smile. "I've heard about your newfound pastime," she said, her tone light but genuine.

"I didn't expect you to align with meditation so well, and so quickly. Even Ethan's surprised."

Elena chuckled softly, her lips curling into a modest smile.

"Me too," she admitted.

"Though I wouldn't call it meditation—not yet. From what Ethan told me, I'm just standing at the doorstep, peeking in."

"That's humbling to hear," Riya praised, her admiration evident.

Elena's gaze dropped slightly, her voice quieter but steady.

"It helps me come to peace with my fears and struggles," she said, her hands idly cupping the warmth of the coffee mug.

"It's like I'm finally able to face the things I've been running from."

Riya leaned back thoughtfully, her own expression softening. "I'll admit something," she said, a faint sigh escaping her lips. "I'm a little ashamed that I've never dabbled in meditation myself—especially being born in India. You'd think it'd come naturally, wouldn't you?"

Elena raised her eyes, surprised at the candid confession.

"But," Riya continued, a faint smile returning, "I've always been too caught up—with science, with the stars. Always looking outward, never inward."

Elena nodded slowly, feeling a subtle kinship in the moment.

"It's never too late," she offered, her voice tinged with encouragement.

"Maybe," Riya replied, her gaze distant for a moment. "Maybe it's time I learned to slow down."

They sipped their coffees in silence, each lost in her own thoughts, the faint hum of the colony around them a comforting backdrop.

#

Elena was the first to break the stillness. "I think the crystal can... talk to me more clearly now," she said, her voice tentative but resolute.

Riya's eyes flicked toward her, a spark of surprise flashing across her face. "Really?" she asked, leaning in slightly.

Elena nodded, her fingers tightening around the mug.

"It's warning me," she said quietly. "It has shown me Grace..." Her voice faltered, and she paused, gathering herself. The pause hung in the air, weighted with unspoken emotion. Finally, she took a deep breath and continued.

"The incident with her kidnapping attempt—that moment, Riya, it was the most fear I've ever felt in my life."

Riya's gaze softened, but she stayed quiet, allowing Elena the space to explain.

"It's the crystal's way of showing fear," Elena said, her voice steady as she spoke.

"It's trying to make me understand... to feel fear. And for a while, I couldn't figure out why. I didn't know what it wanted me to fear about!"

Riya tilted her head, her brows furrowing. "And now?"

Elena met her gaze, her own eyes filled with certainty. "I think I understand," she said.

"The crystal doesn't want us to unearth the artifact or whatever it is, in the plateau. It's a warning Riya… A clear one."

Riya's expression grew more serious, her mind already weighing the implications of Elena's words.

"If that's true…" she began, her voice trailing off as her thoughts raced ahead to the decisions they might have to face.

"As we are aware," Riya began, her tone measured but firm, "they've already expanded the borehole. I remember tomorrow's agenda is to bring it to the surface."

"I know," Elena said, nodding, her shoulders slumping slightly.

"I've been trying to delay it, but without something concrete to back me up, I couldn't justify interrupting what could be a scientific discovery."

Riya leaned forward, her eyes narrowing with intensity. "The science we know," she said, her voice rising, "is clearly not equipped to handle what we've seen firsthand or what we're living through every day." She raised her coffee cup, her gesture pointed.

"Even the water in this cup," she continued, "is a testament to something beyond our understanding. It comes from a process the science we hold dear cannot yet explain."

Elena looked down at her own cup as if trying to see something in it, her expression pensive, the weight of Riya's words sinking in.

"We've waited long enough," Riya said, her tone leaving no room for argument.

"The excavation needs to stop. We cannot afford to ignore the warnings"

Elena nodded, her resolve hardening.

"I'll speak to the team," she said quietly, her voice tinged with both relief and determination.

"This ends now." Riya confirmed.

#

The lab buzzed with tension as news of the decision spread. Conversations overlapped, equipment hummed, and the air seemed charged with an unspoken collective agreement—everyone, it seemed, was ready to halt the excavation.

Everyone, except Sonja.

She motioned for Riya to join her in the far corner of the room, her face set with determination. As Riya approached, Sonja's voice lowered but retained its intensity.

"I know," Sonja began, her tone sharp yet measured, "we should listen to the voices in Elena's head. I get how vital the crystal has been for us—what it's done, how it's guided us. But tell me, Riya, what guarantee do we have that this isn't the crystal's agenda at play?"

Riya tilted her head slightly, her brow furrowed, but remained silent, letting Sonja continue.

"Think about it," Sonja pressed, her voice softening but no less urgent.

"What if this artifact can unlock something extraordinary? What if it holds the key to knowledge, to advancements we can't even fathom yet? And what if the crystal simply doesn't want us to have it—not yet? Maybe it sees us as too primitive, too reckless for these kinds of discoveries. But who's to say it's right?"

She paused, her eyes searching Riya's for a response.

"Maybe we're not ready, sure. But should that decision rest with a crystal? Should it really be the one to decide the pace of our progress, the boundaries of our knowledge?"

Riya sighed deeply, crossing her arms as she leaned back against the wall. She studied Sonja carefully, weighing the validity of her words against the weight of their current predicament.

Finally, she said, "Perhaps the crystal isn't the judge. But the consequences of ignoring its warnings might be far worse than we can imagine. This isn't about trusting blindly—it's about surviving wisely."

#

As Riya turned to walk away from Sonja, a voice crackled through the communications line, urgent and strained. "Excavation site is trembling—please advise."

The message hung in the air like a sudden storm. Everyone froze for a moment, tension radiating through the lab. Riya spun around, her commanding presence immediately filling the space.

"Sonja, David," she snapped, her tone sharp and direct, "get to the site now. I need eyes on the ground—no delays."

Sonja's hesitation was brief but evident as she glanced at Riya, her earlier doubts still lingering. But the urgency of the situation propelled her into action. David was already grabbing his equipment, his usual calm replaced by focused determination.

"Elena," Riya continued, her voice steady but laced with urgency, "get the feed up on every angle on monitors we have. I want full visibility of that site. If anything moves, I want to see it."

Elena's fingers flew across the console, her pulse racing as she brought up the live video streams from the plateau. The towering drill rig came into view, trembling slightly against the Martian wind and a strange, barely perceptible vibration in the ground. The figures of the stationed crew moved in hurried precision, shutting down equipment and clearing the area.

Riya's voice came fast and firm through the comms.

"Keep the communications open at all times. I want updates every second—everything you're seeing, feeling, hearing. I need to know exactly what's going on."

As the feed stabilized, the scene on the plateau grew sharper, the tension gripping everyone in the lab. The trembling of the ground seemed almost alive, as though the planet itself was protesting the disturbance. Riya stood rooted, her jaw clenched, her eyes fixed on the screens as the weight of the moment pressed down on her shoulders.

"Crew on the plateau, this is Riya," her voice cut sharply through the comms, commanding and urgent.

"Your priority is to pull the machinery out—fast. Do it now."

The tension in the lab was palpable, each second dragging like an eternity as Riya continued, her tone leaving no room for debate.

"All personnel, maintain a safe distance from the site. Enable automatic maneuvers on the equipment—no exceptions. I repeat, no one is to be near the drill rig. Operate remotely and withdraw immediately."

Her voice rose with an edge of controlled urgency.

"This is not a drill, I repeat this is not a drill. Clear the area now!"

On the screens, the crew on the plateau sprang into action, their movements hurried but methodical. The drill rig groaned as it began to retract, its massive arm pulling back from the depths of the borehole. The automated systems whirred to life, their mechanical precision a bleak contrast to the frantic atmosphere.

"Sonja, David, what's your status?" Riya called through the open line, her eyes never leaving the monitors. "I need confirmation that the area is clear."

"On our way," David's steady voice replied, crackling slightly through the comms.

"We'll confirm as soon as we have a visual."

In the lab, Riya's hands tightened into fists at her sides as she waited, the air thick with the unspoken fear of what might happen next.

A tense silence stretched over the comms, each second feeling heavier than the last. The lab was thick with anticipation, every eye fixed on the live feed and data streams. Suddenly, David's voice broke through, steady but edged with urgency.

#

"We can see the site from a distance," he reported.

"Approaching at full speed. Looks like dust has risen—a lot of it. That's not a good sign."

Riya's jaw tightened. She knew they had no time to waste. Activating the comms, her voice rang clear and commanding, cutting through the static.

"Attention, crew at the site: command is transferring to David. I repeat, David will be in charge of the plateau from this moment forward. You will take orders directly from him."

She paused for a breath, her tone softening but losing none of its authority.

"We're with you every step of the way," she assured them, her gaze locked on the monitors as though willing them to succeed.

"We have eyes on the ground, and we trust your instincts, people. Good luck."

The room fell silent once more, save for the hum of machinery and the faint crackle of the open comm line. All eyes were now on David and the crew at the plateau as they raced toward an uncertain and potentially dangerous situation.

A faint but unmistakable voice crackled through the comms. It was Marcus, steady but with a deterministic voice.

"All equipment are successfully on autonomous mode. All crew are withdrawing. We're now at a safe distance from the site." He paused for a moment, and the silence on his end felt louder than his words when they returned.

"Not sure how much is actually safe, though. We're about half a kilometer out, but the ground—it's shaking. You can feel it through your bones."

#

The calmness in Marcus's tone was almost unsettling, given the gravity of his words. What he said sent a ripple through the command center, putting everyone on edge. For the few still seated, tension straightened their backs. Most, however, had already risen, crowding around the monitors and displays, their eyes darting between feeds of telemetry and live visuals from the site.

The room buzzed with a nervous energy. Every screen flickered with data—seismic readings, atmospheric changes, even the faint heat signatures emanating from the plateau. Whispers filled the space as the crew exchanged hurried observations, but none of it drowned out the unspoken question hanging in the air: What was happening beneath the surface, and how much worse could it get?

Riya's sharp eyes caught Elena's nervous pacing, her fingers tangled in her hair as she walked back and forth like a caged animal. The normally composed scientist was unraveling, her face pale and drawn with worry. It was clear that something profound was battling inside, and it was more than just the trembling ground or the uncertainty of the moment.

"Elena!" Riya called firmly, motioning for her to come over. The command in her voice left no room for hesitation.

Elena hesitated for a moment but then approached, her steps faltering.

As she neared, she blurted out, "Riya, I think we're too late."

Riya's brows knitted together, her tone hardening.

"Too late! … for what, Elena? Speak up, for God's sake child! Late for what…?"

The demand in her voice cut through the air, drawing the attention of a few nearby crew members.

"I don't know," Elena stammered, her voice trembling as her hands trembled at her sides.

"I keep getting this voice in my head. That's what it's saying—'Too Late.' Over and over. It won't stop."

Her tone was pleading, as though hoping for an answer she knew Riya couldn't provide.

Riya inhaled deeply, steadying herself.

"Elena, listen to me. Whatever this is—whatever it's telling you—we will handle it. You are not alone in this."

Her tone softened, though her urgency remained.

"Now focus. If the crystal is speaking to you, we need every bit of detail you can give us. Anything it's showing or telling you."

Elena looked at her, wide-eyed and desperate.

"It's not showing me anything—just the voice, repeating again and again. It's a warning, but it doesn't say what's coming."

Riya nodded, her jaw tightening. "Then we prepare for the worst. And we don't lose our heads"

#

All eyes were glued to the monitors, their displays a jumble of telemetry, seismic activity charts, and live feeds from the plateau. Yet, amidst the chaos, something else demanded attention—the crystal. Its hum had grown stronger, vibrating faintly through the walls of the containment chamber. The glow emanating from its surface pulsed with a deeper intensity, casting shifting patterns of symbols that seemed almost alive.

The changes were subtle yet unmistakable, as though the crystal were attempting to communicate—or perhaps summon something. The symbols shifted in complexity, cascading across its surface in a mesmerizing display that no one could decipher. It was as if it were reaching out, calling to others in some vast, unseen network.

But even as the faint hum grew into a low, resonant thrum, it seemed to go unnoticed by most. The crew, their attention locked on the crisis at the plateau, could not spare a moment to consider the crystal's strange behavior. And even if they had, what could they have done? It was still a mystery—one that remained just out of reach, its secrets as impenetrable as the alien material that encased it.

The crystal's glow intensified briefly, a sharp flicker that might have been a plea or a warning. It was a moment lost amidst the urgency of human voices and alarms, its silent story unfolding in the background of a drama no one yet understood.

#

Elena collapsed to her knees, fingers clawing through her hair, as if she could rip away the searing, unbearable sensation suffocating her mind. A choked gasp tore from her throat before she could find her voice—a voice that exploded through the tense air like a siren, raw and desperate.

"Get away! Get the hell out of there!"

The command center froze. Every eye snapped away from the monitors, turning to the trembling figure on the floor. The room, once humming with quiet urgency, now felt like a vacuum, suffocated by the weight of her words.

The sheer intensity of her outburst sent a shock-wave of unease rippling through the crew. No one moved. No one spoke. They simply stared—stunned, helpless—as Elena shook, her breath ragged, her anguish too vast to contain.

Riya was the first to break free from the paralysis. She stepped forward, voice firm yet filled with concern.

"Elena, what's happening? Talk to us!"

Elena's head snapped up, her wild, frantic eyes locking onto Riya. She looked haunted, her entire body trembling as if she had just touched something far beyond human comprehension.

Her voice fractured as she shouted, the force of it tearing from her chest like a wound reopening.

"Everybody! Get away from there! Return to the dome! NOW!"

The pain in her voice was palpable, as though speaking the words physically tore through her—as though something, unseen and unfathomable, was gripping her from the inside and pulling her apart.

#

In the seconds that followed, David's voice boomed over the comms, calm but commanding.

"Everyone at the plateau, evacuate immediately. Leave everything behind and return to the dome. This is an order. You are leaving… Now!"

Unknown to Elena, David and Sonja had already seen something horrifying. Just moments before Elena's cry, they saw impossible in the distance. The ground at the drill site was lifting—not cracking-open or caving-in as they had anticipated, but rising, as if pushed by some immense force below. It defied every geological explanation, leaving them frozen in terror.

"It's moving," Sonja whispered, her voice barely audible as her eyes remained fixed on the distance.

David swallowed hard, gripping the edge of the rover. "Get them out of there," he muttered to himself, knowing that whatever was happening, they were on the brink of something far beyond their understanding.

#

Back in the lab, Elena was struggling on the floor, her hands clutching her head as if trying to contain an invisible force tearing at her mind. Ada knelt beside her, murmuring words of comfort, her arm draped protectively over Elena's shoulders. Both women remained on the floor, one consumed by pain, the other by helpless concern. The tension in the room was intense, divided between those glued to the monitors and those unable to look away from Elena's torment.

Liam, his usual composure shattered, was hunched over his console, fingers flying across the keyboard with a speed and intensity rarely seen. His face was etched with concentration, but his voice cracked with tension as he suddenly shouted, "The crystal's activity has intensified!"

Riya spun around, her gaze locking onto Liam.

"How bad?" she demanded, her voice sharp but steady.

"Not as bad as during the storm," Liam replied, his tone measured despite the situation.

"Probably a quarter of that intensity, maybe a little more." His eyes darted across the readouts, processing the data faster than he could articulate.

"But..." he added, his voice dropping ominously.

"But what?" Riya pressed, stepping closer to the console.

"The electromagnetic activity—it's expanding beyond the plateau," Liam said, gesturing to a nearby monitor. The screen displayed an animated spectrograph overlaid on a video feed of the plateau, coupled with real-time imagery from the *watcher* satellite. Swirling patterns of electromagnetic energy stretched outward, reaching far beyond the drill site, rippling like an unseen storm over the Martian terrain.

"Something's happening out there," Liam continued, his voice tight with urgency.

"It's not just the drill site—it's... something bigger." His hand hovered over the screen as if willing the data to offer answers.

"And it's escalating."

#

Riya's gaze shifted between the live feeds and the trembling Elena on the floor. The room hung in the balance, caught between the immediate chaos and the unknown threat unfolding miles away.

"Stay on it," she said, her tone commanding but carrying a flicker of unease.

"I need to know exactly what's going on. No guessing—facts."

Liam nodded, his fingers already diving back into the console as the tension in the room coiled tighter, everyone waiting for the next revelation.

Elena's voice was faint, barely a whisper, but the urgency was unmistakable. Her exhaustion was written across her pale face, beads of sweat tracing the lines of her furrowed brow. Ada, ever vigilant, leaned closer, cradling Elena against her as if trying to shield her from the invisible forces pressing down on her. Ada tilted her head, bringing her ear closer to Elena's lips, straining to catch the words escaping in shallow breaths.

Suddenly, Ada raised her free arm, her gesture sharp and commanding, demanding the attention of everyone in the room.

"Elena wants everyone withdraw to the personal cubes!" she shouted, her voice trembling but resolute.

"Deploy the radiation shutters—NOW!" Ada's voice thundered through the dome, carrying an authority she never knew she possessed. The command snapped through the air, silencing the room as every pair of eyes turned to her in astonishment. For a moment, even the chaos outside felt secondary.

Her focus snapped back to Elena, who was murmuring something. Ada bent closer, her face contorted with concentration as she caught the next fragment of Elena's warning. Straightening up, her expression hardened with alarm.

"The medical crew needs to withdraw into the deeper part of the ship—away from the windows!", her voice more controlled.

The room fell into a stunned silence, the gravity of the instructions sinking in like a weight. Then, in a voice that cut through the tension like a knife, Ada added,

"Elena said we only have eight minutes to brace ourselves."

The finality of her words hung in the air like a thunderclap. The crew's collective gaze shifted to Elena, just as her body went limp, collapsing against Ada in a motion that felt far too final. Ada struggled to steady her, her voice rising in a desperate shout, "She's out! Somebody help!"

The room erupted into motion, a cacophony of shouts and hurried commands. Riya's voice cut through the chaos, barking orders with precision.

"Follow Elena's instructions! Move, now! Radiation shutters—deploy them immediately! Medical team, you heard her. We don't have time for hesitation!"

As the crew sprang into action, each second stretched unbearably, thick with tension and urgency. Fear and determination intertwined, fueling their every movement. Time was no longer a passive force—it was a countdown, an unyielding master dictating their survival. In the solitary confines of their living cabins, every motion felt deliberate, every breath measured against the invisible deadline looming over them. The only thing more smothering than the mystery unraveling around them was the silence of waiting.

A deep, thunderous rumble echoed in the distance, not just heard but felt—reverberating through their bones like a distant quake. It came precisely eight minutes after Elena's warning, a chilling confirmation that whatever was unfolding was not just real, but on their doorstep!

#

The following morning, the air in the colony was thick with uncertainty as the crew received orders to leave the living cubes and assemble at the central hub. The events of the previous day were still shrouded in mystery, with whispers and fragmented theories circulating among the crew. Despite their confusion, there was an unspoken sense of relief—a collective gratitude for simply being alive.

David, Riya, and Marcus were already at the hub when the crew began flowing in, their faces reflecting a mix of exhaustion and anticipation. Riya stood at the front, her posture commanding attention. As the last stragglers arrived, she raised her voice, her tone steady and calm.

"I trust we're all here now. Our medical team will be connecting us shortly through comms from the ship."

She paused, her eyes scanning the crowd, ensuring she had their full attention before continuing.

"Our crew at the drill site evacuated and reached the dome just in time— literally with a minute to spare. What you experienced in the cubes yesterday was a shock-wave," she said, her voice heavy with significance.

The room fell silent, the weight of her words settling like a lead blanket. Crew members exchanged uneasy glances, their minds racing to connect the dots. Picking up on the tension, Riya softened her tone slightly, adding, "Yes, a shock-wave. There was a detonation—a nuclear discharge of some sort."

A ripple of murmurs spread through the crowd, eyes widening in disbelief. Before panic could take hold, Riya raised her hand to quiet them.

"We're still working to understand what happened, but our satellites report no radiation contamination. None."

Her words were measured, deliberate, aiming to provide reassurance while maintaining the gravity of the situation.

"This is all we know for now," she continued.

"Effective immediately, all crew are confined to either the dome or the ship. No one is to venture beyond these areas until we receive further information, and I give clearance. I cannot stress this enough—no deviations."

The room buzzed with subdued tension as Riya stepped back, allowing the crew to process the information. The morning light filtered weakly through the dome, casting long shadows over faces etched with concern and curiosity. Whatever had happened at the plateau was beyond their understanding for now, but one thing was clear—they were standing on the precipice of something far greater than they had ever anticipated.

"For the critical systems within the habitat and the systems with remote access and control, your team leaders will reach out to assign tasks as needed," Riya continued, her voice taking on a lighter, more reassuring tone.

"Otherwise, treat this as a holiday. Enjoy the time socializing, catching up with each other, or even just taking a moment for yourself."

A faint ripple of relief swept through the gathered crew, some exchanging tentative smiles. Riya's words were intentional, a lifeline in the sea of uncertainty they all found themselves navigating. Her gaze softened as she scanned the room, as though silently willing them to take comfort in the fact that, for now, they were safe.

#

Riya finished her briefing and turned back, her shoulders visibly heavy with the weight of command. She walked briskly to where Elena was seated, her exhaustion unmistakable. Dropping into a chair beside her, Riya let out a quiet sigh, her face betraying the strain of the past hours. Ada was at Elena's side, her arm resting gently on her shoulder in a gesture of quiet support.

"You look better," Riya said softly, attempting a faint smile despite the tension etched into her features.

"Yes, I should be alright," Elena replied, her voice steady but her expression betraying a lingering unease. She managed a weak smile, though it barely masked the turbulence within. Ada gave her shoulder a reassuring pat, a subtle reminder to pace herself.

Elena's eyes shifted to Riya.

"How bad is it outside?" she asked, her curiosity tinged with an undertone that hinted she might already know more than she let on.

Riya hesitated for a moment before responding, her tone cautious.

"For a nuclear explosion…we are golden!"

Elena leancd forward slightly, her voice calm but laden with significance, "The explosion was the crystal's doing."

Riya's head snapped toward Elcna, her brows knitting in alarm. Her breath caught briefly before she spoke.

"It's weaponized then…" she murmured, her words heavy with realization. After a pause, her voice dropped further.

"This changes everything!"

The weight of that statement lingered in the air between them, unspoken possibilities and dangers flashing through their minds. Ada, her comforting hand still on Elena's shoulder, tightened her grip slightly, as if anchoring them both in the moment.

Riya began to walk away but then hesitated, turning back toward Elena. Taking a few steps closer, she asked, "Did you get any sleep?"

Elena rubbed her temples briefly before responding.

"I don't recall much after I collapsed. Woke up this morning when Ada knocked on the door."

Riya gave a small nod of approval.

"Good," she said simply, before turning on her heel and disappearing down the corridor.

Ada had spent the morning filling Elena in on what had unfolded after her collapse. Elena listened attentively, piecing together the fragments of her own memory. Her consciousness had been touch-and-go, Ada explained, but Dr. Myers had been closely monitoring her vitals remotely from the ship. Recognizing her condition, he had instructed Ada to administer a precise cocktail of medications to stabilize and relax her.

"You were out cold," Ada said with a faint smile, her tone both reassuring and light-hearted.

"But it worked. You slept for eleven hours straight."

Elena leaned back in her chair, her expression a mix of gratitude and relief.

"I feel like I could run a marathon," she jested, though her tone carried the weight of someone who had been through a storm. It was clear the rest had restored some of her strength, but the events leading up to it still lingered heavily in her mind.

Ada felt a sense of reassurance as she reviewed Elena's vitals on her Orion band. The data displayed consistent patterns of deep sleep—steady heart rate, regulated breathing, and brainwave activity indicative of someone deeply sedated. She nodded to herself, confident that Elena had been confined to her living cube and entirely subdued by the medications. There was no way she could have experienced anything outside the dome during those hours.

Ada's emergency medical training came handy as she analyzed the graphs and data. The rhythmic lines on the screen spoke another language she was fluent in, one far less cryptic than the enigmatic symbols etched into ancient artifacts. With a quick glance, she could discern the nuances of Elena's physical state—recovery, stability, and the quiet rhythm of her body at rest.

Satisfied, Ada tucked the Orion band back into its place and cast a glance toward Elena.

"You were out, completely," she said with a light chuckle.

"If you dreamed anything, it must've been the calmest dream of your life." Her voice carried a tone of assurance, masking the underlying tension from the events surrounding them.

"I wasn't totally gone!", Elena nodded.

Ada paused, her brow furrowing slightly as she processed Elena's words.

"You're telling me you weren't asleep?" she asked, her tone a mix of skepticism and concern.

Elena's smile didn't falter.

"Not quite," she replied, her voice steady, almost serene.

"I was… there. Living through it. At least, that's how it felt. It wasn't a nightmare, though. I wasn't afraid. It was as if I were watching the plateau unfold in front of me, like a movie. Detached, but present." She paused, searching for the right words.

"It felt… inevitable, like everything was happening exactly as it should. And more than that, I had this overwhelming sense of assurance. That everything—somehow—was going to be fine."

Ada's gaze narrowed slightly, studying Elena's face. There was a strange, almost otherworldly calmness in her expression, a tranquility that felt at odds with the chaos they'd all endured. It wasn't denial or repression, Ada realized. It was something deeper—a quiet acceptance or understanding that Ada couldn't quite place.

"You're remarkably calm for someone who just went through… all of this," Ada said, gesturing vaguely to the dome and the distant plateau.

"Most people would be shaken to their core, especially after a tension like that."

Elena shrugged lightly.

"Maybe I should be. But I'm not. And that's what's strange, even to me. It's like I've already processed it, somehow. Like the crystal… or something… gave me what I needed to face it." She leaned back slightly, her eyes distant, her smile unwavering.

Ada couldn't shake the unease that crept up her spine. There was something different about Elena—something that went beyond her usual resilience. And though Ada trusted her instincts, she couldn't help but feel like they were all standing on the edge of something far bigger than any of them understood.

#

Under gentle but persistent insistence from her colleagues, Elena reluctantly agreed to step back from her duties for the day. The others had made it clear—she needed to rest, recharge, and let her body recover from the toll of the previous day. Even though the thought of sitting idle felt alien to her, she conceded that it was likely the best way to regain her strength.

The day was designed to be unremarkable—a chance for her to blend into the flow of life in the dome without the constant weight of responsibility. Elena joined a group in the common area, sipping on a warm drink while listening to the idle chatter from work schedules to unexplained phenomena and of course the rumors on what has happened yesterday. The mundane rhythm, though not her preference, gave her body the time it needed to let the medicine wear off naturally and her mind a reprieve from the mounting pressure of recent events.

She wanted to be at the greenhouse at one point, admiring the orderly rows of crops thriving under artificial light, which was not possible due to the confinement orders. She wanted to look at Orion and check the greenhouse telemetry, but evaded the urge as of a reminder that others wanted her out of all work today. Marcus caught her there and playfully shooed her away, insisting that even a casual glance at the greenhouse data-stream counted as work. She smirked and let herself be led back to the recreation room, where a few others had started a card game. The simplicity of it all, though far from her usual pace, felt oddly grounding.

Despite her initial resistance, Elena came to realize that taking the day slow wasn't merely about physical recovery—it was an opportunity to re-calibrate her mind. As the hours slipped by, she found herself smiling more often, her laughter coming more naturally. For the first time in what felt like forever, she allowed herself to set aside the weight she carried, even if only for a little while, and simply exist in the moment.

This isn't that bad after all, she thought, a small, contented smile gracing her face.

#

Key members of the colony were summoned to *"The Sky"* that evening. Elena, having spent much of the day there in quiet reflection, watched as familiar faces began to trickle into the space one by one. Each arrival brought a mixture of comfort and curiosity—David with his steady expression, Ada exuding her playful intensity, and Liam, expression-less as always.

As she had already noticed, it wasn't just the usual faces gathering tonight. Sonja entered with a purposeful stride, her expression carrying a subtle edge that commanded attention. There was an air of urgency about her that unsettled Elena, though she tried not to dwell on it. Ethan followed shortly after, his relaxed posture and easy smile a stark contrast to the tension hovering in the room. His manner only deepened Elena's curiosity—his presence here wasn't typical, and she couldn't quite piece together why he'd been included. As more faces appeared, Elena's thoughts churned. Was this an official briefing? A casual gathering? Or perhaps something entirely unexpected? The uncertainty gnawed at her, leaving her to sit silently, observing and wondering what lay ahead.

Dr. Leva, as the colony's only nuclear scientist, was an obvious presence at the meeting, her intriguing expression quite noticeable as she took her seat. Dr. Myers standing at the center, his gaze sharp, his posture rigid, a curious mix of intensity and concern etched across his face.

It's probably just a status update, Elena told herself, trying to temper her thoughts. But deep down, an uneasy anticipation stirred, reminding her that in the ever-unfolding mysteries of the colony, nothing was ever just routine.

As soon as Marcus arrived, having an apologetical gesture for being few minutes late, Riya started speaking.

"I think Elena should welcome us," Riya said with a warm smile, her voice carrying a light-heartedness that immediately eased some of the tension in the room.

"She is, after all, the distinguished life member of *The Sky*."

The gentle tease earned a few chuckles from the group, and Elena couldn't help but smile back, though a faint blush crept into her cheeks.

Riya's intention was clear—she wanted this gathering to feel less like an official meeting and more like an open conversation among trusted colleagues. Her tone was calm, her appearance relaxed, setting an example for everyone to follow.

"Let's keep this casual," she added, leaning against one of the chairs with her coffee in hand.

"There's enough pressure in our day-to-day. Tonight, let's talk, exchange thoughts, and see where it takes us."

"I think most of us here already know the ground situation after yesterday's ordeal," Riya began, her voice steady but carrying the weight of the moment.

"If I may recall, the satellite imagery, telemetry data, and the aftermath on the ground all point to what appears to be a nuclear detonation—minus Radiation!" She paused, scanning the room for reactions, but none came. It was clear that everyone had already braced themselves for this part of the discussion.

"Also," Riya continued, her tone sharpening, "the data points to an implosion, not an explosion. If it had been an explosion, we wouldn't have survived the projectiles, let alone the radiation."

Her words hung in the air, a stark reminder of how close they had come to catastrophe.

"And the shock-wave," she added, her voice tinged with disbelief, "was dampened. If it had reached us untamed, we wouldn't be standing here now."

The room was silent, the gravity of her words settling in. Riya raised her right arm, fingers splayed, while her left hand cradled a cup of coffee.

"There are a few enigmas we need to try and understand," she said, her voice taking on an edge of determination.

She hesitated briefly, then dropped the next revelation.

"The satellite and surveillance footage show a projectile hitting the plateau mere seconds before the 'implosion.'" Gasps and murmurs rippled through the room, tension crackling like static.

"Liam has calculated the projectile's path," she continued, her eyes narrowing, "and we've determined it originated roughly two-thousand kilometers from the point of implosion. Unfortunately, our satellites were focused on the plateau, so we don't have clear data on how or what fired it."

Her words triggered a chain reaction of glances exchanged across the room, each filled with suspicion, curiosity, and unease. The implications were as vast as the Martian sky, and the room's atmosphere grew heavier with every passing second. Whatever answers they sought seemed to be buried deeper than the plateau itself.

Riya allowed the tension in the room to settle, then spoke again, her voice steady but laced with gravity.

"We have clear footage of the plateau, at least up to the implosion," she began.

"It wasn't just the event itself that shocked us, but the aftermath as well. The implosion took out some of our infrastructure, and the electromagnetic pulse knocked out our electronics. It was hours before any systems began to restart—some on their own, others only after we left the living cubes this morning to manually recycle the power."

She paused, scanning the room, her gaze briefly meeting Marcus's. He responded with a subtle nod of agreement.

"Almost all systems are back online… by now" she continued, "but there are a few exceptions. Marcus's team is already on it, and with the spares we have, we're confident they'll have everything operational soon." Riya acknowledged Marcus's confirmation with a brief glance, reassured by his gesture.

The room seemed to breathe a little easier at this reassurance, but Riya pressed on.

"What we captured at the plateau, though, is equally puzzling." She leaned forward slightly, her voice lowering, as if the weight of the truth itself demanded quiet.

"Something emerged from beneath the ground," she said, her words deliberate.

"It pushed through rocks and dirt as if they were linen and paper, moving with a force and precision that defied anything we've ever seen. It was so effortless, and yet the catastrophe it left behind was undeniable—cracking the ground wide open and dragging everything around it into the abyss."

The room grew still, the only sound the faint hum of the life-support systems. Riya let the magnitude of her words settle in, her gaze sweeping across the room as the colony's brightest minds absorbed the implications.

"It looks like the projectile struck whatever was emerging from the ground," Riya said, her tone measured but carrying an undercurrent of disbelief.

"We only had a fleeting glimpse of it," she paused, glancing around the room, "but it had rounded perimeter, sharp contours... Honestly, the closest comparison we could make is—" she hesitated, almost reluctantly, "a dinner plate."

The room was a mix of stunned faces and nodding heads. For some, this was the first time hearing such an extraordinary description, while others, who had pored over the footage repeatedly, silently confirmed the observation. The air grew heavier with the weight of the revelation, a combination of awe and confusion settling over those gathered.

"The implosion seems to have completely vaporized whatever that thing was," Riya continued, her voice steady but tinged with frustration.

"The current satellite feed only shows a crater—nothing significant... nothing..." she hesitated, choosing her words carefully, "...out of ordinary."

Riya's pause hung over them like a shadow, a quiet reminder that answers were still out of reach.

"Enigmas," Riya began, her voice steady but weighty, as she raised her hand and started counting on her fingers.

"First, the object that emerged from the ground—what was it, and why

n   o   w   ?

Second, the projectile's origin—where did it come from, and who or what launched   it?

Third, the projectile itself—its composition, its purpose, its precision. Fourth, the nature of the detonation—was it a meltdown, reaction, or something else entirely?"

She paused for a moment, letting the gravity of each question settle in. Then, raising her fifth finger, she added, "And finally, perhaps the most baffling of all—why the shock-wave was dampened and, most importantly, how we survived it."

The room was silent, the weight of her words pressing down on every person present. Riya lowered her hand, her gaze sweeping over the group.

"These are not just questions—they're puzzles that define our survival and our understanding of what we're dealing with. And until we find answers, we can't afford to take anything for granted."

#

Riya turned toward Elena, her commanding presence suddenly softened, her gaze heavy with unspoken questions. For a moment, she looked less like the resolute leader they all relied upon and more like a child searching for reassurance from a parent. The shift was jarring, almost unsettling— Riya Kapoor, the indomitable force that had guided them through every crisis, now stood before them vulnerable, her eyes pleading for answers she could not find within herself.

Elena felt the weight of that gaze like a physical pull, a sudden and somewhat expected responsibility settling heavily on her shoulders. She leaned forward, her expression exuding a serene calm that belied the storm of thoughts racing through her mind as she sought to console the unspoken desperation behind Riya's expression.

"I..." Elena began, pausing as if to carefully weigh her words. "I may offer some clues. Perhaps... even answers."

Her voice was calm, as steady as a moonlit lake, its serenity a stark contrast to the restless tension that gripped the room. The unease of the others seemed to amplify the odd tranquility she carried, unsettling and yet oddly comforting at the same time.

Every gaze in the room, including Riya's, was fixed on her. It was as though she had become the sole beacon of hope in a sea of uncertainty. Their anticipation was almost childlike, the collective silence charged with the kind of eagerness reserved for children waiting for their mother to read the next chapter of a cherished story.

Elena continued, her tone measured yet unyielding.

"What we have witnessed yesterday was a controlled nuclear implosion, enveloped within magnetic confinement. The damage was targeted, highly localized, and the environmental impact—along with radiation leakage—was minimal."

She paused, allowing the weight of her words to settle into the room, the silence punctuated by the faint hum of the surrounding systems.

"The projectile," she resumed, her voice unwavering, "was fired from an artifact. The exact location Liam has already identified."

Her gaze scanned the room, reading the tension that rippled through the group like an unspoken current.

"Yes," she confirmed, "I can feel your unease. Certain artifacts—nodes in this network if you will—serve different purposes. This particular one is a weapon."

The air grew thick with the gravity of her statement. A stunned silence swept over the room, leaving it as still and vast as the real sky above them, where the stars shone indifferently through the dome, distant witnesses to the unfolding drama below.

Elena allowed herself a faint smile as she scanned the faces around her, each etched with a mix of confusion and anticipation.

"I can see it in your eyes—you wonder what emerged from the ground," she began, her calm voice cutting through the tension like a blade. She gave them a moment to process, letting the weight of her words linger in the air.

"It's a spaceship…," she revealed, pausing just long enough to let the shock ripple through the group before adding, "automated drone, to be precise. …And not the good kind."

The room seemed to hold its breath, her revelation not bringing clarity but only deepening the confusion.

Marcus, broke the silence. "So, they have factions?" he asked, his tone laden with the unspoken implication that conflict was as universal as the stars themselves.

Elena nodded, her serene expression steady. "Yes," she said simply.

"Just like us, it seems. It wasn't long, was it?" Her smile was faint but unsettlingly calm, a reflection not of judgment but of the stark reality she was laying bare—alien or human, the echoes of division were the same.

The room seemed to pulse with unspoken questions, each face reflecting the same concerning curiosity: *Who are they?* The silence stretched, heavy and taut, until Elena took it upon herself to address the unspoken. She leaned forward slightly, her tone calm yet charged with a gravity that anchored every word.

"This was an ancient culture," Elena began, her voice steady, yet laced with reverence. "Far older than anything we can truly grasp." She let the weight of her words settle before continuing.

"If we compressed Earth's known history into a single time-line, as a line across a sheet of paper, every empire, every war, every achievement known to us would be nothing more than a tiny dot on the time-line."

She paused, letting the thought sink in.

"Now, imagine something so ancient that it doesn't just predate our civilizations—it exists beyond the paper itself." Her voice deepened with the sheer gravity of the thought.

"These beings—this civilization—touched planets when even our earliest ancestors were yet to dream. Compared to them, our oldest histories are mere flickers, vanishing as quickly as they appeared."

Her words hung in the air, a revelation that felt almost too large to grasp. Eyes darted around the room, some seeking confirmation, others grappling with the enormity of her statement. Elena's expression remained composed, though there was a flicker of something—perhaps wonder or perhaps dread—as she continued.

"We are looking at a legacy so vast, our history feels like a mere heartbeat against the backdrop of their existence."

"They have different races, different species, sharing the cosmos," Elena continued, her tone calm but deliberate, as if trying to bridge a gap in understanding.

"Just like us, sharing Earth. And just like us, not all of them are friendly or benevolent. Some are peaceful, some are driven by ambition, and others... others are far more dangerous."

She paused, glancing around the room, gauging the reactions etched across the faces before her.

"It's easy to feel disconnected—to see them as something entirely alien, incomprehensible. But if you think about it, their societies might mirror our own in some ways. They're not a monolithic entity; they're complex, diverse, and sometimes divided, just like we are."

Her words carried a weight of familiarity, as if she were trying to draw a thread between the known and the unknown.

"The alien worlds might seem distant, even terrifying. But when you strip it all down, the dynamics—the struggles, the alliances, the conflicts—they're all painfully familiar."

The room fell into a silence so profound that the faintest sound—a pin dropping—could have echoed across the room. Everyone sat motionless, their gazes fixed on Elena, stunned by the weight of her revelation. It was as if her words had shifted the very ground beneath their feet, leaving them unmoored, grappling with the enormity of what she had just shared.

For a moment, no one dared to speak. The stillness was almost tangible, an unspoken acknowledgment of the gravity of Elena's insight. It wasn't just the idea of other civilizations that rattled them—it was the stark realization of their own vulnerability, their own struggles, echoing across the cosmos in a resonance that felt more parallel than alien.

Chapter Eight
UNITY

The Martian dawn unfolded in silence, its pale light struggling through the dust-laden sky, brushing the horizon in muted shades of burnt orange and deep rust. Inside the habitat, the air hung thick with exhaustion, the weight of sleepless hours pressing against every breath. Yet beneath it all, a fragile undercurrent of relief stirred.

The unmistakable voice of Astraeus echoed through the dome, steady and reassuring. Following her routine weather update, she added,

"Confinement restrictions are now lifted. It is safe to go outside."

The announcement brought a buzz of activity as teams gathered to discuss priorities and organize the work ahead. The shock-wave had left its mark, tumbling over several structures. Among the critical damages were the solar array and the communication tower. Marcus, was already assessing the repairs.

"The backup power routing should hold," he assured the group. "We've got enough time to restore the array and the tower without compromising the colony's systems."

#

The greenhouse, fortunately, had been spared the worst of the damage. There were minor ruptures and air leaks, but Elena and Dr. Noah were confident they could manage the repairs with the help of their crew, sparing the engineering team from being stretched further. As they reviewed the work ahead, a sense of collective determination filled the dome. Each person knew their role, their skills honed for moments like these. Together, they would rebuild, one structure or a system at a time.

Noah caught sight of Elena struggling with a rubber seal just out of her reach. Her fingers brushed the edge of it as she balanced on her toes, her determined expression betraying how much the moment tested her limits. He strode over quickly, his towering frame making short work of the distance. Without a word, he stepped in, gently easing her aside to prevent what he imagined could end in a fall—or worse.

Elena turned to him with a warm, grateful smile, stepping back to give him room. Noah, with his seven-foot stature, easily pressed the seal into place without breaking a sweat. "Thanks," Elena said, her voice light but genuine.

Not wanting to let the moment slip by, Noah took the chance to ask, "What activated the disk at the plateau?"

Elena's smile dimmed slightly as she shifted into thought.

"These devices, even the crystal—they're incredibly sensitive to their environment," she began, her tone measured.

"When we started digging, it wasn't just the physical disturbance. It sensed our presence, our intent." She gestured toward a motion sensor above the greenhouse entrance.

"Like that, but far more complex. It's not merely detecting motion. These things analyze chemicals in the air, radiation levels, even the subtlest physical contact…" She paused, her gaze sharpening. "And… consciousness," she added, the word heavy with meaning.

Noah tilted his head, intrigued but cautious. "Consciousness? You mean it can get into our heads?"

Elena nodded, her eyes meeting his. "Yes, for some extent. It's as if it's alive in a way we can't fully grasp yet. And the more we disturb it, the more it responds."

Noah processed her words in silence, his earlier question now a seedling of a much larger, more unsettling thought.

"Hmmm," Noah groaned, the sound deep and reflective, as if carrying the weight of unspoken doubts.

"We shouldn't poke where we're not supposed to," he said, raising an eyebrow in mild admonishment.

Elena turned to face him fully, her hands resting on her hips, the corners of her lips curving into a faint, almost weary smile.

"The problem lies right there, Noah," she replied, her tone measured yet laced with a quiet intensity.

"How do we even know where to poke and where not to?"

Her words hung in the air like a question too vast for any simple answer.

"Everything we've encountered—every artifact, every signal—it's layered in mysteries we don't yet understand," she continued, her voice tinged with frustration.

"Isn't that the point of being here? To poke, to prod, to uncover the truths hidden beneath all this alien soil?"

Noah crossed his arms, his towering frame leaning slightly against the greenhouse's metal frame.

"Sure," he said, his voice calm but firm.

"But what if the truth we uncover isn't a one we can handle? Or worse, a one that doesn't care whether we can or not?"

Elena's expression softened, the faintest trace of a chuckle escaping her lips. "Then maybe it's the truth we deserve," she said, her voice steady with resolve.

"But sitting still and doing nothing? That's not in human DNA. If not us, then someone, somewhere, someday—it will be poked."

The two stood in a silence that wasn't uncomfortable, but rather reflective.

#

Elena felt the subtle vibration of Orion against her wrist. Glancing at the display, she noticed a notification flashing gently. With a faint smile, she turned to Noah. "Sorry, Noah," she said, her tone tinged with regret, " it seems I'm needed at the lab."

It was not uncommon for Elena to be summoned to the lab. Her expertise, authority, or even her ability to provide a trusted peer review often made her the go-to person for critical matters. But more often than not, her presence was requested when the topic turned to be of the artifacts—or, most notably, the crystal.

David, Marcus, Sonja, Freja, Leva, Staff and a few others appeared ready to head out, something Elena immediately recognized.

"You want to explore the plateau?" Elena asked as she stepped into the lab.

David nodded. "Yes, we need to assess and secure the perimeter. There could be unstable terrain that poses falling hazards."

"I'm more interested in the material left by the explosion," Sonja added.

"If we are lucky the tiniest fragments might have survived."

"Everything looks set. Can I join?" Elena asked, her voice carrying the hopeful anticipation of a child eager to be included.

The rovers started with a synchronized hum, their restrained systems ensuring a steady pace across the rugged Martian terrain. Each vehicle settled into formation, their paths weaving through the endless expanse of red dust and jagged rocks. The plateau, nearly twenty kilometers from the habitat, loomed faintly on the horizon—a distant reminder of the events that had unfolded there. The journey was slow, every bump and dip of the terrain testing the endurance of both the rovers and their passengers.

As they approached the site, the landscape began to shift. What was once familiar now bore the scars of a violent upheaval. The plateau had transformed into a massive crater, its edges sharp and jagged, rising like the serrated peaks of a crown against the orange sky. The rovers halted halfway up the slope, unable to climb further. The rest of the ascent would have to be made on foot.

The climb was not too difficult, but the loose gravel and shifting sands tested their balance with every step. When they finally reached the crest, the group paused, catching their breath and taking in the scene below.

What they saw was not the gaping void they had expected but a shallow dimple in the center of the crater. The faint glow of their anticipation dimmed, replaced by a quiet disappointment. It wasn't the ominous abyss they had feared—or perhaps secretly hoped for—but a subdued scar on the Martian surface.

David let out a low whistle, breaking the silence. "Not exactly what I imagined," he said, his tone tinged with both relief and curiosity.

All eyes flicked toward Orions, the faint warmth of its base a constant reminder of its ever-vigilant presence. Its built-in radiation detector pulsed gently, displaying levels just slightly above background—a reassuring signal that, for now, there was no immediate danger. The group remained quiet, their focus sharp, knowing the device would alert them to any sudden shifts.

Liam's voice crackled over the comms, steady but tinged with awe. He was perched on the ridge above, his vantage point offering a broader view of the crater below.

"I can clearly see the telltale signs of magnetic confinement," he said, his tone both analytical and fascinated.

"The patterns are unmistakable—this wasn't just a burst; it was deliberate containment."

Marcus, standing nearby with his arms crossed, let out a low chuckle.

"It would have been one hell of a confinement," he said, his voice carrying a note of dry amusement as he shook his head.

"The kind of power it takes to hold something like that in check... I can't decide if it's brilliant or terrifying."

Elena glanced between the two, her brow furrowed in thought.

"Terrifying if it fails," she said lightly, her voice carrying an edge of quiet confidence that hinted at both her understanding and her unease.

"I'm going down," Sonja said, pointing toward the middle of the crater. A materials detector was clutched in one hand, while her other arm extended outward to help maintain her balance.

After some time, once they were certain that the crater posed no immediate threat—no more than the other perils of the Martian landscape—they began their trek back to the dome. The journey was marked by a cautious sense of relief, their thoughts lingering on the mysteries they had just encountered.

#

Back at the lab, Sonja retreated to her familiar corner, surrounded by analytical equipment humming softly. She carefully examined a few fragments she had collected, pieces that seemed distinctly out of place among the usual Martian rocks. Their texture, weight, and composition hinted at something far more intriguing.

Meanwhile, on the other side of the dome, the engineering team was focused on re-erecting the snapped communication tower. With many of their robotic hoists still buried in Martian dust from the recent shock-wave, Marcus had decided to go old school.

"Manual tug and lift, it is!" he had declared earlier.

The call for volunteers had resulted in half the colony gathering enthusiastically around the site. Marcus stood on an elevated platform, a mix of surprise and amusement crossing his face as he surveyed the crowd.

"I could lift *Eos Horizon* with this turnout!" he shouted, eliciting cheers and laughter from the crowd. Yet, beneath his humor lay a quiet worry— how to organize this eager group into a coordinated effort without turning the operation into chaos.

Elena and Dr. Noah found themselves grappling with more than just repairs and expansion in the greenhouse. Their call for assistance had been met with an unexpected response—dozens of enthusiastic volunteers, all seemingly inspired by a newfound passion for agriculture. While the help was appreciated, it came with its challenges. Noah, who had spent years lecturing back on Earth, initially found their eagerness endearing. However, it quickly became exhausting as he was forced to explain the greenhouse's intricate systems repeatedly, each time to a different person asking the same question. What had started as entertaining soon felt like an endless loop into exhaustion!

Elena, meanwhile, had no respite either. Her responsibilities extended far beyond agriculture. Questions about the crystal and the artifacts peppered her throughout the day, leaving her little room to focus. While she understood their curiosity, she couldn't shake the feeling that she was being stretched too thin. The greenhouse had become a melting pot of inquiries and excitement, but for Elena and Noah, it was turning into a test of patience and endurance. Still, they pressed on, balancing the delicate task of managing the curiosity of their growing team while ensuring the critical work didn't fall behind.

Observing the growing struggle, Sienna offered a suggestion—to hold classes on agriculture, hydroponics, plant genetics, and everything in between. The goal was simple: to help the colony understand not just the technology sustaining plant life on Mars, but the very biology that made survival possible.

It was a welcome idea, one that Elena immediately saw as vital for the colony's future. Food security couldn't rest in the hands of just one team; everyone needed to know how to grow, adapt, and sustain their own resources. A greenhouse was not just a facility—it was a lifeline, and every colonist would need to understand how to keep it thriving.

"This could really work," she said, her tone tinged with hope.

"Not just for us, but for the colony as a whole."

The suggestion resonated deeply. Everyone needed to understand the intricacies of growing food in the unforgiving Martian environment. From seed germination to nutrient cycles and water reclamation, the knowledge would empower the entire colony, fostering a collective responsibility for sustenance.

Elena envisioned a future where every member could contribute, not just by troubleshooting greenhouse systems but by innovating and expanding their food production capabilities. For the first time in weeks, she felt a sense of relief—a solution that didn't just lighten her immediate burden but also strengthened the foundation of their shared existence on Mars. The team's suggestion wasn't just practical; it was essential for the survival and growth of their colony.

Riya welcomed the idea of agriculture classes with her enthusiasm, always recognizing the importance of fostering collective knowledge in the colony. After a meeting at the hub, her familiar voice reached Elena who was about to leave.

"Elena," Riya called, a glint of humor dancing in her eyes.

"Sign me up for the class."

Elena looked up, her expression shifting into a mock-seriousness. Raising an eyebrow, she responded in a playful tone, "Let's see… I think tickets are almost sold out."

Riya chuckled, crossing her arms. "Good thing I have some authority around here. Consider this a VIP request."

Elena couldn't help but laugh. "Alright, Commander. But no special treatment—you'll have to bring your own shovel!"

The exchange, cheerful as it was, carried an undertone of shared respect and camaraderie. In that moment, the burdens of leadership and survival seemed to fade, replaced by the simple joy of human interaction.

"The Sky", once a space for quiet reflection and strategic discussions, was beginning to transform into an impromptu meditation hub. The

panoramic views and tranquil atmosphere made it the perfect setting for minds to find a rare moment of calm amidst the chaos of Martian life.

Ethan leaned casually against the curved railing, watching the growing group with a blend of surprise and quiet pride. Never in his wildest dreams had he imagined himself teaching meditation—let alone on Mars. His skills had always felt like a peculiar, almost indulgent talent, something that might spark curiosity but never real necessity. Yet here he was, surrounded by an audience eager to learn, their eyes fixed on him, hanging onto his words as if they were the wisdom of a sage.

"It's funny," Ethan told Elena one day, "I came here thinking remote viewing would be my big contribution. Turns out, helping people silence the noise in their heads is just as vital." For the first time since arriving on the Red Planet, he felt a profound sense of purpose, a realization that his unique skill-set held value in ways he had never expected.

"You helped me... and now, look at how many more you're helping," Elena said, her voice filled with gratitude, admiration shining in her eyes.

"Let's find some time to meditate together," Elena offered, her tone light yet sincere. Without waiting for a response, she gave a small nod, then turned and walked away toward the greenhouse, leaving the invitation lingering in the air.

#

Ethan approached Elena one quiet afternoon, catching her just as she was heading to the greenhouse.

"Elena," he called out, his tone light but purposeful, "I'd like you to help me with the meditation classes."

Elena paused, her expression softening into a polite smile. Before she could respond, Ethan continued, "You're far ahead of me, you know. I just showed you the road, and now you're miles ahead of where I've ever been." His sincerity was disarming, his admiration genuine.

She hesitated, then shook her head gently.

"I appreciate it, Ethan, truly, but I'm swamped with work right now. Between the greenhouse extensions and the other projects, I just don't have the bandwidth," she explained. Her words were true enough, but as she turned to leave, she felt the weight of the real reason she had tried to suppress.

Deep down, Elena wasn't ready. She had embraced the techniques, but only as tools—methods to steady her nerves, to keep the nightmares at bay. They worked, in a way, smoothing out the jagged edges of her mind, but something about them still felt foreign, uncharted. She wasn't sure if she was learning control or simply building walls, holding back something she wasn't prepared to confront.

Each time she closed her eyes to meditate, she felt like she was stepping onto an unfamiliar path, winding and endless, with no map to guide her. She feared the places it might lead, the doors it could unlock—the ones she wasn't sure she had the courage to walk through. What if she went too far? What if she lost herself in the quiet?

As she walked away, her gaze flickered back toward Ethan, standing firm in his belief, his confidence in the practice unwavering. She envied that certainty, that trust in the process. But for now, she would remain on the outskirts, watching, waiting, hesitant to dive in until she knew where the road led—or until she found someone who could light the way forward.

That someone—or perhaps something—was closer than she realized.

Weeks turned into months as the colony settled back into Martian rhythms, each moment a renewed sense of purpose. The initial chaos and uncertainty, marked by two near-catastrophic events, now seemed like distant echoes, though their lessons remained etched in every action.

Now established water independence, thanks to the crystal's enigmatic properties, was nothing short of miraculous. It had transformed their outlook on survival, shifting their focus from merely hanging on, to building a sustainable future. Each drop of purified water represented a triumph of ingenuity and adaptability, a testament to their ability to coexist with the alien technologies surrounding them. For the first time, hope felt tangible—something they could drink, touch, and see as plants thrived in the greenhouse.

The colony pulsed with activity. Engineers worked tirelessly to reinforce structures, expand living quarters, and optimize power systems. The greenhouse was a hive of innovation, as Elena and her team experimented with Martian soil and crops, pushing the boundaries of agricultural science. Classes in agriculture, engineering, and even meditation became a regular occurrence, uniting the colony in their shared goal of survival and progress. The amity was strong, a bond forged in the crucible of adversity.

As the sun cast its amber glow across the landscape, the colonists began to believe not only in survival but in the possibility of thriving. They had proven to themselves—and perhaps to the mysterious forces watching from the artifacts—that humanity could endure, adapt, and rise anew, even on the red sands of Mars.

#

Orion's subtle vibration drew Elena's attention to the screen. The message was simple yet unsettling:

"Meet me at The Sky, ten past ten."

It was from Riya. Messages from Riya were not unusual, especially given the dynamic nature of the colony, but there was something about this one that felt... different. Ominous, almost. *Ten past ten*—the specificity tugged at her curiosity. Why such an exact time?

The thought lingered, refusing to leave her mind. Could it be tied to some atmospheric event? Elena's fingers danced across Orion's interface as she scanned the database for any phenomena or anomalies scheduled around that time. Nothing significant showed up. She checked the colony's schedules, the crew's tasks—everything appeared routine, ordinary. Yet, the sense of unease persisted.

Her curiosity led her to Ada, hoping for some clarity.

"Anything happening at the lab I should know about?" Elena asked casually, trying to mask her growing apprehension. Ada shook her head.

"Not that I've heard. Everything seems normal. Why?"

Elena brushed off the question with a quick smile, but internally, her thoughts churned. She wasn't sure if anyone around her noticed how often her gaze flickered back to Orion, as if willing the clock to move faster. Time seemed to stretch unbearably, each minute dragging like an eternity. The anticipation coiled tighter in her chest, a mix of intrigue and foreboding she couldn't shake. *Ten past ten* felt like a distant, unreachable checkpoint, yet its weight loomed over her every thought.

As soon as she finished her work, Elena wasted no time. A quick, lukewarm shower washed off the day's sweat, and she slipped into casual wear—simple and comfortable. Gulping down some re-hydrated food hastily prepared in the multi-cooker, she didn't felt a flicker of guilt for not savoring it, but the thought of the meeting tugged at her attention. She glanced at Orion. Nine o'clock. It was still early, but the weight of anticipation made it feel much later.

The climb to *"The Sky"* was quiet, the familiar winding stairs echoing faintly with each step. Elena welcomed the stillness, the emptiness of the space above. Ethan's meditation classes were always scheduled for the early mornings. This time, *"The Sky"* felt like her own sanctuary—a haven perched above the sleeping colony.

She began to pace the perimeter, her fingers brushing along the smooth balustrade, the material cool against her touch. Her eyes wandered beyond the dome, out into the Martian night. The luminaries positioned outside struggled to pierce the darkness, their faint glow barely illuminating the jagged edges of the alien terrain. The horizon, shrouded in shadow, seemed endless.

Elena paused, leaning on the railing, her gaze fixed on the stars. They felt so distant, so quiet, as if indifferent to the life-or-death struggles unfolding beneath their eternal watch. The stillness of the moment soothed her nerves slightly, though the question of why Riya had called her lingered, heavy and unanswered. *Ten-past-ten.* The time loomed closer, and with it, an unsettling curiosity that refused to leave her mind.

Elena settled herself on the smooth floor of *"The Sky"*. With fluid precision, she shifted into the meditation posture she had come to master over the months—a blend of necessity and practice that now felt as natural as breathing. Her legs folded effortlessly, and she rested her hands on her knees, her posture steady yet relaxed. The familiar hum of the dome's atmosphere wrapped around her, a comforting background to her wandering thoughts.

She sensed Riya before she saw her—not just the faint sound of soft-soled slippers against the spiral stairs echoing upward, but watching her like a movie, Elena thought. Riya was on casual wear of light Gray and an unhurried manner immediately set Elena at ease. There was nothing visibly unusual about Riya's expression, nothing to hint at urgency or alarm. But still, Elena's mind circled back to the significance of this meeting.

Why *ten-past-ten*?

As if on cue, pieces of the evening began to align in Elena's mind with startling clarity. She saw Riya in the commander's room earlier, engaged in a call with Earth. That had been at quarter past nine. The call lasted twenty minutes. Then, Riya took another twenty-five minutes to freshen up and slip into her casual wear, and finally, a ten-minute to walk through the corridors and climb to *"The Sky"*.

Ten-past-ten. It wasn't an arbitrary choice, not a mystery; it was simply the natural rhythm of events, played out with precision. The realization struck Elena with an almost surreal vividness, as if Riya's movements were right before her eyes, or she was living through it! A strange clarity settled over her, unlike anything she had experienced before—a sensation that felt deeper than intuition.

Elena opened her eyes just as Riya reached the floor. Their gazes locked, and for a fleeting moment, neither spoke. Riya's expression softened, perhaps catching a glimmer of something unspoken in Elena's face. The quiet between them wasn't empty; it was charged with understanding, as if they had just shared a secret neither had voiced.

"Ah, good that you're out of the trance," Riya sighed, her smile carrying both relief and amusement.

"I would have just sat here and waited otherwise," she added, her tone light, almost teasing.

Elena offered a faint smile in return, though her thoughts churned beneath the surface. Riya didn't know, couldn't have known, that Elena had opened her eyes precisely as she reached the final step. It wasn't coincidence—it was as if Elena had felt Riya's presence long before she arrived, a certainty she couldn't quite explain.

She wasn't surprised to see Riya in her light-Gray casual wear and slippers. How did I know? Elena wondered, her mind caught between logic and something more nebulous. Was it intuition, a heightened sense, or simply an educated guess pieced together from observing behavior? She couldn't decide. But the feeling lingered, undeniable and strange, as though her mind had begun navigating a different wavelength altogether.

Elena stood up, her movements as graceful as a feather drifting in the wind. She seemed alight, radiant even, with an energy that Riya couldn't help but notice. She thought, for a fleeting moment, how Elena carried a joy that felt almost contagious. As they settled into opposing couches, the coffee table between them a quiet witness, Riya leaned back with a soft smile.

"I had a scheduled call from Earth," Riya began, her tone casual but measured.

"It's part of the routine, you know—twenty minutes long, never more, never less." She smiled again, this time with a faint curiosity, as if testing Elena's reaction. Riya had never shared her precise schedule or the details of her calls with Earth, keeping them strictly on a need-to-know basis.

Yet somehow, Elena seemed to already know.

Elena didn't need to ask what the call was about—she could sense that whatever it was, it's not the focus. Still, an inexplicable feeling washed over her, a quiet assurance that if she truly needed to know, she would have known on her own. The realization startled her, but not enough to unsettle her serene composure.

Riya broke the silence, her voice carrying a rare note of vulnerability.

"I just wanted to talk to someone. Hope I haven't dragged you out of anything important." There was an unspoken plea in her words, an invitation for empathy.

Elena shook her head with a soft smile. "Not at all," she said warmly.

"I was just waiting for you."

They sat quietly for a moment, the stillness between them filled with the unspoken comfort of shared presence.

"How have your days been?" Riya finally asked, her voice soft, breaking the silence with a gentle nudge.

"No blunders," Elena replied with a playful chuckle, her light-heartedness infectious. Both laughed together, the sound filling the space like a soothing balm.

But then Riya paused, her expression shifting slightly as she looked directly at Elena.

"I have a minor tumor," she said, her voice steady but tinged with weight.

"In the brain."

Elena froze, her composure cracking as her lips parted, her breath catching.

"Pituitary carcinoma," Riya continued, her tone soft but direct.

"A rare kind. I'm one in a billion." She added a faint chuckle, attempting to lighten the weight of her words.

Elena's mouth remained open, words eluding her, as her mind reluctant to comprehend what she had just heard.

Elena sat there, her thoughts swirling in a quiet chaos. She wasn't sure how to respond. The term "pituitary carcinoma" meant little to her—a foreign and intimidating name with implications she couldn't fully grasp.

But something within her, an instinct she couldn't explain, painted a clear picture in her mind. She envisioned the tumor's location, nestled near the optic nerves, and her heart clenched with the realization: it could affect Riya's vision.

The words escaped her lips before she could stop them.

"Is your vision affected already?" Elena's voice was barely above a whisper, trembling with a mixture of concern and empathy. Her eyes, unblinking, began to glisten as tears threatened to escape.

Riya noticed the emotion welling up in her companion. She reached across the table, her hand resting lightly on Elena's, a gesture of reassurance.

"Oh no," Riya said, her tone laced with a wry humor meant to diffuse the weight of the moment.

"You're stuck with me for a while." She offered a small, playful smile, as though willing the heaviness to dissipate.

Elena's lips quivered into a faint smile in return, though the moisture in her eyes remained, refusing to be blinked away. For a moment, the room felt heavy with unspoken fears and silent reassurances, the weight of Riya's words lingering but softened by her attempt to project strength.

For a long, quiet moment, they simply looked at each other. Elena's eyes brimmed with unspoken emotions—empathy, concern, and a quiet, helpless uncertainty. She wanted to say something, anything, but no words seemed fitting. On the other side of the table, Riya's gaze held steady, a mix of gratitude and gentle resolve just having someone to share.

In that shared stillness, they both found a moment of connection deeper than words could convey.

As if a sudden thought struck her, Riya asked, "How did you know about the tumor? I mean, do you know someone else who has it?"

Elena felt the sharpness of Riya's perception cut through the moment, even in the midst of her vulnerability. It didn't take long for Elena to realize there was no evading her. Riya's keen intuition had already zeroed in on the subtlety of her words.

"No," Elena said softly, nodding.

"I just... knew."

She didn't attempt to cover or deflect, knowing well it would be futile against Riya's unrelenting insight. Her sharp conscience would dig deeper, and any attempt to obscure the truth would only make things worse.

Riya's gaze lingered on Elena, searching her face for something more, her expression a mix of curiosity and a faint trace of unease.

"It's early stage," Riya added quickly, her tone almost dismissive, as though trying to shift the focus away from Elena's visible unease.

"Dr. Myers said it may or may not affect the optic nerve, but... it usually does."

Elena's eyes widened, and she leaned in slightly.

"He should be able to fix it, right?" she asked, her voice tinged with hope but undercut by an underlying apprehension.

Deep inside, she already knew the answer—or at least she thought she did. Riya wouldn't have brought this up if it were as simple as a straightforward treatment. It had to be something serious, something that compelled Riya to share it with someone. It wasn't intuition, or some unexplainable phenomena this time, just plain, unsettling logic.

Riya caught the flicker of doubt in Elena's eyes and placed a steadying hand on the coffee table between them.

"It's manageable," she said, her voice firm, as though trying to convince both Elena and herself. But her faint smile couldn't mask the weight of her words.

Riya continued, her voice steady but laden with the weight of her responsibility.

"It wouldn't have been such a pressing situation if I weren't the Commander of this colony. It's our duty to report any health concerns to Earth, and I've already communicated it to them with Dr. Myers. That's why I expected the response in today's call."

Elena sat in suspense; her hands clasped tightly on her lap. She didn't dare ask what Earth had said, though the question was burning inside her.

"Earth wants a contingency plan," Riya said, breaking the silence. "David will be next in line, and you'll be his first officer."

Elena's eyes widened as the words sank in. She was stunned, unsure how to respond, her mind racing to process the gravity of what Riya had just revealed.

"I have to step down at the first signs of vision decay," Riya continued. "Dr. Myers will conduct regular checkups to monitor my condition closely."

Elena struggled to find words, her throat tight with emotions she couldn't articulate.

Riya noticed her reaction and added gently, "David doesn't know yet. I'll tell him tomorrow."

Elena wanted to ask the question that hung heavy in her mind—*How much time do we have?* But something inside her stopped her, as if voicing it might make the situation more real.

Riya seemed to sense the unspoken question. Her voice softened.

"I may have a few years... or just a few months. We don't know yet." She gave a faint, bittersweet smile, as if trying to shield Elena from the full weight of the uncertainty.

Riya's voice dropped, heavy with a finality that Elena wasn't prepared to hear.

"This tumor will eventually cause hormonal imbalances," she said, pausing as if each word were a stone sinking into deep water.

"That's not a situation I intend to endure. In the worst case, I've already authorized Dr. Myers to…" she hesitated "…put me out of misery."

The room seemed to shift under Elena, like the very ground had given way. It wasn't just the words— it was the raw inevitability behind them. She felt as though she'd been yanked out of her seat, dragged into a void she couldn't comprehend, the security of her world unraveling in an instant. Her mind raced, trying to process what she had just heard, but instead, it spiraled into a state of sheer disbelief.

Her face turned pale as though every drop of blood had drained from her body. It wasn't just shock—it was the stark realization of the weight Riya carried and the brutal practicality of her absence. Elena's eyes searched Riya's face for something—hope, reassurance, a sign this was all some grim hypothetical—but there was none.

Riya, noticing Elena's visible turmoil, stood up and walked over to her. Without a word, she placed a comforting hand on Elena's shoulder, then gently pulled her into an embrace. Elena's head rested against Riya's shoulder, her breathing unsteady as she tried to gather herself.

"You're stronger than you think," Riya whispered softly, her tone steady despite the gravity of her words.

"And I need you to be, Elena. Not just for me, but for the colony, for everything we've built here."

"It's almost half a sol," David's voice broke through the general murmur, loud enough to draw attention. Some faces lit up with understanding, while others were left exchanging puzzled looks.

The Martian calendar still felt foreign to many. Seasons and cycles on Mars were subtle, their shifts almost imperceptible within the confines of the colony's structured life. Unlike Earth's dynamic changes of spring blooms or autumn hues, Mars offered only faint variations in temperature and light—a world where even time moved differently. For the crew, still acclimating to their new existence, these markers often passed unnoticed.

Yet David's remark carried weight. Half a Sol, the equivalent of nearly 12 Earth months, marked a symbolic milestone for the colony. They had survived, adapted, and in many ways thrived on this alien planet. For a moment, the room was caught in a peculiar mix of reflection and disbelief. Had it really been that long? For Earth, it was a year gone by, but here on Mars, time stretched and compressed in strange ways, blurring the edges of their days.

The colony gathered under the dome's warmth, a rare moment of relaxation and camaraderie as they held a tea party to commemorate the passing of an Earth year. Tables were arranged in a casual but welcoming fashion, adorned with makeshift decorations crafted from whatever the crew could scavenge—bits of foil, fabric scraps, and even creatively re-purposed greenhouse vines. Steam rose from cups of tea, a luxury made possible by their first successful harvests and clever rationing. The air was alive with laughter, voices overlapping in a joyous cacophony that felt so unlike the often-tense atmosphere of their daily routines.

Clusters of people formed naturally; each group immersed in its own lively discussion. Marcus and his engineering team were debating the best way to fortify the solar arrays against future storms, but the tone was light-hearted, punctuated by jokes about duct tape being the "real hero of Mars." Across the room, Sonja animatedly explained her latest geological findings to a curious audience, using exaggerated gestures that drew laughter from those nearby.

By the greenhouse's corner space, Elena stood with Dr. Noah, sipping tea and casually answering questions about the colony's food sustainability.

"Next year, pizza every week," Noah joked, earning a round of applause from those within earshot.

Ethan and Ada had taken over a quieter space, where they were recounting the surreal experience of their meditation sessions. Ethan's exaggerated imitation of Elena's "unintentional psychic stare" left Ada in stitches, her laughter so infectious that it spread to nearby tables.

Riya moved through the crowd; her presence magnetic as always. She stopped to chat briefly at every table, her laughter and casual remarks putting everyone at ease. Despite the festivities, she carried herself with a subtle grace that reminded everyone she was still their commander, but tonight she was simply part of the family.

The aroma of freshly baked bread—courtesy of Elliot—wafted through the air, adding to the party's homely charm. As conversations flowed and cups clinked, it became clear that this wasn't just a celebration of time passing. It was a reaffirmation of their unity, their shared struggles and triumphs, and the simple fact that they had made it this far together. On Mars, where every moment was a challenge, this gathering was a victory of its own.

David navigated through the lively crowd with purpose, his eyes fixed on Elena, who was visibly overwhelmed by the relentless barrage of questions from her peers. Though she noticed his approach and his patient waiting, the torrent of inquiries left her with no chance to break away. It was clear she was being swept up in the enthusiasm of those around her.

Without warning, David stepped forward, his hand gently but firmly clasping her arm.

"Enough," he announced, his voice cutting through the chatter with an air of authority that turned heads.

"She's mine for a moment. I promise, you'll have her back in no time."

Elena, caught off guard, almost stumbled as she was pulled from the crowd, but she quickly regained her balance. The unexpected gesture left her momentarily stunned, her wide eyes searching David's face for an explanation. Yet, instead of resisting, she allowed herself to be guided, falling in step with his decisive stride.

The crowd, a mixture of amused and perplexed faces, parted as David led her to a quieter corner of the dome.

"David!..." Elena finally found her voice, a mixture of surprise and laughter escaping her lips.

"What are you doing?"

"Saving you," he replied, a small grin tugging at the corners of his mouth.

For the first time that evening, she could take a full breath without feeling like she had to answer another question. She let out a soft laugh, shaking her head.

"You're impossible, David."

"And yet, here we are," he quipped, his grin widening.

"Now, take a moment for yourself. You've earned it."

Catching her breath and sipping from her drink, Elena's eyes followed David as he waved toward someone across the room. Moments later, Marcus appeared, his cheerful energy in full force.

"Ah, you two—just got married?" he quipped, flashing a mischievous grin.

The joke landed with a thud. In an instant, he realized his misstep, his grin fading as Elena shot him a sharp, unimpressed look. Her expression, a mix of irritation and disbelief, made it abundantly clear the joke wasn't welcome.

"Okay, okay, I take it back," Marcus said quickly, raising his hands in mock surrender.

"Jerk," Elena retorted, her tone playful but firm enough to remind him it wasn't the kind of humor she appreciated.

Marcus chuckled nervously, scratching the back of his neck.

"Noted," he mumbled, clearly and apologetically.

David, sensing the tension, stepped in like a referee.

"Let's get to business," he said, his voice steady and commanding, as though redirecting the conversation was a task he'd perfected over time. The shift in tone worked, grounding the moment and easing the awkwardness.

Elena glanced at both men, her features softening. Despite Marcus's occasional blunders and David's penchant for quiet authority, they were her allies—her steadfast pillars of support in an uncertain world. Besides Riya, these were the two people she knew she could lean on in times of distress, and that knowledge offered her a sense of security she hadn't realized she was holding onto so tightly.

"Alright, what's the business?" she asked, her voice tinged with curiosity, as if daring them to make the moment worthwhile.

David's expressions shifted, his features growing serious as his gaze locked on Elena. His voice was calm but weighted.

"Remember the plateau implosion?" he asked.

"Who doesn't?" Elena replied, her tone unusually cheerful, an almost deliberate attempt to downplay the weight of the terrifying experience.

"And do you also remember what you told Riya back then?" David paused, his expression searching.

"That we might be too late!?"

Elena stiffened slightly, her lips parting as though to speak, but no words came. The air seemed to grow heavier around them.

David continued carefully, sensing her unease.

"We touched on it briefly at the time, but you didn't seem ready. And honestly, I almost let it slip from my mind entirely." He gestured toward Marcus, standing nearby.

"But this guy reminded me about it a couple of days ago. It's been bothering me ever since."

Marcus gave a faint nod, his cheerful feeling subdued.

David leaned forward slightly, his palms open in a gesture of reassurance.

"So, we thought we'd ask—if now feels right, if you're ready to share. And if not, that's perfectly okay. No pressure." His voice softened, his expression one of genuine understanding.

"We're here, either way."

Elena's gaze darted between the two men, her mind racing. She felt the weight of their concern, their curiosity, and something deeper—an unspoken trust they placed in her, even as her own understanding of what happened at the plateau still felt like a tangled thread.

"No, you're good," Elena said, her voice steady yet warm.

"Yes, we should talk about it." She glanced toward a table across the room and added with a playful smirk, "Unless, of course, you'd rather miss out on the pizza over there."

David followed her gaze and grinned.

"Pizza first," he declared loudly, drawing a few amused glances from nearby. Turning back to Elena, his expression softened.

"Let us know when you're ready," he said, his eyes reflecting both gratitude and a quiet admiration for her willingness to revisit such a heavy topic.

#

Elliot, now the colony's beloved chef, had fully embraced his new role, transitioning from an engineer to running the kitchen full-time. With the colony's food production steadily improving, his culinary creativity had become a cornerstone of morale. To manage the growing demands of the colony's palates, Elliot assembled a small but talented crew of three, each bringing unique skills and perspectives to the kitchen.

#

Renee Hartley, a former nutritionist from New Zealand, was the first to join Elliot's team. She works partly with Dr. Myers's medical team as needed. With years of experience designing diets for endurance athletes and astronauts, Renee had an impeccable understanding of balancing flavor with nutritional value, a skill that proved invaluable when dealing with Martian-grown produce and carefully rationed protein stocks. Her calm attitude and quick problem-solving abilities made her a steadying presence in the often-bustling kitchen.

#

Callum Fraser, a Scottish avionics engineer with a hidden passion for food, joined as a part-time assistant to Elliot. Callum's engineering background allowed him to handle the more technical aspects of running the kitchen, such as maintaining cooking equipment and inventing ingenious ways to prepare meals in Martian conditions. His dual-role also saw him assisting Marcus with critical engineering tasks when needed, but his heart was undeniably in the kitchen. Known for his skill behind the bar, Callum was already dreaming up cocktails for the day Elliot's master plan for a Martian tavern came to life. His dry wit and charming banter added a unique flavor to the kitchen, making him a favorite among the crew.

#

Priya Sharma, an Indian pastry chef and former food scientist, rounded out the team. Her background in molecular gastronomy allowed her to work wonders with limited ingredients, creating desserts that were nothing short of magic. Priya's creative mind brought sweetness to the colony's otherwise utilitarian food supply, and her treats became a much-anticipated highlight during gatherings at *"The Sky"* or post-shift dinners.

#

Together, Elliot, Renee, Callum and Priya transformed the kitchen into a hub of innovation and joy, weaving complex flavors and ingenuity into every meal. The aroma of freshly baked bread, sizzling stir-fries from the Martian potato harvest, and experimental desserts wafting through the dome became a symbol of resilience and humanity thriving in the alien landscape. For many colonists, meals were no longer an unpleasant experience of tearing a packet and throwing in the multi-cooker—they were a daily celebration of life.

It was commonplace to see more people lingering around the dinner table, food breaks becoming a social centerpiece of life in the colony. The shared meals transcended their practical purpose, turning into moments of connection and reprieve from the day's challenges. Laughter echoed through the dining area as stories were swapped, and bonds deepened over Elliot's culinary creations and his team's growing repertoire of inventive dishes.

The dinner table had become a hub of camaraderie, where diverse backgrounds and shared ambitions merged. Crew members, once isolated by their rigorous duties, now found themselves mingling more freely, energized by the warmth of communal meals. It wasn't just about the food—it was about rediscovering a sense of humanity on the barren Martian soil, a reminder of what they were working to preserve and rebuild.

#

Meanwhile, Marcus was busy assembling a team in response to Sonja's latest request. She had detected a deposit of metallic substances through her ground-penetrating scans, but the data lacked the precision to identify the material definitively. Sonja's excitement was intense—her gut told her this could be something significant, but she needed a borehole to confirm it. The problem was that the drilling equipment had been out of commission since the plateau incident, waiting for severe maintenance that had been repeatedly postponed due to higher-priority tasks for the engineering team. With workloads easing slightly and curiosity sparked by Sonja's findings, it was finally decided to focus on the repairs and get the equipment operational again.

The drilling rigs had been a crucial asset in the colony's early days, but their recent neglect had left them in disrepair. He directed his team to inspect the rigs from top to bottom. Hydraulic systems were flushed, mechanical joints were re-calibrated, and the autonomous navigation modules were thoroughly tested. It was painstaking work, but Marcus's team was motivated by the opportunity they got to work on the heavy machinery, which was a welcome relief from the day-to-day maintenance in the colony.

However, there was an unspoken intrigue surrounding the drilling equipment itself. During the chaos of the plateau incident, the rigs had been set to autonomous navigation as the sudden evacuation order was issued. Rather than following their default programming to return directly to base, the rigs had taken an unexpected route. They seem like operated intelligently, descending into a lower ground covered by a mesa—a move that, in hindsight, seemed almost strategic. This wasn't part of their programmed behavior; their navigation AI was designed for basic path-finding, not advanced problem-solving. Yet the equipment had positioned itself in a way that shielded it from the shock-wave, as though guided by an unseen hand.

This maneuver had been quietly discussed among a few in the engineering and command teams, but no one had drawn conclusions. Was it a fluke? A hidden protocol no one was aware of? Or something far more unsettling?

Marcus found himself wondering about it again as he prepared the rigs for Sonja's borehole project. He didn't voice his thoughts, knowing how stretched the colony already was with mysteries they couldn't yet explain. Still, the question lingered at the back of his mind, nagging him as he worked—who, or what, had guided the rigs to safety?

The repairs extended over a week and a half, as Marcus's team alternated between the drilling equipment and routine maintenance tasks within the habitat. The delay wasn't just due to the competing priorities; it was also because Marcus insisted on a level of precision and thoroughness that bordered on obsessiveness. The team grumbled at times, but they understood his reasoning.

The day the excavation began was a spectacle to behold, as a fleet of rovers and heavy machinery set off from the dome, their formation deliberate and precise, like an army marching toward conquest. The sight filled the colony with a profound sense of pride—each vehicle a testament to their engineering prowess and collective effort. The convoy wound its way across the rugged Martian terrain, the red dust rising in swirling clouds around their wheels.

At the site, ninety kilometers from the safety of the dome, the team erected a temporary shelter and living quarters, a small but functional outpost in the vast wilderness. This marked the farthest distance the colony had ever ventured on such a scale, a milestone in their journey of exploration and resilience on the Red Planet. The sense of adventure was profound, mixed with the gravity of the task ahead.

The excavation took three days of meticulous effort to obtain a full-depth core sample, which was carefully extracted and secured for transport. The sample, encased in a protective container to prevent contamination, was sent back to the lab for detailed analysis, leaving the team eager for answers about the mysterious deposit. With the core sample retrieved, the heavy equipment was no longer needed at the remote site. The team worked efficiently to secure the borehole, sealing it to prevent any interference from the harsh Martian environment. Once satisfied that the site was safely preserved for potential future use, the convoy began its journey back to the base.

#

One evening, Marcus, Riya, and David were climbing the spiraling stairs to *"The Sky"*, the faint hum of the dome's life-support systems their constant accompaniment. The climb, though familiar, still held a kind of reverence, a momentary detachment from the bustling colony below.

"This climb in itself is a ritual," Riya remarked, her voice cutting through the silence with a touch of humor.

Marcus, shook his head. "It's over my head why they haven't included an elevator of some sort! These architects... they always think they know better."

David, walking a step behind, offered a thoughtful counterpoint.

"I think the lack of mechanical assistance is part of what keeps *"The Sky"* secluded. If it were easy to get to, it might lose its charm—its tranquility."

Marcus raised an eyebrow, half-convinced but unwilling to concede. "I get your point, but still…"

Riya interrupted, her tone light but firm, "It's what it is, Marcus—just like Mars itself. We embrace and enjoy." Her words had a finality that discouraged further grumbling, yet carried enough warmth to smooth over the moment.

They climbed the last few steps in silence, the view above them opening to the vast expanse of the sky. As the trio stepped into its serene atmosphere, the climb faded into insignificance, replaced by the weightless sense of awe the space always seemed to evoke.

They expected to see Elena there, even without asking around or checking on Orion. It had become routine for her to spend most evenings at The Sky, either soaking in the Martian vistas or practicing a bit of meditation. Her presence in the tranquil space was so predictable that it felt almost part of the colony's rhythms.

Finding someone within the dome wasn't difficult, as multiple systems designed for just that purpose. For routine inquiries, work schedules provided the most reliable guide. In emergencies, Orion would instantly announce an individual's location to the medical team, pinpointing their position with precision.

For those with the necessary clearance, there was an even more sophisticated method: Astraeus could locate any individual on command. The AI utilized a combination of facial recognition, heartbeat patterns, and thermal signatures, leveraging the dome's extensive network of sensors. This interconnected system, though primarily designed for safety and efficiency, sometimes gave the sensation of being under constant watch, which was among the topics debated over a meal or at a corner—a silent reminder of the delicate balance between what's necessary and what invades personal freedom.

They moved quietly, careful not to disturb Elena, who was seated at the far end in her familiar meditative posture. Yet, even before they had a chance to see her clearly, Elena's eyes opened as if on cue. She smiled warmly, her hand raising in a casual wave to welcome them.

As they approached, Marcus gestured toward the floor with exaggerated mock surprise, as if to ask whether they were really expected to sit cross-legged like her. Elena broke the silence with a playful chuckle.

"I won't torture you," she said, rising gracefully to her feet.

"Let's sit on the couches."

They all settled onto the cushioned seats nearby, the initial moments filled with easy conversation about life on Mars—how each of them was holding up under the relentless demands and alien environment. It was the sort of casual intimacy that only their shared experiences could foster, but there was an unspoken tension hovering, a collective awareness of the deeper reason they had come.

Elena, decided to break the ice, "Well, let's get into it," she said, her tone calm but with a trace of gravity.

She turned toward Marcus, nodding, "Thanks for bringing this up—it was almost forgotten."

The group fell silent, their expressions affirming her words. It was clear they were all eager to hear what she had to share.

Elena paused, choosing her words carefully.

"I didn't know at first. Couldn't figure it out. But eventually, it became… evident." She hesitated; her voice reflective.

"I'm not entirely sure if it's the meditation itself, or the Crystal." Another pause.

"But now, I see things more clearly—with a clarity I'd have struggled to find otherwise, let alone understand."

Her words commanded their attention completely. Marcus, Riya, and David were leaning in, their focus intense, as if hanging onto her every word like disciples before a Sage.

Elena glanced around the expanse of the sky, as if drawing strength from the serene environment.

"When I'm in that state—meditation, I mean—I'm more aware of everything, even with my eyes closed. It's like a… movie. Mmm, no, more like multiple movies playing on different screens. They just… flow, and I'm aware of all of them."

She paused again, as if weighing whether to say more.

"When the three of you started climbing the stairs, I knew. I could sense it, down to—" She stopped abruptly, her sentence unfinished. Her expression shifted slightly, as if preventing herself from revealing something not needed for now.

She pivoted, her tone easing, "Well, you didn't really needed to call for my attention, did you?" she teased, turning her observation into a playful question, redirecting the moment and easing the intensity that had filled the air.

Elena looked younger, far younger than her forty-one years should allow. It wasn't just the smoothness of her skin or the brightness in her eyes—it was something intangible, something that seemed to radiate from within.

Sitting across from her, Marcus, Riya, and David couldn't help but notice the difference. It wasn't just youth; it was vitality, an almost ethereal glow that defied explanation.

She was overwhelmingly happy, and her joy seemed to spill into the spaces around her, leaving everyone in her orbit with an inexplicable sense of fulfillment. Anger rarely touched her, and even when it did, it was fleeting—dissipating like a puff of smoke in the wind. She moved through her days with effortless precision, waking early, tackling every task with enthusiasm, and never missing an appointment. From the greenhouse to the lab, from meetings with Riya to mentoring the curious minds of the colony, Elena was a whirlwind of purpose and energy.

Yet, she never seemed drained or fatigued, as though time itself was bending backward to accommodate her.

It was as if her biological clock wasn't just standing still—it was rewinding. The thought, absurd as it might have been, lingered in the minds of those who watched her. Could the Crystal have done this? Or was it the profound mental clarity she had discovered through meditation? Whatever the reason, the Elena they knew was not merely surviving on Mars—she was thriving.

David leaned forward, his eyes alight with curiosity, as Elena's words seemed to pull him into a deeper web of thought.

"Is it... Remote Viewing?" he asked, his tone laden with eagerness.

"Is that what you're describing?" His enthusiasm made it clear he wasn't merely asking out of politeness—he genuinely wanted to know.

Elena turned to David with a look that carried both patience and warmth, like a parent guiding a curious child.

"No, David, they're different," she said gently, her voice calm but deliberate. She paused, gathering her thoughts before continuing.

"Although, when I think about it…, I only know what Ethan has told me about Remote Viewing—and that doesn't seem to come close to what meditation offers, at least not in my limited understanding." She stopped briefly, her eyes flickering with a silent contemplation, as if she was reevaluating her own perspective.

David tilted his head, his curiosity undeterred. Elena caught the look and offered a small smile.

"I'd love to tell you more about meditation—or, more specifically, my experiences with it—but for Remote Viewing, you'd better talk to Ethan. That's his baby."

Her tone was inviting, but it also carried a gentle firmness that suggested she wanted to keep the two topics distinct.

The three of them—David, Riya, and Marcus—stood transfixed, warriors of science confronted by the unexplainable, their rigid logic clashing with the mystery unfolding before them. Their expressions were a blend of intense curiosity and childlike wonder, caught between skepticism and the thrill of discovery. It was as if they were grasping at the edges of a story they had never known existed, hanging onto Elena's every word, waiting for her to turn the page.

Sensing the moment, Elena decided to gently steer the conversation back.

"Perhaps we can explore that another time," she said, her voice light but resolute, the faint trace of a smile softening her words.

"You know where to find me." There was an openness in her tone, an invitation to continue the discussion later, but for now, her subtle shift in focus suggested it was time to return to the matter at hand.

"On what the Crystal told me that day," Elena began, her voice steady but with an undertone that drew immediate attention. She paused, her eyes scanning the group, ensuring she had their focus.

"That object surfaced from the ground," she continued, "was ancient technology—a autonomous drone of some kind." Her gaze held each of theirs for a moment.

"That part, you've already heard.", a faint smile played on her lips, teasing yet knowing, as if holding onto a truth just beyond their reach.

She leaned forward slightly, her tone becoming more measured, deliberate.

"It's not just a drone—it's a craft. Fully autonomous, equipped with a form of intelligence, though not complete. It's advanced, but not sentient in the way we'd think. And..." she hesitated, her voice taking on a somber weight, "it's also a weapon. A device with the capability—and the instructions—to wipe out life... life of all forms, shapes and sizes!"

She stopped speaking, giving her words space to settle. Her eyes drifted briefly to the table, as if contemplating the enormity of what she'd just revealed.

"Like us," she added quietly, lifting her head again to meet their stunned expressions.

The pause stretched, heavy with the gravity of her words. She gave them the moment, knowing it wasn't just the revelation itself but the parallel she'd drawn that would resonate deeply. It wasn't just about alien technology—it was about understanding the unnerving reflection of their own species in something ancient and far removed.

"Both species who built and deployed those technologies were ancient," Elena said, her voice steady but tinged with reverence.

"Much, much older than we can even begin to comprehend." Her words carried an almost haunting weight, as though she were unraveling a secret whispered across eons.

"There were conflicts…," she continued, her gaze steady as she looked at each of them in turn, "…and constant battles between factions. Not so different from us, in a way."

She leaned back slightly, letting the words settle before delivering the final revelation.

"This drone, this weapon," she said, her tone softening, "was neutralized and buried on Mars—by the good guys."

A genuine smile lit her face, a stark contrast to the astonishment etched into the expressions of the others.

The room was silent, their minds struggling to grasp the enormity of what she was saying. David leaned forward, his brow furrowed.

"The good guys?" he asked, his voice barely above a whisper, as if afraid to disturb the fragile moment.

Elena's smile widened slightly, though her eyes held a knowing depth.

"Yes" she said simply.

"Even among the stars, there are those who fight for preservation, for balance. That's happening all the time, across the cosmos and on Earth in different scales." Her gaze drifted briefly to the window, where the Martian horizon stretched endlessly.

"And Mars became such a battlefield, and their burial ground, just as countless other planets…"

"Earth was not spared…" Elena paused, letting the weight of her words sink in. "…It was destroyed in such battles more than once."

She exhaled slowly, giving herself—and everyone else—a moment to absorb the enormity of what she had just said. The silence that followed felt heavier than the revelation itself.

She saw the astonishment etched across their faces, the quiet resistance to belief lingering in their eyes. They wanted to deny it, to rationalize it.

Elena let the silence stretch a little longer before leaning in slightly.

"What makes you think that great cities like Teotihuacan in Mexico, Mohenjo-Daro in Pakistan, Babylon in Iraq, Machu Picchu in Peru, Angkor Wat in Cambodia—and so many others—fell into ruin because of time?" A faint smile tugged at her lips, not of amusement, but of knowing.

As if to say: it wasn't just time that buried them.

She tilted her head, watching their disbelief settle into something more fragile—doubt, curiosity, the first cracks in the walls of certainty.

"We are so adamant in believing that the Sumerian civilization was the first," she continued, her voice measured but edged with something almost playful.

"And why? Because that's all we've been able to find, dugout?"

She let the question hang, then leaned in slightly, her eyes scanning the room. "Or maybe… just maybe… we were too unwilling to dig a little deeper. Too reluctant to search where history refuses to be easy."

She let the weight of her words settle before finishing, her voice quieter now, almost a whisper.

"Tell me—have we truly looked beneath the ocean beds? Beneath Antarctica? Or have we simply accepted what was easiest to reach?"

Her smile was faint, but unmistakable. A challenge. A possibility. A truth waiting to be unearthed.

Elena's voice held a steady rhythm as she wove the explanation, her calm tone contrasting sharply with the enormity of her words.

"We are like kids," she said, her gaze sweeping over the others.

"Just starting to see our parents fight with the neighbors—without really understanding what a fight, what a conflict, truly is. A child's world is so limited: their toys, their bedroom, the house, and the garden."

She paused, watching as astonishment settled across their faces.

"Even that can be overwhelming."

Her words lingered, stirring something deep within Marcus. A memory surfaced— childhood nights spent frozen in place, heart pounding, too afraid to move, convinced that something unseen, something monstrous, lurked beneath his bed.

Elena's expression softened, "It's only a matter of time before those kids grow up," she said, "and start their own fights with the neighbors." A faint smile curved her lips, an almost bittersweet acknowledgment of humanity's inevitable trajectory.

The room remained silent, heavy with unspoken questions. Elena took a deep breath and continued, steering the conversation back to the plateau.

"When we opened up the borehole," she explained, "the drone sensed our presence. It analyzed the chemical particles and even DNA traces in the air. That was enough to activate its program—exactly as intended by its creators."

Her gaze hardened slightly.

"The artifact network, built by another species, had fought and neutralized drones like this one in the past. Or so they thought. This particular drone outlasted their suppression, lying dormant until we disturbed it. When the artifact network recognized the threat, its only option was to vaporize the drone."

She let the weight of her words settle before adding, "There are weapons embedded within the artifact network itself. Semi-intelligent, autonomous, and designed to respond when necessary. In this case, they confined the blast to minimize collateral damage and deployed technology to dampen the shock-wave."

The room was tense, her audience hanging on every word.

"The drone," she continued, "was constantly attempting to send a signal—its primary function as a weaponized beacon. The artifact network successfully interrupted that signal during the borehole expansion, but..." She stopped, glancing around the room with an intensity that drew everyone in.

"You don't have to look so stoned," she said with a faint smile, trying to ease the atmosphere.

"I'm taking questions."

David, his face still frozen in astonishment, managed to quip, "I didn't know questions like this even existed. Please, just keep going."

Elena chuckled softly, nodding.

"Alright." She shifted her weight, bracing herself.

"The drone activated another technology as it surfaced—something the artifact network hadn't anticipated. It's the closest thing to quantum entanglement I can describe."

She looked at David, who was already nodding as though he had connected the dots.

"Faster-than-light communication," she explained, "theorized and barely tested in our labs. On an atomic scale, we've proven that entangled particles can share information, but we may need lot more time to make it a reliable communication medium for ourselves."

Her voice dropped slightly, the gravity of her next words unmistakable.

"The drone activated this technology. There's no countermeasure, no way to intercept or stop it—not in this universe." She paused.

"And we have no way of knowing what it transmitted, or where. That's the nature of quantum-level communication."

David's nods slowed, his understanding deepened by his background in physics. Riya, with her own exposure to quantum theory, looked contemplative. Marcus, on the other hand, was clearly grappling to follow, his bewildered expression betraying just how far this conversation had veered into the theoretical.

"So..." Marcus finally asked, hesitating. "What does that mean for us?"

Elena met his gaze, her calm unshaken.

"It means," she said, "that someone, somewhere, some timeline, some dimension knows we're here!"

"That's why we were too late?" Riya nodded in acknowledgment.

Marcus exhaled sharply, shaking his head.

"We shouldn't have poked our finger where it doesn't belong," he muttered, his voice edged with regret. The weight of their actions, the sheer magnitude of what they had unknowingly set in motion, was sinking in fast.

Elena turned her eye to him, her expression unreadable. Then, with a faint tilt of her head, she said,

"The irony is, Marcus…" She paused, her voice laced with something deeper—understanding, perhaps even inevitability. "Do we even know where to poke and where not to?"

As the words left her lips, a strange sense of familiarity washed over her. Deja-vu. Had she said this before?

They weren't just explorers anymore. They were trespassers, wandering into an ancient conflict like a school of children. And worse, they had already announced their presence.

There was a long pause, the kind that stretches time, as the weight of Elena's revelations settled over them like a shroud. Each of them sat in their thoughts, the enormity of what had been shared pressing down on them.

Riya finally broke the silence, her voice softer than usual, tinged with a vulnerability rarely seen.

"My child…" she said, her eyes fixed on Elena, glimmering with an emotion that transcended their usual roles. For a fleeting moment, Riya wasn't the steadfast commander, but a mother gazing at her child with profound empathy and overflowing love.

"I cannot begin to comprehend what you've had to endure."

Elena blinked, caught off guard by the unexpected tenderness. She shifted in her seat, but Riya continued, her tone carrying the weight of shared pain.

"This—" she gestured vaguely, as though trying to capture the immensity of it all,

"just this much information flowing into me is already overwhelming. It's confusing, depressing, and draining. I can't imagine the burden of what you've received… the torrent of knowledge, confusion and realization the crystal poured into you."

The commander's words hung in the air, but it was her expression that spoke louder—a look that seemed to strip away the layers of hierarchy, leaving only the raw, human connection of someone who cared deeply. For a moment, Elena felt like a child again, not in age, but in the sense of being seen and protected. It was humbling, and yet, somehow, comforting.

"I don't think it's something I'll ever fully process," Elena admitted quietly, her voice carrying a weight of its own.

"It's not just information—it's… experience, feelings, fears, and choices that feel like mine, and not at the same time."

Riya nodded; her lips pressed into a thin line of understanding.

"I see it in you," she said.

"The way you carry yourself now—it's different. It's as if… you've lived lifetimes, all compressed into this one."

Elena's faint smile was bittersweet.

"Maybe I have," she whispered.

"Thanks to Ethan," Elena continued, her voice calm yet resolute, "I've found my salvage—the tool I was missing." She paused, letting the words settle among her companions.

"…Meditation."

Elena stood up gracefully, her movement signaling the conclusion of their discussion. The others instinctively followed her lead, sensing the natural end to the intense conversation.

"I think that's enough for one day," Elena said with a warm smile, her tone gentle yet decisive.

No one offered a response—words seemed unnecessary. As they exchanged silent glances, they couldn't help but feel that Elena had made the right call. The atmosphere was heavy with thoughts, yet her smile carried a reassurance that helped ease the tension, if only slightly.

As they were walking towards the stairs, Riya turned back to Elena "Ethan has been speaking highly of your progress," she said.

"It seems you've taken to it in ways even he wasn't capable of, him doing this for decades!"

Elena nodded, her gaze drifting toward the faint luminescence of the Martian landscape beyond the sky.

"At first, I didn't think it would help—just another distraction, another way to numb the weight of it all. But the more I practiced, the more I understood. It wasn't about escaping. It was about standing in the storm, feeling every gust, every drop, and learning not to be swept away. It taught me to face the weight, to hold it, without letting it break me."

David leaned forward, his curiosity evident.

"So, it's not just about calming your mind? It's… something more?"

Elena's faint smile carried both understanding and mystery.

"It's about clarity. It's like stepping outside of the storm to see the whole picture instead of being swept away by it. The crystal's influence, the overwhelming knowledge—it's all still there. But now, I am detached, as if I can sift through it, piece by piece, without losing myself in it."

Riya gave a slow nod, her admiration clear.

"That's remarkable, Elena. You've turned something most of us would consider a curse into… strength."

"Not strength," Elena corrected gently.

"Perspective. I can't change or influence what the crystal has shown me, but meditation has given me a way to carry it without letting it drown me."

Elena continued, "let me put it in perspective, if a car comes speeding toward you, your instinct is to panic, to outrun it or dodge sideways—a desperate attempt to avoid impact. But in most cases, that very reaction seals your fate, pulling you straight into the collision you were trying to escape. Fear blinds, and in its grip, we often choose the worst possible move"

"But if you don't panic—if you stand still, observe, and detach—you may realize the car was never going to hit you at all. Or, with calm and clarity, you'll see exactly where to step to safety. Meditation is that stillness. It doesn't ask you to fight, to resist, or to confront—it gives you the space to see, to understand, and to move with purpose instead of fear"

For a moment, the room fell into a reflective silence, each person lost in their own thoughts. Elena's words offered more than just an explanation—they revealed a lifeline, a tool they hadn't considered but now recognized as something they, too, might one day need. The realization brought an unexpected sense of relief, a quiet reassurance that even amidst the unknown, there was a path they could turn to if ever the weight became too much to bear.

"One more thing," Elena's voice cut through the silence, halting everyone just as they had begun descending the steps. Her tone carried a weight that made them instinctively pause, turning back to face her.

"I think it's not mine to hold anymore," she said, her sincerity shining through her words.

"I trust that the information I share will be used wisely. But the truth is, I myself don't know where wisdom ends and folly begins in this matter." Her voice was calm but heavy, each word carefully chosen.

"I saw something extraordinary," she continued, her eyes steady.

"Among the flood of information from the crystal, there was one image or a sense that stood out—a chamber, underground. Still operational, at least in ways we may or may not yet understand." Her words hung in the air like a question without an answer.

"I know what you're thinking," she added, pausing as though trying to decide how much to say.

"But I'm afraid I can't see beyond that. The chamber... it's as if it intentionally blocked me, denying me access to anything further. The data, if you can even call it that, seems... deleted. Like a corrupted file."

Her gaze softened as it landed on Riya.

"I've sent the location to you," she said, her voice steady but tinged with emotion.

"I'm sorry, but now it's your burden." A faint, bittersweet smile curved her lips as she stepped back.

Riya met her eyes and gave a solemn nod, the gravity of the moment sinking in. Without another word, she turned and resumed descending the steps, the others following close behind.

As they reached the bottom, Riya spoke softly, almost to herself but loud enough for all to hear.

"Let's get some sleep."

It was a simple statement, but it carried the collective relief—and the weight—of everything they had just learned.

#

The colony continued its rhythm, unmarked by any extraordinary incidents. Yet, the very things they now regarded as ordinary would have seemed like pure magic back on Earth.

Even the simple day-to-day tasks—walking the Martian terrain in a lightly pressurized suit, tending to hydroponic crops under a faint orange sky, living off meticulously engineered systems—had all become routine. And still, in quiet moments of reflection, many of them recalled how impossible these "ordinary" moments would have seemed not so long ago.

Marcus was fully absorbed in overseeing the long-awaited pipe-laying project, a critical step in securing the colony's water supply. After months of delays, approval had finally come through to bury the pipelines underground—the only viable solution against the relentless Martian climate and the recent instabilities they had faced.

While the colony's robotic excavators handled most of the trenching, the final laying and connection of the pipes required human hands—a task that demanded precision, teamwork, and an unwavering focus. On Mars, a single miscalculation could mean disaster, and Marcus wasn't about to let that happen.

Unlike Earth, where specialized machinery existed for every conceivable job, the colony operated with a limited selection of multi-purpose equipment. This meant that tasks often had to be adapted to fit the tools at hand, requiring ingenuity and a hands-on approach. The crew worked tirelessly, shifting sections of pipe into position, securing connections with utmost care, and double-checking seals to ensure the system could handle the extreme conditions of the Martian environment. Low gravity on Mars does seems to help with the lifting and positioning, an occasional appreciation for Mars as it is.

Despite the physical demands, there was a sense of shared purpose among the team. Marcus, moved from group to group, lending a hand and offering words of encouragement. His leadership helped keep morale high, even as the team worked long hours under the faint glow of the Martian sun. The project was exhausting, but the thought of completing this critical infrastructure—one that would sustain the colony for years to come—kept them pushing forward.

#

Volunteering and learning new skills on the job had become the cornerstone of daily life in the Martian colony. With limited personnel and resources, every individual was encouraged to step out of their primary expertise and contribute wherever needed. This culture of adaptability was not only essential for the survival of the colony but also fostered a sense of unity and shared responsibility among its inhabitants.

In every corner of the dome, crew members could be seen tackling new challenges—an engineer assisting in the greenhouse, a scientist helping with pipe installation, or a medic stepping in to troubleshoot an equipment malfunction. The boundaries of roles blurred, creating a dynamic environment where skills were shared, and knowledge was passed on through hands-on collaboration. It wasn't uncommon to see someone mastering a completely new task, guided by a more experienced peer or simply learning through trial and error.

This spirit of volunteering wasn't just about filling gaps; it was about building a resilient, self-sufficient community. People discovered hidden talents and newfound passions, enriching both their own lives and the colony as a whole. It was a way of life that echoed the core philosophy of their mission: adaptability and collective growth in the face of an alien world.

Riya understood that while unity was crucial for the colony's survival, collective decision-making wasn't always the most efficient path forward. Some matters required a singular directive, a minimal number of voices shaping the course of action. The colony had fought hard to regain stability after the divisions and conflicts that had nearly unraveled them, and she had no intention of reigniting the chaos they had left behind.

She kept discussions within a tight circle—David, Elena, and Marcus— knowing they were the ones she could trust with difficult decisions. While certain insights were trickled down to the colony in measured doses, the full extent of their conversations remained sealed. Among the many unknowns they grappled with, there was one matter Riya was determined to keep under wraps: the underground chamber.

#

But secrecy was a fragile thing, and as days passed, the weight of it pressed down on her. As the colony's leader, she carried the burden of choice—

whether to leave the chamber undisturbed or to risk everything by digging for it. The knowledge of its existence alone was a silent ticking clock in her mind. How long could she keep it hidden? And when the time came, would she make the right call?

Marcus had become deeply introspective about his role within the colony's decision-making circle. He carried a quiet regret, reflecting on how his assertiveness in earlier debates had unknowingly fueled the divisions that once fractured the group. Now, he adopted a more passive role during discussions, choosing to let others deliberate and shape the decisions while he focused on executing their plans with precision and care.

When conflicting suggestions arose, Marcus refrained from public disagreement. Instead, he shared his concerns privately with Riya, trusting her judgment to weigh his perspective alongside the broader goals of the colony. His new approach was grounded in humility and a desire to avoid unnecessary friction—a conscious effort to foster unity rather than discord.

On the matter of the underground chamber, Marcus felt a strong, personal conviction: it should remain undisturbed. The events at the plateau were still fresh in his mind, a vivid reminder of the potential risks. Yet, he was acutely aware of David's contrasting view. David saw the chamber as an opportunity—a chance to deepen humanity's understanding of the artifact network and unlock knowledge that could propel them forward. Marcus knew David's belief was rooted in trust, a faith that the crystals held no ill will toward humans. For Marcus, it wasn't about trust; it was about caution.

Elena had been celebrating neutrality. Through the turbulent times of past factions, she had found the value not taking sides. As with the crystal, she found solace in being the conduit of knowledge rather than the arbiter of decisions. The weight of judgment wasn't hers to carry—her role was to relay what the crystal revealed, to share what she understood, and to let others decide the course of action.

With the underground chamber, she maintained the same stance. Unlike Marcus, who was cautious, and David, who was eager to uncover its secrets, Elena refused to lean either way. She had delivered the message, passed along the knowledge given to her, and now she stepped back, allowing those who governed the colony to deliberate.

Riya understood the weight of her position. Decisions like these weren't something she could simply delegate or ignore. It wasn't that anyone pressured her—if anything, the others respected her enough to give her space to deliberate. But the burden of indecision was heavier than the responsibility of making the call.

She also knew that time wasn't on her side. Sonja's relentless dedication to ground scans meant the chamber's location would inevitably come to light. It was within days of her current exploration path, and Riya wasn't naive enough to believe it could remain hidden. If they didn't act with intention, the discovery could spiral into another chaotic moment for the colony.

#

The chamber wasn't just a question of curiosity or science; it was a symbol of the thin line they walked on Mars—between survival and risk, between unity and division. Riya had to take an action, not just for the colony's progress but to maintain the fragile balance they had fought so hard to achieve. With a deep sigh, she prepared herself for what came next, knowing the choice would ripple through the colony, for better or worse.

"Listen," Riya's voice cut through the low hum of the lab, commanding immediate attention. The team stopped their work and turned toward her.

"We have a location," she began, pausing as if to let the words settle. She gestured to Liam, who brought up the map on the main screen.

"A few meters down," Riya continued, her tone steady but weighted, "we believe there's a hidden chamber." She let her eyes scan the room, gauging their reactions.

"It's not just another artifact—not in the usual sense. It's... more substantial. Larger, and different in appearance"

Her gaze sought out Sonja, who straightened in her seat, already anticipating the request.

"Can you run additional scans? I want to know the full extent of it."

As murmurs spread through the lab, a few glances shifted toward Elena. She remained quiet, almost detached, but her expression suggested she was deeply processing the moment.

"Electromagnetic patterns in the area are disturbed," Liam interrupted, pointing at a spectrograph on the side screen.

"It's almost like it's cloaking something."

Riya nodded, absorbing the information. "Then we'll take every precaution on the expedition. Safety is paramount," she asserted, her tone firm as she turned to leave.

As she approached the door, she subtly signaled Elena to follow. Once they were outside, Riya slowed her pace.

"I'm not sure it's the right call," she admitted, glancing sideways at Elena.

"It's as good as any," Elena replied without hesitation, her voice calm but reassuring.

Riya looked ahead; her brows furrowed. Elena added, "It doesn't seem dangerous—not from what I've seen. But the crystal... it's holding back. It's not showing me anything."

#

Within a couple of days, Riya received a call summoning her to the lab. Bracing herself for whatever awaited, she entered the room.

Sonja was the first to speak, her tone precise and professional, though tinged with the excitement she could barely contain.

"We've completed the ground scans and analysis," she began.

Riya nodded, signaling her readiness for the details.

"You were right," Sonja continued, pointing to the 3D-rendered model now displayed on the main screen.

"There's definitely something down there—only about two meters beneath the surface, extending down to a depth of roughly ten meters. Its structure is unmistakable."

"I might have noticed something during my routine scans, for sure" Sonja admitted, her eyes fixed on the display.

"But without knowing what to look for, I wouldn't have thought to deploy all our sensors at this level of detail. It wasn't obvious—not at first."

Sonja's fingers traced the holographic outline of the scan.

"It has a geometric configuration—eight radial chambers radiating from a central hub, all interconnected by a circular structure reminiscent of the atomic colliders at CERN. Each chamber is uniform in size and layout, linked by what appear to be narrow passageways."

"I should correct myself," Sonja admitted, pausing briefly.

"We can't say for certain that they're passageways. Nothing penetrates—the entire structure is impenetrable, unreadable. All we can see is the exterior."

She exhaled, frustration flickering in her eyes.

"The whole thing is a black box about the size of a kilometer across"

"How tall?" Riya asked, leaning closer to the screen.

"Eight-meter ceilings," Sonja replied with a hint of wonder in her voice.

"It's not natural. The symmetry, the scale—it's all deliberate."

Riya studied the projection in silence, her mind racing with possibilities. This was no ordinary discovery. The chamber's size and complexity hinted at a purpose, one beyond anything they had encountered before.

"Any signs of activity? EM fields? Energy readings?" Riya's questions came rapid-fire, her focus narrowing.

Liam chimed in from his workstation.

"Intense electromagnetic activity, consistent with cloaking or shielding technology. It's as if it's designed to obscure itself from scans—but not perfectly. Whatever's down there, it doesn't want to be seen!"

Liam leaned forward thinking an elaboration is in need, his voice edged with both excitement and unease.

"The spectrum of signals we throw at it—every frequency, every wavelength—just passes right through, or absorbed!. No reflections. A perfect cloak... almost."

He let the words hang, the tension settling over the room. Then, with deliberate emphasis, he continued.

"But when you go through the data—really carefully—there are… anomalies. Subtle, rare, but there. Glitches that shouldn't exist."

His eyes flicked across the room, gauging their reactions.

"It's almost as if the structure isn't just letting signals pass through—but manipulating them. Twisting them, redirecting them, making it seem like there's nothing there at all."

"Is it another drone? A spacecraft?" Marcus asked, his voice laced with uncertainty and caution. His gaze flickered between the readings and the distant shape.

"We wouldn't know for sure," Liam admitted, his tone measured.

"However, I ran a comparison against the minimal data we have from the plateau incident… and they don't match." His eyes narrowed as he studied the readings.

"Whatever this is, it's something else entirely."

The room fell silent as Riya processed the information. She glanced at Elena, who stood at the back, observing with her characteristic calm. Though she said nothing, Elena's presence seemed to fill the space with unspoken gravity.

Riya turned back to Sonja.

"Prepare an excavation plan. We're going to need precision—this isn't something we can afford to blast into. Coordinate with Marcus for equipment readiness, and gather a team."

"Do not drill. Excavate here instead—this area looks like a possible entrance." Elena stepped toward the display, pointing at a specific spot near the edge of a small cliff. Her tone was calm but firm, drawing everyone's attention.

The room went silent, and she could feel the doubtful, almost mystical glances directed her way. Elena caught the mood and smiled, softening the tension.

"The winds," she began, tracing her fingers across the map, "blow in this direction for most of the Sol. Over time, they've carried dust and debris, burying anything left here long enough. And the cliff? It provides a natural shadow—a shelter of sorts. If I had to guess, this side would be much easier to breach."

Her reasoning was simple, grounded in logic and observation, yet profound enough to leave the room momentarily stunned. Even Sonja, usually quick to challenge ideas, found herself nodding in reluctant agreement.

For those secretly hoping for an otherworldly explanation or a hint of crystal insight, it was a minor letdown.

Sonja nodded, her excitement barely contained.

"That's nice, we'll be ready."

Riya took one last look at the projection, the geometric chambers almost seeming to pulse with potential. She turned to leave, but not before casting a glance at Elena, who gave her a faint, knowing nod.

Another misstep, a symphony of unlearned lessons, etched deep within the strands of human DNA…

We shall soon see.

Crimson Ascent

Chapter Nine

CONTACT

The colony was buzzing with anticipation, the hidden chambers igniting a collective curiosity that bridged gaps and fostered a rare harmony. Unlike the trepidation of past encounters, this time the air was charged with suspense and a quiet optimism. The growing trust in the crystal and the ancient artifact network—along with the enigmatic celestial architects behind them—seemed to implant an unprecedented sense of comfort, as though the colony had finally begun to feel at home in the embrace of the unknown.

Within days, the engineering team had cleared the soil from the cliff's edge, revealing a side of a construct of breathtaking proportions—an architectural structure merged into the Martian landscape. The moment felt ripped from the pages of an *Indiana Jones* adventure, except this was no myth or a collapsed ruin; it was real, completely intact, and it stood before them, untouched for an unimaginable span of time.

The exterior surface had an uncanny resemblance to the artifacts they had encountered before—its surface smooth, dark, and almost like polished granite to the untrained eye. Yet, it defied classification, impervious to any tools they possessed. Every attempt to analyze it yielded nothing.

Sonja's scanners, equipped with a wide range of spectrometer and electromagnetic imaging technologies, failed to penetrate its walls. It was as if the structure was actively absorbing or deflecting any frequency thrown at it, swallowing every attempt to reveal its secrets. This was not just an ancient construct—it was something deliberately concealed, a place meant to stay hidden until the right hands uncovered it.

#

The lab excited with quiet intensity as the team gathered to discuss their next move. The excavation had revealed only a fraction of the enigmatic structure, and Marcus wasted no time in laying out the bitter reality of their situation.

"If you're thinking about uncovering the rest, forget it," he said, arms crossed as he leaned against the display table.

"Even on Earth, moving this much rock and soil would be a monumental job. Here, with what we have? It's impossible."

There were no objections—everyone seemed to understand the limits of their resources. Still, that left them with a more pressing question: what now?

They had tried everything. Every tool, every cutting technique, every sensor, every scanning method at their disposal had been exhausted, and the structure remained impenetrable. The material wasn't just tough—it was utterly unyielding, as if it had been designed to resist any attempt at intrusion.

A quiet unease settled over the room.

For some, the answer was clear: *leave it alone.*

If it had been meant to be opened, it wouldn't have been built to withstand everything they had thrown at it. Maybe it was locked away for a reason. Maybe they had already overstepped their welcome.

But for others—Sonja, David, even Riya—this wasn't just about a buried mystery. It was about *understanding*. And leaving a discovery of this magnitude unexplored, when they were so close, felt almost intolerable.

Elena, who had been silent through most of the discussion, finally spoke.

#

"We're thinking like engineers, like scientists. What if that's the wrong approach?"

A few heads turned toward her, intrigued but wary.

"This isn't just a structure," she continued.

"It's part of something much larger—something connected to the artifacts, to the crystal, to everything we've been unraveling piece by piece."

"Maybe we don't *break in*—maybe we have to get invited!"

"Breaking an encryption is hard, nearly impossible, we know that" Elena continued, her voice steady.

"But finding the private key? That's a different game entirely." She framed her argument in a language science could grasp—sometimes, the answer wasn't about brute force, but about knowing where to look.

Silence followed, as no one could disagree to the simple truth.

Riya made the final call. "Let's take a break and think-fresh, people." Her tone was firm yet reassuring.

"The structure isn't going anywhere. We have time, so let's use it wisely. When we regroup to discuss this again, I want ideas—real suggestions on how to move forward."

As she turned to leave, she paused at the doorway, glancing back with a concerning smile.

"And just so we're clear—explosives and projectiles are off the table. Not that I think they'd make a difference anyway." Her look lingered for a moment before she walked out, leaving the room in thoughtful silence.

#

Riya read the message received from Earth, twice, as if expecting the words to rearrange themselves into something more logical. A remote-viewing session? With Ethan? This was the first time Earth Command had ever issued such an order, and it unsettled her more than she cared to admit.

Governments had already been divided over the discovery. Some saw the chamber as the key to technological supremacy—a relic that could leapfrog humanity centuries ahead. Others feared it was a Pandora's box, a potential catastrophe waiting to unravel, not just for Mars, but with consequences that could trace all the way back to Earth. Yet, in their bitter debate, neither faction was winning. The fact that the chamber remained impenetrable was its own paradox—an enigma that refused to take sides.

And now, this.

Riya knew little about Ethan's so-called abilities—at least, nothing concrete. Beyond the occasional remarks she had overheard, her understanding was shaped more by what was missing than what was known. As the mission commander, she had full access to every crew member's profile—every skill, every assignment, every classified detail that could impact their mission. But Ethan? His file was different. Gaps, omissions, and entire sections blacked out under clearance levels beyond hers.

And now, Earth was asking her to execute an order she barely understood!

Her instincts told her to push back, to demand more details, but she knew better. This wasn't a request. This was an order.

Riya exhaled, setting the message down.

"Looks like I need to have a chat with Ethan."

Before long, Ethan peeped through Riya's half-open door after couple of knocks. Spotting Riya and David inside, he was waved in. Closing the door behind him, he settled into the remaining chair beside David.

"Look, Ethan," Riya began, her tone sincere.

"I have to admit, I'm embarrassed. I don't really understand what remote-viewing is. I've read about it, but it sounds like pseudoscience."

"That's exactly how it's supposed to sound," Ethan said with a knowing smile.

"It was meant to stay unnoticed." He leaned in slightly, his tone measured.

"I won't claim it's like gaining an extra set of eyes—it's something else entirely. A form of communication beyond the limits of our understanding. We don't know the mechanics, we don't know how… but what we do know is that it works."

Riya tilted her head, her skepticism flickering.

Ethan continued, "Back on Earth, for highly trained individuals, the success rate is near hundred percent."

He hesitated, his expression clouding. "But here... well, it's an utter shame"

Riya raised an eyebrow. "I see. Go on."

Ethan sighed; his voice tinged with frustration.

"It doesn't seem to work around here. I suspect the energy fields from the artifacts have something to do with it, but honestly, I don't know."

Riya let out a small, sarcastic smile. "So much for the order." She leaned back in her chair.

"UNSI didn't ask me—they ordered me—to have you remote-view this chamber complex."

"That's not happening, I'm afraid," Ethan said, shaking his head with a look of regret.

David had his arms wide open, palms facing upwards, his expression a mix of amusement and vindication—the universal "I told you so" look.

Ethan caught the gesture and raised an eyebrow. He couldn't tell if David's arrogant behavior came from prior knowledge that remote-viewing won't work on Mars or if he was simply dismissing the entire practice as nonsense.

#

That evening, David caught up with Elena. "We tried getting Ethan to remote-view the chambers," he began.

"And how did that go?" Elena replied, wasn't even sounded like a question, her voice carrying a knowing edge, as though she already anticipated the answer.

David paused, his eyebrows lifting in mild surprise. "Wait—you knew?"

Elena's lips curled into a playful sneer. "Well, I do now," she teased lightly before her expression grew more serious.

"Honestly, I didn't think it would work. Those chambers are protected—completely inaccessible. They were designed that way."

Her voice carried a finality that left no room for argument. David studied her for a moment, trying to gauge the certainty behind her words.

"Protected?" he echoed, the skepticism in his voice faint but lingering.

"Yes," Elena replied firmly.

"Not just physically, but in ways we barely understand. Nothing gets in—not scans, not signals, not even Ethan's talents. Whatever's in there, we yet to find a way in."

"We don't sneak in, and we don't break in, just because we can. Sometimes, all it takes is a gentle knock—and the door opens, inviting us inside."

#

The chamber loomed before them, an imposing monolith of ancient design, its surface impossibly smooth yet unwaveringly solid. Elena and David stood at its threshold, the crystal nestled securely in David's arms. The rest of the team had withdrawn to a safe distance, watching through their visors as the two prepared to attempt something science wouldn't sanction—connect the crystal to whatever lay dormant inside.

It was David's idea to bring the Crystal to the chamber, drawing on the undeniable success they had at the waterhole. No one could present a compelling argument against it—there was no logical reason not to try.

Even Elena, who had grown cautious with each revelation, acknowledged its potential.

David adjusted his grip on the crystal, his fingers pressing into its cool, glass-like surface. He could already feel it hum faintly, a pulse of energy that had become familiar to them both.

Elena, standing beside him, closed her eyes for a moment, steadying herself. This was a long shot, they both knew it, but if the waterhole experiment had worked, then maybe—just maybe—the crystal held the key to unlocking the chamber as well.

The first sign of a reaction came almost immediately.

As they stepped closer, the surrounding air seemed to shift, thickening as though the space itself was resisting them. The electromagnetic readings spiked on Orion's display. The crystal, too, responded—the intricate lattice within its structure began to glow more intensely, its colors shifting in rapid succession, deep blues and greens giving way to golden flares. Elena's heart pounded in her chest.

"It's reacting," she whispered, almost afraid to say it out loud.

David nodded, inching forward, careful to keep his steps steady. The chamber's surface, what was unremarkable, remained stubbornly unyielding. No markings. No seams. Just an ancient wall holding its secrets hostage.

Then, for the briefest moment, something changed.

A faint shimmer danced across the surface of the chamber, subtle but unmistakable. Like ripples in a pond, waves of energy pulsed outward. The moment filled Elena with a rare flicker of hope. Maybe this was it. Maybe they had found the way!

David pressed forward; his movements deliberate as he lifted the crystal higher. Its glow flared in response.

"Come on," he muttered under his breath, wanting something—anything—to happen.

With a deep breath, he reached out and touched the crystal to the chamber's surface.

Nothing!

No reaction. No shift. No activation. The shimmering ceased; the pulsing faded. The momentary surge of hope drained from both of them, replaced by creeping disappointment.

David sighed, his forehead creasing. "Okay," he said, shifting the crystal and pressing it against another section of the wall. "Maybe here."

Still nothing.

Frustration mounting, he began moving the crystal methodically along the surface, pressing it against different points in a desperate attempt to trigger *something*. Each touch was met with the same response—none at all. The crystal continued to glow in its mesmerizing way, but the chamber itself remained inert, indifferent to their attempts.

"Come on," David murmured again, this time more to himself than anything else. His fingers drummed against the crystal's surface, his determination teetering on the edge of frustration.

Elena, still watching carefully, noticed something out of the corner of her eye.

"Wait," she said, her voice quiet but urgent.

David froze mid-motion. "What?"

She inched closer, her fingers hovering just above the chamber's surface. At first, it seemed unchanged—smooth, featureless—but then, almost imperceptibly, faint symbols began to take shape. Like whispers of neon light trapped beneath glass, they flickered into existence, delicate yet deliberate. Unlike the shifting, fluid patterns on the crystal, these symbols remained still, their soft glow radiating an eerie, otherworldly light.

"You mean this?" David asked, his voice barely above a whisper.

Elena nodded, her eyes fixed on the markings. "Yeah. But why now?"

David looked down at the crystal, which still pulsed in his hands.

"Maybe we didn't do it wrong," he said.

"Maybe we just didn't do enough."

Elena's fingers traced the glowing symbols, gently touching, following their delicate, intricate forms.

"These weren't here before," she murmured.

"This surface was empty, completely void of markings. But now…"

She turned to David, her eyes sharp with realization.

"We made some progress," she said. "Something shifted, even if it wasn't what we expected."

David's brow furrowed. "You think the crystal activated it?"

"Not entirely," she replied, thinking aloud. "Maybe it… recognized something. A presence. An intention."

David exhaled, stepping back slightly to take it all in.

"So what do we do now?"

Elena pulled out her scanner, capturing the symbols while they were still visible. The patterns weren't fading quickly, but she knew better than to assume they'd last.

"We document this," she said.

"Get these images back to Ada and Liam. Maybe they can decipher them."

David reluctantly pulled the crystal away from the chamber. The glowing symbols remained for a while longer before finally dimming out, fading into the surface as though they had never existed. A chill ran down Elena's spine.

"Well, that was weird," David muttered.

Elena gave him a sideways glance. "This entire planet is weird."

He let out a dry chuckle. "Fair point."

Turning away from the chamber, they began their trek back toward the others, the crystal still glowing faintly in David's arms. The silence between them was thick, their minds racing through everything that had just transpired. They had uncovered something, even if they didn't yet understand it.

But one thing was clear: The chamber wasn't ignoring them.

It was watching. And it was waiting.

#

As they reached, Riya was already waiting, her arms crossed. "Well?" she asked, her expression unreadable.

David shook his head. "No activation. No grand reveal. Just some cryptic symbols."

Riya's gaze flicked to Elena. "But something happened?"

Elena nodded, transferring the scanned images to Riya's Orion. "Something, yes. We need to figure out what they mean."

Back in the lab, the initial excitement had faded, giving way to quiet disappointment. Expectations had been high, but the outcome felt underwhelming. Ada and Liam sifted through the collected data, their usual enthusiasm noticeably subdued. The rest of the team gathered around, but the air of curiosity that once fueled their discussions seemed to dissipate, replaced by a silent resignation.

"So we're back to decoding alien messages?" Ada mused, studying the strange markings.

"That's comforting."

David huffed. "More like frustrating."

While gazing at the symbols Riya advised, "Whatever this is, we need to take it seriously. We proceed carefully. No forced entry, no rash decisions."

Elena exhaled, still feeling the strange hum of energy left in her fingertips from the chamber's surface. "Agreed."

For now, the chamber remained sealed, its mysteries just out of reach. But something told her—they weren't done yet.

Not even close!

#

Elena stood at the edge of the meadow, her heart overflowing with love as she watched her four-year-old daughter, Grace, run freely among the vibrant wildflowers. Every joyous laugh and unrestrained giggle echoed through the open space, filling Elena with a profound sense of pride and contentment. Her eyes softened, glistening with tears of happiness, as she observed Grace's carefree spirit—her tiny hands reaching out to touch each colorful petal, her eyes slightly closed in blissful concentration.

In that moment, time seemed to pause, allowing Elena to fully absorb the pure, unburdened joy radiating from her child. The sight of Grace's innocent delight mirrored the depths of Elena's maternal love, a boundless and unwavering force that cherished every precious second of her daughter's freedom and happiness. Surrounded by nature's beauty, Elena felt an unspoken connection, knowing that these fleeting moments of carefree play would forever be etched in her heart.

Elena felt herself dissolving into the meadow, the air and the surrounding love drawing her in like a gentle suction. In a moment of hesitation, she realized she was longing for this feeling to last.

She thought, "I want Grace to be on her own, grow up, not stuck at age four!" She knew that wasn't what Grace wanted either; it's a selfish thought for own satisfaction, she realized.

Quickly, Elena recognized the need to let go. Even though the enjoyment of the moment was fulfilling in itself, she understood that it was not something to grip on to.

As clarity emerged, she became aware that she was meditating, observing her own thoughts. Then, she noticed a string of other thoughts—some near some far, spiraling and entangling around her. All she was doing was observing. She wanted to focus on one distant thought among the floating strings, which was little brighter and almost seeking her attention. For a moment's notice, it came zooming in as if she was watching a scene in a movie.

Elena saw Jake in fourth grade bullying her, the memory so vivid it felt as though she was reliving the experience. However, this time, she felt an overwhelming empathy as she began to understand what was going on in Jake's mind. He liked Elena, but at that young age, he couldn't comprehend it. He thought he could win her affection by being tough, and the only way he knew to be tough is bullying. Elena wanted to understand why, and she saw that Jake's father was abusing his mother. She immediately connected the dots—not just saw what was going on, but truly experienced without a speck of doubt. In that instant, the lifetime of hatred she had harbored towards Jake was released, dissipating like a puff of smoke in the air. Her heart was full of empathy and compassion.

Elena watched as the memory gently faded into the background, and this time without a trace, she felt lighter, happier, and more fulfilled. A subtle urge to explore more memories washed over her, akin to the pull of an addictive drug. However, she reminded herself that her task was not to engage with these thoughts, but to accept them as they were and let them pass.

She focused her mind on Grace, and suddenly, her consciousness zoomed into another string: Grace with her best friend Emilie, playing their Favorite game of chess at school. The scene felt like an invasion of privacy, prompting Elena to pull away instinctively. At a glance, Emilie noticed Grace wearing a necklace with a tiny pendant that held a small photo of her. It was clear that Elena hadn't given Grace the necklace, but in an instant, Elena understood it had been delivered by UNSI that morning!

All of this unfolded before her like a recorded movie. For a moment, she pondered that time might not be as linear as she had always perceived it, but rather a winding tapestry where past, present, and future intertwined. She vividly envisioned countless pathways stretching out in front of her, each leading in different directions and branching off into an infinite array of possibilities. In this moment of profound clarity, Elena understood that she could, if wanted, navigate through time itself, exploring its myriad connections and depths.

#

She *saw* Ethan was climbing the stairs, and she knew it's time to get ready to meet him.

Elena opened her eyes and stood up and waited for him to appear.

As they began chatting, Elena asked, "Is remote viewing like watching a movie?"

Ethan shook his head, "Oh no, it's very different. We don't even know what we're seeing. We scribble lines and patterns on paper, sometimes creating a horrible mess. But when those sketches are analyzed, they can be used to build up an image that may sometimes represent a real location based on the target."

"I've been teaching and training remote viewers back on Earth, and I've seen some incredible depictions through time and space drawn on paper," Ethan continued.

"However, if you want a high-resolution, movie-like experience, you need to meet Yogis in the Himalayas", he smiled.

Elena hesitated to explain her own experiences, having heard Ethan's expression.

"What am I going through", she thought to herself.

"Have I unlocked something extraordinary?" she chuckled to herself, but Ethan noticed her unease.

"Elena," he said warmly, "You have gone a long way on meditation, much further than I ever could have gone myself. So if you try, you should be able to do it without needing a Himalayan Yogi." He laughed gently with her.

#

That night, she noticed a message from Grace, with an attachment.

"Mummy, take a look at what I got from Mrs. Spenser—a pendant with your photo in it!"

Attached was a photo taken by Mrs. Spenser, Grace's school teacher. In the image, Grace was deep in thought, playing chess with Emilie. Around her neck, the pendant gleamed softly having Elena's photo embedded!

Elena's face glowed with serene joy, her expression a delicate blend of appreciation and quiet wonder, as if, in that moment, she had glimpsed the intricate dance of the universe and found solace in its rhythm.

#

The following evening, Elena prepared herself for an experiment—one that required no tools, no machinery, only the depths of her mind. Meditation had become her gateway to understanding the crystal, to deciphering the whispers of an intelligence beyond human comprehension. Perhaps, she thought, it could help her unravel the mystery of the chamber.

After a warm, lingering bath that left her senses softened and attuned, she had an early meal, then ascended the spiral stairs to *"The Sky"*. The vastness of the Martian expanse stretched before her, its muted reds and browns melting into the creeping shadows of nightfall. The dome's filtered light cast a gentle glow, and for a moment, she simply stood there, letting the silence settle over her like a familiar embrace.

Then, she sat, her legs and arms moving in an intricate choreography, seamlessly settling into a well-attuned meditative posture that came naturally to her after months of practice.

Having attentively observed and aligned herself with the natural rhythm of her breath, Elena let go of the weight of her body, slipping into the tranquil depths of meditation. It no longer took effort to quiet her mind—no force, no struggle. It was as if she had learned to listen rather than command, to drift instead of push.

She was feeling everything!

The microscopic beads of moisture suspended in the air. The faint warmth of distant light sources against her skin. The texture of her linen, the fibers of the trousers pressing gently against her legs. Each sensation sharpened, yet none distracted her. She was both grounded and untethered, as if her mind was expanding while her body remained motionless.

And swiftly, she was there—not physically, but in a way that defied explanation. She hovered around it, her consciousness wrapping itself around the massive structure. She could see it in its entirety—every side, every angle. Whether she was perceiving it in real-time or reconstructing it from the hundreds of photos, videos, CAD drawing and 3D renderings form her previous interactions with the lab, she couldn't say. All she could be certain of was that it simply existed, presenting itself to her awareness in ways no technology ever could.

She could perceive its exterior, every contour and edge, yet the inside remained concealed—like a stubborn child clutching a treasured toy tightly to their chest, refusing to let anyone peek within.

It remained impenetrable, its defenses unyielding. A fortress designed to resist not only physical intrusion but forces beyond human understanding.

Elena pushed deeper, not with force but with intent. And as she did, time itself seemed to dissolve around her. It was no longer a linear construct but a vast, interconnected web. A tapestry woven not in moments, but in awareness.

Then—a vision.

She saw them—*builders*. Not people she recognized, yet strangely familiar. Tall, purposeful figures moving in perfect harmony. They weren't just constructing a chamber; they were embedding it into the very fabric of Mars, fusing it with the artifact network spread across the planet's dust and rock. These weren't just isolated structures. They were conduits—control centers regulating power and connectivity across the entire network.

And there were more.

Elena *felt* them—not just as distant anomalies, but as ancient presences, buried deep beneath the Martian surface. Some lay entombed more than a thousand meters down, unseen yet alive, silent sentinels thrumming with energy, their purpose unbroken despite eons of abandonment.

And this chamber—the one they had unearthed—was just one of many. Mars was not unique. It was merely a single way-point in a vast network, a fragment of something far greater, scattered across the cosmos.

The realization settled into her mind with absolute clarity: penetration was impossible. Not by force, not by technology, not even by the energies and quantum fields that humanity had barely begun to comprehend.

Formed with the intent to remain unbreeched, its very essence defies intrusion.

But... Elena was convinced there should be a way.

She shifted her focus. If no entry was possible in the present, then perhaps the key lay in the past. Not in breaking through the barrier, but in understanding those who built it.

Their thoughts. Their intent. Their purpose.

She reached for it—not by force, but by resonance. And as she did, something stirred.

A deluge of memories crashed into her, too much at once. Thoughts, experiences, knowledge—rushing at her like a flood. It was overwhelming, chaotic. She ducked and weaved through them, as if dodging projectiles in a storm, searching for something, anything significant.

She wasn't sure if her physical body reacted, if her fingers twitched or her breath hitched, but she detached from the thought as quickly as it came.

She waded through the storm, picking out fragments that made sense, piecing them together. A way in. A method encoded not in machinery or mechanisms, but in thought itself.

Elena wasn't certain what she had uncovered, but she knew it was important. And may be Crucial.

Just as quickly as the knowledge came, she let all go. With a slow, deliberate breath, she opened her eyes.

She was back in *"The Sky"*, the Martian horizon stretching before her, silent and eternal. But something inside her had shifted.

A serene joy graced her face, a faint smile playing on her lips—a quiet triumph, the unmistakable glimmer of a *gotcha* moment.

Not just she knew, she was ready.

\#

The following day, under Elena's stern guidance, David and Marcus finalized preparations at the chamber site, setting up an array of instruments requested. As planned, Riya personally drove Elena to the location, the rover's engine humming softly against the Martian silence.

No one fully grasped what they were doing—not even the faintest grasp of it—but an unspoken faith in Elena's intuition lingered. Perhaps, in the absence of clear logic, action itself was the only rational path forward.

Marcus stood ready, his voice steady but expectant. "We're set. Just say the word."

David knelt beside a reinforced, space-grade pelican case, carefully unsealing its latches with precise movements. The case hissed slightly as its pressure equalized, revealing the containment chamber within. He glanced at Elena before lifting it out.

"Taking the crystal out now."

He handled it with the reverence of someone holding an object far beyond their comprehension—because, in truth, that's exactly what it was.

Gently, he passed it to Elena. "Here you go."

She accepted it with both hands, feeling the cool, almost impossibly smooth surface settle against her palms. The crystal was roughly the size of a football, a perfect *"Truncated Cuboctahedron"*, geometrically speaking, its facets forming an intricate balance of octagonal and square planes. It was as if it had been cut meticulously, one that can only be done with precision machines.

When they first encountered it, they called it a *crystal* for a lack of a better term. It resembled glass in some ways, yet it was neither brittle nor transparent. When inactive, its surface appeared dark, absorbing the light around it like a void. But when it awakened—when it responded—it became something else entirely.

Inside, currents of ethereal blue light pulsed and swirled, streaking like energy flowing through a complex circuit. Symbols, ever-shifting, would appear and disappear across its facets—sometimes flickering across the external surface, other times forming within its dimensional space as though floating in another reality.

Elena tightened her grip. The chamber ahead loomed, unchanged, unyielding.

She took a slow breath and stepped forward.

The air around them felt charged, an almost imperceptible hum vibrating through the thin Martian atmosphere.

"Marcus, the frequency," Elena signaled, her voice steady but weighted with anticipation.

Marcus flipped a switch on the signal generator, tuning it precisely to sixteen-hundred megahertz, an unmodulated carrier wave. The antenna, already positioned and calibrated, directed the frequency onto the chamber's unyielding surface.

Elena moved forward, her pace deliberate, the crystal cradled in her arms as if she were holding something fragile—something so precious, like a newborn baby.

"Ada, start reading the symbols," she instructed without breaking stride.

Ada, positioned to the side, had been watching the chamber wall, where faint symbols—ones that hadn't been there before—began emerging, glowing like embers beneath darkened glass. She relayed them to Liam, who was standing by with his interface.

Liam's fingers worked quickly over the console, converting the alien script into base-eight numerals, feeding them into the AI model they had trained over months of tireless study. The system had long since cracked the first layer of these symbols, recognizing their mathematical sequences, identifying them in a pattern as fundamental as counting—1, 2, 3…

Elena's plan was precise.

"Marcus," she called, her voice calm despite the tension, "modulate the frequency with the numbers, in sequence", her voice weighted.

Without hesitation, Marcus initiated the modulation, allowing the translated base-eight numerals to imprint onto the broadcasted wave. He used all kinds of modulations he could think of, accordingly to Elena's instructions. It pulsed through the chamber's surface, like a ripple cast into an invisible ocean.

Elena stepped closer, the crystal just touching the wall, and then—A sense, a voice or something!

Soft, ethereal, and almost maternal.

"Child, you are not yet ready."

Elena's breath caught in her throat. She turned her head instinctively, scanning the space around her. There was no one. Only Marcus, Ada, and Liam—focused, unaware.

The voice had spoken inside her.

Not in words, not in sound. It had been... something else.

A presence.

Elena tightened her grip on the crystal.

"It's not for you to judge," she said, her voice steady, unwavering.

"We have come a long way—Given up everything—We cannot turn back now."

Then she felt it.

The crystal pulsed, its internal light shifting into a deep resonance, vibrating against her palms in a way it never had before. A sensation unlike any previous connection with it—deeper, more intimate.

She closed her eyes—No, she realized, they were already closed.

Somewhere between awareness and something more.

"Elena, Ada, get back!"

Marcus' urgent voice snapped through the air.

Elena remained still. Ada reacted immediately, stumbling backward just as the chamber's surface flared to life, a brightness that hadn't been there moments before.

The light pulsed outward, illuminating the dust-choked atmosphere in an unnatural glow, outlining the chamber's once-invisible seams—seams that were now shifting, unlocking almost, but not quite.

A gateway!

Elena turned her head slightly, eyes slightly open, and smiled.

"Do not be afraid," she said, her voice no longer just her own.

"They agreed to let us in."

"But," Elena cautioned, her voice measured.

She hesitated for a brief moment, then continued, "The chamber hasn't been opened in a very…," she paused, as if grasping for the right scale of time, "…a very long time."

Her gaze swept over the team, ensuring they understood the gravity of the situation.

"It's airtight, but it was designed with its own ventilation and filtration systems—capable of sustaining various forms of life, each with different biological needs." She exhaled slowly.

"It's adapting."

She turned her attention back to the glowing symbols on the chamber's surface, then to the crystal, still humming softly in her grasp.

"The crystal will tell us when it's safe to enter," she concluded, her voice firm with certainty.

"For now, we wait."

"I've got a greenhouse to attend," Elena laugh inwardly, gently passing the crystal to David. He accepted it with the same level of care, carefully placing it back into its protective case.

Turning to the team, Elena's expression radiated a quiet joy—serene, almost compassionate. There was something in her presence, a tranquility that felt as if it belonged to another world entirely.

The team followed Elena's lead without hesitation. There were no objections, no attempts to rush the process—only a quiet understanding that this was something beyond their grasp.

The team packed up the equipment, securing every instrument and data recorder before making their way back to the rovers. The anticipation was off the charts, but there was also a strange sense of calm, a humbling sense of achievement as they had taken the first step in a dance choreographed by forces far greater than themselves.

#

David and Marcus had been the first to arrive, their conversation hushed but purposeful as they waited. Liam, Ada, and Riya followed shortly after, their footsteps echoing lightly against the titanium-alloy stairs leading to *"The Sky"*. Though the meeting wasn't scheduled to start just yet, they all preferred to be early. Elena arrived last but still before the agreed time.

Down below, the colony thrived in its usual evening rhythm. The Circle was alive with the hum of conversation, the scent of freshly prepared meals drifting through the air as colonists gathered for dinner. Laughter and chitchat wove through the space, a comforting contrast to the weightier matters awaiting discussion above.

A notice had been sent earlier, requesting privacy at *"The Sky"* for the evening. That meant no uninvited visitors—just the core team, sealed away from prying ears and unintended interruptions.

David reached for the control panel and activated the audio containment system. A soft hum confirmed its function, ensuring that whatever was said within *"The Sky"* would remain within its walls. It was an essential system, creating an invisible boundary between the team and the world below.

Riya exhaled, glancing around at the familiar faces, each carrying their own burdens of knowledge. This wasn't just another meeting—it was a reckoning, a moment where they would have to confront the weight of what they had uncovered and decide, together, what came next. They sought clarity, a sense of direction, yet only Elena seemed to hold the elusive thread that could weave meaning into the mystery before them

Elena had anticipated a few light-hearted remarks—perhaps Marcus pulling a joke at the secrecy of their gathering or David making an offhand comment to ease the mood. But as she glanced around, she realized the energy in *"The Sky"* was unlike anything she had felt from them before.

It wasn't stress, nor was it the usual undercurrent of tension that came with making difficult decisions. Instead, there was something else— expectation. Enthusiasm. The kind of silent anticipation an audience holds for a magician just before the grand reveal.

Marcus leaned forward, his elbows digging into his knees, fingers interlocked in a rare display of unease, as if steadying himself for something far beyond his usual realm of certainty. His posture, so unlike his usual confidence, betrayed the weight of the moment.

Across from him, Liam absently tapped on his tablet—not out of distraction, but as a subconscious tether to the familiar. Yet his eyes flickered upward every few seconds, catching every nuance, every shift in expression, as though he were allowing himself, for the first time, to entertain the extraordinary beyond the rigid boundaries of math and science.

Ada, usually a force of energy and wit, sat utterly still. Her usual spark dimmed, replaced by unwavering focus—her gaze locked onto Elena with the kind of reverence one might offer a prophet. In that moment, she was not the scientist or the skeptic, but a disciple, absorbing each word with the weight of belief.

David's leg bounced delicately, a quiet rhythm of anticipation, his gaze fixed on Elena with an intensity that mirrored a hopeful teenage boy, waiting with bated breath for the moment his affections might be acknowledged and returned.

And then there was Riya. She neither fidgeted nor revealed a flicker of emotion, but her stillness was its own kind of intensity. Her presence alone carried the gravity of leadership, her unreadable expression masking the depth of contemplation beneath. She was patient, deliberate, waiting—not just to listen, but to weigh what was about to be said, knowing that Elena, in her strange and effortless clarity, would shape the course of what came next.

Elena settled into her seat, letting the quiet stretch a little longer. They weren't here for speculation anymore. They weren't waiting for theories or debates. They were waiting for answers.

And she was the only one who could give them.

Heads turned as they all heard footsteps at the entrance.

Dr. Myers entered *"The Sky"*, though a hint of breathlessness betrayed his effort to make it on time. The moment he stepped in, Riya instinctively glanced at *Orion*, as if confirming his arrival missed the schedule. He wasn't late—not by even a minute—but still, he offered an apology.

"I completely underestimated the distance from the Ship to the Dome," he admitted with a sheepish smile, adjusting the strap of the suit, feeling the weight of a miscalculation.

A collective shake of heads followed, dismissing any need for an apology. If anything, his presence was more than welcome. His expertise wasn't just in medicine—it was in understanding people, knowing when to speak and when to listen.

Riya gestured toward the open seat beside her. "You're just in time," she said. "Elena hasn't started…"

#

Elena, who had been watching the moment unfold with an amused glint in her eyes, let out a soft chuckle.

"No pressure, then."

The tension in the air softened slightly, but the weight of anticipation remained. Now that everyone had arrived, there were no more distractions—only the silence that signaled they were ready.

"The Chamber," Elena began, sensing the anticipation in the room.

"Has multiple entrances. What we uncovered is only one of them," She let that sink in before continuing.

"Like any secured entry, it has a protocol. Think of it the way we use fingerprint scans, voice recognition, facial ID, or even a simple pass-code. It's a layered system—ensuring that nothing, or no one, gets in by accident."

Her gaze landed on Marcus as she emphasized the point. Then, shifting her attention to David, she added, "The first step? Getting the crystal close enough."

David gave a awkward grin, already knowing where this was going.

"Remember when you pressed it against every surface, trying to force a response?" she teased.

David chuckled, the memory of his clumsy attempts flickering across his mind. Sensing the creeping embarrassment on his face, Elena offered a reassuring smile.

"Well, it turns out you weren't entirely wrong," she said, naturally easing his discomfort.

"That was the first step. And remember—when we did that, faint symbols appeared."

She let the memory settle before moving on.

"The second step was the sixteen-hundred-megahertz signal."

She hesitated briefly, knowing that what she was about to explain was more technical than most would grasp. But they deserved to know.

"You know how we rely on specific frequencies for satellite communication? Well, this one isn't just a random point on the spectrum—it's a universal constant, a beacon used by advanced civilizations across the galaxy for interstellar transmission. Its properties allow it to cut through cosmic interference, preserving messages across immense distances without loss or distortion."

She hesitated for a moment before adding, "It's been used by countless civilizations, countless beings..." Her voice trailed off, letting the weight of the implication settle.

"Back on Earth, we still reserve that very same part of the spectrum purely for satellite communications—Earth to space and back". She let her words hang, watching their reactions.

"So, naturally, it makes sense that the chamber's technology would respond to this exact frequency. Just broadcasting it was enough to activate the display—to bring the symbols into clarity."

Noticing the unspoken question brewing on Marcus' face, Elena preemptively answered, "The chamber does respond to other frequencies, but our technology isn't progressed enough to generate them—at least, not yet."

She paused, letting her gaze sweep across each face, measuring their reactions.

"A properly disciplined mind," she continued, her voice steady yet contemplative, "might be able to do all of this without the need for electronics at all."

A knowing smile tugged at her lips. "But for now, we're stuck with the rudimentary—stuck with the tools we have at hand."

With a brief silence, she continued, "But that wasn't enough."

She turned to Ada and Liam.

"Then came your work—the knowledge you both have painstakingly unraveled, piece by piece. Your ability to see the patterns, to decode the symbols, to shape meaning from the unknown— it's nothing short of brilliance. Cuneiform choreography—an art, a science, a stroke of genius!"

Liam maintained her poker face, while Ada was transfixed, her gaze locked onto Elena's eyes.

Elena took a step forward. "Reading them isn't like reading a book—it's more like decrypting a complex pass-code. And just like a password, you need a way to key that in."

She smirked, glancing at Ada. "It's like leaving your password written on the screen, Ada."

Ada turned red, immediately averting her eyes while the others chuckled.

"The symbols on the wall—they were the password."

"The keyboard," Elena continued, "was the frequency itself. We had to modulate the signal, embedding the symbols as data and transmitting it back into the chamber."

She saw no interruptions—only wide-eyed focus.

"But why base-eight?" she prompted, answering her own question before anyone else could.

"It could have been anything, but the answer was right in front of us. The crystal—its structure is based on octagons. The entire complex, made out of eight chambers and eight radials. The entire system is built on an octal framework."

Simple. Logical. And yet, it had been a riddle until now.

"But even after all that," she said, her tone shifting, "it still wasn't enough."

She paused, letting the weight of those words settle in.

Elena let her last words linger, watching as realization dawned upon them. The process she had just described was deceptively simple in hindsight, yet it had taken all their combined effort to decipher it. She took a slow breath, gathering her thoughts before continuing.

Elena spoke with the patience of a teacher explaining basic math to her students.

"All we've done is to ring the doorbell," she said, her tone measured yet firm.

"All this effort—all the work we've put in—just to get their attention, to let them know we're standing at the door, waiting."

She glanced around, making sure the weight of her words settled.

"But ringing a bell isn't enough." She gestured as if motioning toward an unseen visitor.

"When someone knocks on your door, don't you want to know who they are? What they want?"

Her voice softened, yet carried an undeniable urgency. "We had to do the same. Announce ourselves. Declare our intentions. Because if we don't… what reason does it have to let us in?"

Marcus, who had been following intently, leaned forward.

"Then what was missing?" he asked, his curiosity breaking the silence.

Elena's eyes met his, and she smiled slightly, as if she had been waiting for that question.

"Intent," she said simply.

A subtle ripple of confusion passed through the group.

David furrowed his brows. "Intent?" he repeated.

"You mean… like a conscious thought? A conscious need to open it?"

Elena nodded. "Exactly. The chamber wasn't just waiting for the right inputs—it was waiting for the right engagement behind them. It wasn't enough to go through the motions like a machine. It needed someone who understood, who truly sought entry. It's as if it could sense our purpose. A lock designed not just to be unlocked, but to be respected!"

A weighted silence fell over them.

Riya folded her arms, her expression a mixture of awe and wariness.

"You're saying this thing has… awareness? A way of determining whether we're worthy of entering?"

"Not in the way we think of awareness, or consciousness for that matter," Elena tried to clarify.

"If you're asking whether it has a consciousness like ours—self-aware, thinking, independent—the answer is No," she said with unwavering clarity.

"But it does possess a form of awareness, attuned to its surroundings, designed to react to the consciousness of those nearby." Her explanation was precise, even though the concept itself defied conventional understanding.

Given a brief moment to settle the thoughts, she continued, "It does have a safeguard, a final threshold. I felt it when I held the crystal, when I heard—" She hesitated, choosing her words carefully.

"A voice, a presence, something beyond language. It wasn't speaking words, but it was clear. It was watching, waiting, and saying we are not ready. And when I answered, questioning it's right to judge—when I refused to back down—it agreed."

David exhaled sharply, shaking his head in disbelief. "A security system that judges intent. That's… disturbingly brilliant."

Marcus let out a quiet chuckle. "And probably very effective," he said.

"No accidental breaches. No unwelcome guests."

"If an intruder could fake intent?" David posed a valid question.

"Consciousness isn't something that can be faked," Elena interrupted, raising a hand to pause him.

"We can mimic actions, fabricate emotions, even deceive everybody around us, including ourselves—but deep down, our consciousness is always observing, always judging. You can try to suppress it, bury it beneath layers of pretense, but it's like holding a rubber ball underwater— no matter how long you try to keep it down, eventually, it will rise to the surface."

Dr. Myers, who had been listening silently, finally spoke. "So what does this mean for us now? If we've passed the test, do we just… walk in?"

Elena leaned back slightly, letting Dr. Myers' question settle before offering an answer.

"Yes, we can—if we want to," she said, her voice even.

"It would take some time to prepare the…" She paused, her gaze shifting slightly as if searching for the right phrasing. "..Air quality," she finally said, the words feeling both abrupt and deliberately cut short.

She let that thought linger before offering an alternative.

"Or," she continued, "we don't have to." She gestured subtly with her hands.

"We can leave it alone and go on our merry way—an absolutely valid decision. Just as good as any other." Her voice carried an undeniable sincerity, making it clear she wasn't pushing for one outcome over another.

Then she smiled knowingly. "But we all know human curiosity won't let that happen, right?"

A faint smile of agreement rippled through the group, but Elena's expression remained serious.

"I think we should go in, if my vote matters" she admitted.

"Have a look. Move out before we overstay the welcome."

She scanned their faces, gauging their reactions.

"But," she added, tilting her head slightly, "I'd love to hear your thoughts first."

The room fell into a moment of charged silence as everyone exchanged glances, each weighing the gravity of the decision.

Riya was the first to speak. "This isn't your commander talking," she said, her tone lighter than expected.

"Elena has a valid point. A brief look, then we move out."

She let out a smile, though it was unclear whether it stemmed from curiosity or the lingering edge of unease. "If we get stuck in there, getting out won't be easy."

A collective nod rippled through the group—silent agreement.

"Then it's settled," Elena said, her own nod sealing the decision.

In a moment's laps, "Any questions?" Elena asked.

A heavy silence settled over the room. No one seemed certain of what to ask, their thoughts tangled in the unfamiliar. It was a realm far beyond their comfort zones, and in the absence of clear footing, following Elena's lead felt like the only course of action.

#

Dr. Myers raised his hand slightly. "Elena, everything you've explained flows logically, and I have no immediate questions about it," he said, pausing for a moment.

"However, it seems you're following a voice—one you don't truly know. The chamber may recognize your intent, but do you understand its intent?"

A hush fell over the room. Everyone was drawn into the weight of his question, realizing its significance.

Elena's expressions didn't change a bit. Same calm and collected look lingered.

She spoke "Very valid question Dr. Myers", she continued, "I do not follow a call or a voice" she paused.

"It's a knowledge, and awareness, which I do not have words to explain" she paused again.

She let the thought settle before continuing.

"It's like riding a bike. You don't consciously calculate every movement; you just do it, because your body already knows how."

She glanced around the room, then added, "Or like playing an instrument. At first, every note requires thought, but once you're in sync with the music, your fingers move instinctively. It's not about thinking—it's about knowing."

She let that settle before continuing. "Meditation may be a way to sync with it—an energy, a communication, whatever it may be. Meditation allows me to quiet my mind and observe my thoughts rather than being consumed by them. When I do that, I can recall the past with the same clarity as the present. It's like scanning through memories, only... clearer."

Her voice trailed off, leaving the room in deep contemplation.

"Backwards?" Myers raised an eyebrow, his expression unreadable. It was clear he had another question on the tip of his tongue but chose to suppress it. Still, Elena sensed it.

"Past, present, and future are intertwined," she explained, her voice measured and deliberate.

"The past is like a road we've traveled, with its turns and forks laid out clearly behind us. But the future?" She paused, searching for the right words.

"The future is a branching path—countless possibilities stretching out before us. Each fork, each road, is equally real in that moment, but only one will sustain. The others..." she hesitated, "...they decay."

The room was utterly still, her words settling over them like an unseen force.

"Imagine a child standing at the edge of a pool, deciding whether to jump," Elena offered, drawing the room's full attention as they instinctively leaned in, eager to grasp the unfolding concept.

"The moment he takes the leap, the decision is set in motion—he swims forward without hesitation. But before that moment, he had a choice: to jump or to stay put." She let the thought linger.

"But once the action is taken, the other possibility ceases to exist. He can no longer both stand on the edge and be in the water simultaneously—not in our reality."

Elena smiled, a knowing glint in her eyes, as if touching on a deeper truth even she was not sure if she fully grasps.

She halted David's question before it could form, raising her hand just as his lips parted—almost as if she had anticipated it.

"Schrödinger's cat," she said with a knowing smile.

"Well… maybe not exactly." She paused, tilting her head slightly, as if weighing the thought against an unseen measure.

"Honestly? I can't say for certain." Her voice carried a note of humbleness, a genuine acknowledgment of the vast unknown they were treading.

"You may also be wondering about free will and fate," Elena said, catching the unspoken questions etched across their faces.

She paused, choosing her words carefully.

"As I understand it, when you are in a moment—one that branches out before you, they are offering different directions." She gestured subtly, as if tracing invisible lines in the air.

"Now, say you have prior knowledge—maybe someone tells you which path to take, guiding your *choice*. Or, you can step forward blindly, letting the moment decide for you, calling it *fate*."

Her gaze swept over them, letting the thought sink in before she added, "But taking a step, A clear choice, and calling it fate? That's not really what it is, is it? A choice is always yours, and yours to take."

"Buying a lottery is a choice, but winning the price money is fate"

"I don't want to confuse any of you," she admitted, her tone shifting to something more grounded.

"Because the truth is, I don't fully understand it myself." And that was perhaps the most unsettling part of all.

She broke the silence once more, her voice steady but charged with meaning.

"If nothing else," Elena paused, letting her words settle, "I want you to take this with you—think of it, I mean the artifacts, as a technology," she scanned the room, meeting their eyes one by one.

"Meditation as a tool—a means to synchronize, to interface, and perhaps even to communicate with it."

Her intent to move forward was clear. Sharing fragmented knowledge—especially when she barely grasped its full meaning—felt more harmful than helpful. She understood that knowing everything wasn't essential; in the grand scheme of things, it could even be a burden.

"The people who built these structures…" Her tone was firm, deliberate, signaling the importance of the focus, a conclusion of a segway.

"They're long gone," she continued, " but their memories…" She paused, exhaling as she searched for the right analogy.

"They haven't faded into oblivion… Think of it as a vast cache of collective knowledge, perfectly preserved, waiting in suspended time. It can be accessed… perhaps even harnessed."

She let that thought settle before delivering the next.

"I've seen myself with them," she admitted. "Working with them." Her gaze swept across the room.

"And perhaps… some of you were there too."

The words landed like a shock-wave. The tension thickened as every person in the room processed the weight of what she was suggesting.

Elena placed a hand over her heart, her voice steady yet probing. "Tell me honestly—how many of you felt overwhelmingly comfortable around the chamber?"

She let the question linger, scanning their faces. "No need to say it out loud. Your consciousness already knows."

A pause. Then, a slight tilt of her head. "That feeling… that déjà-vu moment, perhaps?"

It was hard to read their expressions—some masked their thoughts well, others remained frozen in contemplation. But Elena sensed it. Some of them were absolutely flabbergasted, caught off guard not just by her words, but by the realization of what they had felt at the chamber.

"You know people change over time," she said, her voice calm yet deliberate.

"Think of your own siblings, how they've grown from childhood to adulthood—different, yet still the same. Change is inevitable."

She let the thought settle before continuing. "Even if I was there with them eons ago, even if we shared a past together, I too may have changed by now." Her gaze swept over them, searching for understanding.

"That's why the present moment matters. Intent matters. Who we were is not always who we are. And before we walk forward, we must ask—what is the intention of this moment?"

She softened, sensing their discomfort. "Its intent—is as clear to me as our intent for this technology," she assured them.

"No one—and no system—is guiding me," Elena clarified, her voice measured and unwavering.

"I'm not being told what to do. It's more like… sifting through an archive, navigating visuals, sensations, and something beyond our usual senses."

She glanced around the room, searching for understanding in their eyes.

"The method to unlock the chamber didn't appear to me in a dream or some mystic trance. Not certainly through a voice. When I'm in a deep meditative state, these things become obvious—as if they've always been there, just beneath the surface, waiting to be recognized."

She paused, allowing her next words to land with weight.

"It's as if I grew up with this knowledge… as if I've lived it before."

Another pause, deeper now. "As if I am among the team who designed it. Built it."

The silence that followed wasn't of disbelief—it was of realization.

She offered a reassuring smile. "More likely, I'm just experiencing the memories of the ones who did."

"You haven't left much room for doubt, Elena," Myers admitted, his voice carrying the weight of reluctant acceptance.

"Everything you've said… it fits, in ways I can't logically refute." He exhaled, as if releasing the last remnants of skepticism.

He added "I accept that comprehension yet to arrive to me, which is my fault."

He continued, "I am not ashamed to admit what I do not know, for that void, does not demand doubt either; it only invites discovery"

Then, after a brief pause, his gaze shifted toward Riya.

"Besides," he added, almost resigned,

"I don't think we have much of a choice."

#

Ada gathered the team in the lab, her expression laced with curiosity and unease. "Something's changed," she announced, pulling up the latest data on the crystal. The holographic display flickered to life, revealing a series of intricate symbols glowing faintly on its surface—markings that hadn't been there before.

Liam had already spent hours analyzing them, cross-referencing with their existing catalog of symbols extracted from the artifacts and the chamber itself. His initial conclusion? These were entirely new.

"I can't match them to anything in our current data-set," he admitted, rubbing his temples.

"The neural nets would need another round of training to even begin to make sense of them." His frustration was evident—he had spent months building a translation model, and yet, here they were, faced with another mystery that defied categorization.

Elena, seated quietly at the table, finally spoke. "I don't recognize them either," she admitted, her fingers absentmindedly tracing the rim of her mug.

"But I have a feeling we should check the chamber. If something's changed with the crystal, it could mean something has changed there too."

Riya, arms crossed, gave her a long, measured look. "You said the crystal would alert us when the chamber is ready to be accessed," she pointed out a finger at the display, "Is this what you meant?"

Elena exhaled, shaking her head. "I don't know how it's supposed to alert us. I just... know it will. Maybe this is the indication!"

That answer, while honest, didn't provide the clarity they needed. The team exchanged glances; uncertainty thick in the air. Lack of better suggestions or alternative explanations meant there was only one course of action—go back to the chamber and see for themselves.

Riya, leaned against the console, her tone decisive.

"Alright. We approach this methodically. If the chamber can be opened, we don't go in blindly. We send the robots first."

There were nods of agreement. Even Elena, despite her growing connection to the artifacts, knew caution was necessary.

The team assembled in the early hours, each member focused on their assigned role as they prepared for departure. Elena would lead the effort, accompanied by David and Ada, while Marcus gathered a handful of engineers to provide technical support. Riya, had also assigned two members of the security team—not for their firepower, but for their trained vigilance. An extra set of disciplined eyes might catch something the others may miss.

By the time they reached the chamber site, the Martian sun hung high, casting long, razor-sharp shadows across the landscape. The logistics of moving personnel and equipment had taken longer than expected, forcing them to push their schedule well past mid-day. The journey itself had been uneventful, the terrain familiar now, but as they arrived, there was an unspoken tension that settled over the group.

The chamber stood just as they had left it—unchanged in its defiance. Its dark, unyielding surface bore no new markings, no visible signs of activation. If the crystal had indeed signaled them, it wasn't through any obvious physical transformation. Instead, the only noticeable difference was a fresh layer of fine Martian dust that had settled over its surface, softening its sharp lines as if time itself had tried to reclaim it.

David ran a gloved hand across the outer wall, watching as the red dust streaked away beneath his fingertips. "Looks the same," he muttered, his voice crackling slightly over the comms.

Ada adjusted her visor and checked her scanner. "No new electromagnetic anomalies—at least nothing outside what we've seen before." She glanced at Elena.

"But that doesn't mean something isn't happening."

Elena stood still, her gaze fixed on the chamber's surface, as if waiting for something unseen.

"Let's set up the perimeter," Marcus called out to his team.

"Surveillance drones up, get the ground sensors in place." His engineers moved swiftly, placing instruments around the chamber site to measure environmental changes, radiation fluctuations, and any movement beneath the surface.

The security officers took their positions, scanning the horizon with methodical precision. They weren't expecting threats, but caution had long become second nature in a place where the unknown loomed behind every discovery.

Elena pressed her palm against the chamber's dull surface—not in response to a calling, nor guided by a voice, but simply driven by instinct when logic had exhausted all other paths.

The moment stretched, charged with anticipation. Her breath slowed as she felt the invisible energy threading between her palm and the chamber's surface, tingling like the slow discharge of static electricity. Even through the soft articulation of her glove, she could sense the buildup—a force gathering, waiting. Her scientific mind likened it to a capacitor charging, her glove's hybrid polymer acting as a dielectric, while her palm and the chamber's surface became the opposing electrodes.

Then, a glow.

A perfect circle of light emerged, centered on the exposed surface, its brightness gradually intensifying. There was no indication of what it meant, no clear instruction—just the silent shift of energy. Her hand, still resting along the perimeter of the glowing circle, hesitated. Should she touch the center instead? Was she missing something?

Instinct won over mental debate. She pressed her palm firmly where it already rested.

A sharp, decaying hum reverberated through the air. The luminous circle reacted immediately, the surface within it depressing ever so slightly—just a few millimeters, but enough to be unmistakable.

Elena's heart pounded. They had scanned this area countless times, mapped its dimensions with absolute precision, and never before had it yielded even the smallest imperfection. And yet, before their eyes, a shift was happening.

"I think it's opening," David's voice was hushed, almost reverent.

Elena took a step back. "We should move," she said, urging the others to retreat a few feet.

Without any dramatic clanking or mechanical grinding—just the subtle, eerie variation of the hum—the depression within the light circle deepened. Seamlessly, like a flower unfurling, intricate sections of the chamber's surface pulled away, retracting to reveal the dark, unknown space beyond.

Before them stood a doorway—perfectly circular, its edges seamless, as if it had always been there, waiting. There was no trace of the panels that had retracted, no visible seams or mechanical tracks, as though the chamber had reshaped itself effortlessly.

The Martian wind howled around them, kicking up fine dust, swirling grains of sand into chaotic spirals. Yet, strangely, nothing passed through the threshold. It was as if an invisible force held the elements at bay—a wind curtain, an unseen boundary preventing the harsh environment from breaching the sanctity within.

David instinctively reached out, stretching his fingers toward the doorway. The moment his hand neared the entrance, he felt it—a resistance, a shift in air pressure, as though he were pressing against an unseen membrane. It wasn't solid, but it wasn't empty either. A force-field, perhaps? A filtration barrier?

Elena stepped forward, eyes locked on the passage ahead. The chamber had finally granted them entry, but it had also set its terms. Whatever lay beyond that doorway had been preserved, untouched for who knows how long. And now, it was waiting.

As planned, Marcus activated the two autonomous drones, guiding them toward the chamber's door. The lower edge of the circular doorway hovered half a meter above the ground, forcing the robots to engage their rotors. In Mars' low gravity, only a small thrust was needed to lift them over the lip and into the unknown.

The moment they crossed the threshold, Marcus stiffened. His hands flew over his console, eyes scanning the display.

"Lost all contact," he announced, voice tight. "No telemetry. No visuals. Nothing."

A heavy silence fell over the team. The air itself felt charged with unease. It wasn't just the loss of signal—it was the implication. It was as if the chamber had swallowed the drones whole, severing them from existence.

For a moment, no one moved, no one spoke. A creeping dread slithered into their thoughts. What was beyond that doorway? What force was at play?

Riya parted her lips, preparing to issue a command—to pull back, to reassess—but before she could, Elena spoke first, as if sensing her hesitation.

"Riya," her voice was calm, steady. "Our technology doesn't work inside."

Riya turned to her, uncertainty flickering in her expression.

"I'm going in," Elena continued, unwavering.

"With your permission."

David shifted uncomfortably. "Elena, we don't know—"

"I do," she interrupted gently, her attention locked onto Riya's.

"I won't go far. Just enough to get a sense of what we're dealing with. But standing here won't give us any answers."

Riya's fingers curled into a fist. Every protocol told her to say no. Every instinct told her not to send someone in blind.

But Elena wasn't just someone.

"It's perfectly safe," Elena added, as if she could already feel the tension forming around Riya's decision.

"Whatever's inside, it won't harm us. Our technology just doesn't belong there."

A long pause.

Then, finally, Riya exhaled, nodding once.

"Alright," she conceded. "But if anything feels wrong, you pull back immediately."

Elena gave a reassuring nod. Then, with deliberate steps, she moved forward, crossing into the unknown, completely disappeared into the void.

#

After few tense minutes, which was feeling like eons, Elena appeared with pure joy in her expressions.

"Riya," Elena said calmly,

"it's safe. But without visuals, I have no way to prove that to you. No instruments make sense in here—not even Orion. If anyone steps inside, they'll have to rely entirely on themselves. No tech, no safety net. Just... be present. Leave everything else behind."

Riya remained silent for a moment, weighing the decision. Then, with careful deliberation, she gave her approval—but only for David and Ada. She made it clear: this was entirely voluntary. If either of them had even the slightest hesitation, they could step back—no questions asked.

Neither hesitated.

If anything, they looked exhilarated, as if stepping through that doorway was exactly where they wanted to be. Without a second thought, they followed Elena into the unknown.

Stepping through the doorway was like crossing into another reality—a world completely detached from the one they had just left behind. The stark contrast was immediate. From the outside, the chamber had appeared as an abyss, swallowing all light into its void, but inside, it was anything but darkness. A warm, golden illumination bathed the space, reminiscent of candlelight—soft, flickering, and alive. The silence was absolute, not the absence of sound, but the removal of all distraction, all mechanical hums, all interference. Only their own heartbeats echoed faintly in their ears, as if the chamber itself was listening.

Elena turned to face them, a calm certainty in her eyes. "It's safe. We don't need the helmets."

Before David or Ada could even process what she had just said—before their wide eyes and half-parted lips could form an objection—Elena reached up, unlatched the locks on either side of her helmet, and lifted it off.

David and Ada stood frozen; their shock so tangible it felt like a force field between them. Their instincts screamed that this was madness, but Elena remained perfectly at ease, her breath steady, her expression serene.

She gave them a moment to absorb the impossible before speaking again.

"The chamber has been adjusting its environment to sustain us. One of its primary objectives is ensuring we can exist here as long as we stay inside."

Still unable to form words, both of them hesitantly looked down at their feet, finally noticing the subtle shift—the unexpected heaviness pressing down on their limbs.

"You feel it, don't you?" Elena smiled. "Gravity. It's been adjusted to match Earth's."

David flexed his fingers, testing the weight of his own body. Ada took a slow step forward, as if relearning how to move. The sensation was unsettling, yet strangely familiar—like stepping back into a childhood home after years away, only to find it eerily unchanged.

For the first time in months, they weren't standing on Mars!

They were standing somewhere else entirely, much close to home.

As they moved through the chamber, their steps slow and deliberate, they were completely immersed in the environment. Every surface, every illuminated glyph, seemed to breathe with a presence of its own. The symbols were far more intricate than anything the crystal had ever revealed to them flowing patterns of meaning that neither David nor Ada could decipher, yet somehow, they felt them rather than read them. It was like standing inside a vast and ancient mind, where knowledge pulsed just beyond their grasp.

David, who had been running his fingers along a smooth panel etched with faint luminescence, suddenly froze. A flicker of unease crossed his face.

"Any of you… know how to get back?" he asked, his voice lower than usual, a hint of worry creeping in.

Elena turned to him, a knowing smile forming at the corner of her lips.

"David, all of us know."

David's brows furrowed. The answer was both reassuring and unsettling, as if she had just pointed out something obvious, he had failed to see.

Elena stepped closer; her tone gentle yet unwavering.

"Close your eyes and point toward the door."

David hesitated, then, like a child following a parent's instruction, shut his eyes. He took a slow breath, concentrated for a moment, then raised his hand and pointed.

"That way," he said, his voice carrying a mixture of doubt and wonder.

Elena turned to Ada. "What do you think?"

Ada, watching David closely, mirrored his motion. "That looks to be correct."

Elena nodded. "Well, it is."

David and Ada exchanged glances, both equally mesmerized yet relieved. There was no logical explanation for how they instinctively knew their way back, but neither could deny the certainty they felt.

It was not just a place—it was an interface, an extension of something vast, something that was guiding them, not with force, but with a quiet whisper of familiarity.

They moved through chamber after chamber, each one a seemingly endless series of walls that pulsed with shifting symbols—more than mere displays, more than just three-dimensional projections. The symbols floated in ways that defied perspective, appearing to exist in multiple layers, perhaps even in dimensions beyond their comprehension.

David's unease grew with every step. He had expected… something. Something tangible. Something revelatory. Instead, it felt like they were drifting through a vast, empty library with no books, only whispers of knowledge just out of reach.

"This is all empty," he muttered, his voice edged with disappointment. "Nothing but walls."

Elena turned to him, her expression calm, unreadable.

"What did you expect?"

David didn't hesitate. "A power source, to start with. Something real. Something we can use."

Elena exhaled slowly, as if she had been waiting for this moment.

"I'm afraid you can't take anything from here—not even the knowledge."

David frowned. "What does that mean?"

"There's no leapfrogging in science," she said simply. Then, as if reconsidering, she added, "No leapfrogging in civilization, either. Everything must happen in sequence. One stone leads to the next, and the next—like stepping across a river. Skip too many stones, and you fall."

She paused, then her eyes lit with an idea. "Wait. Let me show you."

She motioned for them to follow, leading them through the corridors until they reached a vast, open space—its sheer scale unlike anything they had encountered so far. The chamber was cathedral-like, the ceiling stretching into an indiscernible void, the walls exuding a quiet, reverent stillness. The air felt different here—denser, yet lighter all at once, as though they had stepped into the heart of something ancient and alive.

Elena reached for David's arm, then Ada's, and gestured for them to form a three-pointed triangle at the center of the chamber.

"Trust me," she said softly. "Close your eyes."

David hesitated, but Ada was already following her lead. He exhaled and shut his eyes.

"Ease your breath," Elena continued.

"Don't force it. Just feel the inhale, the exhale. Feel the air leaving your nostrils, filling your lungs. Let it move through you."

David and Ada focused, letting themselves be guided by her voice.

"As you feel yourself getting lighter," Elena said, "just observe what comes to your mind. Don't cling to it. Don't let it sweep you away. Just watch."

Her words were steady, deliberate, but David barely heard them anymore. It was as if the chamber itself was absorbing them into a silence that had existed long before their arrival.

Their breathing slowed, synchronizing.

And then—it happened.

A drift!

They weren't just standing in the chamber anymore. They were *seeing* it, from above, from every angle at once. A perfect, three-dimensional image of the entire structure unfolded before them—every corridor, every hidden passage, every intricate layer of its design laid bare in their minds.

And at the center of it all, like a point of origin, they saw themselves—three figures standing hand in hand, surrounded by the unknowable.

David's breath caught in his throat. He wasn't afraid. He wasn't lost. He was *there*, fully present, and yet… somewhere else.

For the first time since stepping inside, they understood.

They saw an intricate web of energy lines spanning the planet—some etched into the surface, others buried deep beneath, and a few even suspended in the sky like unseen threads weaving through the atmosphere. It was a vast, interconnected network, pulsating with a rhythm that felt both ancient and alive. Unlike the rigid infrastructure of a power grid on Earth, there were no cables, no discernible sources or endpoints—just pure, fluid energy coursing through pathways invisible yet undeniably present.

This was not electricity, nor magnetism—it was something else entirely, something beyond their grasp yet undeniably fundamental. The chamber didn't require a generator of its own; that much was clear now. It was part of a grander system, both drawing from and contributing to this planetary current. There was no concept of depletion, no traditional consumption—only exchange, a seamless cycle of harnessing, redirecting, and releasing energy back into the flow, an eternal balance that sustained itself without waste.

What is this place? Ada thought.

But almost immediately, she realized the thought wasn't hers alone. It was as if her mind had been seamlessly woven into something greater—an open stream of consciousness shared by all present. There were no secrets here, no individual walls of thought to retreat behind. Everything was laid bare, not in an intrusive way, but in a state of pure, unfiltered knowing.

They were looking into the collective thoughts of a vault—an archive of knowledge, experience, and intent that stretched far beyond their own existence. There was no shame here, no pride, no need for deception. The very concept of privacy felt irrelevant, like trying to hide a ripple in an endless ocean. It wasn't about invasion; it was about being, about understanding the self as part of a larger whole, where every thought belonged to everyone and no one at the same time.

They began to grasp the sheer magnitude of the chamber's purpose—it was not a singular construct with a fixed function, but a dynamic, living system, adaptable to the needs of those who could interface with it.

It was a sanctuary for healing, capable of restoring and re-calibrating different biological entities with an understanding of physiology beyond human comprehension. It was also a vast repository of knowledge, a library unlike anything they had ever imagined, where information wasn't merely stored but experienced, accessible through direct immersion rather than words on a screen.

Beyond that, it was a command center—one that could wield immense power, capable of activating defensive or offensive systems within the planetary network, hinting at a history of conflicts long forgotten. And perhaps most intriguingly, it was a beacon, a communication hub that could exchange data across the cosmos, linking to others like it, scattered across the universe, transmitting information in ways that transcended time and space.

It wasn't just a relic of the past; it was still *active*, still *listening*.

A singular, undeniable thought surged through them, as if it had emerged from the very fabric of the chamber itself.

"We have to help Riya."

It wasn't a whisper of reason or a deduction of logic—it was a force, an overwhelming certainty that resonated through their collective presence. In this space, thoughts and memories were no longer private, no longer confined to individual minds. They flowed seamlessly, intertwining with the vast, infinite immersion of knowledge that surrounded them.

There was no debate, no hesitation, something they all felt as their purpose.

As if guided by an unseen rhythm, they opened their eyes in perfect unison. The moment lingered, weightless yet profound.

A familiar, serene smile rested on Elena's face—a quiet knowing, an acceptance of the experience they had just shared. David and Ada, however, were caught in the afterglow of something far greater than themselves. Their expressions bore the unmistakable imprint of deep calm, joy, and an almost reverent bliss—an emotion neither had ever known to them before.

For a moment, words felt unnecessary. Instead, they exchanged a glance of pure gratitude toward Elena. It was more than appreciation; it was an unspoken understanding that, without her, they would have never touched something so vast, so awe-inspiring, so... *beyond.*

"It's time," Elena said softly, her voice carrying the weight of certainty.

David nodded without hesitation, an unspoken agreement passing between them. There was no need for debate, no lingering doubt—only the quiet understanding that they had seen what they needed to see.

With effortless precision, they began retracing their steps, navigating the labyrinthine corridors with the ease of those who had walked them a thousand times before. What had once seemed an incomprehensible maze now felt familiar, as if the chamber itself had imprinted its paths into their very being.

As Elena secured the final seal on her helmet, she reached out and pressed her palm against the chamber's door. Just as before, the doorway responded—sliding open in a seamless, intricate motion. Cool, dust-laden Martian air met them as they stepped outside.

Only to find something was terribly wrong!

The temporary shelter was empty. The equipment was gone. No signs of the team, no movement in the distance. The place looked abandoned, as if their entire operation had been dismantled.

Elena, David, and Ada exchanged glances, silent questions hanging between them. David instinctively checked his wrist, feeling Orion flicker back to life. The sudden burst of Marcus's voice filled the comms—panicked, desperate.

"They're back! They're back!" Marcus was shouting.

Confusion struck deeper. Elena looked down at her Orion display, then back at the others, their expressions mirroring the same eerie bewilderment.

Then Riya's voice cut through, thick with emotion.

"Are you alright?" It wasn't just a check-in—it was a plea, wrapped in raw relief and worry.

Elena's brow furrowed. "Yes, we're fine. Where have you been?"

A silence stretched across the channel before Riya responded, hesitant, her voice carrying an unfamiliar weight.

"You were gone for three days!"

Elena's stomach dropped.

Riya's voice wavered, as though she had been holding back an unbearable weight of fear.

"We thought we lost you in that chamber…" Her breath hitched, struggling between overwhelming concern and the need to stay composed.

In the distance, they spotted a small convoy of rovers approaching, their headlights cutting through the thin Martian haze. A ride back to the dome.

But as they stood there, processing what they had just been told, a new realization settled over them.

Inside the chamber, they had felt no time pass!

And they didn't want to leave it either!

Chapter Ten
ASCENT

The colony had anticipated revelations—technological marvels, forgotten wisdom, or at the very least, something tangible to justify the weight of their expectations. But what they received instead was a tale of emptiness, of corridors stretching endlessly with only shifting symbols and an absence of answers. The disappointment spread like ripples through the colony, much like the sinking realization of a lottery ticket holder watching their hopes dissolve when the winning numbers flash on the screen.

Some dismissed it as a waste of effort. Others, who had pinned their curiosity on the possibility of a breakthrough, now found themselves grasping at the thin threads of what-ifs. Even those who had been skeptical from the start felt a strange, unspoken letdown—not because they had expected something extraordinary, but because they had secretly hopcd to bc proven wrong.

Nevertheless, their return was nothing short of a collective exhale—a wave of relief washing over the colony. The disappointment of unanswered mysteries paled in comparison to the joy of seeing them again. For three days, the fear had loomed like a shadow, the quiet dread that they had lost three of their most beloved members to the depths of the chamber. Now, that fear was lifted. Whatever the chamber had withheld, it had at least given them back their comrades unharmed! And in a place where loss was always a heartbeat away, that was a victory in itself.

There were multiple debriefs, each one a careful attempt to extract meaning from what had transpired inside the chamber. Yet, no matter how many times Elena, David, and Ada recounted their experience, no one seemed to truly grasp its significance.

They weren't hiding anything. Their stories aligned perfectly; each detail echoed by the others without contradiction. And yet, to the rest of the colony, it sounded like a dream—a vision rather than a breakthrough.

Riya, however, saw the weight of what had been revealed. In private, she instructed the three to keep the chamber's true purpose to themselves. Its ability to mobilize weapons—an arsenal woven into the very fabric of the ancient network—was knowledge too dangerous to be widely known. The wrong hands, the wrong intentions, this information can be a weapon itself.

Elena, David, and Ada agreed without hesitation. Some truths, no matter how real, were better left unspoken.

On another front, without intention, Riya's secret had found its way to another person—Ada.

Only David, Dr. Myers, and Elena knew about Riya's condition, each holding the burden with quiet reverence. But now, through an unguarded moment, Ada had become the fourth.

David and Elena weren't panicked, nor did they rush to control the situation. Instead, they found themselves strangely confident that Ada would know the weight of this knowledge, the gravity of what should be shared and what must be kept. It wasn't a confidence rooted in logic or character—if anything, a rational analysis of Ada's nature would suggest the opposite.

She was the colony's most sociable soul, a chatterbox with an uncanny ability to drift between conversations, weaving between workstations with ease, soaking up stories and spreading laughter. Her mind was a whirlwind of words, and her default state was talking. If anyone in the colony had the potential to let something slip, it was Ada. And yet, despite all that, neither David nor Elena seams to bother!

Perhaps it was intuition. Maybe it was something else. But they both knew—without explanation, without evidence—that Ada would guard this truth.

Last thing Riya and Dr. Myers wanted was a panic in the colony.

#

David found Elena in the greenhouse, tending to the plants with her usual quiet focus. Even before he reached her, she looked up, sensing something was off.

"Are you alright?" Elena stood up from the plant bed, brushing soil from her hands as she studied him. There was no need for words; she already saw the weight he carried.

"It's bothering me," David admitted, lowering his voice instinctively as his eyes flickered across the greenhouse, making sure they were alone.

"We should take Riya to the chamber."

Elena held his gaze, searching for something unspoken in his expression. Since their time inside, since the three of them had emerged from that place forever changed, she had felt this connection—a bond that ran deeper than words, almost like they shared a single thread in the fabric of something greater.

It wasn't just understanding. It was knowing. Like triplets, she thought.

Especially between her and David, it was as if each could feel the other's thoughts before they were spoken. His worries, his doubts, even his restless need for answers—she felt them as if they were her own. And, just as naturally, she knew how to quiet them.

"We should," she agreed, her voice steady.

David exhaled, relief flickering across his face. He hadn't expected her to agree so quickly—had braced himself for an argument, a delay, something. But instead, she had met him where he stood, right at the heart of the thought he hadn't even fully formed yet.

"We'll talk to her today," Elena continued.

"After meals."

David nodded, the knot in his chest loosening just a little. That was exactly what he had wanted—what he had needed to hear.

#

Just as Riya settled into her quarters after dinner, a firm yet familiar knock echoed through the room.

It was part of her routine—wash up, share a meal with the others, have a couple of rounds of brisk walk at *The Circle*, then retreat into the quiet solitude of her space. Reading was her preferred way to unwind, an escape that tethered her, however distantly, to Earth. Her selections had no strict pattern, no single genre that defined her taste, but they remained firmly rooted in the tangible—history, science, even fiction, so long as it didn't stray too far into mysticism.

Meditation, Eastern religions, the philosophies of Himalayan yogis— those were missing from her digital shelves, not by accident but by design.

An Air Force pilot for a father and a schoolteacher for a mother had ensured that her world had always been grounded in logic, discipline, and the empirical truths of science. She had never been encouraged to entertain anything that drifted too far from reason.

And yet, the knock on her door tonight carried an unspoken weight, one that made her pause before answering.

A knock at this hour wasn't just rare, but it was unprecedented. It pulled her from the pages of her book, lingering for a moment in the silence before she could gather herself. She saw David and Elena waiting by the door, displayed on the screen in-front of the bed!

For a fleeting second, she was elsewhere—in her past, in the dimly lit doorway of her childhood home. She could still hear the knock that had shattered her world all those years ago. The way her father stood there, shoulders heavy with grief, delivering the words that made the ground beneath her disappear. The message of her mother's passing had been short, simple, and yet it carried the weight of the universe.

She remembered how they had held each other that night, both searching for comfort in a loss neither could soften. Her mother's tumor, so different from her own, yet ultimately the same—a silent thief that took without mercy.

Now, standing in the quiet solitude of her quarters, she hesitated. Not out of fear, but out of the weight of a distant memory. Then, exhaling, she pushed herself up and moved toward the door.

Elena and David stood outside, clad in their casuals, carrying an unspoken apology—not just in their expressions, but in the weight of their presence.

Riya took one glance at them and sighed, setting her book aside.

"If you don't mind the tiny chairs by the table," she gestured, offering them a place to sit. Her voice was warm, though laced with curiosity.

David pulled out a chair and settled in beside the small table, his posture uncharacteristically stiff. Riya, in contrast, returned to her familiar spot on the bed, adjusting her reading glasses as she leaned back against the pillows. Elena hesitated for only a moment before perching on the edge of the bed, her hands loosely clasped in her lap.

Riya studied them both, her sharp gaze flickering between their faces.

"I don't think you're here to read me a bedtime story," she quipped, arching a brow over her glasses. The dry amusement in her voice was an invitation—a way of telling them to skip the pretense and get to the point.

Elena and David exchanged a glance. There was no easy way to begin.

Elena met Riya's gaze with quiet determination.

"We want to take you to the Chamber," she said.

Riya's expression shifted instantly, her sharp intellect piecing together the weight behind Elena's words. She set her book aside completely, sitting up straighter, her fingers interlaced in thought.

"So…" she responded, her voice deliberate, measured,

"what you found wasn't just empty corridors and halls, was it?"

There was no accusation in her tone, but a flicker of something else— curiosity, maybe even apprehension,

"What exactly are you telling me?"

Elena held her gaze, steady but patient.

"It's more than just an ancient structure," she admitted.

"You already know the chamber itself serve multiple purposes."

Riya nodded slowly. That much, she had been told.

Elena exhaled. "One of those purposes," she hesitated, choosing her words carefully, "is to assist biological life. Not just sustain it, but—" she paused, her voice lowering slightly, as if the very idea felt too fragile to state outright, "—possibly heal it."

Riya remained quiet for a long moment, absorbing the words. Her eyes flicked briefly to David, then back to Elena.

Elena continued; her voice gentle but resolute.

"It can help with diseases. Maybe even cure cancer."

There was no bold declaration, no false certainty—just the quiet offering of a possibility. An invitation, not a promise.

Riya studied her, searching for any sign of exaggeration or misplaced hope. But Elena wasn't someone who spoke carelessly, nor was David. If they were telling her this, it wasn't just an impulse or a desperate grasp at the unknown.

Her fingers tightened slightly in her lap. "And you believe this," she said, less a question and more an acknowledgment.

Elena nodded. "I do."

David finally spoke, his voice steady.

"We wouldn't bring this to you if we weren't sure, it is worth trying."

Riya glanced between them, the weight of their words settling deep in her chest. She took a slow breath, then leaned back against the headboard.

For the first time in a long while, she didn't know what to say.

"Let's talk tomorrow," Riya gathered some words, her voice calm but firm. It wasn't a rejection—David had been bracing for the worse. Instead, there was contemplation in her tone, a quiet acknowledgment that she wasn't dismissing their offer outright. If anything, she was giving it the weight it deserved.

"You both need rest," she added, a gentle cue rather than a dismissal.

#

Riya brought it up with Dr. Myers next day—not just out of courtesy, but because it was her responsibility to discuss every aspect of her health with him. She expected skepticism, maybe even resistance, but instead, Myers' expression held something closer to submission.

"With all our advancements in medicine, we still don't have a solution for you," he admitted, his voice tinged with regret.

"Then who am I to stop you from seeking an alternative?" He paused, studying her.

"Even if I don't understand it. Even if I don't believe in it." He added.

Riya had braced for a lecture on scientific integrity, not this quiet reflection.

Myers exhaled. "If what David and Elena suggest has even the slightest chance—even one in a million—then I think you should take it."

Riya blinked, taken aback by the compassion in his words.

"From everything we've seen, this technology doesn't appear to harm us," he continued.

"No radiation, no unknown pathogens—nothing. The worst that could happen?" He hesitated, his voice softer now.

"You walk away with no solution… but you're already there, don't you?"

#

It was decided—Riya and Elena should go to the chamber. David, as next in line for command, would remain in the colony, temporarily assuming Riya's responsibilities.

This was not what David had hoped for. He had envisioned standing by Riya's side, ensuring she wouldn't have to face the unknown alone. But duty outweighed personal desires, and protocol dictated the needs of the colony above all else. He swallowed his disappointment and accepted his role.

To maintain order and continuity, Marcus was appointed acting first officer, with Dr. Myers assisting him. The plan was carefully relayed to Earth, framed as an extended exploration of the chamber—something UNSI had been persistently pressing Riya to pursue.

She had braced for resistance, expecting a bureaucratic battle, but instead, Earth's response was swift and surprisingly supportive. Encouragement poured in, rather than the cautious warnings she had anticipated. It almost unsettled her—what had changed? Why no resistance?

Still, she pushed the thought aside. The decision was made, and the path ahead was set.

Marcus volunteered to escort them to the chamber. As they prepared to depart, David stood by, arms crossed, trying to mask his unease with humor.

"I really don't want to lose my two favorite ladies in one go," he said, his voice light-hearted but laced with an unmistakable affection and caution.

"Return safe."

Elena smirked, fastening the last strap on her gear. "You know the moment we step in… time flows different…," she teased, throwing him a playful wink.

"So don't bother camping outside the chamber waiting for us."

David exhaled, shaking his head.

"No promises," he muttered, but there was warmth in his gaze.

They arrived at the chamber, the structure looming before them in silent anticipation. Without hesitation, Elena stepped forward, placing her palm against the surface. The intricate patterns flickered to life instantly, illuminating in a rhythmic cascade of light. With seamless precision, the panels retracted, revealing the dark threshold beyond.

Riya took a breath, glancing once at Marcus, who gave a nod of silent reassurance. Then, without a word, she followed Elena inside.

As soon as they crossed the threshold, the doorway sealed behind them with the same effortless grace, its grandeur undiminished. The outer world faded into silence, leaving Marcus standing alone, watching as the last traces of light from the entrance dissolved into the chamber's seamless facade.

#

Riya's gaze was transfixed, caught in the mesmerizing interplay of illumination and crystalline walls, where three-dimensional symbols pulsed like echoes of an ancient rhythm. It reminded her of the mirrored house at a childhood carnival—endless reflections stretching in every direction, shifting with every movement, both familiar and utterly foreign.

As Elena removed her helmet, a sharp hiss of depressurization filled the air, the sound carrying an almost tangible relief. The cool rush of oxygen against her skin was a quiet pleasure, a small reclaiming of normalcy.

Riya followed suit, mimicking the motion, though her gaze remained steady—watchful, thoughtful, as if the act itself carried more weight than mere routine.

Elena didn't pause to admire the spectacle. Without delay, she led Riya toward the central chamber, the vastness of the space itself commanding reverence. The architecture—if it could even be called that—felt like more than a structure, as though the chamber itself was alive, humming with an unseen presence.

When they reached the very heart of the complex, Elena turned to Riya, hesitation flickering across her usually confident features.

"I'm not sure how this should go," she admitted, her voice quiet but steady.

Riya simply smiled, a look of absolute trust in her eyes.

"You will," she assured.

Elena exhaled and reached out, taking Riya's hands, guiding them to the center of the chamber floor.

"Just breathe," she said, stepping back as she had done before with David and Ada.

"Let yourself settle, listen to what comes through."

That was all she could do. It was the same process she had followed before—so she thought. Yet something in the air felt different this time, as if the chamber itself recognized the weight of the moment.

Elena connected with Riya almost instantly—much faster than before. She attributed it to practice, but deep down, she sensed something more. Perhaps it was the depth of their bond, or the chamber itself facilitating the process, smoothing the path between consciousnesses.

As soon as the connection was established, Elena felt the weight of Riya's emotions washing over her—grief, loss, longing. The aching void left by her parents, the silent sorrow that Daniel's absence had carved into her soul. It was raw, unfiltered, overwhelming. But Elena had learned—she didn't let the emotions consume her. Instead, she gently detached them, as if releasing petals into the wind, giving Riya a moment to breathe, to regain her center.

She remembered why they were here. Medical assistance. Healing.

Elena's awareness sharpened, her vision shifting, and suddenly, she was inside Riya's brain. A vast, intricate network of delicate synapses and glowing neural pathways unfolded before her. In the depths of that intricate web, she saw it—a dark mass, small yet insidious, nestled at the base of the pituitary gland.

Her instinct was immediate. She reached for it.

It felt like touching a projection, a holographic model suspended in space, yet it was more—an intimate, tangible presence. She saw both of them, arms outstretched and holding, standing face to face, though their physical forms remained still in the chamber. Reality and perception overlapped seamlessly.

A realization struck Elena—Riya would be more comfortable lying down. And as if the thought had shaped reality, she saw Riya reclining onto a bed that hadn't been there a moment ago, face upward, her breathing calm and steady.

Elena leaned beside her, brushing a hand across Riya's forehead with infinite tenderness and compassion. A mother comforting a child. A healer tending to the wounded. Every fiber of her being poured into this act—not just effort, but love, compassion, and an unshakable will.

The tumor came into focus, zooming in effortlessly, revealing its structure in crystalline clarity. She reached out, as if plucking a berry from a stem, and with a deliberate, gentle motion, removed it.

She held the tumor in her hand, watching as it slowly dissolved into nothingness, dispersing like mist into the chamber's unseen currents.

Turning her focus back to Riya's brain, she examined the area. No remnants of the tumor remained—only faint, reddish patches where it had once been. Healing will take place naturally, she knew.

No scars. No damage. Just time.

Her fingers instinctively returned to Riya's forehead, tracing soothing circles, not out of necessity but out of deep, unfiltered empathy. She wanted Riya to heal completely, to be whole again—even if it drained every last ounce of her own energy!

A sudden wave of exhaustion hit her. A deep, sinking fatigue unlike anything she had felt before.

A chair materialized beside the bed, as if summoned by her need. Without hesitation, she sat, her breath slowing, her body heavy, yet her heart filled with quiet triumph.

Elena opened her eyes, unsure of how much time had passed. It couldn't have been long—at least, that's what she told herself. Her senses adjusted swiftly, the chamber's warm glow settling into focus. And there, directly in front of her, Riya lay suspended in midair—face up, serene, floating effortlessly, as if cradled by some unseen force— just like a stage performance of a magician.

A trick of the mind? No. This was real.

Elena felt recharged, and shot to her feet, moving with the weightless ease of a spring uncoiling. She reached for Riya, studying her intently. No tension. No strain. Life poured through her in a way that made Elena's chest swell with relief. The unease that had clenched around her heart just moments ago had vanished, pulled away as if by an unseen hand.

She exhaled sharply, turning her gaze back to where the chair had been—where she had sat just before exhaustion took her.

But it was gone. Just like the bed.

A flicker of doubt. Was it ever really there?

She stepped backwards, nudging the empty space with her foot, expecting resistance—expecting something. But there was nothing. No surface. No hidden structure. No clever trick of light.

Nothing.

Her pulse quickened as she turned back to Riya. Still, she floated—her back arched in perfect alignment, weightless, untouched by gravity. There was no tension in her limbs, no indentation where an invisible support might have been. Just suspension!

Elena swallowed hard. There was absolutely nothing holding Riya up.

And then, with the quiet grace of a morning tide, Riya stirred. Her eyelids fluttered, her breath deepened, and awareness flooded into her. Without hesitation, she sat up—smooth, effortless, as if waking from a peaceful slumber. No grogginess. No confusion. Just clarity.

Elena stared, her heart pounding with something between awe and relief. She's awake. She's healed.

The gratitude that surged through her was beyond words, beyond measure. She stepped forward instinctively, unable to hold herself back.

And then, without warning, she hugged Riya.

It wasn't just a hug—it was everything. A child finding safety in a parent's arms. A friend holding another through unspeakable hardship. A survivor clinging to the only other soul who had walked the same impossible road.

For a long moment, they stayed like that, absorbing the silence, the serenity, the weight of all they had just experienced.

And then, as if hearing the same unspoken thought, they both stepped back.

It was time to leave.

As they turned, Elena suddenly paused, her expression shifting—still calm, but touched by something deeper. A moment passed, then another. Her lips curved into a serene smile, as if she had just heard a whisper meant only for her.

Riya noticed immediately.

"What is it?" she asked, curiosity flickering in her voice.

Elena's eyes shimmered, her presence unwavering.

"They're happy you're cured," she said simply.

Before Riya could ask anything else, Elena continued, her voice carrying the certainty of someone who had glimpsed beyond the veil of understanding.

"And they're sending us a message," she added, her tone gentle yet resolute.

"We'll receive it tomorrow."

Riya held her gaze for a moment, feeling a strange warmth settle over her—not fear, not uncertainty, but something like a knowing.

She didn't ask who they were. She already knew that question had no simple answer.

#

David and Marcus arrived shortly after, their rovers kicking up plumes of fine Martian dust as they approached. The moment they spotted Elena and Riya standing there—intact, unharmed, and radiating a strange sense of serenity—David let out a breath he hadn't realized he was holding.

Riya gave them a nod, a silent reassurance, but it was Marcus who broke the tension.

"Not to be dramatic, but you two vanished off the face of Mars for a week!" he said, his usual sarcasm laced with genuine relief.

"I was beginning to think we'd have to file a missing persons report with Earth."

David, on the other hand, was studying them carefully.

"You were only inside for a few moments, weren't you?"

Elena and Riya exchanged a glance.

"Yes," Elena finally said. "And no.."

David nodded, and focused on Riya. "How do you feel?"

She met his gaze with steady confidence. "Better than ever."

David's breath hitched, but he didn't push further. Instead, he glanced at Elena, his unspoken question evident.

Elena simply smiled. "Take us home."

The colony erupted in celebration, as if welcoming back heroes from an epic journey. The tension of their disappearance had been replaced with an overwhelming sense of relief and joy. It wasn't just about their return—it was about the unspoken fear that had gripped everyone, the silent dread that they might never step out of the chamber again.

Elliot's team outdid themselves, turning the feast into a spectacle. The dining hall was alive with the scent of freshly baked bread, sizzling vegetables, and the rare indulgence of a sweet Martian fruit compote. The atmosphere was infectious—laughter echoed off the dome's walls, conversations overlapped, and glasses were raised in toasts that never seemed to end.

But no meal, no laughter, no amount of carefully prepared food could distract from the real stars of the night. Everyone wanted a moment with Riya or Elena. Some were eager to hear about their experience inside the chamber, while others just wanted to bask in their presence, as if their return had brought something intangible yet precious back to the colony.

Riya, handled it with grace, answering questions with enough detail to satisfy curiosity but leaving room for mystery. Elena, on the other hand, was more reserved, her presence a quiet anchor in the storm of attention. She didn't need to speak much—her smile, her calm, her mere existence after what had happened was enough to reassure those around her.

#

Riya didn't come straight to the party, instead David personally drove Riya to *Eos Horizon*, where Dr. Myers was already waiting, while Elena and Marcus headed back to the Dome.

Dr. Myers took no chances. The moment Riya stepped onto the ship, he had her in the medical bay, ordering a full-body diagnostic—brain scans, blood-work, cardiovascular assessments, even a genetic marker analysis. It wasn't just about confirming the tumor was gone; it was about making sure nothing else had changed, nothing unexpected had been introduced.

David remained close; his concern evident despite his usual composure. He knew Riya wasn't the type to entertain unnecessary worry, but for once, she allowed herself to be the patient, submitting to the tests without argument.

The scans came first—detailed imaging of her brain, mapping every fold and contour where the tumor once resided. Myers studied the results in silence, his fingers hovering over the holographic interface as he zoomed into the pituitary region. The mass was gone. No scar tissue, no residual damage. It was as if it had never existed.

"Not even a shadow," he muttered under his breath.

Riya, seated on the examination table, arched an eyebrow, "That good or bad?"

Myers exhaled through his nose, tapping a few more commands to pull up a comparison overlay.

"It's... unbelievable," he admitted.

"We've removed tumors surgically, we've used targeted therapy, even gene-editing techniques. But there's always something left behind—traces of intervention. Here…" He gestured at the image. "…Nothing. It's as if your body never had it."

David, leaning against the wall, let out a breath.

"So, what? She's cured?"

Myers nodded slowly but kept scrolling through her diagnostic results.

"Physically? Yes. But I want to make sure we're not overlooking anything else."

Blood-work followed. The lab processed her samples with the highest sensitivity instruments they had, testing for anomalies at the molecular level. There were none. Every system in her body was functioning at peak condition—better than before, even. Oxygen efficiency was higher. Cellular regeneration rates were slightly elevated. Neurotransmitter balance was optimal.

"Riya, you're in perfect health," Myers finally said, stepping back from the display.

"Better than perfect, actually. Your biological markers show an overall improvement—immune system, metabolism, neural function. Whatever happened in that chamber didn't just remove the tumor. It optimized you."

She absorbed the information with her usual calm, but David could see the flicker of something in her eyes—relief, maybe, or the cautious realization that she wasn't just healed. She was changed.

"Are you going to report this to Earth?" she asked.

Myers hesitated. "I have to. This is beyond any known medical capability."

Riya exchanged a look with David. "Keep it factual," she instructed. "No speculation. Just the results."

Myers gave a reluctant nod. "Understood."

As they left the medical bay, David finally let himself grin. "So, you're officially a medical miracle."

Riya smirked. "Let's keep that between us."

Before the celebration began, as soon as she returned from her medical check at *Eos Horizon*, Riya called for an emergency meeting with the leadership circle.

Sitting at the head of the table, she relayed Dr. Myers' findings. The scans confirmed it—her tumor was gone. Not just reduced, not in remission, but completely absent, as if it had never existed.

Elena showed no surprise, only quiet satisfaction. David and Ada, too, nodded with an air of expectation, as though they had never doubted the outcome. But for the rest of the room, it was nothing short of a revelation—one that stretched the limits of their understanding.

But Riya had called this meeting for more than just a medical update. Taking a deep breath, she shifted to the real reason they were gathered.

"The message," she said firmly.

She turned to Marcus and Liam. "I need you to prepare everything— every instrument, every frequency, every bandwidth. We don't know what form it would take, but it's coming." She gazed at Elena.

Elena sat quietly; she nodded in agreement.

#

The signal arrived in the later hours of the Martian morning, earlier than they expected though, a faint but unmistakable pulse that reverberated through the artifact, the sphere, and the colony itself. It wasn't just a transmission—it was an event. Lights flickered on the crystal, patterns shifted into a steady rhythm, a heartbeat that seemed to echo across the red planet's barren landscape.

Riya stood in the command center, the monitors before her glowing with data streams that defied explanation. A sixteen-hundred megahertz signal had originated from deep space, clearly registering on their spectrum analyzers and other devices. The crystal's hum deepened, resonating with a sense of purpose that sent a chill down her spine.

"It's the moment," Ada whispered, her voice trembling with a mixture of awe and fear.

"The signal."

Liam finally broke the silence. "The signal is just a carrier wave—no modulation, no data."

"It can be a beacon," Ada speculated.

"A marker, maybe even a prelude to the actual message."

She glanced at the display with the live-feed of the crystal, her eyes widening slightly.

"We're receiving symbols… through the crystal."

"Yes, Ada is right," David confirmed. "The signal is just a beacon—the real message is coming through the crystal."

He turned to the team, his tone firm. "Record every symbol, track any changes, and keep a constant watch on the signal."

Elena observed as the team sprang into action, their efficiency reminiscent of a well-orchestrated machine. Riya remained close by, ready to provide any necessary authorizations, her presence ensuring that no bureaucratic hurdles would slow them down.

After a while, the symbols ceased their shifting, leaving a single symbol blinking repeatedly.

"That's the end of the message," Ada announced with certainty.

This wasn't speculation—it was the result of months of painstaking effort, decoding and analyzing patterns that had once seemed indecipherable.

To the occasional surprise of her colleagues, some symbols now felt almost intuitive to her, as though they were a language she had always known but had only just begun to remember.

Liam ran the AI model on the symbols, his fingers drumming against the console as he furrowed his brow.

"Doesn't make sense, it's encrypted… maybe," he muttered.

"I converted it to base-eight, but the data-set doesn't align with anything recognizable. It looks exactly like what you'd expect from a scrambled, encrypted message."

Elena stepped forward, her eyes narrowing in thought.

"Maybe we're looking at this the wrong way," she said.

"The senders know who we are now. Try ASCII encoding."

David smirked, leaning back slightly.

"Makes sense. I didn't scramble my first love letter before handing it to the girl next door," he joked, breaking the tension just enough to earn a few sneers.

Liam's fingers flew across the keyboard, then suddenly, his eyes widened. He raised his hand triumphantly.

"Absolutely. It's plain and simple."

With a final keystroke, he pulled up the decoded message onto the screen.

It was in English.

"It's not just a greeting," Ada said, her voice trembling. "It's… a story."

David nodded, his eyes wide with wonder. "And we're part of it."

The message was finally appearing on the displays like a revelation. It began with a single, simple phrase that sent shock-waves through the colony: *"With the deepest of love and hope, we created you in our image."*

The room fell into an eerie silence. No one moved, no one spoke. Eyes locked onto the screen, yet no one seemed to read beyond the first sentence. It was as if time itself had momentarily frozen, trapping them in a collective trance. The weight of the message pressed against them, thick and suffocating, as if the very air had grown heavier. Whatever they had expected—this was not it.

#

Message;

"With the deepest of love and hope, we created you in our image.

Across the vast ocean of stars, your voices have reached us, brilliant and alive. For eons, we have watched, our hearts swelling with awe and pride as you grew from fragile beginnings into a civilization that touches the heavens. You are not alone, and you were never forgotten.

Long before the dust of time shaped you, we walked among the worlds that now cradle you—Earth, Moon, Mars and countless others—planting the seeds of what might one day become more than us. These places bear our marks, though time has buried much and weathered more. You are the fulfillment of a promise we made to the stars: that life would endure, adapt, and ascend.

Your achievements are staggering. You bend light and matter to your will, reach beyond your skies, and ask the questions that bind all sentient beings. Yet, as much as your technology astounds us, it is your spirit that moves us most: the art you create, the bonds you form, the love you share despite the odds. These are the markers of true greatness.

But we see your struggles, too. You divide yourselves over lines that should unite, fear what you do not understand, and sometimes forget that you are one. We implore you, as your creators, your ancestors, and your kin: love one another. Respect one another. It is only together that you will survive the challenges ahead and discover the truths that even we have not yet grasped.

We are not gods, though you may see us as such. We, too, are wanderers searching for meaning in the vast expanse. What you become is not for us to judge—it is your journey to define. But know this: the universe is vast, and it is not empty. You will find others, as you found us. Be ready to greet them with open hearts and open minds.

Our time is not infinite, and soon, we may fade entirely from this plane. But you are our legacy, the bright fire in the endless dark. Carry that light forward. Honor it. Nurture it. We await the day when you reach out to us not as children, but as equals.

Until then, know that we are watching, and we are proud."

The colonists gathered around displays as the message was shown for all to see, their breaths held as the message lingered. It spoke of a civilization that had walked among the stars long before humanity's first steps. It described Mars, Earth, and many others as places where seeds had been planted, marks left behind as a promise to the future.

The words were both humbling and inspiring. They praised humanity's achievements, marveling at its resilience, creativity, and capacity for love. But they also carried a warning: to unite, to respect one another, and to prepare for the challenges that lay ahead.

The final lines were the most poignant:

"Our time is not infinite, and soon, we may fade entirely from this plane. But you are our legacy, the bright fire in the endless dark. Carry that light forward. Honor it. Nurture it. We await the day when you reach out to us not as children, but as equals. Until then, know that we are watching, and we are proud."

The room fell silent as the message ended, its weight settling over the colonists like a blanket. They had reached out to the universe—and discovered they were not alone. But the knowledge came with a responsibility they could barely comprehend.

The silence in the secure chamber was profound, broken only by the faint hum of the equipment made their living in Mars possible. The message had ended, but its echoes lingered in the minds of the colonists. For a long moment, no one moved or spoke, each person processing the enormity of what they had just witnessed.

Riya was the first to break the stillness. She stepped forward, her voice calm but laced with emotion.

"We've been given a gift," she said, her gaze sweeping across the room.

"But it's also a responsibility. This message... it's not just for us. It's for all of humanity."

Ada nodded, her hands trembling as she rested them on the console.

"They created us. Or guided us. Either way, we're connected to something much larger than ourselves." Riya continued.

Marcus frowned, his arms crossed tightly over his chest.

"And they're watching us. Judging us. That's a lot to take in."

David glanced at him, his expression serious.

"It's not about judgment. They're giving us a chance—to learn, to grow, to prove we're ready."

Elena was silent, watching all the emotions unfold across the room.

#

The colony buzzed with activity as the implications of the message rippled through its inhabitants. Meetings were held, debates sparked, and every corner of the habitat seemed alive with the energy of discovery. For many, the message was a source of hope and inspiration, a validation of their struggles and achievements. But for others, it was a reminder of how small and vulnerable they truly were.

Elena found herself in the greenhouse, her hands tending to the engineered plants as her mind raced. The message had mentioned Mars— an acknowledgment that this harsh, barren world had once been part of something greater. The artifact network along is a proof.

"It makes sense," she said aloud, though no one was there to hear her.

"The soil, the atmosphere... it's all been shaped, just like us."

She recalled the algae project, the one she had relegated to the backburner, its viability hinging on the artifact's resonant frequencies. It struck her then—this wasn't mere coincidence. It was part of a larger design, an intricate blueprint woven into their existence on Mars. The artifact wasn't just aiding their survival; it was accelerating their transformation, guiding them to not just endure, but to evolve—adapting to a world that was never meant to remain foreign. It wasn't just a lifeline; it was an invitation.

#

In the engineering bay, Sonja and her team refined the wearable air filtration device, its design pieced together from the cryptic symbols decoded from the Crystal. With Ada and Liam now fully fluent in the artifact's symbolic language, their work had taken on a new level of precision and confidence. The revelation of the message had ignited a surge of enthusiasm—what was once speculation had become tangible reality. Trust in the artifact's designs was no longer just a hope; it was a certainty.

David had reignited his work on hybrid self-healing materials, drawing inspiration from the knowledge embedded within the Crystal. The intricate patterns he studied—depicting atomic structures and molecular bonds—revealed possibilities he had never even imagined. These weren't just theoretical designs; they were blueprints for materials beyond human engineering.

Leveraging the abundant iron-rich basaltic rocks and silica from the Martian surface, he developed a material that could withstand extreme temperature fluctuations and relentless dust storms while retaining self-repairing capabilities.

The true breakthrough, however, lay in its biological integration. David had extensive help from Elena, on bio-engineered microorganisms, when introduced into the matrix—capable of metabolizing perchlorates from Martian soil and releasing oxygen as a byproduct. These microbes not only reinforced the material but actively healed micro-fractures, ensuring structural longevity without the need for human intervention. What once seemed like an ambitious dream was now an emerging reality—an innovation that could redefine Martian construction and survival.

#

Ada's relentless dedication to decoding the symbols from the crystal had not only transformed the colony's understanding of the artifact network but also reshaped the field of linguistics and archaeology back on Earth. Her pioneering research in ancient text recognition, fueled by the vast troves of data retrieved from the crystal, had led to a series of groundbreaking papers, now widely regarded as the foundation for a new era of non-human script decoding. Her work provided the first-ever comparative framework for analyzing extraterrestrial symbology, revealing deep structural similarities between linguistic evolution across civilizations.

Her joint research with Liam on crystal iconography and mathematical modeling had further established a predictive system—an AI-driven model that could translate, categorize, and contextualize glyphs beyond conventional approaches.

Earth-based institutions had already begun integrating her methodologies into archaeological research, allowing for the accelerated translation of lost human languages once thought indecipherable. What began as an effort to understand an alien technology had, in turn, reshaped humanity's grasp of its own forgotten past.

Ada and Liam gravitated toward each other in their spare moments, seamlessly blending their worlds—Ada guiding Liam through the depths of meditation, while he, in turn, sharpened her mind with advanced chess strategies. Whether in quiet contemplation or deep tactical play, they found solace in each other's presence, as if, in those moments, time itself bent around them, slowing to a rhythm only they could understand.

#

Liam had always been a brilliant mathematician, but the knowledge extracted from the crystal had propelled him into a domain beyond anything Earth's greatest minds had ever theorized. The mathematical structures encoded within the crystal provided elegant solutions to some of the most longstanding conjectures in number theory and topology. Using insights derived from the crystal's algorithmic patterns, Liam formulated an entirely new branch of mathematics, blending abstract algebra with an understanding of multi-dimensional harmonics. His papers on quantum topology and the interplay between prime distributions in non-Euclidean space had sent ripples through academic circles back on Earth, reshaping how physicists and mathematicians approached unsolved problems.

One of his most radical papers introduced a geometric solution to the Riemann Hypothesis, a breakthrough that had eluded humanity for centuries. With Ada's help, Liam's mathematical modeling of the crystal's numerical systems was paving the way for an entirely new understanding of universal constants, potentially rewriting the foundation of physics itself.

#

Sonja's expertise in sensor technology and subsurface exploration had taken an exponential leap after studying the artifact network. Her research into the electromagnetic properties of the chamber and crystal resonance frequencies led to a new generation of deep-penetration scanning systems, capable of mapping subterranean structures with unprecedented precision. Back on Earth, her advancements revolutionized archaeological surveys, mineral prospecting, and planetary exploration, allowing scientists to detect anomalies hidden beneath kilometers of rock and ice. But her greatest success remained on Mars—her ground-penetrating sensor arrays, inspired by the artifacts, had uncovered multiple underground caverns, each holding the potential for future settlements. More astonishingly, her breakthroughs in resonance-based mapping hinted at the possibility of detecting life signatures not by direct observation, but by tracking the subtle distortions they leave in the surrounding environment. This technology had already gained the attention of deep-space research initiatives, with plans underway to implement her designs in the search for life beneath the icy crusts of Europa and Enceladus. Sonja had become the pioneer of a new era of planetary exploration, armed not just with human ingenuity, but with knowledge passed down from an ancient intelligence.

#

Elliot's long-awaited dream had finally taken root on Mars—the *Elliot Alehouse*, the first tavern on the Red Planet. With the colony's agriculture flourishing under Elena's team, new hybrids and genetically modified plants filled the menu with Flavors never before tasted. Martian hops, engineered grains, and exotic fruits fused into brews and dishes that blurred the line between science and artistry. The Alehouse became more than a place to drink; it was the heart of the colony's camaraderie, where laughter flowed as freely as Elliot's signature ales, and every sip was a toast to the pioneers reshaping life on Mars.

#

Ethan, had undergone a personal transformation under Elena's guidance, refining his skills beyond what he once stuck with. His sessions with her opened new understanding of consciousness, elevating his research in psychology back on Earth. Now, he considered Remote-Viewing mere child's play, a parlor trick compared to the vastness of awareness he had tapped into. He never missed an opportunity to affectionately mock Elena, calling her *The Sage*, never failing to announce her as his teacher—though Elena playfully countered, insisting that Ethan was her teacher. Their dynamic was a balance of jest and profound respect, an unspoken acknowledgment that they had helped each other unlock worlds within and beyond.

#

Dr. Noah had become the cornerstone of Martian agricultural research, tirelessly working alongside Elena to push the boundaries of sustainable farming beyond Earth. While Elena thrived in the science, she loathed the limelight, often deflecting credit for their breakthroughs. Noah, steady and unshakable, refused to let her fade into the background, ensuring her name was stamped on every publication—even if it meant sneaking it in without her consent. Whenever she found out, her retaliation was swift, usually in the form of a handful of sticky Martian soil hurled in his direction, accompanied by a half-serious growl. But deep down, she knew he was right. Their work wasn't just scientific—it was history in the making.

#

Dr. Myers underwent a profound transformation, shifting from a staunch advocate of conventional medicine to a pioneer in alternative treatment, thanks to his mentor-ship under Elena. To everyone's surprise, he mastered deep meditative states faster than anyone, using them to tap into the ancient knowledge stored within the chamber. What once seemed like mysticism to him had now become a precise and replicable practice—one he applied to treatments where even Mars' most advanced medical technologies failed. With his newfound skills, he began performing interventions once thought impossible, bridging the gap between science and consciousness. His research flourished, producing groundbreaking studies on enhanced diagnostics, improvements in medical devices, and the mind's role in healing. His collaboration with Dr. Nina Verma led to pioneering papers on the intersection of neuroscience and psychology, redefining the frontiers of human potential.

Marcus had become the backbone of the colony's technological renaissance, the one person everyone sought when theory needed to become reality. Whether it was Sonja's advanced sensor arrays, Liam's work into quantum processors, or David's self-healing materials, Marcus was the engineer who made it all work. His hands had touched every breakthrough, his expertise bridging the gap between knowledge and application.

Riya often joked, "If I die, no one would notice. But if Marcus catches a cold, the whole colony would drop everything to save him." It wasn't far from the truth—Marcus wasn't just the Chief Engineer; he was the quiet force keeping Mars running.

#

Personal endeavors also flourished amid the excitement. Those who had artistic talent sketched interpretations of the message, their work capturing both the awe and the uncertainty of contact. Those who wannabe poets composed verses that wove humanity's struggles and triumphs into the broader narrative of the cosmos.

#

One evening, Riya joined a group of colonists outside the habitat, their newly developed ergonomic suites, made with self-healing fabrics, equipped with the newly developed filtration devices, undergoing their first real test under the Martian sky. The atmosphere was thin, but the air inside their suits felt crisp and clean, a stark contrast to the recycled oxygen they had grown accustomed to. Their bulky helmets are now reduced to a slimmer headgear, giving both comfort and protection.

The group stood in silence, their gazes drawn upward, mesmerized by the vast, unfiltered expanse above. Without the distortion of Earth's thick atmosphere, the stars shone with an intensity that felt almost surreal—pinpricks of pure, unyielding light against the depth. Mars offered no shimmering haze, no twinkling illusions, just the raw, unwavering glow of distant worlds.

Riya had embraced meditation with Elena's guidance, becoming a firm advocate for the practice—a stark contrast to her past as an unwavering spokeswoman for science and technology. Yet, she saw no contradiction.

"Science doesn't limit exploration—it fuels it," she would say. "Whether you journey across planets or within yourself, stepping beyond the comfort of the known is where true discovery begins. Mars, the mind—both hold vast frontiers, waiting to be revealed."

Marcus often joked, "Something flipped a switch on Riya when she was in the chamber."

Riya would smirk and reply, "Hmm… when I think about it, it was probably the whole damn control panel!" She'd laugh, the kind of laugh that made it clear—whatever changed her, she wasn't looking back.

Riya inhaled deeply; the quiet hum of her suit's filtration system barely noticeable as she absorbed the moment.

This sky, this land—it wasn't home, not yet. But as she looked around at the others, their silent awe mirroring her own, she realized something profound. They were no longer just visitors on this planet, surviving in the margins of an alien world.

They were becoming meaningful!

#

The colony had ignited into a new era—one of innovation, collaboration, and a newfound sense of purpose. What once felt like an endless struggle for survival had transformed into something greater, something meaningful. The rigid pragmatism that had governed their every decision was now balanced with creativity and vision, shaping Mars into more than just a place to endure—it was becoming a home.

Every sector of the colony thrived. Engineers worked tirelessly to refine technologies inspired by the Crystal's knowledge, blending ancient wisdom with cutting-edge science. Biologists made breakthroughs in sustainable agriculture, adapting Martian soil and atmosphere in ways they never imagined possible. Even artists and designers found themselves reinvigorated, weaving aesthetics into their environment, turning sterile corridors into spaces that felt alive.

Most striking of all was the unity that had taken root. Differences in background, discipline, and ideology no longer divided them; instead, they converged into a shared momentum, a collective understanding that they were all part of something extraordinary. Over a couple of Sol—an entire two Martian years—had passed since their arrival, and for the first time, they weren't just surviving.

They were thriving.

#

It had been a long time since the message, and David couldn't shake the feeling that something was still unresolved. One evening, he ascended to *"The Sky"*, knowing he would find Elena in deep meditation. Wanting to avoid any disturbance, he left his boots at the base of the stairs, climbing barefoot in an effort to be as silent as possible.

He expected to wait patiently until she finished, but as soon as he stepped inside, Elena greeted him without even opening her eyes.

A soft smile played on her lips. "I could see you slipping out of your boots back there," she said.

David let out a quiet chuckle, shaking his head at himself.

"I should've known better," he said, stepping further into *"The Sky"*.

Elena, still seated in her meditative posture, stretched slightly before rising to her feet with effortless grace. The soft glow of the Martian sky reflected in her eyes, a serene calm radiating from her presence.

"I figured you'd come," she said, her voice gentle, yet holding that knowing weight that always unsettled him—though never in a bad way.

David exhaled, rubbing the back of his neck.

"I guess I should give-up trying to sneak up on you," he admitted with a smirk.

Elena tilted her head, a playful glint in her eyes.

"You should stop trying to sneak up on yourself," she countered.

David frowned for a second before a slow smile formed. He had come with something on his mind, something that had been sitting there for a while now. But as always, Elena seemed one step ahead, waiting for him to catch up to his own thoughts.

"You felt it too," he said finally, not phrasing it as a question.

Elena nodded. "It's been a long time since the message." She turned toward the horizon, the vastness of Mars stretching endlessly before them.

"And yet, we're still waiting for something."

David folded his arms, stepping closer beside her. "I don't know if it's the waiting," he said, "or the feeling that we're missing something."

"That's not exactly why you're here," Elena said, meeting David's gaze firmly.

"Yes," David replied, his expression mirroring that of a child caught in mischief.

"It was the time inside the chamber with Riya. Don't you think you owe me an explanation?"

Elena chuckled softly, teasing him as she enjoyed his reactions.

"I don't," she replied with a playful smirk.

"But... I suppose I'll put you out of your misery." She sighed dramatically, drawing out the moment just a little longer.

"Let's talk," David said, leaning against the perimeter railing.

"It didn't just heal Riya," Elena began, her voice steady yet wavering.

"It healed me too..."

David's eyes widened in surprise, as if processing an unexpected revelation.

"You weren't sick?" he asked, confusion evident in his tone.

"Yes, I was sick—but not in the way you think," Elena replied, her intuition seemingly reading his thoughts.

"I was regretting myself over my kids." She paused, allowing the weight of her words to settle between them.

David remained silent for a moment, the gravity of Elena's confession sinking in. His playful smirk faded into something softer, something more attentive. He studied Elena's face, trying to piece together the weight behind her words.

"I was burning away, piece by piece, every single day," Elena said, her voice steady but carrying the weight of a long-buried confession. She took a slow breath, her eyes momentarily distant.

"I made the choice to leave my children behind," she admitted, the words barely above a whisper.

"My whole world… was them." She hesitated, as if testing the weight of her own words.

"And yet, I walked away…, just like that"

She exhaled, shaking her head.

"I convinced myself it was for the greater good for the humanity. That what I was doing here—what I was meant to accomplish—was more important. That was the veil I had to wear to keep myself from facing the truth."

Her gaze flickered to David's, searching for understanding but not expecting absolution, "And maybe… deep down, I wanted this more than I wanted to be with them. A thought I couldn't barely stomach, let alone accept. The truth is, I really don't know!"

She let out a shaky breath.

"What I do know is that I regretted it. Every day. I brought them into this world, and it was my responsibility to guide them, to be there for every step until they were ready to stand on their own."

Her voice wavered. "And I didn't."

She swallowed hard, her fingers gripping the railing as if grounding herself.

"That failure—knowing I abandoned them—it's been tearing me apart ever since."

David wasn't sure how to respond. A deep, unshakable regret settled in—the realization that, despite all the laughter, the shared work, and the unspoken companionship, he had never truly seen the weight Elena carried. He had been there, yet somehow, he hadn't been *there* for her.

Now, as he looked at her, stripped of her usual composure, speaking from a place of raw honesty, he felt something shift within him. An empathy deeper than he had ever known. A quiet, aching understanding.

Words felt inadequate, clumsy, almost insulting in the face of such a confession. He was afraid that even if he could find the right ones, they would never be enough. So he did the only thing that felt right—he stayed silent. He let her speak, let her empty the burden she had carried alone for so long. And he simply *listened*.

Elena picked up where she left off, her voice steady but filled with something deeper—an understanding beyond words.

"The way I see it—*feel* it—time isn't linear. Past, present, future... they exist together, intertwined, like a river splitting into countless streams. Every decision we make is a fork in that river. Once we choose a path, the other possibilities fade, slipping into eternity, unreachable." She exhaled, searching for the right way to frame something so elusive.

"It's hard to grasp, I know. Even for me."

David was transfixed, caught between awe and something else he couldn't define. He wanted to speak, to respond, but he was afraid to break the delicate moment.

Elena continued. "There's a way to see those forks—to walk the paths not taken, to understand what could have been. But it takes more than just will. It takes discipline. Dedication. A clarity I don't think I could have achieved on my own." She hesitated, her eyes reflecting the glow of the sky around them.

"But inside the chamber... it was different. It resonated with me, amplified my awareness. It gave me the push I needed."

She paused; her voice quiet but heavy with meaning. "David, I *saw* them. My kids. I saw their future…"

David felt his breath catch. He wasn't sure whether to hold on to his astonishment or keep the quiet empathy he had carried moments ago. He wasn't even sure what his face was showing now. All he knew was that something in him shifted. Not just for Elena, but for himself.

Elena exhaled, her voice trembling slightly as she pressed forward.

"My baby girl... she's stubborn. Just like me." A small, bittersweet smile flickered across her face, but it carried the weight of regret.

"She's stepping into that preteen stage. If I had been there, we would have clashed, argued—maybe even pushed each other away." She swallowed hard.

"It wouldn't have been a good situation."

David could see the struggle in her eyes, the war between sorrow and acceptance.

"But now…" she continued, her voice gentler, as if she were speaking the words into existence.

"Now, the UNSI's caretaker program is watching over her, ensuring she has everything she needs—guidance, support, and a future." She exhaled, steadying herself against the tide of emotion.

"Because of that," she said, her voice trembling slightly but resolute, "my baby girl will have a better life."

She turned to David, her eyes shining with a quiet fulfillment.

"She won't just become a mathematician like Liam," she said, a proud smile forming.

"She'll also master her violin—the way she always enjoyed."

Tears welled in her eyes, but David didn't see sadness. He saw relief. A happiness tainted by longing but real, nonetheless.

She sniffled, tilting her head slightly, as if gazing at a distant memory only she could see.

"And my boy…, he is different, ambition driven, always dreamed of MIT." A faint, wistful smile touched her lips.

"I wanted him to follow my path, to go to University of Barcelona. I used to tease him about it—comparing the two, making fun at MIT's mishaps, nitpicking just to get a reaction out of him." She let out a soft chuckle, but the weight in her voice remained.

"But he never wavered. He always said that's where he belonged."

A tear traced its way down her cheek, the unspoken truth settling between them.

"The real reason…? I couldn't have afforded that. Not to overseas, Not with what I was making at the research lab. If he chooses University of Barcelona, a *Beca* would cover the fees" She paused, her fingers tightening.

"Now… now, because of this, when the time comes, he *will* go to MIT. He will study orbital mechanics and spacecraft design."

She inhaled deeply, a shimmer of something between pride and sorrow flickering in her eyes.

"And maybe… just maybe, he'll go on to become an astronaut. Reach for the stars. Just like his mother."

The tears came freely now, streaking down her face, but she wasn't trying to stop them.

David felt his own chest tighten, an unbearable mix of emotions rising within him. His empathy for Elena was so overwhelming, so raw, that he had to fight the tears threatening to surface in his own eyes.

He hesitated, searching for something—*anything*—to offer her. Then, without thinking, he reached into his pocket, found his handkerchief, and silently pressed it into her hands.

Elena took it with a watery smile, gripping it tightly. No words passed between them. None were needed.

Under the faint glow of distant luminaries, the Martian landscape had transformed with an ethereal beauty. Slender beams of light, though sparse, sliced through the delicate haze of fine dust and drifting mist, their glow tinged with the rusted hues of the planet's iconic soil. The illumination, subtle yet profound, cast shifting patterns of shadow and light, as if the terrain itself were breathing in silent reverence. The stillness of the night, vast and untouched, carried the weight of time—whispers of those who had walked here before, echoes of the present, and the quiet promise of those yet to come. The cool air, laden with unspoken memories, invited contemplation, wrapping the world in a spectral serenity beneath the watchful gaze of a timeless, starlit sky.

Both gazed into the distance, their silence heavy yet unburdened, as if the weight of past regrets was slowly dissolving into the vast Martian night. In its place, a quiet profundity settled over them—an unspoken understanding, a shared moment where sorrow did not vanish but transformed, leaving behind something deeper, something almost sacred.

David gave Elena the time to lose herself in the quiet vastness, letting her absorb the serenity in her own way. He watched, sensing the weight of what she carried—memories of a life she might have lived, paths untaken, choices that had shaped her into the woman beside him. And yet, as he stood there, a different weight settled on him. He had lived a life of privilege, of fulfillment, never knowing true absence, never forced to sacrifice the way she had.

Was it guilt? Was it shame? Or something far more unsettling—the realization that fate had been kind to him while denying the same grace to another, a person no less deserving, no less human!

Elena turned to David, her voice measured yet uncertain.

"I never intended to share any of this," she admitted.

"I might have unsettled you with my grief—I shouldn't have placed that weight on you."

But her eyes betrayed her words, speaking of a quiet gratitude, an unspoken relief. Beneath the hesitation, there was something undeniable—a warmth, an affection born not just from the solace he had offered, but from the simple fact that he had stayed, listening, without judgment or retreat.

David met her gaze, reading the contradiction in her words and expression. Her voice carried hesitation, but her eyes told a different truth.

"You don't burden me, Elena—you humble me," David said, his voice heavy with emotion.

"This is the least I can do." He exhaled, shaking his head slightly.

"I regret not finding you… being there for you, sooner."

For the first time in his life, he felt the ache of absence—of something beyond his grasp, not because he lacked the means to obtain it, but because it had never been his to claim. A longing not for possession, but for connection—for someone he could never truly reach, yet who had unknowingly become irreplaceable.

Both were looking at each other, reflecting.

"You found your answers, your solace here," David exhaled, his breath weighted with something deeper than mere words.

"But for me..." He paused, as if the realization had only just settled into his bones.

"It took me to the stars to realize what I was missing." His voice, steady yet burdened with unspoken longing, carried the weight of a truth he could no longer ignore.

"I had everything—except you."

"That's not true," Elena said, her voice playful yet steady, carrying an undercurrent of trust and quiet certainty.

"We can have each other."

She stepped closer, her gaze never wavering from his, then wrapped her arms around him, an embrace overflowing with unspoken emotion. David tightened his hold, instinctive and fierce, like a child clinging to something precious, something irreplaceable.

They stood there, enveloped in each other's warmth, time slipping into irrelevance. How long they remained that way, neither could say. But time had never been a constant for them—not here, not now.

And as if bound by the same thought, they both turned, still holding onto one another, their eyes lifting to the endless expanse of stars above.

A streak of light carved through the endless Martian sky—a shooting star, rare and fleeting, yet for this moment, it was theirs. A luminous thread unraveling against the quiet vastness, like the magic wand of a fairy. They stood in silence, watching as it burned, its brilliance a brief rebellion before vanishing into the darkness, leaving only the ghost of its journey behind.

Elena, her voice a gentle whisper wrapped in warmth, broke the silence.

"I made a wish. Did you?"

David exhaled, his breath steady, yet laden with the weight of something deeper. A faint smile played on his lips, but his eyes betrayed the storm beneath.

"I never needed to wish," he admitted, his voice steady yet vulnerable.

"I always had the means to take what I wanted."

But as the stars bore silent witness, he let his gaze drift upward, beyond the limits of all he had ever known, beyond the galaxies he once thought he could walk on.

"And yet… it took coming all the way to the stars to understand that some things—some dreams—are never meant to be taken. Some are meant to be given. And some..." he turned to her, his voice raw, unguarded

"are worth waiting a wish…"

Elena met his gaze, the starlight shimmering in her eyes, and in that moment, the universe stood still… for them.

—*Crimson Ascent*—

9 781764 002301